BY ADRIENNE YOUNG

The Unmaking of June Farrow

Spells for Forgetting

Sky in the Deep

The Girl the Sea Gave Back

Fable

Namesake

The Last Legacy

Saint

The
UNMAKING
of
JUNE FARROW

The

UNMAKING

of

JUNE FARROW

A NOVEL

ADRIENNE YOUNG

DELACORTE PRESS

NEW YORK

Published in the United States by Delacorte Press, an imprint of Random House, a division of Penguin Random House LLC, New York.

DELACORTE PRESS with colophon is a registered trademark of Penguin Random House LLC.

ISBN 9780593598672

Printed in the United States of America

Book design by Caroline Cunningham
Title page and chapter ornament: iStock/KatyaKatya

For Meghan Dickerson and Kristin Watson

You are my true north.

The

UNMAKING

of

JUNE FARROW

ONE

When Margaret Anne Farrow died in her sleep on June 10, 2023, I became the last living Farrow on earth.

The setting sun fell behind the hill that overlooked a wide expanse of the Blue Ridge Mountains, a rolling sea of soft violet peaks. Only a few of those who called the town of Jasper, North Carolina, home had gathered to bid Margaret farewell.

Put me to sleep with the fiddle at sunset, she'd said, because she'd known she was dying. We all did. We hadn't planned to say any words because she hadn't wanted that. There weren't many things that were clear, especially in those final years when Gran's mind had all but slipped away, but a burial on this hill at sunset with a fiddle playing in the wind was one of them.

The headstone was made of simple, rough-cut white marble to match those of the other Farrow women who were laid to rest only feet away. Mildred, Catharine, Esther, Fay, now Margaret. One day, my own name would stand beside them—June Farrow.

To the town of Jasper, I was first known as the Market Street Baby, words made eternal the day the *Chronicle* put them on the front page. Just before daybreak on October 2, 1989, Clarence Taylor was on his way to open the cafe when he heard the sound of a baby's cry coming from the alley. It took only hours for the whole town to hear about the baby girl in the basket with the birthmark beneath one ear and the locket watch tucked into her blanket.

The necklace was an heirloom that had been passed down in the Farrow family for generations. The last woman to wear it around her neck was my mother, Susanna. Susanna—the only name missing from the cemetery because Gran had refused to raise a headstone over an empty grave.

There was no mistaking who the baby was when they found that locket watch. It had been almost fourteen months since my mother disappeared. There was no shortage of theories on the matter, but no real answers. Susanna had simply walked into the woods one day, her belly swollen with child, and never returned. There were those who thought she'd met a tragic end. That she was a victim of some unspeakable crime. Others believed she'd lost her way in the deep woods and was never found.

The easiest and most widely accepted explanation for my mother's strange disappearance was madness—the same affliction to befall every woman in my family for as far back as anyone could remember. We were cursed—the Farrow women.

By the time night had fallen, the sheriff was knocking on my grandmother's door, and that's where the story ended. My mother was gone. She wasn't coming back. So it was just the two of us, Gran and me.

Two finches arced across the darkening glow of the horizon, drawing my gaze up from the headstone as Malachi Rhodes drew the bow down his fiddle. The notes stretched deep and long, sending a melody into the air that made my heart twist painfully. The same tweed flat cap he wore fly-fishing on the river every morning was pulled low over his wrinkle-framed eyes, but he was one of the few in town whom Gran had considered a true friend, and he'd made the effort of wearing his nice jacket.

The windows of the little white wooden church at the bottom of the hill were still lit. On Sundays, it was filled for service, when everyone in Jasper piled into the pews. Most everyone, anyway. I'd never set foot in the place; neither had Gran. That was one of the reasons the young minister, Thomas Falk, had pretended not to watch as we'd made our way through the cemetery gates. It was also one of the reasons that only four other souls stood on that hill besides me and Malachi.

Ida Pickney, our next-door neighbor, dabbed at the corner of her eye with the tissue balled in her fist. Her daughter, Melody, was at her side, and Mason Caldwell stood a whole head taller than her only a few feet away. He'd had the misfortune of being the only kid in grade school foolish enough to sit beside me at lunch, and he'd eventually grown into the only fool who'd jump from the river bridge with me in the summers or cut class with me our senior year. Then there was Birdie Forester, Gran's oldest friend, who was more like family than anything.

Her hand found mine, squeezing, and it was only then that I could feel how cold my fingers were. I blinked, pulling my eyes from the narrow steeple of the church to look over my shoulder. Birdie stood at my back, the lace neckline of her black dress fluttering along the curve of her collarbones. Her silver hair was pulled into old-fashioned pin curls, making her look exactly like the photographs of her and Gran when they were young. There were dozens of them in the basement. Arm in arm in front of the soda shop. Perched like chickens atop hay bales on the farm. Standing knee-deep in the river in only their underwear.

"Made it to holy ground after all," Birdie whispered.

A smile pulled at the corner of my mouth, my eyes flitting again over the five white headstones of the Farrow women. There was a time when this corner of the cemetery didn't exist. When Gran was little, the Farrows were buried outside of the fence because they weren't baptized. But eventually, as the need for more burial plots grew and the fences of the churchyard were moved, the banished graves fell within its borders. Gran had found an endless humor in that, saying she'd make it to holy ground after all.

There were things that made this town what it was. The scent of honeysuckle blooming along the black tar roads and the rush of the Adeline River, which cut through the land like the scrape of a knife. The curious gazes that followed me and Gran on the street and the rumors that skipped in the air no matter how much time had passed. Their stories were nothing compared to the ones that Gran had regaled me with when she tucked me into bed as a little girl. The town of Jasper had no idea just how different and strange we were.

The wind picked up, and goosebumps surfaced on my skin, tracing from my wrist to my elbow when the feeling of eyes crept up the back of my mind. I swallowed hard before I followed the movement at the corner of my vision back down the hill. The square of golden light on the lawn beside the church was painted with a sharp black shadow.

My gaze rose to see the silhouette of a man framed in the window, shoulders squared to the cemetery. Even from here I could feel those eyes focused on me. But the parking spot where the minister's car had been an hour ago was now empty. So was the church.

It's not real, I told myself, tearing my eyes away. *There's nothing there.*

When I blinked, he was gone.

The notes of the fiddle slowed, drawing out against the wind as the last bit of light disappeared in the distance. The trees swayed in a balmy summer evening breeze that made my skin sticky to the touch, and a moment later, there was only the sound of the footsteps on the damp grass as the others made their way through the headstones and back to the road.

I stared at the dark, crumbled earth that filled the grave. Gran had taught me how to work the farm, to weave flower crowns, and to make her grandmother's biscuits. She taught me how to ignore the whispered prayers women uttered beneath their breaths when they came in and out of the flower shop. How to read the coming seasons by the intuition of the trees and predict the weather by the look of the moon. I hadn't let myself really think about the fact that it was what came next that I most needed her for. But she wouldn't be there.

Birdie and I waited for the last of the headlights to bleed away before we finally started the walk back, following the bridge over the river to the single block that was downtown Jasper. I chanced one more look at the church and found the window still empty, like I knew it would be. But that sick feeling still swirled in my belly.

I unbuttoned the top of my black cotton dress, letting the cool night air touch my skin before I pulled off my shoes, a pair of black slingback heels Gran had probably had in her closet since 1970. The same was likely true for the pearl earrings I'd fished from her jewelry box that morning.

The crickets woke with the darkness that fell over the thin strip of town that lined the road, not a car in sight. Small communities like this one usually went to sleep with the sun, and Jasper was mostly farms, which meant its residents would be up when the roosters crowed.

The main street had some other name no one ever remembered, a combination of four or five numbers that only showed up on maps. In Jasper, it was known as just the river road, the only way to town from the remote stretches that were tucked into the surrounding mountains. South took you to Asheville. North took you to Tennessee.

A banner for the upcoming Midsummer Faire was stretched out across the only intersection, catching the wind like a sail. The redbrick-faced buildings were more than 150 years old. They snaked along the Adeline River, which, that time of night, with the moon waning, just looked like a wall of black. The only reminders that it was there were the hiss of it running over the rocks in the shallows and the distinct smell that the churn of mountain water put into the air.

The lights of the cafe, the feed store, the grocery, and the bank were dark, and the poorly marked side streets were quiet. One after the other, the tilting signs reflected the moonlight as we passed. Bard

Street, Cornflower Street, Market Street . . . I let my eyes drift to the shadows that striped this last narrow alley. It was there that Clarence Taylor had heard those cries in the darkness and found me.

Then there was Rutherford Street, named after one of the Jasper's more sinister tales, the only one I knew of that overshadowed my mother's disappearance. Decades ago, the town's minister had been brutally murdered at the river, though I wasn't sure what truth there was to the grisly details I'd heard murmured over the years. There were people who still left flowers on his grave and his picture hung in the cafe like the patron saint of Jasper, still watching over his flock. My missing mother, on the other hand, had barely warranted a search party.

"Did Mason lock up?" Birdie asked, eyes finding the dark windows of the flower shop across the street.

I nodded, watching our reflections on the glass as we walked side by side. Birdie had taken over running the shop when Gran got so sick she couldn't work, and now Mason had pretty much taken over things at the farm. My days for the last year and a half had been spent looking after Gran, and now that she was gone, I wasn't sure where I fit anymore. I wasn't sure it would matter much longer, either.

The porch light of the little house I'd grown up in was the only one lit when we turned onto Bishop Street. Even from the outside, it looked different without my grandmother in it. Older, somehow. Birdie, on the other hand, looked younger in the moonlight. She un-latched the gate to the once-white picket fence, holding it open for me before she followed.

She'd sold her house and moved in three years ago, taking the spare room downstairs when Gran's decline worsened, and the two of us became the three of us. But in a way, that had always been true. Even before Birdie's husband died, she'd been a fixture, a rare constant in my life. That was one thing that wouldn't change now that Gran was gone.

I climbed the steps to the porch and opened the screen door. For no other reason than it was habit, I reached into the letter box, tucking the little stack of envelopes under my arm. With a pang of guilt, I realized it was one of those mundane things that went on, even when your world stopped spinning. Edison's Cafe still closed at 8 P.M., the morning glories still bloomed at dawn, and the mail was still delivered every day but Sunday.

Birdie pushed through the door, and that smell—old wood and decades' worth of brewed coffee that had baked itself into the walls—made my throat constrict. She hung her sweater on one of the hooks, where Gran's hand-knit scarf was still buried beneath an umbrella and a rain jacket. I suspected that the ache of missing her would mostly come from those little things. The holes that were left behind, empty places I'd stumble upon now that she was gone.

A narrow hallway stretched past the sitting room to the bottom of the stairs. The floorboards groaned, the old house creaking around us as a wind wove through the trees again. Birdie stopped in front of the long, enamel-framed mirror that hung over a little table beneath it. I set the letters down on top of the others that had accumulated there. At one corner, an oval picture frame held a photograph I'd taken of Gran sitting on the porch steps. Beside it was another that held a picture of my mother.

"Sure you don't want me to make you a cup of tea?" Birdie wrung her hands, trying her best not to appear as if she was taking care of me. I'd never liked that.

"I'm sure. I'm just going to go to bed."

"All right."

Her eyes searched the ground, and she reached out, hooking one hand on the banister as if she was steadying herself.

My brow pulled. "You okay?"

That flat line of her mouth twitched just slightly, and she hesitated before she reached into the pocket of her dress. When she pulled out what was inside, I had to squint to make it out in the dark. The glow of the kitchen light glimmered on what lay at the center of her palm.

"She wanted me to be sure you got this," she said.

An ache rose in the back of my throat. It was the locket. The one

Gran had worn every day since the sheriff had knocked on her door with me in his arms. The one that had been tucked into that blanket with me when Susanna left.

The long, faceted chain glittered as I lifted it from Birdie's hand and the pendant swung into the air, cold and heavy. Its round face was etched in a complex pattern, worn from the years of my grandmother's fingers, and her grandmother's before her.

I opened the clasp and the mother-of-pearl watch face stared back up at me. It was set with not two hands, but four, and each of them varied in length. It was a strange piece of jewelry that most closely resembled a watch. But the numbers were off-kilter, some of them missing. Ten and eleven were gone, and a zero stood in place of the twelve. The hands never moved, two of them perpetually stuck on the one, the other two pointing to nine and five. The numbers that were scratched from the mother-of-pearl surface could still be seen if I tilted it toward the light, a defect that Gran didn't know the origin of.

Birdie looked sad, brushing a thumb over my cheek before she kissed it. Her eyes searched mine for another moment before she let me go.

"Good night, honey."

I waited for her bedroom door to close before I turned back toward the mirror. My fair hair was darker in the weak light, and it was already escaping from the bun I'd tamed my waves into. The chain of the locket slipped through my fingers as I dropped it over my head, letting the gleaming pendant come to rest between my ribs. I closed my hand over it, rubbing my thumb over the smooth surface.

I glanced at the picture of my mother nestled at the corner of the table before studying my own face in the mirror's reflection. My light brown eyes were the only thing I'd ever gotten from Susanna, and every time I thought of it, it made me feel like I was seeing a ghost. I traced the dark red birthmark tucked beneath my ear with the tip of my finger. It stretched down around my jaw, coming to a point along my throat.

When I was a child, the kids at school said it was the devil's mark, and though I'd never admitted it to anyone, I'd sometimes wondered if it was true. No one in Jasper had ever seen me as normal because my grandmother had never been normal. She'd never believed she was sick, either, saying that she was simply in two places at once.

Before I'd even registered the sting behind my eyes and the quiver of my bottom lip, a hot tear was falling down my cheek.

"I know," I whispered, glancing to my grandmother's face in the second photograph on the table. "I promised I wouldn't cry."

But that ache inside of me wasn't just the pain of losing her. It was the relief, too, and that was something else I'd never said aloud. In those last years, Gran had all but lived inside of her own broken mind, shut away from our world for weeks at a time. It was one thing to miss her when she was gone. It was another to miss her when she was still here, in this house with me. For the last few months, I'd found myself longing for the end as much as I'd dreaded it.

The pop of wood made me blink, and my head turned to the hallway, where the light from the porch was coming through the front door's oval stained glass window. But the moment my eyes focused, a prick crept over my skin again, making me still. The frame of a man was visible on the other side—the same one I'd seen at the church.

There, behind the glass, eyes as black as inkblots fixed on me as the bright orange glow of a cigarette ignited in the darkness.

It's not real.

I clenched my teeth, jaw aching as I willed myself to blink. But this time, he didn't disappear. A curl of smoke twisted in the haze of the porch light, and I was sure for a moment that I could smell it.

I closed my eyes again, counting three full breaths before I opened them. The cigarette glowed again. He was still there.

My fingers slipped from the locket, and I started up the hall, heels knocking like a heartbeat until my hand found the brass knob. I yanked the door open, my vision swimming as the night air spilled back into the house. The place on the porch where the man had stood only seconds before was now empty. Finally, he'd vanished.

I pushed through the screen door, searching the darkness. The yard was quiet, the rocking chair still as the tin light swayed gently over-head.

"Everything okay, June?"

Ida Pickney's high-pitched voice made me jump, and I sucked in a breath. She stood on the porch of the house next door, already changed out of the dress I'd seen her wearing at the burial. An un-opened newspaper was clutched in one hand as her eyes moved over me slowly.

"Fine." I forced a smile, trying to slow my breathing.

Ida hesitated, hands fidgeting with the rubber band on the paper. "Can I get you anything, dear?"

"No, I just . . ." I shook my head. "I just thought I saw someone on the porch."

The look on her face went from hopeful to worried in an instant, and I realized my mistake. That was how it had started for Gran—seeing things that weren't there.

I pressed my hand to my forehead, giving a nervous laugh. "It was nothing."

"All right." She forced a smile. "Well, you just call over if you or Birdie need anything at all. You will, won't you?"

"Of course. Night, Ida."

I slipped back inside before she'd even answered, locking the dead bolt behind me. My steps were slower as I made my way back toward the stairs, but my palms were slick, my unraveling hair curling with damp. When I reached the mirror, the locket caught the light, and I saw that the trail of the tear that had fallen a moment ago still striped my cheek. I wiped it with the back of my hand.

"It's not real." The words were barely audible under my shaky breath. "There's nothing there."

I ignored the sick, sinking feeling in my gut again. The one that whispered at the back of my mind the thought that I wouldn't let fully come to the surface. A year ago, I would have told myself it was just a trick of the light through the glass. Not a wrinkle of the mind.

Not a fine crack in the ice. It was the porch light swinging. The shadow of a tree branch.

But I knew. I'd known for some time now.

My eyes trailed down the dark hallway, to Birdie's bedroom door. I hadn't told her about the flashes of light that had begun to appear at the corner of my vision last summer. I hadn't told her about the echo of voices that drifted in the air around me or the fact that more and more each day, my thoughts felt like sand seeping through the floorboards.

It came for my grandmother, as it came for my mother, and now it had come for me.

For years, the town of Jasper had been watching me, waiting for the madness to show itself. They didn't know it was already there, brimming beneath the surface.

My future had never been a mystery. I'd known since I was very young what lay ahead, my own end always so sharply visible in the distance. That was why I'd never fall in love. Why I'd never have a child. Why I'd never seen any point in the dreams that lit the eyes of everyone else around me. I had only one ambition in my simply built life, and that was to be sure the Farrow curse would end with me.

It was as good a place as any to end a story. I wasn't the first Farrow, but I would be the last.

TWO

The larkspur was blooming, and that was the first real sign of
summer in the mountains.

I worked my way down the narrow row, wedging myself against
the wall of dahlias at my back that wouldn't wake for another couple
of weeks. Not until midsummer, Gran had always said, and every year
she was right.

I tugged at the collar of my coveralls, pulling it up against the heat
of the rising sun. The mornings were cool, the best time to cut, and
they were also quiet. Birdsong and the sound of the river behind the
tree line were the only companions in the fields at that time of day.
Most of the hands were down at the barn getting ready to work, but
I'd been at it for hours, happy to have a reason to leave the silence of
the house on Bishop Street.

Bright golden pollen covered the knuckles of my worn leather
gloves as I found the end of the flower stalks by memory. One by one,
I worked down the groupings of leaves until I reached the place to
cut. I'd been using the same snips since I was thirteen, a pair of wood-
handled clippers I'd notched my initials into and refused to replace.

The Farrow women had a *touch*. When farms had sprung up from valley to valley and everyone else in North Carolina was planting tobacco, the Farrows were growing flowers. It had kept the farm working for the last 118 years, and long before there was internet or travel guides, it had been one of the things that Jasper was known for—a peculiar little farm that was growing flower varieties even the richest growers in New England hadn't been able to get their hands on. The mystery had made the farm something of a legend, even if the women who ran it weren't exactly considered polite company.

My great-great-grandmother Esther had never come clean about where she'd gotten those seeds, though people in Jasper had their guesses, including some local lore that she'd made a deal with demons. It was more likely that at some point, someone who'd come to work on the railroads had sold them to her. But that wasn't the kind of story that people liked to tell.

The rattle of a bucket landing on the ground sounded on the other side of the dahlias, and I looked up to see the top of Mason's hat. The wide-brimmed canvas was stained across the brow with a few growing seasons' worth of sweat.

"Wasn't sure you'd come in today," he said, not finding my eyes over the row.

I cut another bunch of the larkspur, and when my grip was full, I tucked them under one arm, pinning them there so I could reach for the next. "Are you checking up on me, Mason Caldwell?"

He pulled the snips from his belt and got to work, cutting into the rainbow of bloomed ranunculus on the other side. "Do you *need* checking up on?"

Mason still had a bit of that wry, boyish demeanor he'd had when we were kids fishing on the bank of the river and sneaking out to watch the sunrise up at Longview Falls.

I half laughed. "No. I don't."

"Did you look at the schedule?" he asked.

I sighed. "You know I didn't."

"The larkspur is tomorrow."

"Well, it's getting cut today," I said, a monotone note creeping into my voice.

I wouldn't tell him that the tinge of pink at the tip of the petals had told me they were ready, and that tomorrow just a little of their color would be gone. I wouldn't tell him that the amount of dew on the stalks this morning had me worried about the leaves, either. Mason didn't believe in the wives' tales Gran had taught me. He put his faith in plans and data and forecasts, and I'd resolved myself not to argue with him. He was running things now, and that was best. There was no telling how long I had before I ended up like Gran or my mother.

"We have schedules for a reason, Farrow."

I rolled my eyes before I found the joint of the next stem, not bothering to look back at him. Again, I wouldn't argue, because there was no point. That was one of the benefits of working with your oldest, and in my case—only—friend. You got good at not wasting energy where it would be badly spent.

"Well?"

"Well, what?" I echoed.

"You okay?" His voice softened a little, but I could still hear him cutting.

I took the bundle underneath my arm and followed the row to its end, where a bucket was waiting. The memory of those eyes on the porch last night made me clench my teeth. Even now there was a part of me that thought I could still smell that cigarette smoke in the air.

"I'm good." I dropped the larkspur into the bucket, returning to the place I'd left off.

Every woman in the Farrow family was different, but the end was always the same. Gran hadn't started showing signs until she was in her sixties, and it had progressed very slowly. Her mind had crumbled in those last years, the light in her eyes all but flickering out. In the end, I lost her to wherever that other place was. She faded. Disappeared.

But the town had already begun to see it in my mother before she went missing, and by all accounts it had been a fast-growing, hungry thing.

The statements collected during the investigation were filled with accounts of inexplicable behavior. Speaking to someone who wasn't there. Confusion about things that had or hadn't happened. There was a particularly concerning story about her walking barefoot in the middle of the night during a snowstorm. And it wasn't the first time she'd disappeared with no explanation. But the day she left me in Jasper was the last of her. After that, there was nothing left.

This time, the ease of Mason's voice gave way to hesitation. "What are you doing later? I'm going into Asheville if you want to come."

I glanced over my shoulder. He was still hidden behind the towering thicket of dahlias. "You're never going to find someone if you spend your weekends babysitting me."

He was quiet for a moment, and I wished I could see his face. We were both thirty-four, and for most of those years, the town had speculated that we were more than friends. We were, I suppose. We were family. In the few times I thought there might be something beyond that, it was smothered by the reality of what we both knew was coming. I'd made promises to myself a long time ago that kept me from ever crossing that line. Mason hadn't crossed it, either.

"I'm all right, Mason," I said again, hoping I sounded more convincing this time.

"I'm just saying . . ."

I made the next cut, irritated now. "I said I'm all right."

Mason's gloved hands lifted into the air in a gesture of surrender, and he fell quiet, making me instantly feel guilty. The truth was, he was waiting for me to fall apart just like Birdie was. He didn't know that the waiting was over. I just hadn't figured out how to tell him yet.

We worked in silence, keeping pace with each other as we moved down the row, and when I reached the end of the larkspur, I slipped the clippers into my belt and sank down, taking hold of the full buckets at my feet. When I rounded the corner of dahlias, Mason was crouched low, cutting away the yellowed stalks from where a section of drip line had busted and flooded the roots.

The rim of his hat was low over his eyes, his denim shirt already wet and darkened down the center of his back. When he finally looked up at me, his blue eyes held the question he wasn't going to ask again. He wanted to know if I was okay. *Really* okay.

"Want me to take those?" He stood, wiping his brow with the back of his arm, but his gaze was on the buckets I was holding.

"No, I got it," I said, readjusting one of them into the crook of my elbow so I could take the one he'd filled with the ranunculus.

Before he could think better of biting his tongue, I ducked past him, heading for the peak of the barn's rusted rooftop, visible in the distance.

"You look at that schedule tomorrow before you come out here hacking away," he called out.

A smile broke on my face, and I waved a hand in the air, not looking back.

It was one of the slow days, and I was grateful for that. The barn doors were open to the sunlight, and inside, a few of the farmhands were tying up the blue hydrangeas we hadn't used up in the shop last week. There they would hang until winter, when there was frost on the fields and the only things to sell were evergreen wreaths and dried flowers.

The old green Bronco that had once belonged to my mother was parked between the barn and a wall of sunflowers that were days from blooming. The engine still ran, and it was more farm truck than anything these days. I set down the buckets on the gravel drive and opened the back, not even flinching at the painful screech of rusted hinges. Withered blooms that had broken off in previous shop runs littered the bed, along with a burlap cloth and the old milk crate bolted into the metal that served as the only real storage space.

I loaded the buckets, taking care not to let the flower tops scrape along the roof, and then unzipped my coveralls, letting them fall to the ground. I stepped out of my boots, reaching for the sandals that were waiting in the milk crate.

"Morning, June." A few of the field workers passed with sympathetic smiles, the greeting too sweet to pass for normal. It would be like that for a while, I guessed.

I gave them a nod, shaking out the coveralls before I dropped them into the crate. The farmhands were disappearing into the rows of bachelor's buttons and soapwort up ahead when I shifted the truck into gear and backed up onto the road.

The road curved into the trees, the summer vines already creeping onto the cracked pavement. It was like that this time of year, as if the woods were nibbling at the edges of town, just waiting for a chance to swallow it whole.

There was a quiet in the mountains, even when the cicadas and the crickets were singing and the wind was howling. It was the sight of those rolling blue peaks in the distance that made me feel like maybe the earth wasn't really spinning.

None of the farms that were still operating grew tobacco anymore. The river had kept the land fertile, carving through the fields before it began its descent into the lowlands, and now, the families in Jasper mostly raised hogs or grew sweet potatoes. There were even a number of Christmas tree farms now.

The radio cut in and out with bits and pieces of Billie Holiday's "I'll Be Seeing You," and I breathed through the tight feeling in my chest, eyeing the cracked display. I reached for the knob, turning it just to be sure. But it didn't matter how many channels the dial scrolled past, the song was the same. The radio had been busted for years, but I could hear the static-muffled notes and butter-smooth voice buzzing in the speakers.

Sometimes, if I focused, I could push the episodes from my mind like tightening the tap on a faucet to stop the drip. But that was becoming less and less easy to do. The man I'd seen on the porch and in the church window last night had been proof of that.

I steered the truck down the winding roads and let one hand fall out the window, splaying my fingers so that the wind could slip through them like warm water. The song faded from my mind as the cool morning burned out of the air and the sun rose higher.

When town appeared in the distance, I saw the doors of the flower shop were already propped open. The engine groaned as I came to a stop at the only traffic light in Jasper, which hung from a tenuous wire over the main intersection in town. A right turn would take me over the bridge that crossed the river, now sparkling with sunlight. I could see the steeple of the church, and I resisted the urge to search the cemetery's green hill for the freshly dug grave we'd stood by the night before.

To the left of the stoplight stood the county courthouse. The red brick was the same that had been used for all the buildings, but its white dome top and marble floors were too grand for Jasper, built at a time when the farms in these hills were producing the east's best tobacco. No one had known this town wouldn't ever become anything more than a few farmers and their local gossip, bypassed by an inter-state that would run all the way from California to the coast of North Carolina.

The traffic light clicked off and then on again as the bulb lit green, and I let my foot off the brake, pulling into the parking spot in front of the shop. The old metal sign that hung above the door read ADELINE RIVER FLOWER FARM.

Birdie was at work behind the counter, a pen clenched between her teeth as she read the order taped to the wall. Ida's daughter, Melody, spotted me from the front counter before I even had the gear in place. She'd been our summer hire for the last two years when she came home from college and we needed extra hands for wedding season. We might be in the middle of nowhere, but the brides that came in droves to be married with a mountain view in Asheville wanted Ade-line River flowers in their bouquets and boutonnieres.

Melody came outside, her linen apron tied with a perfect bow at her waist. She was eleven years younger than me, and hers was a face that had always reminded me just how much I'd never really fit. Not in this town, my life, or even in my own skin. She was always smiling. Always polite in that way that southern people were taught to be. Like nothing dark had ever touched her.

She made her way around the truck, giving the back a few jerks until it opened. "Morning, June." Her singsong voice was a pitch even higher than her mother's.

"Morning."

"The service was so beautiful last night. Me and Mom both thought so."

I found Melody's eyes in the rearview mirror as she slid the buckets toward her. The look on her face made me wonder if Ida had told her to keep an eye on me. I wouldn't put it past her.

"Thanks." I tugged at the rolled handkerchief tied around my head, dropping it to the seat beside me before I pulled my hair from its knot. The sun-warmed waves spilled over my shoulders.

"I didn't know you were cutting the larkspur today." She said, "This everything?"

"That's it. They'll be by with more in a couple of hours, and there should be room in the cooler."

"All right." She swayed from left to right as she lugged the buckets to the sidewalk. "Want me to get Birdie?"

"No," I said, working the stubborn gear back into reverse. "I'll catch her later."

She gave me a dutiful nod as I pulled back onto the road, and I drove the rest of the way to the house, the truck jostling as I turned into the uneven drive. I came to a stop in front of the cottage. It was painted in a sunlit peach color, and the garden was in full bloom, making the house look like a page from a storybook or one of the postcards on the counter at the grocery. It still didn't feel like that, though.

The screen door of the house squeaked as I worked the keys from the ignition, and I climbed out of the car as Ida appeared on our porch.

"Oh hey, honey." She came down the steps as I pushed through the gate. She had the house key Birdie had given her dangling from a hooked finger. "I was just on my way to the courthouse, but I left some dinner in the fridge for y'all. Didn't want to leave it out here in this heat."

"Thanks, Ida."

She hesitated, hands fidgeting with the keys. "I was a little worried about you last night. Looked like something gave you a fright."

I could see that look in her eyes as they narrowed on me. To her, I'd always be the little girl in a torn dress stealing ripe cherries from the tree in her backyard, and I had a feeling she considered herself something like my keeper now that Gran was gone. That would become a problem, especially if I wanted to keep those flashes of light and vanishing sounds to myself.

I shook my head. "Just tired. It's been a long few days."

"Well, of course it has." She softened, smile turning sad.

I stepped around her on the pavers that led to the porch, climbing the steps. "Thanks again."

"No problem, honey."

I watched her in the reflection of the window as I unlocked the door. She stood there a beat too long before she finally went out the gate.

Any other day, I'd walk into the house to find the smell of Gran baking pound cake or the sound of her humming from the sitting room, but this time, there was only silence. It didn't sting like it had the night before, but it was still there—that emptiness.

I dropped the keys into the bowl on the table and took the pile of mail from its corner before I climbed the stairs. My legs felt heavy, and the tingle of sun still bit my skin. The bathroom I shared with Gran was at the top of the steps, lit by another stained glass window that painted the white penny tile with yellow and orange light. I propped the window open and turned the faucet to fill the tub before I raked a hand through my hair, holding it back from my face. There was still dirt beneath my fingernails. Somehow, there always was.

I rinsed my hands in the sink, studying the dark circles beneath my eyes. I was thinner. More pale than usual despite the morning in the fields. I sighed, folding my hands together beneath the water as it heated, and when I glanced down to turn off the tap, I froze, fingers dripping. A red swirl circled the drain like a ribbon of crimson in the water. It almost looked like . . .

I lifted my hands before me and turned them over, bringing them close. There were still little dark half-moons beneath my nails, my cuticles a mess from the cutting and digging. *Just dirt*, I thought. *Only dirt.*

I squeezed my eyes shut, blinking furiously as I reopened them, and when I looked into the sink again, the water was clear. I turned off the faucet, forcing my exhales to slow before I pulled the towel from the hook. I counted slowly, pressing a wet hand to my face.

Most of the time, I could feel the episodes coming. It was like static in the air, the details of the world sharpening and brightening like the surge of a lightbulb just before my mind slipped. Other times, it snuck up on me.

I turned away from my reflection, taking the mail from the sink and making my way down the hall to the bedroom. It was the same one I'd slept in since I was a girl, a small corner of the second floor with a slanted, wood-paneled ceiling and a window that looked out over the electric purple blooms of the weeping cherry tree in the yard.

I tossed the stack of envelopes onto the bed and stripped off my clothes, leaving only the locket around my neck. I instinctively opened it, as if to check that the little watch face was still inside. Then I slipped it over my head and set it gently on the dressing table before taking my robe from the hook on the back of the door.

I wrapped it around me and sat down on the bed, reaching beneath the mattress. The notebook was right where I'd left it, the pen making the binding bulge.

July 2, 2022, was the date scribbled on the first page, and I still remembered the feeling that had climbed up my throat when I wrote it. It was a journal, for lack of a better word. A record of every single episode I'd had since they started. The ones I knew of, anyway. I'd begun to wonder if they were happening more often than I was aware of and I just hadn't caught them. Maybe the man I'd passed on the road this morning wasn't really there. Maybe Ida hadn't just been standing on my porch. How would I know? At what point would it all just bleed together, like it had for Gran?

Dr. Jennings had been the one to call them episodes, but I didn't like that word, and neither had Gran. I understood why she said it was like being in two places at once. It felt like two slides of film placed one over the other. Like an overlap that got clearer and more real each time it happened.

I flipped to the page I'd written on the night before, when I got home from the funeral.

June 13, 2023
Approx. 7:45 P.M.—I saw a man in the window of the church who wasn't there.
8:22 P.M.—I saw someone on the porch. The same man, maybe? I could smell cigarette smoke.

I stared at the smudge of ink where I'd set the tip of the pen down for too long on the last letter, remembering that pinprick orange glow in the darkness.

I swallowed down the lump in my throat, turning to the next blank page. The clean, lined paper was the color of milk, a contrast to the creased and stained cardboard cover.

I picked up the pen, writing the date at the top.

June 14, 2023
Approx. 11:45 A.M.—Song on the radio again.

I glanced at the clock on my bedside table.

12:12 P.M.—Blood in the sink, beneath my nails.

I couldn't stop myself from stretching my hand out to check them again. I'd tasted it—that sharp tinge of copper in the warm air. I'd seen the bright red curling into the drain like a snake.

When my fingers started to tremble, I stuck the pen back into the notebook and closed it, shoving it beneath the mattress. They'd been sparse at first, a few episodes a week, at most. But for the last three months, there were entries nearly every day. Soon, the notebook would be filled.

I took up the stack of mail from the corner of the bed, desperate to put my mind to something else. It was mostly bills to pay and invoices for the farm, but when I spotted the corner of a speckled brown envelope, I paused. It was the same kind we used at the shop, but that wasn't the strange part.

I slid the other envelopes out of the way, staring at the script.

June Farrow
12 Bishop Street
Jasper, North Carolina 28753

It was Gran's handwriting.

I picked it up, inspecting it. There was no return address, but the stamp matched the ones we had in the desk drawer downstairs, and the postage was dated only two days before she died.

How long had it been sitting on the entry table?

I turned it over, tearing the envelope open. The scalloped edge of what looked like a small white card peeked out from inside. I pulled it free, brow furrowing when I read what was written there.

Nathaniel Rutherford and wife, 1911

Rutherford was a name I knew because it was the subject of almost every ghost story told in this town. He was the minister who'd been murdered at the river.

It wasn't a card, I realized, feeling the thickness of the paper between my fingers. It was a photograph.

I flipped it over, and an old black-and-white image that was yellowed at its edges stared back at me. A man in a white button-up shirt leaned into the side of a brick wall with one shoulder, a cigarette in hand. The memory of the figure on the porch the night before resurfaced in my mind. Those broad shoulders set on a narrow frame.

He was handsome, hair combed to one side, with a sharp jaw and deep-set eyes that looked straight into the camera. A faint, painful twinge crept into the tips of my fingers.

A woman stood beside him, turned in his direction with one hand tucking her waving, windblown hair behind her ear. The other was hooked into the crook of his arm. There was a smile on her lips.

The running water in the bathroom down the hall bled away into silence as I studied her. Every inch of her outline. Every detail of the simple dress she wore. I was looking for something, anything, that would explain the feeling that erupted in my chest.

Because it was a face I'd recognize anywhere, even if I couldn't remember ever seeing it myself.

It was the face of my mother.

THREE

My feet paced the length of the upstairs hallway until they were taking me down the staircase, my eyes still glued to the photograph. I held it out before me, tracing the tip of the woman's nose. The shape of her chin. When I reached the bottom step, I pried my focus from the picture, finding the one that sat framed on the table below the hall mirror.

It was the only photo of my mother displayed in the house. I passed it every time I came down the hallway, its image burned into my mind like a brand. I stared at it. The chill that had raced up my spine was now a cold blanket wrapped around me. I wasn't imagining things this time. It looked just like her.

My eyes drifted through the sitting room to the basement door, and then I was walking again, pacing past the fireplace, the afternoon light pooled on its wide, flat stones. My hand tightened on the photograph, and I pressed it to my chest as I reached for the glass knob and turned it. The door swung open, bringing with it the cool, damp air. The basement smelled like fresh mud in the summer, and it thickened as I went down the steps, reaching into the darkness for the string that hung from the single lightbulb.

I gave it a tug, and the tinny fizz of electricity filled the space, making the small room come to life around me. There wasn't much down there except for the peaches and plums we'd canned last season and the clothes washer, but Mason had built metal shelves along one wall for us after the basement flooded a couple of years ago. We'd transferred everything from disintegrating cardboard boxes to clear plastic bins. I pushed the first few to the side, looking for the only one that wasn't labeled. It had been intentional on my part because I hadn't wanted to draw Gran's attention to what was inside.

I was sixteen years old when I first started looking into my mother's disappearance. I'd figured out at a young age that Gran didn't want to talk about it. In fact, she didn't want to talk about my mother at all. That framed photo on the table by the stairs was the only evidence in this house that Susanna had ever even existed.

It began with a newspaper clipping I'd found at Birdie's. That single tether to the mystery had turned into an obsession. Before that, Susanna had been no more than another town rumor to me. Part of the folklore that lived in these mountains. Seeing it in print, her name inked onto paper, had somehow made her come alive in my mind. It took some convincing, but I'd enlisted Ida at the courthouse to help me meticulously compile every bit of information that could be found on my mother and what had happened to her.

I slid the bin from the shelf and lowered it to the ground, my bare feet now cold on the basement floor. The lid came off with a pop, and I peered inside at a large accordion folder. The file was thick, its edges worn. I hadn't opened it in years, but it was heavier than I remembered. The feel of it brought back memories of the summer afternoons I'd spent in Mason's garage. I'd sprawl out on the old, tattered sofa, notating and cross-referencing and cataloging every piece of paper while he played video games on an old box TV set.

The research had taken over my entire life for the better part of a year, something I'd had to keep hidden from Gran. There had been a feeling of urgency to it. Like it was my only chance to understand what happened. Only, it didn't matter how much I colored in the picture or filled in the blanks. All these years later, I only had more unanswered questions.

I sank back and pulled the folder into my lap, unlacing the twine and bending the flap backward so that I could read the labels. It was everything I'd collected. Stacks of articles, photographs, and copies of the police report were arranged with dates and sources.

The sheriff gave me what few answers he could. There were statements filled with stories about Susanna that turned my stomach— glimpses of what I imagined would be my own future. Then there were little things, too, like library records of the last book she'd checked out. The purchase agreement for the Bronco, which she'd paid cash for after years of saving. A bill from the cafe showed what she'd ordered the morning she disappeared: pancakes. There had been something so heartbreaking about that particular detail. In a matter of hours, Susanna would be gone forever. But that morning, she'd eaten pancakes.

There were several newspaper articles, mostly about her disappearance, from the *Jasper Chronicle,* the *Citizen Times* in Asheville, and *The Charlotte Observer.* But there was also one announcing that a twelve-year-old Susanna had won the sixth grade spelling bee.

I fished the stack of photographs from one of the sections and clumsily spread them out on the floor beside me, my eyes searching the many faces of Susanna Farrow. A baby in Gran's arms. A toddler in a pair of overalls, chest bare beneath the sagging straps. A young girl blowing out birthday candles. A teenager with wide, wire-rimmed glasses in the fields at the farm. My frantic hands finally stilled when I found the one I was looking for—a Susanna who was in her early twenties, I guessed.

She stood beneath the dogwood tree in the front yard, one hand absently reaching for the low-hanging branch beside her. Her hair was long and down, face turned to the street as if the picture was snapped the moment she saw someone coming down the sidewalk.

On the outside, she looked so normal. So ordinary in the kind of way I'd always longed for. No hint or shadow in her eyes of what was to come.

I slid the photo across the floor, placing it beside the one I'd found in the envelope, and shivered. The two pictures sat side by side, different sizes, one in black-and-white, and one in faded color. But the two women were like perfect symmetry. They weren't just similar. They were *exactly* the same.

I pulled my hand back, finding the pound of my heart beneath my robe and pressing my hand to it. It couldn't be her. My mother had been born decades later, and the resemblance wasn't so strange when you took into account that the woman's face was turned a little to the side. There was also the age of the photograph. It wasn't in bad condition, but it wasn't as sharp and clear as the one I'd taken from the folder.

It wasn't her, I told myself again. I pulled my hair out of my face, tucking it behind my ear. Of course it wasn't her, but where did Gran get it? And why had she sent it to me?

I tried to think back to the week before she died, my mind skipping over the days. They'd been ordinary. Runs to the shop and the farm, the grocery. She could have mailed it from anywhere. But why mail it at all? Why not just give it to me? Those were the kinds of logical questions I'd stopped asking the worse her mind got.

The more the years drew on, the more time Gran spent in that *other* place. She'd be standing at the sink and washing dishes, kneeling in the garden, or sitting in the rocking chair on the porch, but in her mind, she'd slipped away to somewhere else. She'd talk to people who weren't there. Hum songs I'd never heard. She'd go out to the shed looking for something that didn't exist. Over the years, she drifted back and forth over that line. For the last six months of her life, she all but lived on the other side of it.

In those last few weeks, Gran was slowing down. Getting quieter. She was sleeping longer and not wanting to leave the house. I'd had a sense she was coming to the end, even though she didn't say it and neither did Dr. Jennings. But there'd been something different about her.

That single thought is what finally made it click—that maybe it didn't make sense because it didn't actually mean anything. How Gran got her hands on a picture of Nathaniel Rutherford, I didn't know. But she probably thought the same thing I did—that it looked like Susanna—and somewhere in the thick mist of her mind she'd decided to mail it to me.

I couldn't see a ring on the woman's finger, but the inscription called her Nathaniel's wife. And then there was the way she leaned toward him, like there was a center of gravity I couldn't see. Or maybe it was the wind giving her a gentle nudge in his direction.

"June?"

A muffled voice upstairs called my name, making me jolt.

"June!"

Birdie. I hadn't even heard her come in. I looked down at the photos on the floor, as if just remembering where I was. The open bin. The basement. My loosely tied robe.

"Shit." I groaned. The tub. I'd left the water running.

I pushed the folder from my lap, dumping it and the pictures into the bin. My hands clumsily got the lid back on before I slid it against the wall and climbed the wooden steps to the sitting room.

"June!"

When I made it back to the second floor, Birdie was pulling towels from the hall closet. Water covered the tile, reflecting the light coming through the window. The old claw-foot tub was filled to the brim, its surface rippling beneath the dripping faucet.

"I'm so sorry." I took another towel from Birdie's hands, crouching to spread it across the doorway before the bath water could spill onto the wooden floorboards. "I forgot it was running."

"Where were you?"

I sopped up the water on my hands and knees, out of breath.

"June? Where were you, honey?"

"Downstairs," I answered.

"But I was just down there."

"In the basement, I mean."

Her eyes focused more sharply on me before moving over the bathroom. That look was scrutinizing. Almost suspicious. The overflowing tub was exactly the kind of thing Gran would have done. I didn't know how many times I'd come home to a smoke-filled kitchen or all the windows propped open during a storm. But this wasn't that, was it?

"I was just changing over the laundry," I lied, stomach turning when I began to worry that she might go and check.

I didn't want to tell her about the picture. Maybe because it felt like something I didn't understand. It had been my name on the envelope; Gran had specifically meant it for me.

It doesn't mean anything, I reminded myself. *She was sick, June.*

I got back to my feet, glancing down the hall to my open bedroom door where I could see the edge of the quilt that was draped over my bed. The mail was still scattered where I'd left it, the journal tucked safely under the mattress.

Birdie's hand lifted, pressing to my cheek. "You're flushed, dear. Are you feeling all right?"

"Fine." I smiled, still trying to slow my racing heart.

Birdie didn't look convinced. "You know, I don't need to go to Charlotte tomorrow. Why don't I cancel?"

"No," I said, too quickly. "We're already behind schedule."

That was true. We were expanding the willow grove at the farm, and she was going to Charlotte to pick up the new trees. With Gran and the funeral, we'd already pushed it a week, and we couldn't postpone again with the Midsummer Faire coming up.

"I'm sure Mason can go," she said.

"He's got enough to do. I'll help him at the farm, you go to Charlotte." When her mouth twisted to one side, I exhaled on a laugh. "It's just a little water, Birdie. Relax."

"All right, if you're sure."

"I'm sure."

I closed the bathroom door, shutting myself inside, and the smile melted from my face. I stood there, silent, as her hesitant footsteps disappeared. A few seconds later, I could hear her filling the kettle at the sink downstairs.

The water on the floor wasn't warm anymore. I wasn't even sure how long I'd been down in the basement. For a fraction of a moment, fear sliced hot through my mind at the thought that maybe I'd imagined it all. That maybe that letter, the photograph, hadn't even been real.

My hand instantly went to the pocket of my robe, desperately searching for the picture. As soon as my fingertips found it, I let out a painful, relieved breath and pulled it free. Nathaniel Rutherford's dark eyes met mine, so focused and calm that I almost expected him to move. For his finger to flick the ash from that cigarette, or for the collar of that crisp white shirt to shift in the wind.

In the mirror, the image of me was a faint echo of the woman standing beside Nathaniel. From this angle, the birthmark that stretched below my ear looked like blood. My reflection was blurred, the glass fogged with steam. I wiped the flat of my palm across it in an arc, watching as the reflection began to fade again.

Second by second, it was disappearing. Just like me.

FOUR

I woke with arms around me.

The first swimming thought that bobbed to the surface of my mind was that I could smell something. A wild scent that reminded me of summer, like fresh wood and new grass and the sweet fragrance of blooming flowers on the farm.

I breathed it in, tasting it on the back of my tongue, and the weight of an embrace gently drew me closer. In the haze of my thoughts, I could feel the warmth of someone behind me, the line of a body pressed to mine. The faint echo of a touch moved over the back of my hand, slipping between my fingers. The tingle of it traveled over my skin, along my temple, down the center of my spine. And when I heard the sound, it was just a whisper, but it was so close to my ear that I could feel breath on my cheek.

"June."

I gasped, choking as I sat up. I threw off the quilts, and the room took shape around me in the first moments of sunlight before I stumbled out of the bed, pressing myself to the wall.

Before me, the bed was empty—a pile of quilts and tangled sheets.

My fingers went to my cheek, and I rubbed the place I'd felt that warmth. My ear still tingled with the sound. It was so close. So real.

I paced back to the bed, slipping my hands beneath the sheets and frantically searching for the heat I'd felt. But it was cold on the other side of the bed. I was alone.

I stood there, staring into space until the churn in my stomach made me swallow hard. My feet clumsily found their way to the corner of the room, and I pressed myself into it. My skin was burning, and it occurred to me all at once that I might be having a panic attack. I went still, pinning my eyes to a small tear in the wallpaper. I had to breathe. I had to slow down my heart rate.

My hand reached out, steadying me against the window's ledge as I sank down, and I pulled my knees into my chest, trying to take deep, even breaths. I pushed that feeling away until my surroundings became reassuringly familiar. I was home. In our house. I was safe.

One, two, three.

I counted my breaths in a repeating sequence until my trembling slowed. The fever that had been under my skin was fading, replaced by a brittle cold.

"It's not real," I whispered on an exhale, forcing myself to count again.

But in that moment, it had been. And it wasn't the first time I'd heard that voice, either.

The deep tone was something I could pick out now, the *U* in my name distinct and bent in a peculiar way. I'd first heard it at the farm the day the episodes began, calling out my name again and again. Now, almost a year later, I knew it the way I knew the sounds of this house or the rush of the river. That voice was an echo across the pages of my notebook.

I'd had dreams that tiptoed along the edge of reality before. Ones that pushed me from sleep with tears streaming down my temples or a scream trapped in my throat. In those dreams, it was as if my body and mind had bled into another world, only to surface too hard and

too fast in reality. But this wasn't like that. This . . . this was like someone had come through that barrier from the other side. Like those
arms around me had reached through my mind, into my bedroom.

The sun had risen by the time I came downstairs, my hair pulled
into a half-hearted bun at the nape of my neck. Birdie's overnight bag
was already sitting at the bottom of the steps, and I was relieved to see
it. After what happened yesterday, I was almost sure that she would
cancel her trip to Charlotte.

She was sitting in her usual seat at the table, a cup of coffee steaming beside the *Jasper Chronicle*. The headline announced the official
schedule of the Midsummer Faire, the town's largest and oldest event,
which took place on the summer solstice. Local makers and crafts-
people set up on Main Street to showcase their goods, and people
came from neighboring towns for the music and dancing.

Birdie pretended not to watch me from the top of her gaze as she
smeared cream cheese onto the toasted bagel in her hand.

"Morning." I kept my back to her, taking the half-full pot of coffee
and pouring it into a mug. The little sugar spoon clinked against the
ceramic as I dumped two spoonfuls into the coffee and stirred.

"Morning, honey." The newspaper crinkled as she turned the page.

I clutched the mug to my chest, leaning one hip into the counter
as I faced her. It was our usual rhythm, except that a week ago, Gran
would be sitting beside her. I couldn't help but notice that Birdie's
plate and newspaper were set squarely to one side of the table, as if
she'd subconsciously left room for Gran's breakfast.

She tore the bagel in two. "When are you going to tell me what's
goin' on in that head of yours?"

"Nothing's going on." I brought the mug to my lips again, trying to
hide the nervous twitch of my mouth.

I was still thinking about the feeling of that body pressed to mine.
I'd known for most of my life that certain things weren't in the cards
for me. The kind of relaxed, lived-in love where you woke up together
in the morning was one of them. I'd been clear on that. With Gran,
Birdie, and Mason. There were times when I'd sensed the slightest

hint of sympathy worming its way into them. Sometimes, I'd catch Gran and Birdie giving each other a silent look in those conversations. But I'd never let any of them feel sorry for me, and I'd refused to feel sorry for myself.

The faint fissure in the ice of my resolve found me in the rarest of moments. The delicate, absent-minded touch of a woman's hand on her pregnant belly. A newborn cradled in someone's arms at the grocery. It would hit me like a train. Because there was only one thing I'd ever kept from them. It was a buried thing inside of me, so deep I could almost always pretend it wasn't there.

It was the truth I couldn't even admit to myself—that I *did* want it. All of it.

At nine or ten years old, I was just beginning to understand that one day, I'd be sick the way my mother had been. I was old enough to realize that she hadn't just disappeared. She'd *left* me.

I tried not to think too much about the part of Susanna that had been broken enough for her to do what she did. I couldn't imagine it, just walking away from your child and never looking back. The question nagged at me, like a finger picking the same string on an out-of-tune guitar over and over until it just became one head-splitting sound. I knew she was sick, but I wanted to believe that there were pieces of us that couldn't be touched by that shadow—the pieces that made us human.

The sharp, deafening ring of the telephone made me jump, sending my coffee cup forward. The liquid sloshed over the lip, spilling over my hand.

Birdie started to stand but I waved her off, flicking the coffee from my fingers into the sink.

"It's okay. I've got it."

I crossed the linoleum floor, wincing when it rang again, and my shoulders drew up protectively around my ears. The old phone's volume had been turned up for Gran when she started refusing to wear her hearing aids, and it sounded like a fistful of quarters shaken in an old coffee can.

The receiver was cold against my hot face as I answered. "Hello?"

A man's voice crackled on the other end, and I adjusted the twisted cord, trying to make it clear.

"Hello?" I said again.

Behind me, Birdie was muttering. "Got to get that damn thing replaced."

"Ah, hi there. June?" The voice finally came through. "It's Dr. Jennings."

I stilled, slowly turning so that Birdie couldn't see my face. "Oh. Hi."

"Sorry to call so early, but I tried your cell yesterday and there was no answer."

"No problem. What can I do for you?"

There was the sound of paper shuffling, followed by a breath exhaled, as if he was getting situated at his desk with the phone pinned between his shoulder and his jaw. "Just wanted to confirm your appointment for this afternoon."

Dr. Jennings's voice faded to the back of my mind, replaced by the hum of the refrigerator and the sound of a fly tapping the window in an attempted escape. I stared at a black knot on the pinewood floor between my feet. I'd forgotten about the appointment.

"June?"

"Yeah," I said, wrapping the phone cord around my hand. "Sure, I'll be there."

"Great. I'll see you then."

"Thanks."

"Bye-bye now."

The line clicked, going dead, and I hung up the phone, plastering a look of calm on my face before I went back to the sink.

"Who was that?" Birdie spoke the words around a mouthful of bagel.

"Just Mason checking to see if I'm coming out today."

She raised a skeptical brow in my direction as she took another bite. I'd managed to keep her from finding out about my episodes, but eventually, she was going to put it together. I'd kept the secret not because I didn't trust her. It was because the moment I told her I was sick, things would change. For her and for me. The further I drifted, the more alone she would be.

She changed the subject. "Ida's goin' to be the death of me with this Midsummer Faire business. You sure you're up for it?"

I nodded. It wasn't the first time Birdie and I had run the show together. The flower farm always donated the excess late spring harvest to decorate at the event, and this year, Ida was the chair. She had Melody working around the clock on the plans.

"First one without Gran," I thought aloud.

A smile stretched up one side of Birdie's face. "Yeah, I was thinkin' that this mornin'."

My thoughts pulled back to that envelope and the photograph that was tucked inside. I'd considered telling Birdie about it last night as we sat at that same table with Ida's casserole between us. I hadn't been able to bring myself to do it, but it was still eating at me, poking at the edges of my mind.

"Do you know if Gran knew Nathaniel Rutherford?" The question formed on my lips before I'd even really thought about it.

Something stiffened in Birdie's posture, just slightly. Almost too subtle to notice. "What?"

"Nathaniel Rutherford. The minister over at the church who—"

"I know who he is, June." Was there an edge to her voice? I couldn't quite tell. "But I was just a little thing when that happened."

"Right. But Gran was older. She might have actually known him."

"She didn't exactly mix with the church folk. You know that."

"But did she ever talk about it?" I tried again.

"No one really liked to talk about it. Not then and not now."

"I just mean, I grew up hearing that story and seeing his picture in the cafe, but I don't remember Gran ever mentioning it. It's strange."

Birdie frowned. "Not all that strange, if you think about it."

"What do you mean?"

"Well, that was a difficult time for this town. A lot of suspicion, a lot of accusations thrown around. Tragedy will do that, I guess." She got to her feet, a little clumsily. "Should probably get on the road."

I watched her carefully as she dried her hands on the towel hanging from the oven. The drive to Charlotte was only a couple of hours, and she'd already missed the traffic. Somehow, I'd hit a nerve.

"You taking off already?" I asked.

"Might as well. Can you stop in at the shop on your way to the farm and check on Melody? She's got a big order today."

"Sure." The answer sounded like a question. I was still trying to read that look on her face. I had the distinct feeling the question had upset her, though I couldn't think why.

When she finally turned to face me, she looked a little like herself again. She crossed the kitchen in three steps, planting a firm kiss on my cheek. "See you tomorrow."

I forced a smile, propping myself up against the wall as she disappeared up the hallway. When I heard the keys jingle in her hand, I called over my shoulder, "Drive safe!"

"Yes, Mother!" The door closed, and a few seconds later, Birdie's car was backing down the driveway.

It wasn't like her to dance around things. She'd always been the one who got to the point and didn't sugarcoat the truth. She was the first to be honest with me about my mother, about the Farrow curse and the grim future that was coming for me. She'd never tried to shield me from any of it, like Gran had. But bringing up Nathaniel Rutherford had rattled her. Why?

My eyes fell to the newspaper on the table, my mind still turning with the question, until my curiosity got the better of me. I rounded the corner to the sitting room, taking the laptop from the desk that sat in front of the picture window. The room hadn't changed a single bit in my lifetime, down to the knickknacks on the fireplace mantel and the blue velvet tufted sofa that looked older than Birdie.

I sank down into it and pulled open the laptop, hitting a key. It whirred to life, illuminating the inbox of the farm's email account. I opened a new tab in the browser, fingers hovering tentatively over the keys before I finally started typing in the search field.

Nathaniel Rutherford Jasper, North Carolina

Dozens of search results pulled up, and I scrolled, my eyes skipping over them until I saw one from the State Archives of North Carolina. The link took me to another search results page, where a number of headlines from old newspapers were listed with Nathaniel's name highlighted in the description.

The earliest ones looked to be no more than small-town news coverage, but in 1950, the headlines took a turn.

BODY FOUND IN ADELINE RIVER
MINISTER SLAIN
SHERIFF ASKS FOR WITNESSES TO COME FORWARD
JASPER REMEMBERS NATHANIEL RUTHERFORD
ONE YEAR LATER: STILL NO ANSWERS

I clicked on the first one, and a high-resolution scan of the *Jasper Chronicle* filled the screen. The front of the paper was different from the one that sat on the kitchen table. The font had changed over time, and so had the layout of the columns.

Thursday morning, the Merrill County Sheriff's Department responded to the call of Edgar Owens, who was fishing on the north fork of the Adeline River, just upstream from Longview Falls, when he discovered a body washed up on the bank. The man was identified as sixty-three-year-old Nathaniel Rutherford, longtime minister at the First Presbyterian Church in Jasper.

Longview Falls was the region's tallest waterfall, where the Adeline River branched. It was a hiker's destination and the site of numerous accidents over the years. There'd even been a few people who'd jumped to their deaths.

The next article was longer.

The sheriff's department has confirmed that the death of Nathaniel Rutherford is being treated as suspicious. Upon examination, the body was found to have a fatal head wound and multiple lacerations on the arms and neck consistent with a struggle. This would mark the first known murder in the quiet town of Jasper, and the sheriff has vowed to find the perpetrator.

The last known location of the minister was at the Midsummer Faire. Rutherford was expected at Frank Crawley's barn afterward for a weekly card game with a group of men from the church. According to Crawley, Nathaniel never arrived. Those who were present at the game are undergoing questioning, but the sheriff has been clear they are not currently suspects.

To his estimation, Dr. Francis Pullman puts Rutherford's time of death at approximately 8 P.M., an hour after he was last seen.

I clicked on the next link.

The sheriff's department is asking for anyone with information about Nathaniel Rutherford's whereabouts on the night of June 21 to come forward. No detail is too small. Anyone who saw anything unusual can call the sheriff's department at 431-2200.

The headline of the last article was printed above a photograph of a man.

ONE YEAR LATER: STILL NO ANSWERS

Nathaniel was standing on the front steps of the church with a hat in his hands. I had to look at him closely to find the similarities between him and the man in the photo Gran sent. The edition date was

1951, exactly forty years after the date written on the back of the photograph.

But there was no mention of his wife's actual name in the articles, and the only pictures were of Nathaniel alone.

I leaned to one side and slid the photo from the back pocket of my jeans, that itch of curiosity growing more insistent. My leg was anxiously bouncing now, making the laptop shake as my eyes lifted to the kitchen. When I was looking into my mother's disappearance, Ida had helped me request copies of old editions of the *Jasper Chronicle*. She'd also been the one to pull the records at the courthouse for me.

I let the laptop slide onto the sofa and stood, my feet taking me back to the kitchen, where the soft sound of wind chimes drifted through the open window. Ida's cellphone number was still scratched on the long list pinned to the side of the fridge, but I had it memorized. I dialed and a chipper voice on the other end answered on the third ring.

"June? Everything okay?"

"Hey, Ida. Yeah, everything's fine."

"Oh." She paused. "Well, good. What can I do for you?"

"I wanted to see if you'd be able to find something for me in the county records."

"Okay. What is it?"

I stared at the numbers on the phone's dial pad, where Gran's fingers had pushed the buttons so many times that they were shiny and smooth. "It's a marriage license, actually."

"For whom?" I could hear her plucking a pencil from the old decorated soup can on her desk.

I clenched my teeth, changing my mind twice before I forced myself to say it.

"Last name Rutherford. First name . . . Nathaniel."

She fell quiet.

"Would have been sometime around 1911," I added, filling the awkward silence.

"Why on earth would you need that?" She laughed, but it was taut.

I smiled, even though she couldn't see it, hoping it would somehow bleed into my voice. "Just doing some historical research."

"All right." The wheels of her chair squeaked before I heard her nails on the keyboard. "Easy enough, I guess."

I could imagine her there behind the high counter, chin tipped up so she could read the computer screen through the bifocal area of her glasses.

"Now, let's see here." Her voice trailed off as she kept typing. "Got it. What exactly are you looking for?"

"The name of the woman he married."

The murmur of her reading under her breath was barely audible over the phone, and the damaged cord crackled again, making me wince. She made a sound that was followed by another silence.

"Sorry, Ida. I didn't hear you."

"I just—well, this is odd, isn't it?" Another nervous laugh escaped her.

"What is?"

"It says right here . . ." She began to read. "'Having applied for a license for the marriage of Nathaniel Rutherford, of Jasper'"—she took a breath—"'age twenty-five years, to resident of Jasper—'"

The phone cut out again and I pinched my fingers to the cord, holding it in place.

"To Susanna. It says Susanna Farrow."

My fingers slipped from the cord, finding the locket around my neck. I was sure the moment it left her mouth that I'd heard her wrong. That the voice in my mind whispering my mother's name was just too loud. It was drowning everything else out.

"I'm—I'm sorry?" I stammered.

"That's what it says, honey. I'm lookin' at it right now." She continued, "'. . . united in matrimony Nathaniel Rutherford and Susanna Farrow the parties likened above, on the ninth day of September 1911 at First Presbyterian Church in Jasper.'"

I stared at the wall, a numb sensation bleeding through me.

"I didn't know you all were related to that family."

"We aren't," I said, the words made of air.

"Well, this woman was a Farrow. Doubt that's a coincidence in a town this small. Your own mother must have been named after her."

I blinked, fitting her words to the fragments of thought that were struggling to come together. Of course. That would explain it. Maybe someone up the line in the family *had* married Nathaniel Rutherford. But I didn't remember Gran ever talking about another Susanna Farrow, and there was no gravestone in the cemetery for one. She'd always been so serious about making sure I knew the family's history.

Except for when it came to Susanna, I realized.

I swallowed. "Can you find her birth record? Something that has her parents' names or . . . ?"

"Let's see." Ida typed away for a few long seconds before she clicked her tongue. "I don't see anything for that name. The only one pulling up for a Susanna Farrow is for your mother back in 1966. But you already have all that."

I did. Thanks to Ida, I had a copy of every scrap of paper on my mother that could be found in the courthouse.

"Not unusual for that time, though." She thought aloud. "That far back, women birthed babies at home all the time and there wasn't much reason to record the birth with the county."

I leaned into the counter, thinking.

"You could try the church," she said.

"The church?"

"It's been here longer than the courthouse, and they kept detailed records on births, marriages, and deaths. It's worth a try if this woman was married to the minister."

When I said nothing, she spoke again. "Want me to call over there?"

"No, that's all right. Thanks, Ida."

"No problem, honey."

I hung up the phone, one hand still gripped on the receiver as I bit down hard on my thumbnail. In the span of a few moments, that compulsive need I'd had to understand the photograph had turned into a slithering thing. As if the second Ida said my mother's name, she'd uttered the words of a forbidden spell. The name carried a hallowed kind of resonance. One that had captured the town's imagination for years and given birth to a hundred stories. So had Nathaniel's.

My eyes went to the window. I could still hear it—that high-pitched tinkle of the wind chimes—and it struck me that I didn't know where they were coming from. The only ones we'd had hanging in the garden had been blown down in a storm more than a year ago. They were still sitting on the potting bench outside, waiting for a new string.

The sound grew louder. More painful. My chest rose and fell as I made my way to the front door, pulling it open. The screen slammed and I went out onto the porch, searching the rafters, where a turtle dove peered over the edge of a nest.

The wind chimes weren't there.

I pressed my hands over my ears when the ringing gave way to a sharp pain in my head. But the chimes didn't stop. They didn't dim. The ringing rose, the notes fusing together until it was one long, ear-splitting scream in my mind.

And then, all of a sudden, like the wind snuffing a candle's flame, it stopped.

FIVE

Dr. Jennings's office was a tall but narrow three-story building downtown, a contradictory combination of old and new. The examination room was painted in a pale shade of green. It matched a row of 1970s cabinets that hung above a small porcelain sink lined with glass jars of cotton balls and gauze bandages, and though the door was still fit with what looked to be its original glass knob, a brand-new ultrasound machine sat in the corner, its screen aglow.

A tray that held three vials of my blood sat beside me on the paper-covered table, my name scrawled across the stickers in blue ink. I stared at them, listening to the scratch of Dr. Jennings's pen on paper as he flipped through my notebook. He was the only one who'd ever looked inside.

Gran had never been one for doctors, but Dr. Jennings had made his calls anyway, insisting that what was happening to her followed no textbooks or standards of practice that he'd ever seen. She thought that he looked at her as some kind of science experiment, but I found the doctor to be more like a man with a chessboard than anything else. He wanted to be the first to solve the riddle of the Farrow women.

He'd failed with Gran. I was his second chance.

"They're definitely increasing in frequency. You're right about that. How many episodes would you say this week?" He looked up, meeting my eyes expectantly.

His once-dark hair was nearly all white, his smooth black skin dotted with tiny moles across his cheekbones. His face had significantly aged in the years since I was a child, but he still had that gentle way about him, as if he feared one wrong word would send me running straight out of the room.

"June?"

"Six, I think." I cleared my throat when the words came out sounding cracked.

"Okay." He scribbled away, the pen looping across the page. I could see the word *hallucination*.

That label had never felt right. The things I saw were different. It was a hollowed-out, floating feeling, like the meandering path a single dandelion seed takes through the air before it eventually lands. A real thing just barely out of reach.

"Have you noticed if any of these episodes have been accompanied by any . . . physical symptoms? Fainting? Vision changes?"

"No."

My eyes focused on the chart that hung on the wall behind him. It was a diagram of the human heart, with detailed renderings of the muscle and tissue, and I immediately thought how fortunate I would be to have something as simple as a heart problem. There were surgeries for that. Clinically proven medications to prescribe. Transplants, even. Labels identified the organ's components in words like *chamber, ventricle, atrium, valve*. It all looked so simple. Like the parts of a machine. But the human brain was like the uncharted depths of the oceans. Science was still wading around in the shallows.

"I think we should take into consideration that you've been under some significant stress. I know that Margaret's death wasn't exactly sudden, but you're grieving, and that takes a toll on both the body and the mind. It's possible that these episodes have been exacerbated by that stress." He looked up from the notebook, setting it into his lap.

I wasn't going to tell him that my stress had multiplied even more in the last twenty-four hours, when I received a letter from my dead grandmother that had a picture from 1911 of a woman who looked exactly like my missing mother. I wasn't going to tell him about the news articles or the call to the courthouse, either. Just thinking of it made me feel off-balance.

"Have you talked to Birdie about any of this yet? Mason?"

"No," I answered.

"Okay, well, we've known for years that if the time came, you'd have a strong, stable support system in place. That's still true. And you'll need to tell them. Soon."

I'd spent the majority of the last twelve years as varying degrees of Gran's caretaker while Birdie took over things at the shop and Mason took over the farm. The thing was, I was happy to do it because I loved her. She'd taken me in and been everything to me. The center of my very small world in Jasper had always been my grandmother. Now someone would have to become *my* caretaker. It wasn't a job that Birdie could do for very long. That left only Mason.

The thought made me feel weak. Fragile. Those two words had never been familiar to me before, but now they felt intimate. So close that there wasn't air to breathe around them.

"It's important that you continue to document things as accurately as possible so that we can keep looking for patterns and triggers," Dr. Jennings continued.

"Gran never had patterns and triggers," I reminded him. That had been the most frustrating part.

He frowned, flipping through the pages of the notebook again. "That's not true. Some of these hallucinations are repetitive. The horse, the door, the voice."

The tingle of that touch reignited on my skin where I'd felt it when I woke that morning. He was right. There *were* patterns. I'd seen the chestnut horse four times now. A red door twice. The man's voice I'd heard countless times.

"The main thing to look out for is any sign of paranoia or delusions," he continued. "You see any sign of that, you call me right away, no matter the time."

"I will." I slid off the table, taking my bag from the chair. I wanted this conversation to be over.

"And you'll need to start thinking about power of attorney."

"What?" The word came out panicked.

Dr. Jennings's hand splayed in the air between us in a gesture that was meant to calm me. "No rush. Just something to consider. Have you thought about who you'll appoint?"

I couldn't pretend that I hadn't. "Mason." I shrugged. "He's already the sole beneficiary of everything, anyway."

"Well, I'd like for you to prioritize rest over the next week. Limit stimulation, maybe take some time off from the farm."

"I can't just stop living my life. Not when there might not be much of it left."

He gave me a sympathetic look, setting a hand on my shoulder. "We'll get these blood tests done and compare them to the baseline. You know the drill. Regular checkups mean regular data. Might give us some insight."

"I don't want anyone to know," I reminded him.

"Of course. Not until you're ready." He nodded. "Completely confidential."

"From everyone?" I lifted my eyebrows, glancing at the door. Dr. Jennings's nurse Camille was Rhett Miller's wife. He was the owner of Edison's Cafe, and that was the worst possible place this information could exist.

"*Everyone.* No one knows what we talk about between these walls unless you tell them, June. We can even switch to house calls, like we did with your grandmother, if you like."

"Thanks."

His hand dropped from my shoulder, and I took a step toward the door, pausing just long enough for him to give me a concerned look.

"Can I ask you something?" I said.

"Sure."

"Did you ever see my mother? When she was pregnant with me, I mean?"

His head tilted a little, as if the question perplexed him. "Well, yes. Margaret brought Susanna in a few times, and I did her prenatal care until . . ." The words sputtered out. "Until she was gone."

"Do you remember anything unusual about it? Anything that you thought could have been connected to her disappearance?"

"Nothing in particular. Mentally, she was struggling, of course. But overall she was healthy. She seemed to be taking care of herself."

"Were you surprised when she disappeared?"

"Yes and no. Her decline was unpredictable, and mental illness isn't exactly uncommon when it comes to missing persons. But if you're asking whether I thought she might hurt herself or run off, the answer is no."

"She never told you anything about who . . ." I couldn't bring myself to finish the sentence.

"No. She never shared anything about who your biological father might be. To my knowledge, she didn't share that with anyone."

I exhaled, disappointment settling inside of me.

"Why do you ask?"

I shook my head. "No reason. I've just been thinking about her."

I could see that he was drawing a straight line in his mind from what was happening to me and what happened to my mother. Maybe I was worried about the same thing.

His tone softened. "Well, it's quite a tangled knot. But I want you to take what I said seriously, June. Get some rest."

"I will."

I opened the door and followed the narrow steps down to the first floor where the receptionist was bent low over the open drawer of a filing cabinet. She didn't look up as I passed, but I could feel myself holding my breath, waiting for the moment her eyes would lift and find me. By the time I made it out onto the sidewalk, the gravity had begun to hit me. Episodes. Data. Blood tests. Patterns. Triggers. They were words I'd used many times when talking about Gran. Now, this was *my* life.

I stepped into the crooked alley between Dr. Jennings's office and the grocery, finding a place to stand beneath an old fire escape that hid me from the street. My hand shook as I pulled my phone from my bag, and as soon as I found Birdie's name in the contact list, my throat began to close up. I dialed the number, pressing the phone to my ear and wiping a silent tear from my cheek as it rang.

"Hello?"

"Hey!" I said, too brightly.

"June?"

I almost laughed. My name was plastered across the screen of her cellphone, but she still somehow acted surprised when it was me. "Yeah, it's me, Birdie. Just making sure you made it."

"Oh, I made it. Headin' over to the warehouse now. Anything I should add to the order?" I wiped another tear, already feeling better now that I could hear her voice.

"Not that I can think of."

"All right. You need anything? I was thinking, if this doesn't take too long, I could come back tonight."

"No, I don't want you driving the mountain roads in the dark."

"You know I've been driving for longer than you've been alive?" I could hear the humor in her voice now and the sound made the knot in my chest loosen just a little. "I'll see you tomorrow. I'll make chicken and dumplings. How's that?"

"Sounds good." I pulled the keys from my bag and started toward the street.

"Love you, honey."

The tip of my finger found the sharp edge of the key, the lump coming up in my throat again. "Love you."

I climbed inside and turned the ignition. The smell of the engine and the hot leather conjured countless memories of summer. Countless memories with Mason. Driving in our wet bathing suits as the sun went down after an afternoon of swimming at the river. Picking him up for his shifts at the farm when Gran finally hired him. Parking under the big oak tree at Longview Falls with an open pizza box between us and our bare feet propped up on the dash.

As soon as I was through the intersection, I picked up the phone again, finding his number. I did that sometimes, impulsively calling him and then having to think of a reason. It was more for comfort than anything, a way to stave off that lonely feeling that had been with me so long. My world was a very small one, made up of only a few people and places, and it felt like it was shrinking by the second.

My thumb hovered over his name a second too long, and I dropped the phone onto the seat, my gaze going to my bag. I reached into the side pocket, hand searching until it found the photograph. I set it onto the dash in front of me, eyeing its reflection on the windshield.

What Ida said was possible. Our family had never been a large one. Each Farrow had but one daughter, and they'd all kept their maternal surname because most of the men who fathered them died young or faded from the picture. Somewhere along the line, one of the Farrow women could have had more than one child, and the Susanna Farrow in the photograph could have been simply lost to history. It didn't seem that unlikely, especially in a small farming town like Jasper.

My fingers tapped the steering wheel as the road grew narrower, my mind sifting through each thought. I knew what I was doing, throwing myself down one rabbit hole to keep from falling down the other. I was distracting myself from what was happening. And deep down, I knew that it didn't matter how deep the hole went. Eventually, I was going to hit the bottom.

I bit the inside of my lip and pulled onto the shoulder of the road, cranking the wheel hand over hand until I was turning around, headed in the opposite direction of home. Downtown passed in a blur as I drove back down the river road, turning at the light to cross the bridge. Seconds later, the steeple of the little white church appeared through the trees.

I followed the sloped, rocky drive along the waterfront, passing the cemetery. Gran's grave in the distance was still darkened with freshly turned earth, the headstone so white that it almost glowed against the green backdrop of the woods. The flowers left there were beginning to wilt, their bright colors fading.

The brakes squealed as I came to a stop, and I pulled the keys from the ignition, setting them onto the dash. The doors to the church were propped open, like they always were during the day. Even from across the river, you could see the light spilling from the entrance and down the steps after the sun went down.

I waited a few seconds before I got out of the truck, giving myself a chance to think better of it. But there was something relentless about my need to know about the woman in the photo. It was a sinking stone inside of me, like something truly terrible was about to happen and the only way to stop it was to know who she was.

The truck door popped as I opened it, and I hooked one hand into the strap of my bag, taking the locket in the other, as if it were an anchor that would calm that stomach-turning feeling. The cicadas were buzzing in the trees, the river rushing at my back as I climbed the steps.

I froze when I felt it. A slow tingle of gooseflesh started on the back of my hand, moving up my arm to my shoulder. The moment it touched my collarbone I forced myself to turn and look at the thing taking shape at the corner of my vision. "It's not real, June." The words were a reflex.

There, in the middle of the cemetery, a single red door stood among the tilted headstones. It was set into a frame, like it had been pried loose from a wall, and yet, it didn't look at all out of place. Like one brushstroke in a painting. The old-style paneling, chipped paint, and brass knob were the same as you'd find in a dozen other places in town.

The minute my heartbeat kicked up, I forced myself to breathe.

"It's not real." My lips moved around the words again, but I couldn't hear them. That was three times I'd seen it now. Once at the farm, once downtown, and now here, in the cemetery. I let myself wonder if Dr. Jennings's theory was right. Maybe there *was* a pattern to unearth there.

I looked at it for another moment, waiting for it to vanish, but it didn't. It just stood there, erected in the grass like it was waiting for me. I could still feel the weight of its presence as I turned my face back toward the church, my toes stopping at the threshold. My eyes ran over the sunlit sanctuary inside.

Oil-stained pews were set into even rows below six pendant lights suspended from the curved rafters. The fixtures were fit with faceted glass shades that made the light look speckled on the ceiling, the only thing in the room that could be considered elegant. It was just a simple country church, but one that had been painstakingly preserved, down to the single-paned lancet windows that lined the walls.

"Ms. Farrow?"

My eyes darted around the room until I spotted Thomas Falk, the minister. He stood in the doorway at the corner of the sanctuary, forehead scrunched like he wasn't sure what he was seeing. His dark hair was freshly cut, and the pressed button-up shirt he wore didn't have a single wrinkle.

"Hi," I said, my voice tight.

He crossed his arms over his chest. "Can't pretend I'm not surprised to see you here."

I looked down at my feet, acutely aware that I didn't actually want to cross the threshold.

"Afraid you'll burst into flames?"

My gaze flickered up, finding his expression changed. Now he looked amused.

I dragged the toe of my boot over the lip of the floor, taking me one step inside.

He walked toward me, hands tucked into his pockets. "What can I do for you?"

I had the sudden urge to look over my shoulder to be sure that no one was listening. "Actually, I was told that the church keeps records— marriages and births, things like that."

"That's right."

"I was hoping you could look something up for me."

"And what is that?"

"I'm trying to track down a birth record for someone. She would have been born sometime before 1900."

"I see." He lifted an eyebrow. "We do have records from that time. Why don't you come back and we'll see what we can find?"

I hesitated before finding my way up the center aisle, past the pews to the doorway that led to what looked like an office. Thomas disappeared inside, his shadow flitting over the wooden floorboards.

The room was small but packed tight with a desk, a wall of built-in shelves that were filled with books, and a few chairs that looked as old as the pews out in the sanctuary. The only thing that didn't belong was the sleek black computer on the desk.

Thomas sat down in the leather rolling chair, giving the mouse a shake. "You can have a seat, if you'd like."

"Thanks." I tried to sound more comfortable than I was, taking the chair against the window and pulling my bag into my lap. The view overlooked the widest part of the river, where a few boulders split the water into four sections that ran white over the rocks.

"Thankfully, most of the records have all been digitized now, which should make this pretty simple," he said, eyeing me over the computer screen. "Who is it we're looking for?"

My mother's name felt like it was lodged in my throat. There wasn't anyone in Jasper who wouldn't recognize it.

"It's Susanna Farrow, actually."

The shape of his mouth changed. He stared at me. "I thought you said it was for someone born before 1900."

"A different Susanna Farrow. Someone further back in the family."

"Oh." He relaxed just enough for me to notice. "Same spelling?"

I nodded.

He typed, hitting the keys in a steady rhythm, but he frowned when his eyes ran over the screen. "I don't see anything here. Do you know anything else about her? Parents' names, maybe?"

"No, that's what I was trying to find out. She was married to Nathaniel Rutherford."

Thomas's expression shifted, and he sat back in the chair, his elbows finding the armrests. "Really."

I waited, unsure of what his reaction meant.

"If that's what you're after, you can just say it, Ms. Farrow. You're not the first person who's come to this church trying to dig up information about that case."

"I'm not trying to dig up anything," I said, only seconds before realizing that wasn't quite true. "A woman with the same name as my mother was married to Nathaniel, and I'm just trying to figure out who she was."

He surveyed me, and I had the distinct feeling he was trying to decide if I was lying.

"Really. I don't care anything about the minister." That *was* the truth.

"Well, I imagine there's not much documentation on her since she died so young."

"What?" I sat up straighter in my chair.

"Oh, yes. Nathaniel is well known because of the murder, of course. But his story was quite tragic long before then."

"What happened?"

"Well," Thomas said on an exhale. "His father was the minister at this church for years, but he died of a heart attack just after Nathaniel married. Nathaniel was just a young man." His hand lifted, a finger pointing to the open door that led to the sanctuary. "He was preaching God's word at that very pulpit when it happened."

I couldn't help but look. The simple white wooden podium stood up a few steps on a small stage that overlooked the pews.

"Nathaniel took over his father's position. But not long after, he and his wife had a daughter and she died."

"Daughter?" My voice bent the word.

Thomas's bottom lip jutted out. "She was just a baby. His wife never recovered. They say she lost her mind."

I cringed. If I'd had any doubt left that she really was a Farrow, that one detail extinguished it.

"She took her own life up at Longview Falls. Like I said—tragic."

A deep, dull pain erupted behind my ribs.

"Nathaniel never remarried, dedicating his life to the congregation of this church. He's buried out there. His wife and daughter, too."

My eyes went out the window again, to the waterfront down the hill. Only a mile and a half downstream, the river dumped over Longview Falls. The idea of the woman in the photograph tumbling over its edge made my stomach drop.

I swallowed hard. "Try Rutherford," I said.

"What?"

"See if there are any records for Susanna Rutherford. Maybe it'll have a birth date somewhere?"

"That could work." He turned back to the computer, typing.

The phone in my bag buzzed and I reached inside, pulling it out. A picture of Mason standing in front of the barn lit up the screen behind his name. I silenced the call and dropped the phone into the bag, rubbing at my temple in an attempt to soothe the ache growing there.

"Here we go," Thomas murmured.

I stood, coming around the desk to see the screen over his shoulder. The website looked like some kind of database, the words *Presbyterian Regional Assembly* visible at the top of the page.

"There's a baptism record linked to her married name." He clicked on the file, and a black-and-white scan of an old log opened, filling the browser's window. Row after row of names and dates were recorded in the same ornate handwriting.

Thomas leaned in closer, eyes roaming over the entries, but he looked to the door when the sound of footsteps echoed out in the sanctuary. He pushed away from the desk, getting to his feet. "Hello?"

"It's me, Tom," a woman's voice called back.

"Excuse me." He stepped around the desk, leaving me alone in the office, and I took his chair, eyes still glued to the screen.

The old style of calligraphy made the words almost impossible to read, and it was made more difficult by the glare coming through the window. I dragged a finger down the rows slowly until I found it.

Susanna Rutherford.

It was listed under the field MOTHER. The record wasn't for Susanna's baptism. It was for her child's.

The name stared back at me, but it didn't look familiar anymore. There was something that felt twisted about it. Distorted, almost.

I reached for the mouse and zoomed in on the page, reading the entire entry carefully. It was dated 1912.

Baptized by Nathaniel Rutherford on the 4th day of April, with her mother, Susanna Rutherford, as witness.

My eyes stopped on the name of the child, my throat closing up. I read it again. And again.

June Rutherford.

June.

I pushed away from the desk, sending the chair rolling backward a few inches. As if that space between me and the computer would somehow change what was written there. But the more I stared at it, the blacker the ink appeared. It almost seemed to be moving on the screen. Rippling like water.

Voices echoed on the other side of the open office door, followed by more footsteps. I pulled the phone from my bag, taking a picture of the document before I closed out of the window Thomas had opened and I deleted Susanna's name from the search field. My hands were trembling as my fingers left the mouse.

"Find anything?" Thomas came back through the door.

"Not really." I smiled shakily. "But thanks anyway." I stood, pulling the bag back over my shoulder before making my way past him.

"You know," Thomas said, waiting for me to look at him. "You're always welcome here. If you ever need anything. Even just to talk."

I pressed my lips together, unable to muster any kind of answer. What would he think if I told him about the photograph and baptism record? What would he say if I divulged the creeping thought that was unspooling in my fractured mind?

His smile faded in the eerie silence that fell over the room.

I turned on my heel, following the aisle back to the open doors. My feet flew over the steps, and I didn't draw in a full breath until I was outside with the sunlight touching my skin. There was a tightening in my chest again. A pinch at its center that made the ache in my throat expand.

I'd been telling myself it was just a photograph. Just a name. But that wasn't true, was it? Something bigger was happening here.

My head turned to the white picket fence that encircled the graveyard, my eyes searching the stones. The red door was gone, but on the hill beside the tree line, I spotted it: RUTHERFORD. The name was engraved on a red marble stone. I took a step, and another, my open hand hitting the fence posts until the splintered wood was scraping my palms.

NATHANIEL RUTHERFORD

The closer I got, the clearer the name on the stone beside it became.

SUSANNA RUTHERFORD

But it was the smaller one beside them that I was looking for.

The grave was marked with a worn, wind-washed granite, and the writing was shallower, obscuring the inscription.

I sank down, jaw clenching when I came face-to-face with it, and my hand lifted, tracing the moss-covered letters with the tip of my finger.

JUNE RUTHERFORD
BELOVED DAUGHTER
MARCH 14TH, 1912—OCTOBER 2ND, 1912

October 2. All at once, the weight left my body. I couldn't feel the ground beneath me anymore. June Rutherford died on October 2, the exact same day of the year that Clarence Taylor discovered me in that alley.

"Five, six, seven," I counted.

There were seven months between the date of birth and date of death on the headstone. I was about seven months old when I was found.

Reluctantly, my gaze drifted to the date of birth on Susanna's headstone. September 19. The same as my mother's.

My thoughts began to poke at the edges of something I couldn't quite bring into focus. I couldn't explain this away even if I tried. What was it that Gran had told me? That she was in two places at once? That the Farrow women were different. Her words swirled inside my head, making me feel like everything was upside down.

I'd chosen the wrong rabbit hole, I thought.

The roaring was so loud in my ears now that it was painful, a widening rift in my mind. Was it possible that my mother *wasn't* missing? That maybe she'd only gone someplace else, a place no one could find her?

Slowly, I turned to where the door had stood in the middle of the cemetery, my eyes lifting from the grass as I strung the idea together. Where, exactly, did it lead? The fact that I was even considering it was only a confirmation that every thought, every inclination I had couldn't be trusted. I couldn't make this fit together. I wasn't sure I wanted to.

SIX

I didn't have a birthday. Not a real one, anyway.

Working backward from Dr. Jennings's guess that I was about seven months old when I was found on Market Street, I'd let Mason choose a day. Partly because it bothered him I had no birthday and partly because something had to be written down on school or medical forms when it was asked. He chose March 20, and Gran figured it was a good date because the spring equinox often fell on that day. A few months later, the state of North Carolina issued me my first birth certificate.

I stood over the desk in the sitting room, staring at the papers that covered its surface. A nearly empty plate with the remnants of Ida's casserole sat beside my birth certificate. Susanna Farrow was listed as my mother, but the space for the father's name was blank.

I'd pulled out every single document and photo in the house I could find. Pictures that hung on walls. Tax records stuffed in the back of the desk drawers. A stack of meaningless invoices that had somehow made it to the house from the shop. They littered the sofa, the coffee table, the fireplace, the floor . . . they stretched to the edge of the kitchen and the hallway.

I'd missed something. I must have. I'd been at it for hours, tiptoeing through the maze and trying to stitch together a story that made sense. But the deeper I went, the more wayward it was. Somehwere along the way, I'd missed something. I must have.

The first time Susanna went missing, she'd returned to Jasper after a few months. There wasn't much documented about it. The family had kept things as quiet as possible, and Birdie told me that it had later come out that she'd been in Greenville, South Carolina, where she'd met someone. The ordeal was mostly chalked up to the fact that Susanna wasn't well anymore. She did strange, unpredictable things.

Not long after her return, Gran and Birdie learned she was pregnant, and only a few months later, she went missing again. During that time, I was born, though no one knew exactly when or where. When Clarence found me on Market Street with no clue as to where Susanna was, the police checked hospital logs within two hundred miles trying to track down any record of either of us. There was none. Not for a June Farrow or an unidentified woman matching Susanna's description who'd given birth to a baby girl.

My bare feet slid over the smooth floorboards as I crouched beside the sofa, picking up one of the xeroxed copies of my mother's picture.

She could have given birth somewhere else, maybe at someone's home or a clinic, but where had she and I been during the seven months after I was born? How did a young woman in her third trimester just disappear and then slip back into Jasper undetected to leave her baby behind?

I stood in the center of the sitting room, turning slowly as my eyes ran over the papers that blanketed the floor. Pictures of the Farrow women were arranged in a chronological line along the edge of the fireplace. Esther, Fay, Margaret, and Susanna.

The framed photograph I'd taken off the wall in Gran's room was of her grandmother Esther. She'd started the Adeline River Flower Farm and raised Gran after Gran's mother, Fay, died of scarlet fever.

In the picture, Esther stood in the eastern field of the farm, which we now called field six. A wall of towering sunflowers bloomed behind her, and her hands were twisted in the apron around her skirt, like she was uncomfortable with the photo being taken. It would have been just a few years before buyers started driving up into the mountains from Knoxville and Charlotte to stock the farm's flowers in downtown shops and hotels.

I moved on to the sheet of paper draped over the arm of the sofa. It was an old purchase order, made back in 1973 by Gran. Seeds, chicken wire, and a new push plow were among the items listed, and her writing was even and flowing. Not like it had been in the last years when her hands shook. Fifty years ago, she was a single mother running the farm, no clue as to what dark fate awaited her daughter.

What if Susanna could have somehow slipped into the past? I was only just beginning to let myself imagine it.

The pieces did fit, but only if I forgot everything I knew to be true about the world.

A chill slithered up my spine. This was far beyond seeing a man in a window or a horse running in an empty field. More terrifying than hearing the sound of car engines on an empty road. It was an entirely different reality. Complete and utter madness.

My thoughts stumbled ahead clumsily. Maybe they'd never found my mother's body because she wasn't dead. Maybe there was no trail to follow because she'd vanished. Not just from Jasper, but from this . . .

"Timeline." I whispered the word.

Was that what you called this? A timeline? Putting it that way made it sound like there was more than one, and even thinking it made my stomach drop with dread. It was the most insane thought I'd ever had. So why didn't I feel crazy?

From the moment I'd seen that envelope from Gran, I'd been pulling at a thread that seemed to have no end. Like the toss of a stone into a well, when you're waiting, breath held, to hear it hit the dark water below. But that silence just kept going.

Dr. Jennings's warning about paranoia and delusions resounded in my head. I'd been recording my episodes in detail for the last year, but this was different territory. It felt dangerous.

I took the laptop from where it was buried beneath the papers on the desk and sat down on the floor. The light of the screen lit the dark room in a pale blue glow as I stretched my hands over the keys.

I swallowed hard before I typed "define delusion" and hit enter.

The search engine instantly populated.

Noun: a false belief or judgment about external reality, held despite incontrovertible evidence to the contrary, occurring especially in mental conditions.

Trying again, I typed "delusion vs hallucination."

A number of articles came up, and I clicked on the first one. An illustrated picture of the human brain filled half the page, but the winding pathways were drawn like roots. From them, a large tree was growing, branches outstretched like uncurling fingers.

I scanned the text until I found what I was looking for.

Therefore, a hallucination includes seeing, hearing, tasting, smelling, or feeling something that isn't there.

My notebook was filled with those, and they seemed to track with Gran's symptoms.

On the other hand, delusions are false beliefs despite evidence to the contrary.

I exhaled, somewhat relieved. There *was* evidence. It was scattered all over the sitting room like confetti. I hadn't made up the coincidences between my mother and Nathaniel Rutherford's wife. I also hadn't imagined the connections between myself and their daughter, June Rutherford.

My hands tightened into fists automatically. That name still felt like a choking vine, but the irrefutable part of this was that people couldn't just travel through time.

I'm not sick, honey. I'm just in two places at once.

I'd never really thought about those words. I'd never had to, because we knew that Gran's mind was broken, just like my mother's was. The pattern was there, and so was the inevitable outcome. But Dr. Jennings had said himself that this form of dementia or cognitive decline didn't follow the rules in textbooks. He didn't even have a theory about what it could be.

When I followed that line of thinking, it led to only one place. One question that felt like the tip of a needle. If I touched it, it would prick me.

What if Gran *wasn't* mad?

I stopped myself, backtracking the speeding train of thoughts before they led somewhere truly horrifying. The idea was a threshold. One I wasn't sure I could come back from if I crossed it. But I didn't feel like I had a choice anymore.

I went back to the desk, finding my notebook. My hands hesitated on its worn cover. I'd lost that apprehensive, nauseous feeling I'd had all the other times I'd opened it. There was something about it now that felt scientific. Clinical.

I turned to the first page, staring at the date.

July 2, 2022
8:45 P.M.—At the greenhouse. Someone was calling my name.

The first time it happened, I was at the farm, in the greenhouse we used for starting our autumn harvest seeds. I'd stayed late after the fieldworkers had all gone home, and I was working when I heard someone calling my name. It was the very first time I heard that voice that was now familiar. The one that covered me in a feeling of warmth. It was so clear and loud that I hadn't questioned it even for a second.

I answered, but the voice only called my name again. And again, until I'd pulled the gloves from my hands and walked outside, searching the darkening fields for a face. But there was nothing. No one. And the voice just went on.

It was several seconds before I realized what was happening, and it was like being hit by a rogue wave, the rush of it coming all at once. It didn't matter that I'd been standing on that shore my whole life, waiting for it. It still felt like the world split in two when it finally arrived.

The next entry was three days later, just when I'd begun to convince myself that I'd imagined the whole thing.

July 5, 2022
2:11 P.M.—*A horse running on the side of the road. She disappeared.*

The pages were filled with dozens of other dates and times. Music. The smell of bread baking in the oven. There were times I'd seen someone in a reflection or heard footsteps in the house. Once, I'd even called Mason out to the farm late at night, convinced someone had broken in.

Each time, I pushed the hallucination away, breathing deep and closing my mind to it until it stopped. I repeated the words. *It's not real, June.*

If Gran really was in two places at once, could that mean that I was, too?

A tap on the door sounded, and I turned to see the shoulder of Mason's jacket through the curtain.

I let out a frustrated breath, closing the notebook and covering it with a few of the pages that were scattered across the desk. I stepped carefully over the documents on the floor until I was in the hallway. His shadow rocked back and forth in front of the window before I opened the door, and he took a step backward when I pushed through the screen.

His gaze went from me to the inside of the house as I closed the door behind me. "Hey."

"Hi." I tried to sound normal.

Mason's clothes were covered in dirt and pollen, which meant he was on his way home from work. "I called earlier," he said. "Was worried when you didn't come by the farm."

"I've been busy."

"Too busy to call me back?"

I glanced at the street, where a car was pulling into one of the driveways. I could lie to Mason, but I couldn't look him in the eye when I did it. "I've just been dealing with some of the paperwork left from Gran."

He wasn't buying it. I could tell by the way his head tilted a little to one side. "June."

"What?"

"What's going on?"

"Nothing," I snapped.

"Nothing?" His eyebrows lifted knowingly. "Really?"

I stared at him, digging my heels in.

He let the silence drag out for a few seconds before he stepped past me to the door.

"What are you—" I caught hold of his arm, but he pulled free, letting himself inside. "Mason!"

I followed, wedging myself ahead of him in the narrow hallway. When he reached the sitting room, I put a hand on his chest to stop him. But he froze as soon as he saw what I was trying to hide.

His eyes moved over the room slowly, landing on every scrap of paper I'd laid out. He was still—not just physically, but something about his countenance changed, making the house feel colder. When he finally looked at me, there was a strange look in his eyes.

"June." His voice lowered. "What is this?"

I exhaled heavily, pressing both palms to my cheeks as if to cool the heat igniting there. "It's just family stuff."

"Why is it all over the house like this?" He was holding back now, being careful.

"I've just been . . . looking into something."

"Looking into what?"

"Just something about my mom."

"What about her?" he pressed, his voice taking on an edge.

"Nothing!" I shouldered past him to the kitchen. When I reached the counter, I folded the foil back over Ida's old Pyrex dish and yanked open the fridge.

From the corner of my vision I could see Mason studying the empty bins and the accordion file that was now lying limp on the table. He was behind me a few seconds later, arms crossed over his chest. The expression on his face was almost angry, but I didn't know what he had to be mad about. I was the one losing my mind.

I traded the casserole dish for an untouched blueberry pie and fished two spoons from the crock beside the stove. I didn't bother grabbing bowls, heading back to the table.

"You need to talk to me. I'm worried," he said.

"*You're* worried?" I muttered, taking a seat. I set the pie between us, handing him a spoon.

"Yes. I'm worried. Something's off with you. It has been for a while. And now I find you shut up in the house with this shit everywhere?"

I smiled bitterly. "You think I'm losing it."

"I don't know what's going on. That's why I want you to talk to me."

I shoved the spoon into the pie, eating straight out of the pan. I'd known it would come to this eventually. Mason knew me too well. I couldn't hide from him.

"You can trust me, June. You know that."

I did know. There wasn't anything I could say that would push Mason away. In fact, I'd tried. We'd made an agreement years ago that he'd be the first person I called when it started, but the moment I told him, the moment I said it out loud, it would all be true. That would make it real.

I dropped the spoon onto the table, pressing my hands to my face again. There was no point in lying anymore. I knew that. But it was just so hard to say.

I drew in a deep breath and stood, going to the shelf on the far wall for the whiskey decanter. "Sit down." I took two of the etched lowball glasses from the hutch, setting them onto the table.

"If you're trying to scare me, it's working."

"Please just sit down." I was exhausted now.

Mason was already pouring the whiskey when I took the chair across from him, and when he picked up his glass, I followed. I took it in one swallow, wincing as the burn traveled down my throat. The smoky smell of it filled the air around us, and as soon as I set down the glass, Mason refilled it.

"It's happening," I said.

My voice was so quiet that I wasn't completely sure I'd spoken aloud. But Mason's face changed, his eyes jumping back and forth on mine. His grip tightened on his glass.

"It's *been* happening," I breathed. "For about a year now." All at once, it became definitive. Conclusive.

"A year."

I nodded.

"Why didn't you tell me?"

"Why do you think?" I smirked, tears biting the back of my throat.

"Okay." The word stretched unnaturally.

I could see it in his eyes. He'd shifted gears to damage control, and I wasn't entirely sure I didn't need it. I wasn't going to be the one to tell him that there was nothing he could do to make this okay. He was a man who needed to feel like he was fixing things. Always finding the loose knots in people and tightening them up before they could unravel. I wasn't going to take that away from him.

"Well, what do you mean *it's happening*. What's happening exactly?"

"I'm seeing things. Hearing things. Getting mixed up about what's real."

"What kinds of things?"

"I don't know." I flung a hand in the air between us. "Everything!"

Mason looked at me a long time before he picked up his glass and drank. I was glad I couldn't hear what he was thinking. Besides Birdie, he was the only person I had in the world, and that filled me with a tremendous amount of guilt.

"Have you made an appointment with Dr. Jennings?" he asked.

"Yes. I've been going to see him for the last few months."

"Well, I'd like to go with you next time. Talk to him about what kind of plans we need to make."

"It doesn't have to be *we*," I whispered.

He waited for me to look at him, and when he spoke, he didn't hesitate on the words. "It's always been *we*."

An acute pain bloomed inside of me, unfurling beneath my skin. This was exactly what I didn't want, and it was also maybe my only option. The truth was, if the roles were reversed, I'd do the same for him.

"It's one thing to say you'll be there when you're an eighteen-year-old idiot who doesn't know anything about life. It's another to be us, now."

"Have things really changed that much?" He was trying to make me laugh, but I couldn't feel any warmth inside of me.

"Don't you . . ." I turned the glass on the table. "Don't you want something more? A family? A different life outside of the farm and Jasper?" It had been years since I'd asked him that question.

Mason shrugged. "Maybe one day. That's not what I want now, though."

I caught a tear at the corner of my eye before it could fall.

"Maybe I'm still waiting for you to suddenly realize you're in love with me."

I did laugh then, because it was tragically funny and sadly, somewhat true. I could imagine a life where we were together, married, maybe even with children. But that life could only belong to a June who wasn't born a Farrow. And I'd somehow managed to keep my heart from getting broken by Mason Caldwell. He'd managed to do the same with me.

"Have you told Birdie?"

I shook my head. "I will. Soon."

It was all settling. Not just what I'd told him, but what it meant. This was the beginning of the end, and even if we'd known it was coming our whole lives, it was still terrifying.

"And what's going on in there?" He gestured to the sitting room. "Really."

"You don't want to know," I muttered.

His eyebrows raised again.

I sighed, getting to my feet, and walked around the corner of the wall. I took the photograph Gran had sent me from the mantel of the fireplace and the one of my mother from the table. When I came back into the kitchen, Mason's glass was empty for the second time. I set the picture from 1911 down in front of him, sinking back into my chair.

"I was opening a stack of mail yesterday and there was an envelope from Gran. It was posted a few days before she died, and this was the only thing inside."

He studied the faces in the photograph before flipping it over and reading the name. "Who is that?"

"Nathaniel Rutherford," I said, watching his eyes widen.

"The guy who—"

"Was murdered," I said. "Yes. And that woman is his wife."

I placed the second photo beside it, and he leaned in closer. "Okay, so it's the same woman. What of it?"

I set a finger on the one of my mother. "Only, it can't be. That's my mother, Susanna."

He looked confused now, trying to track.

I reached across the table, turning the first photo over so he could read the inscription on the back. "This was taken in 1911. This one"— I pointed to the other photo—"was sometime in the eighties."

"So, it's *not* the same woman." He looked up at me.

I said nothing, silently hoping he was about to offer some kind of explanation I hadn't yet thought of.

"Then they just look alike. But why would Margaret mail this to you?"

"I have no idea. So, I started digging, trying to figure out who Nathaniel Rutherford was married to." I paused. "Mason, her name was Susanna Farrow."

He leaned back in his chair, studying me.

"She has the same birth date as my mother, except for the year, obviously. And she had a daughter named June."

I couldn't read the look on his face now. It was as misplaced as I felt.

"Her daughter was born around the same day and month as the birthday you chose for me. And she died the exact same day and month I was found in Jasper—October 2nd."

"June . . ."

"I mean, isn't that weird?" I was looking for reassurance now.

"Yeah. It's weird."

"But . . . I don't know. There's also something *wrong* about it."

"Well, it's not like it's her," he said.

I bit down on my lip, pulse skipping.

"Wait." He set his elbows on the table, his face turning serious again. "You actually think it's *her*?"

I raked my hands through my hair. "I don't know what to think. I mean, tell me how this is possible. What are the odds?"

"I can't explain it to you. It was more than a hundred years ago. Things get lost over that much time."

I opened my mouth to argue, but his hand lifted between us, stopping me. "June, you're throwing a lot at me right now. You just told me my best friend in the entire world is sick and she's not going to get better. And now you're telling me she thinks her mother . . . what? Went back in time?"

"I know it's crazy."

"Yeah." He nearly laughed again, but now it sounded like a panicked thing. Like he was just beginning to reckon with the fact that I was really, truly broken.

We sat there for a long moment before he set a hand on my arm, squeezing gently. "Look, *this* . . ." His eyes dropped to the photos that sat between us. "This isn't what's important right now."

I let out a breath, giving up. His eyes stared into mine, as if he were waiting to be convinced that I'd drop it. When I nodded, he finally let me go. I should have called him that night a year ago, like I'd promised. Maybe then I wouldn't have ended up here, caught in the labyrinth of Nathaniel Rutherford and my mother and a child that had barely existed.

"When does Birdie get back?" he asked.

I could hear the real question behind the words. *When will there be someone here to keep an eye on you?*

"Tomorrow."

"I'm going to stay over tonight."

"You don't need to do that."

"I'm not asking."

He reached for the whiskey, refilling my glass before he filled his again.

The prick behind my eyes didn't fully give way to tears until more than an hour later, as I was lying in the dark of my room, the sound of Mason's deep sleeping breaths drifting up the stairs. And even then, I swallowed them down before they could fall.

I wanted to let it go, like he said. I wanted to focus on what was important. But the photograph felt . . . intentional. Planned. Like Gran was trying to tell me something.

There was too much to think about. Too many swirling words inside of my head. I couldn't draw them into a straight line. Gran. The photograph. The dates. My mother. Birdie. Mason. It was all one never-ending maze, making me feel like my edges were beginning to fray. And they were.

SEVEN

The first thing I saw when I opened my eyes was a note from Mason on my bedside table.

Take an aspirin. Call you later.

I could feel the ache in my head the moment I sat up, my skin sticky beneath my nightgown from the humid morning air coming through the open window. I'd heard him get up at daybreak and I could smell the sharp scent of coffee, but I hadn't been able to bring myself to go downstairs.

Was this how it would be? Mason taking care of me, sleeping on the sofa when I didn't want to stay alone? Going to doctor's appointments and coming by if I haven't called? I loved Mason, but I didn't want that life for either of us.

I stared into the bathroom mirror with the faucet running, the shadows beneath my eyes making me look like a hollow thing. The birthmark below my ear was darker against my skin, my pale lips almost invisible. The fleeting, lightning-quick thought struck before I could pull it back—was this how Susanna Rutherford felt before she threw herself over the falls?

I washed my face with ice-cold water and got dressed, holding tightly to the railing as I came down the stairs. The house was cast in the pink-tinged light of morning, the kitchen tidied. The half-eaten blueberry pie was gone from the table, the crystal lowball glasses washed and drying next to the sink.

The digital clock above the stove top read 8:08 A.M. Mason would be in the fields by now.

I did as he said, taking the aspirin from the cabinet. Then I filled a glass with water and gulped it down, instantly regretting it. I still felt sick, but not from the whiskey. Last night and the string of clues I'd pieced together had changed things. I didn't know how to explain it or how to prove it, but I was certain that all of this meant something. I could feel it. Like the idea had sunk into my bones, becoming as real as I was.

Susanna Farrow didn't just wander into the woods one day, following the breadcrumbs of her broken mind. And Gran wanted me to know it.

My stomach was still turning as my gaze drifted back to the doorway of the sitting room, where the maze of papers and photographs still blanketed the floor.

The window was propped open, most likely by Mason when it had gotten too hot in here last night. At the corner of the desk, the stacked copies of the newspaper articles I'd printed were fluttering in the breeze.

The house creaked against the wind outside as I crossed the kitchen, but I stopped short when I saw a shadow slip over the floorboards in the sitting room. It was followed by a sound. Shuffling paper, maybe.

I came around the corner, eyes going wide when I saw Birdie sitting in the chair beside the fireplace. She had a pile of the pages she'd gathered up from the floor in her lap, a small rectangular photograph in her hands. She didn't look at me as I stopped in the doorway. She was silent. In fact, she didn't appear to be so much as breathing.

"What are you doing here?" I said, the tone of my voice almost defensive.

I was suddenly embarrassed. I thought I'd have hours before she got back from Charlotte, plenty of time to finish going through things and get the mess I'd made out of sight. What had she thought when she walked in to see all of this? What was she thinking right now?

I came closer, eyeing the photograph in her hand. It was the one Gran had sent me.

Birdie's finger moved over the outline of Nathaniel's wife, as if tracing her shape. "Couldn't sleep, so figured I'd get on the road early." Her voice was far and distant. When she finally looked up at me, there were tears in her eyes. Her gaze moved over the room before finding me again. "It's finally started, hasn't it?"

The buzz in the air turned electric as soon as she said it. There was a knowing in her eyes.

"What?" My lips moved, but the movement felt numb. I could hardly hear myself speak.

She knew. She knew I was sick.

Maybe Mason had called her, or maybe walking in to see the chaos of the sitting room only confirmed the suspicions she already had. She'd been watching me so closely, especially over the last six months. I'd thought she was worried because of Gran, but that look she was giving me now was saying everything she wasn't. It was finally out—this thing we'd all been tiptoeing around.

"I thought I'd be ready when the time came," she said.

She stared down at the picture in her hand with an expression I couldn't read. Nostalgia? Affection? Sadness? When she turned it over, her eyes lingered on the inscription longer than necessary. Was I imagining it, or were her hands shaking?

She swallowed. "But I don't know that I am."

I was trembling despite the warmth that filled the house. Every muscle was jumping beneath my skin, my stomach twisting like I was about to fall, and keep falling.

"You've seen the door, haven't you?"

The trembling stopped then. I felt a cold stillness bleed through me. "What?" This time, I did hear myself say it.

She stood, the photograph still pinched between her fingers. "How many times have you seen it, June?"

I instinctively found the shape of the locket watch beneath my shirt, squeezing it so hard that its edges bit into my palm. I wasn't sure anymore what we were talking about, and it didn't matter how long I stared at her face, I still couldn't read it.

"Why are you asking me that?" My voice was unsteady now.

She lifted a hand, reaching for the picture of my mother on the table beside her, but it stopped midair, like she was reluctant to touch it. Then it was almost as if she couldn't help herself. All at once, it came to me. Whatever all of this was, whatever it meant, Birdie knew.

"She said you'd come asking questions." She spoke softly.

I straightened. "Who?"

"Margaret."

As soon as she spoke my grandmother's name, a sinking feeling woke inside me. I was suddenly terrified of whatever Birdie was about to say. That warmth in her voice and that sparkle in her eyes looked different to me now, as if I could feel at my very center that what was about to happen would destroy everything.

Her mouth twisted, deepening the wrinkles on her face, and her eyes shined, taking on a shade of blue that was clearer and brighter.

"Who is the woman in that photo, Birdie?" I whispered.

Her eyes flitted up to meet mine, and she suddenly looked like a little girl to me. Like someone caught with something they shouldn't have. "I have a feeling you've worked that out for yourself."

"Who is it?" The words sharpened to a point.

"It's Nathaniel Rutherford. And your mother."

Susanna. *My* Susanna, I thought. But what did that even mean? There was never a time when my mother had truly been mine.

I shook my head. "That's not possible."

It was true. But wasn't that the exact conclusion I'd already been coming to? Wasn't that precisely the thought that had haunted me through the long, silent hours of the night? Now that she was saying it, I desperately wanted to be wrong.

"Just breathe, June." Her hand was suddenly on my arm, her touch like ice.

I flinched, pulling away from her. "What is happening?"

"How much have you put together?"

Put together? Like I'd been sent on a scavenger hunt blindfolded. Like this was a game.

When I didn't answer, she let out a heavy breath. "I know this is difficult, but I need you to listen to me. There's a certain way this is supposed to happen."

"What does that even mean?" I snapped.

"You're starting to remember." She searched my eyes. "Right?"

Remember.

I stared at her, my mind twisting. My jaw clenched, biting back an answer. That was the wrong word for this.

I put more space between us, grasping at the last shreds of reality I could hold on to. The obvious answer was that this wasn't real. It never was. The photograph, the marriage certificate, the baptism records, the gravestones . . . it was all one long hallucination playing out in my head. That was it. Maybe I was still in my bedroom, tossing the un-opened mail to the bed. There was a very real possibility that none of this was happening.

"This is . . . this is an ep-episode." My words cracked as I said it. "This isn't real." I tried to reason with myself, begging my heart to calm. It felt like the world would go black at any second.

Birdie took me by the shoulders. "You're not sick, honey."

I felt myself still, the air in the room growing thin and dry. It burned in my chest when I drew it in.

"Now, tell me *exactly*. How many times have you seen the door?"

I blinked. "I don't know. Three? Four times?"

Her eyes widened. "What?"

"The first time was about a year ago," I rasped.

"A year ago?" She let me go, her voice rising. "That long?"

"I didn't want to tell you and Gran. Not when Gran was so sick. I thought . . ."

Birdie pressed a hand to her mouth. She was paler now. "That's not how—" She swallowed. "This isn't how it's supposed to happen."

"Birdie, tell me what's going on."

She crossed the room without another word, disappearing into the hallway. Her bedroom door creaked open, and I could hear a drawer opening and shutting. Then she was back, something pressed between her hands. It looked like another envelope.

"You're not sick," she said again. "You, Susanna, Margaret—further back, even." Her words sped up, warping as I bit down on my lip painfully. "The Farrows are different. You know that. Some part of you has always known that, right?"

The pain radiating at my temples was spreading, my own heartbeat like the strike of a hammer in my ears.

"She didn't disappear, did she? Susanna?" The words withered on my tongue.

"No. She didn't."

I looked around the room frantically, my hand finding the skin inside my forearm and pinching hard. I waited for the walls of the house to dissolve. For my eyes to wake to morning. But nothing happened. I was here, in our home, and I could feel the ground beneath my feet. I could hear the birds singing outside.

I pinched harder. "How long have you known about this?"

That childlike look returned to Birdie's eyes. "A long time."

"And what? You and Gran just decided to keep it from me?"

She looked down at the envelope in her hands before she held it out to me.

"What is that?"

"It's something I'm supposed to give to you."

I stared at it, eyes inspecting what I hadn't seen before. It wasn't one of the brown envelopes from the shop, like the one Gran had mailed to me. It was square and wrinkled with damp, the corners soft and worn.

When I didn't take it, Birdie extended her hand further. "I give you this, and the rest is up to you. I can't say anything else. I can't interfere in any way." Her tone wavered as tears filled her eyes. But her mouth was set in that straight line again.

"Tell me what's going on!" I was furious now.

"I made a promise. One I've kept for a very long time. I'm not going to break it now. Not even for you."

I looked at her for a long moment before I finally took the envelope. There was nothing written on it, but it was sealed.

Birdie took a step toward me, and I moved from her reach, headed for the door. I couldn't be here. I couldn't bear to hear what she'd say next.

I'd made it only a few steps before she caught hold of my wrist firmly, and she pulled me into her arms, not giving me a chance to push her away. She held me so tightly that it hurt.

"The next time you see the door, open it." Her voice shook before she finally let me go, but she didn't look at me. She walked straight past me, taking her purse from the hook by the door. Then she left, and it slammed behind her.

I stood there, frozen, as her car pulled down the drive. It was several seconds before I could even feel myself breathing. I stared down at the envelope, hesitating before I tore it open.

Inside, there was another envelope, this one different. It had once been white, now stained with yellowed edges. I slid it free.

There was an address written on the front.

46 Hayward Gap Rd

I knew Hayward Gap Road the same way I knew every road in Jasper. I passed it every time I went to the farm, and I was sure that at some point, I'd driven it. There wasn't a single inch of this town that didn't feel familiar to me, but I had no idea what made that address significant. Most of those farmlands were nothing but empty fields and the crumbling barns once used for drying tobacco. Looking closer, I realized this wasn't Gran's handwriting. This was a hurried, frantic script in smudged pencil. The fleeting, terrified thought that skipped through my mind was one that I couldn't bear to consider. Could it be my mother's?

I slid a shaking finger beneath the seal, and it opened easily. My heart all but stopped beating as I reached inside, but my fingers didn't find a letter or a photograph. There was something else. Something small and spindly. Fragile.

I slipped it out of the envelope, holding it to the light coming through the window. It was a perfectly pressed flower. A stalk of blue-bells. They grew wild all over Jasper each spring.

I held the blooms up to the light, turning them slowly. The petals had almost completely lost their color.

I searched the envelope, turning it upside down, but there was nothing else inside. When the flap fell closed, two words stared up at me.

Trust me.

EIGHT

It was from Susanna. It had to be.

I pushed out the screen door and went down the steps with the envelope still clutched in my fist. The GPS on my phone said that 46 Hayward Gap Road was only twelve minutes away, not far from the farm. From the map, I could see that two corners of the properties actually touched on the farm's northeast side.

The Bronco's engine roared to life, and I already had the truck in reverse when Ida came out onto her porch. She lifted a hand in a wave, and for once, that concern was missing in her expression. As if seeing me go off to work like I did on any given normal day was reassuring. Like maybe I was okay.

But I wasn't. I wouldn't ever be again.

A faint, static buzz flickered from the broken speakers as the road bent and stretched before me. I let my foot fall heavier on the gas pedal. I was headed east, where the hills started to flatten just a little and the trees that lined the road spread apart. Sunlight sparkled on the dew-spotted grass, where wide, flat blooms of water hemlock swayed in the wind along the roadside ditches.

Gran had had thirty-four years. Thirty-four years to tell me what happened to my mother. But she'd let my life pass with the unknowing and the only one Gran had trusted with the truth was Birdie.

It made sense now. This was why she'd never wanted to talk about Susanna. Why she'd never seemed haunted by the mystery of her disappearance, the way any other mother would be. I'd always taken it as grief, like maybe she couldn't bear to think about what had happened. But all this time, she'd known Susanna was in the past, safe and sound. She'd lived a life and died in Jasper. She just hadn't taken me with her.

I stared at the envelope in my lap, those two words like a beacon in the dark.

Trust me.

The turn onto Hayward Gap Road was marked with a makeshift scrap of wood. I slowed down, checking the GPS when I spotted it. The edge of the property I was looking for was at the turn, but the hill in the distance hid whatever was waiting there. The truck rocked over the deep, rain-filled potholes as the pavement gave way to gravel. But it took only a few seconds for me to spot a stone chimney ahead.

The rest of the structure came into view a few seconds later, and my fingers gripped the steering wheel tighter, as if I were bracing myself for something. I couldn't shake that feeling, like every soft thing in my body was turning to stone.

It was an old farmhouse.

The shingled roof was caved in on one side, the rotting wooden siding almost completely gray where the white paint had chipped off. A small porch that wrapped around one side was still standing, but the house clearly hadn't been lived in for a very long time.

I pulled onto the shoulder when I reached it, sliding the gear into park. There was nothing but tall grass in every direction, spanning a dozen acres at least. What had once been a barn to the south was now just a couple of beams left standing and a pile of wood overtaken by blackberry vines. The skeleton of an old tractor was buried in a thicket of hedges by the road. The metal was rusted over, but the manufacturer's name was still faintly visible on the side.

I couldn't remember ever stopping here or stepping past that fence, but there was a nagging, prodding feeling that I *knew* this place. I'd been here before, hadn't I?

I opened the door, getting out of the truck as I studied the land. The view of the mountains from here was a perfect one, with rows upon rows of misty blue peaks reaching far into the distance. The river wasn't far, either. I could hear it behind the tree line that wandered along the property, but this was upstream from town, an area we'd never really ventured to as kids.

I stepped over one of the fallen fence posts, letting one hand touch the tops of the reeds as I walked toward the house. Most of the glass windows were gone or cracked, and the screen door was crooked. It looked like one of the hundreds of farms that dotted the expanse of the Blue Ridge Mountains, but there was something strange about the place. Something almost frightening. The prick that danced on the back of my neck made me feel like someone was watching me from those hazy, broken windows.

In the time it had taken me to get here, I'd all but convinced myself that this was the key. Like this last clue would be the thing that clicked the pieces into that pattern I was searching for. But I couldn't see it. Instead, I was filled with a feeling I couldn't quite put my finger on. It was like hearing a sound and being unable to tell which direction it was coming from.

The clouds rolling in brought a swift wind with them, and the grass bent all around me, making a whispering sound that made my skin crawl. The soft tingle of something moving below my wrist tugged at my mind and I looked down, going rigid. A wide-winged silk moth had landed on the back of my arm, its size stretching wider than my open hand. It was the same as the ones we found clinging to tree trunks in the woods when we were kids, its brown wings swirled with red markings that resembled two sets of eyes.

I lifted my arm carefully, watching in a kind of awe as the moth's black legs climbed to the tip of my finger. There it sat, giant wings opening and closing in a silent rhythm.

I could tell by the pooling warmth spreading in my chest that it wasn't real. I was seeing something that wasn't there. But for once, I forced myself to stand still, pressing into the vision instead of driving it from my mind the way I usually did. I'd always run from it, but now I was leaning in to that feeling, making the sense of familiarity widen inside of me. I could almost touch the thought, as if my mind were reaching into the air for it. But slowly. Carefully.

I blinked.

Behind me, I could feel the crumbling house and the gray sky. I could sense the cooler air and the empty road. But there, in front of me, was another world. The hills were greener, the sky bluer. And the fields—they weren't empty anymore. Rows upon rows of tobacco covered the earth, the wide flat leaves like a sea of green.

I could feel the vision pulling at me, like I was teetering with one foot in this moment and one in another. Like I was standing in two places at once.

When I looked down to my finger, the moth was suddenly gone, and with it, the view of the tobacco field began to disintegrate. In a matter of seconds, it had vanished, replaced by the abandoned farm that surrounded me.

A tight breath escaped my lips as I stumbled back to the truck, my hand clumsily reaching behind me for the door handle. I hit the gas, but I couldn't tear my gaze away from the sinking porch that encircled the house. The chimney. The crooked front door.

A bead of sweat trailed down the center of my back, and I rolled down the window, trying to wash that scent from the cab. The sweet, berry-ripe, wood-rotting smell that swirled around me. I drank in the wind, the speedometer climbing until I was finally able to breathe. And when I got up the nerve to glance in the rearview mirror one more time, the house had disappeared behind the hill.

The truck slid to a stop when I reached the river road and I stared into the empty field on the other side, still breathing too hard. What happened back there—that vision—was different from the episodes that filled my notebook. What had Birdie asked me? If I was *remembering*? That's exactly how it had felt. Like opening a hole in my mind that held something I'd forgotten. But what?

I glanced to the left, where downtown Jasper lay beyond the hills. I didn't care what promises Birdie had made or how things were supposed to happen. She was going to tell me what I needed to know. Right now.

I turned the wheel in the opposite direction, headed for the farm. The urge I had to call Mason was so strong that I had to will myself not to reach for my phone sitting in the passenger seat. What would I even tell him? How could I ever explain this? The person I should really be calling was Dr. Jennings. There wasn't a single moment that had made sense since I'd opened that envelope from Gran, and the image that kept replaying in my mind was of Susanna. Not the woman in the photo or the one in my files in the basement. It was what I imagined she had looked like that night, walking barefoot on that road in the middle of a snowstorm. Lost and confused, just like I was now. I could almost see her up ahead, trailing the edge of the road in her damp nightgown, skin drained of color in the cold. A drifting figure in a sea of white.

I swallowed down the nauseous feeling climbing up my throat. Was it Susanna I imagined there on the side of the road, or was it me?

The road curved sharply, and my fingers loosened on the wheel when I caught sight of something flashing into view through the driver's side window. Just as quickly as it appeared, it vanished behind me. I slammed on the brakes, tires screeching on the blacktop as the truck came to a jerking stop.

I watched as the smoke from the tires drifted past the windshield, and I took three deep breaths before I dared to look in the rearview mirror.

I hadn't imagined it. It was the door. The red door.

The very same one I'd seen in the cemetery. At the farm. On Main Street. The same brass handle. The same chipping paint. It stood erect in the middle of the field, a blot of crimson against the rolling green hills.

I got out, a floating feeling settling over me as I walked slowly toward the trees. The truck rumbled behind me, and the sound of the wind swallowed up the silence, reverberating in every cell of my body. The scent of burning rubber still stung my nose as I waded into the tall grass.

"It's not real," I whispered, out of habit more than anything. The words were a knee-jerk reaction, but they weren't true anymore. They never had been.

I was breathing so hard now that my lungs hurt. At any moment, I was going to wake, I told myself. I was going to open my eyes in my own bed and realize that none of this had ever happened. But the thought was followed immediately by another. That I had to see what was on the other side.

I stopped when I reached it, boots sinking into the rain-softened soil.

Open it, Birdie's voice echoed.

I looked up and down the empty road, eyes lifting to scan the trees in the distance. There was no one to see me standing in that field in front of a door that wasn't there. No one to bear witness to my madness.

Before I could change my mind, I reached out, fingertips tingling when they touched the scalloped doorknob. My hand curled around it, and I heard myself exhale before it turned. With a shaking, terrified breath, I pushed it open.

My eyes widened as the hinges creaked and the door drifted away from me.

On the other side was another field. Beyond it, a blacktop road was carved into the earth against a thick tree line. I could hear the cicadas. The water in the creek.

Again, I looked behind me to the truck parked with the door ajar down the road. The cool metal of the doorknob was still there on my fingers. But I froze when I heard the sound of wind in the trees, the leaves rustling. Because I couldn't feel it.

Carefully, my gaze returned to the open door. On the other side, the branches were bowed, the grass bending beneath a swift breeze. But on this side, all was still.

I lifted a hand slowly, moving closer, and when it crossed the threshold, a brisk wind wove through my fingers. My lips parted in an overwhelming awe as I closed it into a fist and drew it back. As soon as I did, the wind disappeared.

I stared at my palm, my gaze following the lines that spread like tree roots over my skin.

Two places at once.

It was Gran's voice I heard as I counted the inhale. *One, two, three.* I took a step forward, exhaling a shaky breath. *One, two, three.* I don't think there was a moment when I made up my mind. There was no single thought that made me do it. I was just suddenly moving forward until my boot was touching down on that glistening grass.

The wind caught me, pulling my hair across my face, and I filled my chest with the summer-sweet air. Dragonflies danced on the sparkling water below.

But when I turned around, the door was gone.

NINE

I looked around me, turning slowly in a circle. My breath shook when I caught sight of the freshly paved road winding between the fields like a snake disappearing into the hills.

The truck had vanished.

I was standing in the same spot. The exact same place where I'd pulled over only minutes ago. I knew where I was, but this road was . . . new. The air was filled with the smell of black, pebbled tar, the cracked pavement and rusted guardrails gone. The fields surrounding me were missing fences. Barns. There were giant old trees where I'd never seen them. And a tiny wood-framed house sat where there had been nothing before.

"Wake up." I spoke the words aloud, but they were muted in my ears. "Wake up!"

My voice broke through the wind, my vision sharpening on the world around me. It was too clear. Too specific. This wasn't the distant, dreamlike glimpses I'd seen before. It felt real. Visceral and detailed. This was something else. Something impossible.

My eyes focused on the tilted silver mailbox fixed to the fence post on the side of the road. It was painted with the name GRANGER.

My mind stumbled from one thought to the next before a screech echoed out and the screen door of the little house rattled closed. At the top of the steps, a short, gray-haired woman was watching me, eyes wide.

"Excuse me." I lifted a desperate hand into the air, barely getting the words out.

It wasn't until I took another step that I could read that look on her face. Shock. Terror, even. She scrambled backward, catching the door with her hand, and then she disappeared, slamming it behind her.

My eyes jumped from one darkened window of the house to the next. There was no movement, no sounds coming from inside, but I could feel her watching me, eyes peering through the glass.

I pressed a trembling hand to my hot forehead as I tried to think. There weren't any other houses that I could see. No one in the fields or on the road.

I reflexively reached for my back pocket. My cellphone, my keys, everything was in the truck.

Trust me.

The words that had been scribbled on the back of the envelope Birdie gave me were a faint whisper now. The problem was, I didn't trust anyone anymore. Not even myself.

I ran one hand through my hair, pinning it back from my face. If I'd crossed time, like Birdie suggested Susanna had done, then I wasn't in 2023 Jasper anymore. That didn't give me many options.

I started walking in the direction I'd come from, steps faltering when I passed the spot on the road that the Bronco had been. I was almost sure I could hear the rumble of the engine somewhere far in the distance. I could even smell the exhaust on the wind. It was like before, when I'd see or hear things that weren't really there. Except now it felt like I was on the other side of those visions.

I walked toward the cascade of mountains in the distance. Those peaks and valleys, at least, hadn't changed, and the farther I walked, the more I was piecing together my surroundings. The riverbank looked different, more overgrown and wild with the water half-hidden by the thick brush. But there were subtle things that helped me keep my bearings, like a particular curve in the road or a tree I thought I recognized.

When I made it back to Hayward Gap Road, it wasn't marked. The tar crumbled onto the shoulder, where years of tire tracks had worn it down, carving a dirt track. It was lined with a wooden fence, and beyond it was the hill I'd seen yesterday, arcing up on one side before the land came rolling back down.

The rumble of an engine sounded before a truck appeared in the distance, and I squinted, trying to make it out. It was an old model. Not old like the ones in the Jasper I knew, 1990s trucks and station wagons that had been turned into utilitarian farm vehicles. No, this truck was much older, its deep blue paint gleaming as the sun flashed off its fender.

The driver didn't seem to notice me on the side of the road until he'd already passed, and the truck suddenly slowed, as if he'd hit the brakes out of a sudden reaction. But just as soon as I was sure he'd stop, he started moving again, faster this time.

An eerie feeling crept over me, my breath curling tightly in my chest. As soon as the truck disappeared around the bend, I stepped off the shoulder of the blacktop and onto the dirt road. I followed it, wincing when the sight of the chimney came into view. The same one I'd seen not even an hour ago. But now there was smoke drifting from its mouth.

The leaning, termite-eaten structure that had stood at the bottom of the hill was gone. Transformed. The farmhouse was nestled before the tree line that followed the creek stretching into the distance. The red brick still had its color, the wooden siding painted in a pale yellow. And behind it, acres and acres of tobacco grew in rows taller than I stood. The crumbling barn was no longer the bare remnants of a structure. It was whole.

I was frozen, half expecting the entire scene to disappear into a swirl of smoke as it had before, but it didn't. The minutes just kept passing. Time kept moving. And I had, somehow, crossed it.

The overwhelming sense that I knew this place was even stronger now. Almost unbearable. The windows of the house were dark, but the distant sound of a hammer wove through the air, a sharp ping that grew louder the closer I came. When I reached the bottom of the hill, I could see the open doors of the barn, a few chickens scratching in the dirt.

I set both hands on the closed cattle gate, waiting for someone to appear.

"Hello?" I called out, my voice unsteady.

The thud of hooves drew my eyes from the barn to the paddock, where a horse was watching me from behind the fence. Dust kicked up into the air, casting it in a glow, but I knew. It was the same horse I'd seen before. The chestnut. She had one wild eye fixed on me as she stamped the ground, her head craning as she snorted.

The piercing ring of the hammer went on in a steady beat, echoing out over the fields. I lifted the latch of the gate and let it swing open, stepping onto the drive that stretched to the house from the road. Wild, wispy grasses lined the path that led from one side of the porch to an overgrown garden filled with weeds. I followed it, searching for the source of the sound.

The horse trotted along the fence of the paddock anxiously. Her chocolate-colored coat was tinged with bronze, her mane catching the light. When I took another step, she whinnied, nostrils flaring.

"Hello?" I called again, coming around the house slowly as the pounding grew louder. It stopped suddenly as I made it to the corner of the porch, and my eyes landed on a figure standing on the other side of the barn.

A man.

His gaze was on the horse, as if he'd come out to check on her. A hammer hung heavy at his side, and I could hear the low, faint rumble of his voice as he made his way toward her. He reached up, running one hand up the creature's snout.

The mare calmed for a moment, breaths slowing, and the man's eyes followed her gaze in my direction. His dark hair was falling to one side, tucked behind an ear and curling at its ends. The suspenders that hung from his belt were slack against his legs, his white shirt damp. And when his eyes finally focused on me, his whole body went rigid, making me flinch.

I lifted a hand against the harsh light of the glaring sun, trying to make out his face. "Hello?"

He visibly exhaled, his chest deflating beneath the pull of his shirt, but he said nothing as he stood there, staring at me. And then, suddenly, he was walking. The hammer slipped from his fingers, hitting the ground, and he stalked toward me with an intensity that made me move backward. When he didn't slow, I glanced at the road. Then to the house. There was no one else here.

"What the hell are you doing here?"

"W-What?" I dropped my hand as he came closer.

"I said what the hell are you doing here, June?"

I gasped when I heard it. Not just my name, but my name spoken in *that* voice. The one that whispered in the dark. The one that had been like fire on my skin. I knew that voice.

I took another step backward, hitting the porch railing with a shoulder before he reached me. When he finally did, he was so close that I had to tip my head up to look at him.

"I'm sorry, did you say—"

The words sputtered out as I frantically studied his face. His eyes. They were a deep brown, with the same bronze hue that the sun had lit in that horse's mane. And for just a moment, I was sure that I'd seen them before.

"Do you know me?" I whispered.

"What?" He was moving even closer now. So close that I could feel the heat coming off of him.

"You said my name."

His full lips parted, face twisting in confusion. "What the hell is that supposed to mean?"

I blinked, turning the sound of his voice over in my head. There was a faint accent to his speech that pulled at the vowels and sharpened the words. It was definitely the one I remembered.

He stared at me, waiting, but I hadn't figured this part out yet. I hadn't had any time to think about it. I hadn't had a plan when I walked through that door.

"I'm looking for someone." I took hold of the first thing I could think of. "Susanna Farrow."

His eyes narrowed as he drifted back, putting inches of space between us. There was something changing in his manner now. A shift somewhere I couldn't see.

"Rutherford," I corrected. "Susanna Rutherford. Do you know her?"

"What is this?" He said it so softly that it sounded like he was asking the question of himself, not me. He looked almost . . . wary.

"I'm looking for Susanna. Do you know where I can find her?" I sounded even less sure than I was. And it occurred to me all at once that he wasn't asking about what I wanted. He was asking about *me*.

His hand came between us suddenly, snatching up my wrist. Before I could even react, he was pulling my arm long between us.

"What are you doing?" I tried to yank free, but his fingers clamped down harder.

I watched, gasping, as he pushed up the sleeve of my shirt and turned my hand so that the skin of my forearm was bare between us. His breaths were coming faster now, his grip squeezing tighter, but I didn't know what he was looking for. And then, all of a sudden, he let me go, taking several steps backward.

I pulled my arm into me, wrist screaming with pain.

"You've never been here, have you?" he said.

"Been here?"

The muscle in his jaw ticked. "We've never met."

"No." Again, I looked to the empty road. "I told you—"

"Christ, June." He dragged both hands over his face, pressing them to prayer in front of his mouth, and there it was again. That familiar way he was saying my name. "What did you do?"

He wasn't looking at me anymore. He wasn't talking to me, either. Whatever was unfolding behind his eyes was invisible to me. It took him a moment to blink, to come back to himself.

"Did anyone see you?" His attention went to the road. "Have you spoken to anyone at all?"

"Look, I don't understand what—"

"Has anyone *seen* you."

The woman on the porch and the truck on the road both flickered through my mind.

"You need to get inside."

He brushed past me, going up the steps of the porch and pushing into the house. His boots hit the floor in a way that made me remember the ghost of a sound I'd heard so many times before. That steady, hollow beat.

I followed him, stopping in the doorway when I thought better of what I was doing. Walking into the home of a strange man I'd never even met. But it was obvious that he knew something. There was some piece of this that he had and I didn't.

My eyes moved around the small house, finding everything the light touched. The fireplace still glowed with embers, a small sofa covered in a quilt set before it. There was a broom in the corner. A cedar chest. A framed cross-stitch of a bouquet of flowers on the wall. Beyond the living area was a small kitchen and another closed door.

He pulled up his suspenders, tugging on a thick canvas jacket that he'd taken from the hook beside the door. "Stay here."

"You're leaving?" The words came out stilted. I was still standing on the porch, hands pressed to either side of the doorframe.

He took a ring of keys from his pocket, waiting for me to step inside. But he wasn't looking at me anymore. In fact, it looked like he was taking great care not to. "If anyone knocks on the door, don't answer it. Stay in the house."

"But—"

Again, his jaw clenched, the tension of it traveling down to his shoulders. His arms. "You want to know about Susanna?" His voice took on an edge.

I swallowed. "Yes."

"Then wait here."

My eyes moved from his face to the clench of his hand around the keys. The veins that straddled his knuckles were raised beneath the skin.

I'm not sure what made me decide; in fact, I was almost convinced I didn't have a choice. I didn't know where I was or what was happening. But this man knew me. He knew my mother.

He shouldered past me as soon as I stepped inside. "Lock the door."

It closed heavily behind him, making the windows in the house rattle. I went to the nearest one, watching him open the cattle gate and then climb into the truck. He fought with the gears once the engine was running, and a cloud of dirt kicked up into the air as he pulled onto the road.

Then he was gone.

I let go of the curtain, feeling suddenly sick to my stomach. Almost impulsively, I turned the dead bolt lock on the door, pressing my trembling fingers to my lips. What exactly had I done?

I replayed it, step by step. Coming around that corner to see Birdie in the sitting room. That look on her face. The way her hands trembled when she handed me that envelope. I'd done as she said. I'd gone through the door. But now what?

The house was silent around me except for the sound of my own breathing, and I tried to slow it. I was afraid to turn back around. To see with my own eyes any shred of familiarity. The extra pair of boots by the door. The kettle on the counter. The box of matches on the fireplace mantel. A rifle on the wall.

The possibility that this was all in my head was shrinking by the second. If I was imagining this, then I wasn't just having an episode. I was lost in a labyrinth. I was so deep I'd never be found.

I took a tentative step away from the window, making my way across the knotted rag rug that covered the floor. It was made with fabric scraps in every color, faded and frayed along the edges. I took in every detail. The small table between this room and the next was fit with four wooden chairs, one of them missing a spindle from the back. The cast-iron pan on the stove was still just barely warm to the touch.

It wasn't just a house. This was a home.

My hand slipped over the butcher block as I made my way to the closed doorway across the kitchen, something pulling me toward it until I was reaching for the cold metal knob. I pushed it open and the sunlight that was trapped within flooded out.

I studied the small room. There was a simple bed, a small dressing table, a closed wardrobe. It wasn't the kind of space that only a man filled. It was feminine. Gentle. But I hadn't seen a woman out at the barn. Whoever she was, she wasn't home.

My eyes fixed on the bit of fabric closed in the door of the wardrobe, a dusty pink check that couldn't belong to the tobacco farmer. I could still feel something beckoning me into that room. To the wardrobe. I could feel it guiding my drifting hand to that latch. And when I pulled it open, my gaze flitted over what lay inside.

Boots smaller than the ones by the front door. A thick wool coat. A few dresses and a couple of pairs of denim overalls. A small stack of folded colored fabric that looked like the bandanas we wore on the farm.

I turned back to the room, sifting through the items that likely didn't belong to the man. A tortoiseshell comb, a small dish that held a thin gold ring. An hourglass-shaped silver bottle that looked as if it held perfume. I picked it up, bringing it to my nose, and I breathed in the soft scent of rose and orange. My throat constricted, like it might make me cry.

A part of me *felt* the photograph before I actually saw it. In the mirror's reflection, I spotted a small frame on the table beside the bed.

A mother-of-pearl oval with a black-and-white picture behind the glass.

I set the bottle down, turning toward it, and slow, hesitant steps took me across the room. I had to pick it up to believe it. I had to hold it in my hands.

I unclenched my stiff fingers from my damp T-shirt, picking up the frame. There, the man who lived in this house had his arms wrapped around a woman, her face pressed to the crook between his shoulder and his throat. A wide smile was on her lips, but it was the birthmark that made me feel like I had just been nailed to the floor. Below the ear, tucked beneath the jaw.

I reached up, touching the mark that traced down my own neck with trembling fingers. It was me.

It was me.

The picture slipped from my fingers, glass shattering as it hit the ground, and then I was moving through the house. Toward the door. I flung it open, my feet finding the steps, and then I was at the gate. The road. The turn that led to town.

And I ran.

TEN

I followed the river, staying off the road.

Every few seconds, I glanced back, watching the trees with a terrified feeling growing roots inside of me. I needed to forget what I'd seen, to wipe it from my memory. But the image of that photograph was already seared in my mind. This wasn't the obscure, faint recognition of Susanna in the picture with Nathaniel Rutherford. The moment I'd laid eyes on that woman, I knew without any doubt that it was me.

I kept walking, adrenaline flowing hot in my veins. I didn't know where I was going, only that I wasn't headed toward something anymore. I wasn't searching or looking for answers. Now, I was just running.

The water grew louder below as the terrain turned rocky, and again, I scanned the fields that stretched along both sides of the river, desperate to see the door. If I'd gone through it once, I could do it again. I didn't care anymore what happened to Susanna. I didn't want to know what truth the Farrows had kept buried or what Gran had been hiding from me. None of that mattered. Now, I only wanted to go home. To the house on Bishop Street and the farm and Mason.

The sun was beginning to fall by the time I made it to the old railroad bridge that crossed the Adeline River, but it didn't look as old anymore. It wasn't covered in vines, littered with fallen branches. The only thing that was the same was the blue-green river that ran beneath it.

I pushed into the brush and scaled down the bank, scooping up the cold water and splashing my face. My skin was hot and flushed, my eyes swollen, and the sound that broke in my throat made me feel like the ten-year-old girl who'd jumped from this bridge with Mason.

The moment he entered my mind, the cry loosed itself from where it was tangled in my chest. What I would give to be sitting across the table from him, a blueberry pie between us. To rewind that moment and listen to him when he tried to convince me to let go of my obsession with my mother.

I wanted to believe that what I'd seen in the house on Hayward Gap Road couldn't exist, but the mere memory of the image made me wince. That smile on my face. The way the man's arms had been wrapped around me. I could almost feel them, the way I had that morning when I woke up with the feeling of someone in the bed.

I stared into the water, where my reflection rippled, breaking and changing in the light with the patchwork of blue sky and thick tree branches overhead. That image was how I felt on the inside—distorted and broken. A picture that couldn't quite come into focus.

Sweat beaded along my brow and my muscles burned, reminding me that I hadn't actually slept last night. In fact, I'd barely slept for days now. My legs ached as I climbed the slope to the bridge, my center of gravity missing, like I was floating from one place to the next.

I stepped onto the tracks, following them away from the road until I was standing over the water. In the distance, Jasper sat nestled by the riverbank as if it had never changed. On one side of the downtown bridge, I could just make out the redbrick buildings on Main Street. On the other was the spindly white steeple of the church. It was mostly hidden by the trees, but even from here, I could see some of the headstones that dotted the cemetery. It wasn't until that moment that I admitted to myself that I had no idea what to do. If I wasn't in 2023, or even in my own lifetime, I couldn't just walk into town and find someone I knew. There was only one person I could think of on this side of the door who might be able to help me—Susanna.

A low, soft rumble reverberated on the railing beneath my hands, and I blinked, my grip tightening around one of the iron rods. The metal was vibrating with a deep resonance and when I looked down to my boots, I realized the sound was growing. The tracks I was standing on began to quake and I looked to the trees that sat on the other side of the river. When I heard the whistle blow, I sucked in a breath, pulling myself back across the bridge.

The train burst from the tree line, racing toward me, and I scrambled over the tracks, catching the end of the barricade. Then I was sliding down the hill, back toward the water. I landed clumsily, catching a limb with my sleeve and scraping along the thicket of brambles as the train made it to the bridge. Its shadow cast over me, sunlight flitting between the cars as it passed.

It vanished across the road seconds later, leaving a drifting trail of steam behind it. The sound of it bled away before the rumble of another engine surfaced at the top of the riverbank, and I listened, going still as it got closer. The pop of tires on gravel and the screech of brakes drew my eye to the opening in the brush I'd come through, and a few seconds later, I saw him. The man from the house.

His eyes frantically searched the riverbank before he spotted me and he let out a heavy breath. "What do you think you're doing?"

Again, that image of him holding me in the picture painted itself across my thoughts. I wanted to erase it.

When I didn't answer, he walked toward me.

"Stay away from me!" My feet splashed into the river and cold water filled my boots.

"You need to come with me. *Now.*"

"I'm not going anywhere with you." I cast my gaze behind me, to the other side of the river, judging the distance.

"It's not safe, June."

Hearing him say my name sent another chill up my spine. There was no formality in it. No edge of uncertainty. His mouth moved around it like he'd said it a thousand times.

"Who are you?" I asked.

He pressed a hand to his forehead, as if there was pain there. "My name is Eamon," he said, impatient. "Eamon Stone."

"Why do you have a picture of me in your house?" I blurted out. I was cold all over now.

"Come with me and I'll tell you."

"No. Tell me now."

His face changed as he measured his words. "I know you. You just don't know me yet."

"Yet?" I stilled, watching him. The panic I'd felt standing in that bedroom was now terror. "*How* do you know me?"

His hands fell heavily to his sides, fingers curling into fists. "Look, you need to come with me."

I took another step deeper into the water before his eyes snapped up to the road. I could hear another car pulling onto the shoulder behind the trees.

Eamon shifted on his feet before he set the hat back on his head and a car door opened. There were footsteps moving behind the brush.

"Everything all right?" a man's voice called out.

"Yeah." Eamon smiled at whoever stood on the road, but it looked wrong on his face.

"Saw your truck."

A man in an old style of police uniform appeared at the top of the bank, attention on Eamon. He had one thumb hooked in his belt as he wiped a handkerchief across his brow, and the badge on his chest was engraved with the word DEPUTY. He froze when he saw me.

"June? That you?"

I looked to Eamon, the cinching feeling around my lungs now an excruciating pain. What the hell was happening?

Eamon's eyes bored into mine, like he was truly afraid of what I might say. "Just got back," he stammered, turning so that he was half blocking the man's view.

Back? From where?

The man stepped aside, trying to see me. His hand absently moved from his belt, and I had the fleeting thought that it could be drifting toward the gun at his hip.

"Well, it's good to see you. Your mama doin' all right?"

I looked from him to Eamon. My mother? Susanna?

My mouth opened, but before I could speak, Eamon was cutting in again.

"Much better," he answered, eyes shooting to me. The muscles in his throat tightened, and he gave me an almost undetectable nod of his head.

"Yeah." I swallowed, taking my cue from him. I didn't know what else to do.

"Good."

I nodded awkwardly.

The deputy's gaze moved to my feet. "Everything okay?"

I looked down to my boots, now submerged beneath the water.

"Yeah," I said, more loudly than was necessary. I was still out of breath.

The man was clearly confused, but before he could ask any more questions, I trudged back up the rocks, to where Eamon stood. Behind his truck, the glossy black-and-white paint of the police car reflected the sun. A single red light was fixed to the hood.

I didn't even see Eamon moving before his arm came around me, hand hooking my waist. I stared at it, watching his fingers curl into my shirt. He pulled me closer to him, but I could feel the tension coiled tight around his body. Whatever was happening, Eamon was doing his best to smooth it over.

"Well, like I said, it's good to have you back." The deputy was still watching me intently. "Been a hell of a year."

I nodded again, keeping my mouth shut. I wasn't going to risk saying or asking anything that would make this more complicated. Not before I could figure out what exactly was going on here.

The officer tipped his hat before he walked back to the car, opening the door with one more glance in our direction.

"I, uh." He hesitated. "I'll need to let the sheriff know." He said it as if he were apologizing.

"Of course." Eamon nodded, his voice finding a more convincing ease. "Don't worry about it, Sam."

The man got into the car, and Eamon lifted a hand in the air. As soon as the car was out of sight, he dropped his arm from where it was wrapped around me, eyes pinching closed for just a moment. When he finally turned to look at me, it was with a coldness that made me recoil.

"Get in the goddamn truck."

He didn't say a word as he walked up the bank, not even waiting to be sure I would follow. For a moment, I considered refusing, but beneath the anger, that look on Eamon's face had been desperate. He didn't just know me. I also had the sense that he was trying to protect me.

The engine started up as I opened the door and climbed in. Eamon didn't wait for it to close before he hit the gas.

"I told you to stay put," he said, grip tight on the steering wheel. "What the hell were you thinking?"

I studied the inside of the truck. It was an old farm rig with wooden railings fit to the bed and mismatched tires that had probably blown in the fields. Straw and dirt covered the floor where the mats were missing, and the radio dial was fogged over, the numbers illegible.

We were headed back the way I'd come, away from town. I watched the steeple of the church disappear behind us.

"Where are we going?" I asked.

Eamon stared at the road.

"You said that if I came with you, you'd tell me what's going on."

"I don't know what's going on." He ground it out one punctuated word at a time, his accent deeper now.

"You know a hell of a lot more than I do. What did you mean, I don't know you yet?"

He let his eyes land on me for just a moment before he pulled them away again. "We met five years ago. If you don't recognize me, it's because it hasn't happened yet—for you."

"How is that even possible?"

"How is any of this possible?" His voice rose.

And that's when I saw it—the glint of gold on his left hand. A wedding ring.

"Oh my god." I leaned forward, putting my head in my hands and trying to breathe.

"I came home one day and you were gone. I haven't seen you since," he said. "That's all I know."

"When was that?"

"Almost a year ago."

I closed my eyes, trying to breathe. A year ago was when my episodes had started. When everything changed. Could that timing be a coincidence?

"It wasn't me," I choked out. "It couldn't have been me."

"It was you. I think I know my own wife."

I shook my head, wishing I could unhear those words. "I'm telling you that I have never been here before. I've never met you."

He cranked the wheel, and the truck jostled left to right as it turned. I grabbed hold of the handle above my head to keep from hitting the window, and as soon as I saw what lay ahead, I sat up straighter, leaning closer to the glass.

A relieved breath left my lips.

The Adeline River Flower Farm sat back from the road, framed by the mountains in the distance. The house was a different shape, but it was still the same one I'd grown up in. The windows were in the same place, the porch and steps just like I remembered. But the front room that had now become our office wasn't built yet. Instead, that part of the yard was covered in ferns and a chicken coop framed with gridded wire. Behind it, the land was striped with rows of flowers in full or partial bloom.

Eamon pulled into the drive, barely getting the truck parked before he opened the door, then he was slamming it behind him.

He walked toward the house as the front door opened and a woman's face appeared, her hand twisted into the edge of the apron tied around her waist. His voice was drowned out by the sound of the cicadas in the trees, but I could tell the two of them were arguing.

I hesitated before I reached for the handle and pushed the truck door open. My feet found the ground as I watched them on the porch. The woman's eyes jumped from Eamon to me.

I knew who she was as soon as I saw her. I'd seen her countless times in photographs. Esther Farrow, my great-great-grandmother, stood there looking at me with an expression that said she knew exactly who I was, too.

Their voices quieted as I crossed the yard, but Esther's expression didn't change from the deep concern that wrinkled her brow. She was completely still for several seconds before she finally gave Eamon a nod.

"Thank you." His voice was heavy.

Esther Farrow stared at me, eyes trailing from the top of my head down to my feet. When they lifted to meet mine again, they were guarded. Distant.

"Annie!" Eamon took hold of the front door, pulling it wider. A few seconds later, a quick patter of footsteps sounded inside the house. It was followed by the bob of a head behind the window.

A small girl that looked to be at least a few years old came outside, hiding behind Esther's long skirt. Her wild, waving blond hair was pulled into two unraveled braids and the dress she wore came down to her knees, where tall woolen socks were pulled up over her calves. By the time my gaze made it to her face, she was staring at me. No, not at me. *Into* me.

She stood so still, her pink lips the same shade as the apple of her cheeks. I pinned my eyes to the porch steps, unable to look at her for even another second. I couldn't bring myself to ask who she was. I was certain I didn't want to know.

Eamon reached for her and she untangled herself from Esther's skirt so that he could pick her up. The girl tucked herself against him and her eyes found me over his shoulder, but Eamon shifted her in his arms, blocking her view. He carried her to the truck without another word.

"Hello, June." Esther still stood in the doorway, hands clasped at her waist. "We've got ourselves quite a problem, don't we?"

She watched me come up the steps, her sharp eyes not missing anything. They were an icy blue that was brightened by her fair, silver-streaked hair, making her look almost ethereal. Like she was cast in moonlight despite the glow of the late afternoon sun.

"Is she here?" My voice wavered.

"Who?"

"My mother," I said.

The word *mother* was unfamiliar on my tongue, and it sounded strange spoken in my voice. Foreign, even.

She took a step forward, meeting me halfway on the porch. "When you showed up here five years ago, that was the first question you asked me."

Five years ago. Those three words landed one at a time, making my heart race.

"Where is she?" I whispered.

"It's 1951, June." She looked me in the eye, a well of compassion brimming in her voice. "Susanna is dead."

ELEVEN

Thirty years. I was more than thirty years too late.

I don't remember falling asleep. I barely remember walking through Esther's door. The first rooster's cry came before the sun crested the mountains, and the sound was so much like home that for a split second, I forgot where I was.

No, *when* I was.

The bedroom at the northeast corner of the farmhouse was one I'd slept in many nights when Gran was working late on the farm or she had to stay over to keep an eye on morning deliveries. Yet, in the lifetime of this house, this was still the first time I'd woken beneath this roof. The room smelled the same, and in many ways it looked the same, too. It felt as if I was the only thing that was different now, and that was a change that couldn't be undone.

Susanna is dead.

I'd known it for a long time. There was never a thing in me that felt like she was out there somewhere, waiting for me to find her. But ever since I'd seen that photograph, a part of me had wanted it to be true. The abandoned child tucked away and still living inside of me had seen the words *trust me,* and I'd let myself believe, in some small way, that I could find her. And when I did, I would finally understand why she'd left.

I sat up on the edge of the bed, knees drawn into my chest. My fingers nervously fidgeted with the hem of my jeans as I listened to the sounds of the house. Footsteps had been trailing up and down the hallway for at least an hour, but I hadn't made a sound. If I opened that door, it wouldn't be the house I knew. It wouldn't be the farm I knew. This place was an unknown land, and something told me I wasn't safe in it.

The breeze tugged at the curtains that framed the open window. Outside, the tractor that sat rusted and hidden by overgrown brambles at the corner of the barn in 2023 was clearly operational. The farm was laid out differently from the one I'd grown up working. From the second floor, I could see that there wasn't a clear-cut pattern to the plots, and the fields were mostly wild, an old tactic that relied on native species growing between the plants to help with drainage and pests. In 2023 we had modern practices that controlled those things, and even from the road, you could see the orderly layout of the farm.

There were two makeshift greenhouses that no longer existed in my time, replaced by fancy structures with irrigation and aeration systems. These were more like glorified potting sheds where I suspected Esther grew roses. That was one of the things the farm had been known for during this time—year-round roses that you could otherwise get only in New York.

But the thing my eyes kept looking for was the door.

Every time I'd seen it, it had appeared unexpectedly, out of nowhere. And there had been days, weeks, sometimes months in between. But I didn't have that kind of time. I needed to get out of here. Now.

A familiar scent crept into the air, and I closed my eyes when the burn of tears ignited behind them. Biscuits baking in the oven—a smell I intrinsically associated with home. I let my feet fall to the floor and stood, making my way to the door. It opened with a creak, and I came down the narrow wooden stairs to see Esther in the kitchen. Her hair was pinned at the nape of her neck and she wore a fresh, unwrinkled dress beneath her clean apron.

She didn't look up at me as I timidly stepped out of the hallway. "Did you manage to sleep at all?"

I nodded, the chill in the drafty house making me shiver.

"Good. There's coffee if you'd like some."

My eyes went past her, to the percolator on the stove. There was steam pouring from the spout. "Thanks."

Her gaze followed me as I crossed the kitchen. She was straining something through a cheesecloth in the sink. "Cups are up on the shelf."

I searched around me until I saw the one she was talking about. A small, crude plank of wood beside the icebox held four mismatched mugs. For my entire life, there had always been a cabinet on that wall.

I reached up, taking the cup nearest to me and holding it to my chest. "Thank you for letting me stay."

"Eamon didn't give me much of a choice, did he?" Esther smirked. "But you're a Farrow, June. This place is as much yours as it is mine, even if you've ended up on the wrong end of time."

The wrong end of time. Is that what this was?

I set the mug down, taking the percolator up from the stove and pouring. When I took a sip, I winced at the bitter taste. I didn't see a sugar pot anywhere.

Esther hauled the cheesecloth up out of the sink, giving it a shake before she dropped whatever was encased within it into a bowl on the counter.

"I have questions." I sat down in one of the chairs, watching her.

"I'm sure you do. But I'll tell you now that you should be careful which ones you ask. You might not want all the answers."

It sounded exactly like something Gran would say, but I was finished with riddles and half-truths. I wasn't going to play that game anymore.

"I think I deserve to know what's happening to me," I said.

She continued working, almost as if she hadn't heard me. But a few seconds later, she sighed. "You're not wrong about that, I suppose."

She seemed to make up her mind, rinsing her hands in the bowl of water that sat on the counter. The expression on her face was unreadable, and I began to wonder if she was nervous. She fidgeted with the towel tucked into the waist of her skirt before she sat down on the other side of the table.

"So, where should we start?" she said.

"How about explaining how I got here. How all of this . . ." I lifted a hand, gesturing to the kitchen around us. ". . . is possible?"

"Well, I know less about that than you may imagine," she answered. "I honestly don't know how it began. My mother told me what her mother told her—that any woman in our bloodline will see that door at one point or another, and eventually, she'll walk through it."

That choice of words made me sit up straighter in the chair. "What do you mean *eventually*? Like, it's inevitable?"

"There hasn't been a Farrow I know of who's managed not to go through the door. It doesn't stop appearing. Sure, you might decide you'll never walk through it, but it comes again. And then again. Until one day, you've finally got a good enough reason to open it."

Her eyes studied me, head tilting like she was trying to see if I knew from experience what she meant.

"It wasn't like that for me. I didn't even know about any of this until yesterday."

"It wouldn't matter if you were six years old or if you were eighty. We're like moths to the flame, and once you cross, it begins."

"What begins?"

"The fraying."

I waited.

She set her elbows on the table, as if settling, and I found myself wondering if she'd been the one to tell me all of this the last time. "I'll explain it to you the way it was explained to me. Time is like a rope, made of many fibers, and when they're bound up together, they make one strong timeline."

She stared at me, waiting to be convinced of whether I was following.

"But once you cross it, it begins to fray. Those fibers loosen. Unwind. Eventually, they are bound to unravel. Then you don't have one timeline anymore."

Two places at once. Two *times* at once.

"So, they're real? The things I'm seeing and hearing?"

She nodded. "They're just parallel threads."

"But." My mind went to that notebook I'd kept tucked under my mattress. "I only went through the door yesterday. If it starts after you cross, why did the episodes start a year ago?"

Esther squinted. "A year ago?"

"Yeah."

"Exactly?"

"Almost. The first one was July 2, 2022."

There was an unmistakable reaction that rippled through Esther's body, but she recovered well, tucking a stray hair behind her ear and clearing her throat. "Well, this isn't the first time you've crossed, June."

As soon as she said it, I realized I already had the pieces of that puzzle. My mother disappeared when she was pregnant with me. She most likely gave birth to me on the other side.

"Are you saying that I was born here, in this time?"

"Well, not in this time, obviously. You were born in the year 1912, and the fray is different for all of us. Sometimes it takes months for it to begin, sometimes years. Decades."

The explanation sounded practiced and carefully constructed, but Esther still looked shaken. Uncomfortable, even.

"For my mother," she continued, "it began only a few months after she crossed, and it was swift, breaking her mind in a matter of years. For me, it took a long time to come on, and it's been slow and steady."

"So, you're . . . ?"

"Sick? It has nothing to do with being sick. It's more like having two sets of eyes, one that sees this world and one that sees the other. Eventually, they start bleeding into each other, and *that's* where the madness lies."

"But how do you stop it?"

"You can't. The door appears to the Farrow women, and at one point or another, they *will* walk through it. And once you've crossed, your mind never fully crosses back."

I stared into the steam rising from my coffee cup, that familiar, bleak feeling settling back over me. I'd felt it. The draw to the door had been like a tightening thread. Had I even hesitated before I reached for the knob? I couldn't remember now.

"I suppose at one time or another, it was a useful gift." Esther paused. "But like everything else, it comes with a cost."

"And Susanna?"

"Susanna was—" She stopped herself, as if trying to find the right words. "She met him—Nathaniel—the first time she crossed. Only days after. We told people she was a cousin visiting from Norfolk, Virginia. I thought she'd be here a few weeks and go, but those two . . . I'd never seen twin flames like that before, two people dragging each other so deep, so fast."

That's what had kept Susanna here, I thought. Love.

"Nathaniel and Susanna were both a little broken, to be honest, but they were passionate. They were never good for each other. She knew that, but she couldn't help herself. His father was the minister, and our family isn't exactly welcome in the church, so of course, he didn't approve. They were meeting in secret for some time before I ever found out, and then it was much too late. A few months later, she was pregnant with you."

A shadow flitted past the window, and Esther's eyes followed a young man in a flat cap and denim shirt walking toward the barn with a digging fork propped on one shoulder. His olive skin was a deep golden color that only came from long days in the fields.

"I convinced Susanna to cross back, but she returned months later. Once you were born, there was no undoing it."

"But why would she take me back to her time and just . . . leave me there?"

Esther said nothing.

"Why would she do that? Why stay here without me?"

"I told you. I don't know why Susanna did a lot of things."

My hands slipped from the table and I sank back into the chair, staring at her. There was more to the story than she was telling me. I could see that. But this woman was different from Gran. Her edges were harder, her gaze sharp.

"She got sicker, much sicker, once you were gone. The doctors here in this time call it 'hysteria,' and eventually, it became too much for her. A few years later, she took her own life."

The image of my mother standing up at the top of the falls, her eyes drifting over the drop, made me tremble.

"I thought it was over then. But five years ago, you showed up here looking for her."

"And then?"

"Not so different from Susanna, you met Eamon. Fell in love. Got married. And then one day, you were gone."

"And you don't know where I went?"

She shook her head. "You were here one day and then you weren't. This is the first we've seen of you in nearly a year. It's never happened like this before—an overlap."

"Overlap?"

"A younger version of you showing up after an older version does. I don't know what else to call it, and I don't know what to make of it, quite honestly."

Just listening to her say it out loud made me feel dizzy. "So, what? Does that mean there are two versions of me?"

"No, there isn't more than one of any of us. If you cross into a different timeline, you don't keep existing in the other. You're either here or there. But somehow, things have been disrupted. You're the same June I met five years ago, but if you don't remember me, then you're the younger her. You went through the door . . . early. The things that happened here haven't happened to you yet."

"How early am I?" I whispered. "How much earlier did I cross than before?"

"What year was it when you crossed?"

"2023."

"Well, it's early for you, but late for us. That's the problem. The first time you came here, it was 2024 for you."

"2024," I repeated, trying to wrap my mind around it.

That meant I most likely would have been thirty-five. I'd come through the door at least nine months after Gran's funeral, maybe longer. And I hadn't come to 1951. If it was five years ago, it had been 1946 for them.

Esther was studying me again, those pale eyes refocusing. "Why did you choose 1951?"

"What?"

"When you crossed. Why did you choose 1951?"

"I didn't choose anything. I walked through the door, and it brought me here."

A look of disbelief flashed over her features. "The locket, June."

Immediately, my hand went to my throat, fingers searching for the chain of the locket watch. But it wasn't there. I set down the coffee cup and opened the collar of my shirt, searching for it.

"It's gone," she said.

"I must have dropped it in the field, or along the road." I said, anxiously. "I—"

"You didn't lose it." She reached into the collar of her own dress, pulling a chain free. Then she was lifting it over her head. She set the locket watch down on the table between us.

I stared at it. "How did you . . . ?"

"We'll get to that." She opened the locket, turning it so that the watch face was right side up for me. All four of the hands were pointing to the number zero. "So, you were wearing the locket, but you didn't choose the year."

I was so confused now that I didn't have a response.

"Do you remember what the hands were set to?"

"I don't know. I think five? One?" I swallowed. "Yes, there were two hands on one."

"One, nine, five, one. 1951." She said.

My eyes snapped up to look at her. "*This* is how you cross?"

"You fix the four hands into the four digits of a year, starting with the shortest. It was 2023 when you left?"

I nodded.

"All right." She pulled a pin from her hair. Beginning with the shortest hand on the watch face, she moved them to the numbers two, zero, two, and three. When she was finished, she snapped it closed. "As long as the locket says 2023 when you open that door, that's where it will take you."

I turned it over in my fingers, dazed by the flicker of sunlight on the gold. I'd always known the watch didn't work, and I'd found the four hands and missing numbers strange. But there was nothing about it I hadn't dismissed with the reasoning that it was old. Very old. It still looked ancient, but the metal wasn't quite as fogged and smoothed as the locket I'd worn around my neck.

I eyed the calendar tacked to the wall by the back door. It was a farmer's almanac, open to the month of June. Today was the seventeenth, only four days since Gran's funeral. I didn't know how that was possible. How had four days been enough time to completely unravel everything I thought I knew?

"I've never understood why your grandmother never told you any of this," Esther murmured.

Gran.

That's right. If it was 1951, then Gran was here. She'd been raised by Esther in this very house.

My hands slipped from the mug. "Where is she?"

Esther shifted in her seat, and for a moment, I wondered if she was considering lying to me. "She's here." Her hand came down on mine, stopping me before I could stand. "Listen to me." She leaned in closer. "The best thing you can do, for all of us, is go back."

I searched her face. What did that mean, *for all of us*?

"As soon as you see that door again, cross. And stay there."

I wasn't going to argue with that. "When will that be?"

She sighed. "There's no exact timing, unfortunately."

"No exact timing?" My voice rose. "Are you saying that I'm stuck here?"

Stuck. The word made me feel nauseous. Claustrophobic.

"It *will* appear again. You just need to be ready to walk through it."

"There are people who will be looking for me." The image of the empty Bronco on the road flashed in my mind. "How am I going to explain where I've been?"

"The same way the rest of us have explained it every time this has happened. You create a story, and you stick to it. You don't draw attention, and you don't offer explanations. Frankly, the more mad they think you are, the better."

That's exactly what Gran and Birdie had done with my mother— let the town think she was crazy and that was the reason she'd gone missing. The reason she'd never come back. It was much more believable than the truth.

I pressed my fingertips to my temples. I'd always known that they weren't telling me everything they knew about Susanna. I thought it was because Gran was trying to protect me. That she didn't want me to live in fear of what was coming. But really, she was protecting her daughter. And herself.

"Okay, what else do I need to know?"

"Well, there are rules." She stood, going to the stove, and poured the rest of the coffee into another cup. "The door won't open to you if you don't have the locket, and you can cross only three times. After that, it won't appear to you anymore."

"But you just said I've been here before. If I crossed as a baby and then came here five years ago . . ."

She shook her head. "No. The last time you were here, you were older. The younger you has only crossed once—when you were seven months old. You, in this body, have now gone through the door only twice. Then, and now. You have one more crossing left, a choice to make. The same choice every Farrow makes eventually."

I waited.

"Which side of time you want to live on. Which life you want to live." She answered my unspoken question. "After that, there's no going back."

Is that what I'd done? Crossed to 1946 and eventually decided to cross back?

"And that's not all. The second rule is that you may go only where you do not exist." She pointed at the locket. "There's only one of you, June, just like there's only one of those lockets. That will never change. The locket around your neck disappeared when you crossed because it already lives here. It ceased to exist. Your *mind* can exist in two places at once, but your body cannot. So, if you walked through the door right now and went back to a time in which you already exist in the future—say, 2022—you, also . . . disappear."

I swallowed, the gravity of the idea like a weight pressing down on top of me.

"The other thing you need to think about is what kind of information you've brought with you. No talking about what happens in the future to any of us. No warning us of danger or opportunity or anything else. There are too many risks. Too many things that could be affected."

My thoughts immediately went to Gran. There were decades of her life I'd witnessed. I even knew the exact day she died. But the people on this side of time didn't have that luxury.

"Who did people think I was when I came here?"

Esther slid the locket toward me. "It was years after Susanna died that you showed up. I said you were another cousin. Just left it at that, and people didn't act too curious. Not until . . ." Her voice trailed off. "Well, until things got complicated."

"So, where do people think I've been all this time?"

"Taking care of your sick mother back in Norfolk."

"For a year? People believe that?"

"Not really. That's the problem."

That was why the deputy had acted so suspicious, but it didn't explain why that woman on her porch had been so terrified.

"Which is why I'm taking you home as soon as you finish that cup of coffee."

I froze. "*What?*"

"We might have been able to keep this quiet until the door reappeared, but now you've been seen, June. If Sam saw you yesterday, the entire town will have heard that you're back."

"You can't seriously expect me to go back to that house."

"That's exactly what I expect you to do." Esther frowned. "I know your life was turned upside down when you ended up here, and if you feel like all of this isn't fair, then you're right. You should have been told." She lowered her voice, "Margaret should have prepared you. But while you're on this side of the door, I expect you to do everything in your power to make sure *our* lives aren't burned to the ground by the time you leave. It's important that things go on as normal."

She said it with a calm authority that didn't leave room to argue, and that made me wonder just how much trouble the other June had caused them.

"He doesn't want me there," I said.

"No, but he knows that he needs you to be if we're going to keep this town from turning our family inside out."

I felt sick just thinking about the house on Hayward Gap Road. That bedroom. The photograph on the dressing table.

"You need to attract as little attention as possible while you're here, and people will expect you to be at home with Eamon. Once you're gone, we'll figure out something to tell them."

"Why are they so interested? Why do they care?"

"You've come at a . . . *complicated* time." She said that word again.

She crossed the kitchen, going back to the sink. She was avoiding my gaze now.

"Are you going to tell me about that little girl?" I barely got the words out.

Esther stiffened just a little. "She's Eamon's daughter."

The words felt intentionally incomplete. Did that mean she wasn't mine, or that she was, but that I had no claim to her?

A creak popped overhead, and we both looked up to the milk-glass pendant light hanging over the table. The sound traveled across the ceiling until it reached the stairs. A moment later, a young woman was coming around the banister, one hand still struggling to tuck the tail of her blouse into her skirt. She nearly tripped over her own feet when she saw me.

Wide blue eyes the color of storm clouds fixed on me, a blush reaching her freckled cheeks. "June." She breathed my name, and even now, here, over seventy years away, it sounded the same.

Margaret Anne Farrow, the same one I'd buried only days ago, stood steps away.

Gran. Living. Breathing.

A smile broke on her lips, and she walked straight toward me, throwing her arms around my shoulders and squeezing hard. She was shorter than me. Thin and narrow. But it was her. The prick behind my eyes was now a painful burn, and when I inhaled the smell of her, an ache bloomed in my throat.

Without even meaning to, I leaned into her, holding on so tightly that a broken sound escaped me. I was instantly that little girl again, crying into her shoulder. After the last twenty-four hours, with every inch of reality shifting beneath me, she felt like solid, unbreakable ground.

She pulled back to look at me again, her eyes bright with amazement. There was a girlish smile on her lips and a sun-kissed pink that colored her cheeks. She wasn't a woman at all, a girl more than anything else. She couldn't be older than sixteen or seventeen years old.

But behind her eyes and in the air around her I could sense Gran. I could feel her. The woman who'd raised me. Who'd kept me.

I swallowed against the pain in my chest when the memory of standing on that hill for the burial flashed through my mind. Having her right in front of me, warm to the touch, made that ache of losing her tear back open.

There was a knowing in the look that painted Esther's face now. A solemn understanding. She knew that in my world, my time, this girl was already gone. She'd had to have known that the last time I came here.

"There's work to do, Margaret."

Margaret's hands slipped from the sleeves of my shirt, a protest already brewing on her tongue. "But—"

Esther fixed her with her stare, and Margaret's mouth snapped shut.

"We're on sunnies today," Esther said, using the sunflower nickname I'd only ever heard Gran use. "The delphinium we'll cut tomorrow. It's all going to town for the Faire."

The Midsummer Faire.

I glanced to the calendar again. The summer solstice was labeled in red type on June 21, four days from now. With any luck, I'd be gone by then.

Margaret's lips pursed defiantly, but she obeyed, giving me one last look before she headed to the back door. The screen slammed behind her.

Esther's fair eyes sharpened on me. "Be careful. Best not to let her get too attached before you leave for good."

I watched Margaret's shape grow smaller through the window before she disappeared behind the fence.

"Eamon's not the only one who was left with a broken heart. Understand?"

I didn't know if she was talking only about Margaret or if she was including herself in that statement. If she did have some kind of affection for me, then she was good at hiding it. I'd felt little, if any, tenderness from her since I walked through the door.

If what they said was true, I couldn't blame her. There were years of history between all of us, and it had ended with betrayal. Even if she was the only one who remembered it.

"I've got some things you can wear. You'll have to give me those clothes. Anything else you brought with you that shouldn't be here?" she asked.

I shook my head. I'd left everything in the truck.

Satisfied, Esther nodded. "Don't take off that locket. Not even to sleep. You never know when that door will turn up."

I picked it up, closing my fingers around it. "You still haven't told me anything about why I left," I said.

She finally fell quiet, leaning onto the counter with both hands as she reluctantly met my eyes.

I stared at her, waiting.

"It doesn't matter why. That June is gone. Wherever she is, she's years ahead of you now. The question is, honey, what are *you* doing here?"

TWELVE

The drive from our farm to Eamon's was only a few minutes, but in that time, I'd managed to run through a hundred different scenarios in my head.

I'd been gone from my own timeline in 2023 for more than twenty-four hours now. It wouldn't have taken long for someone to come along and find the Bronco, door open and engine running on the side of the road. When I was nowhere to be found, they'd call the sheriff.

Minutes later, Birdie's phone would ring. Then Mason's. They'd be asked when they last saw me. If they knew where I was headed or if they had any clue where I could be. Mason would be terrified. He was probably out combing that field for me right now. Walking the riverbank and calling my name out into the woods. But Birdie . . . Birdie would know exactly where I was.

There was no way for me to be sure just how much she knew, and now I regretted storming out of the house instead of pressing her. If I had, would I have still walked through that door? I didn't know.

The bigger problem was how I would explain myself when I got back. What kind of excuse could I give for leaving my truck in the middle of the road and just disappearing? Would I ever be able to tell Mason the truth? Would he even believe me?

My hands nervously smoothed the soft fabric of the dress Esther had given me as she turned onto Hayward Gap Road. I broke out in a sweat when I saw Eamon walking the edge of the tobacco fields. We pulled into the drive, and he glanced up for only a moment, but I could see the set of his shoulders change. The look in his eyes hardened before he climbed the back steps to the house.

My hand searched beneath my shirt until I found the locket watch. The metal was warmed by my skin, the small clasp familiar to my fingers. I was already scanning the fields, looking for any sign of that faded red paint that covered the door. But there was nothing. No sign of that glint of sunlight on the bronze knob or hinges amid the green.

The engine cut off, and Esther let out what sounded like an exhausted breath. "Let me talk to him first."

"I told you he doesn't want me here."

"Yes, well, want and need are two different things."

She was opening the door and climbing out a moment later. I watched from the passenger seat as she walked up to the porch and disappeared inside the house. It was beautiful against the fields and the hills that gave way to that perfect view of the mountains in the distance.

Here, in 1951, it was a modest but working farm, its roof the shelter to a family. *My* family. Everything about it was tranquil and serene, but in my mind, I could still see the broken skeleton that existed in 2023. The heaviness of it had settled in my bones, as if I could feel the precarious weight of those bowed, sagging beams that wanted so badly to come crashing down on the earth. It was a place that wanted to take its last breaths.

The mare behind the fence paced its length, head shaking and mane flipping as it watched me with that one glistening black eye. The farm was quiet except for the stamp of her feet and the soft tinkle of what sounded like wind chimes.

Slowly, my gaze moved to the porch, skipping over the rafters until I saw them. The sunlight sparkled as it glinted off a string of silver rods suspended from a wooden frame. My hand found the handle of the truck's door and I opened it, feet touching the dirt as I stared.

That tingling at the nape of my neck was back. It was the same sound I'd heard in the kitchen that day. The one that had split my head open with its ringing. And that wasn't the only time I'd heard it, either.

Another wind picked up and the chimes knocked together, sending another throng of high-pitched peals into the air. I walked up the porch steps, until I was standing beneath them.

I was only beginning to work out how the things I'd written in my notebook connected to this place. I could hear the wind chimes just as clearly now as I had when I was in our house on Bishop Street. That moment had been real, but *when* had it taken place?

What Esther had said about the fraying rope made sense where there had never been any before. The things I'd seen—the things that had happened to me—weren't hallucinations or delusions or any of the things that Dr. Jennings had written in his notes. They were actual, real events bleeding through from another time.

Voices sounded at my back and I blinked, tearing my eyes away from the chimes. Eamon stood in the kitchen with his shirtsleeves pulled up to his elbows, where the muscles of his arms were corded under the skin. His hair was damp and falling into his eyes as he looked at Esther, but I couldn't read the expression on his face.

I took a step closer to the window, listening.

"... much choice here." It was Esther's voice.

"He's not just going to let this go. You know that."

The rumble of a car on the road drowned out the next words, and I caught only the end.

"... she'll be gone."

They stared at each other another moment before Esther finally made her way back to the door. When it opened, she seemed surprised to find me there.

Her chin jerked toward the house. "Come on, then."

Again, I looked to Eamon through the window. He was watching me now, in a way that felt both wary and threatening. He was tense. On alert, as if he were ready to protect this place from me.

"Well?" Esther waited.

I took a steadying breath before I gathered the will to step inside. Esther gave me an encouraging smile as I passed, letting the door close behind me.

I found a place to stand beside the fireplace, studying the little trinkets on the mantel. A speckled feather, a seashell. A small bronze box with an engraved lid. Across the room, a curtain half hid a small nook with what appeared to be a bed, where a little rag doll was tossed on top of the blanket. I hadn't noticed it before, maybe because the curtain had been closed. It had to belong to the little girl I'd seen in Eamon's arms yesterday. I'd been careful not to think too much about her.

"Now," Esther began. "The best thing we can do is to act as normal as possible. June, you've been in Norfolk taking care of your mother after a stroke. She's doing much better, so you're home for good."

I stiffened. "For good?"

"As far as the town's concerned, yes."

Eamon watched me, dark eyes moving over my face in a way that made me shift on my feet.

"People will be curious." She continued, "They'll ask questions. So, it's important that you're careful with your words. Don't embellish, don't share details. Do you understand?"

I gave her a small nod. I did understand, but I didn't like the feeling that filled the room. I didn't have any idea what had taken place here in the last five years. The choices I'd made. The people I'd hurt. All of this felt like being dropped into a stranger's life and it was clear I wasn't welcome here.

"I'll take Annie for the night. Give you two a chance to . . ." She paused. "Talk."

She gave me one last, long look before she went out the back door.

Seconds after I heard her call Annie's name, the little girl was standing in the open doorway of the barn. The remains of a half-eaten apple were clutched in her small hands as she followed on Esther's heels toward the truck.

Across the kitchen, Eamon hadn't moved, but the coldness in his eyes seemed to thaw just a little. He looked more curious now. Appraising. Like he was just beginning to let himself take in the sight of me.

"I don't have to stay," I said, my attention dropping to his hands. They were darkened, streaked with something black that had been only half-heartedly wiped off.

"That might have been true if you listened to me yesterday and stayed out of sight." The words were buried beneath the deep tenor of his voice. The accent was easier to pick out now, a dim Irish lilt that had lost its most recognizable traits. "But everyone in town will know by now that you're here. There's no getting around that."

I folded my hands together, unsure of what to do with them. He wasn't trying to make me more comfortable or put me at ease, the way Esther had. This man was angry, and he didn't care if I knew it.

"You'll stay here until . . ." He didn't finish, as if he couldn't even bring himself to say it.

"The door," I murmured.

He nodded. "When it comes back, you'll leave, and we can all get back to our lives."

My whole body went rigid at the thought that followed. "And if it doesn't?"

"It will. It always comes back." He dropped his gaze from mine. It sounded like there was more meaning to the words than I knew. "You can take the bedroom. I'll sleep out here."

My eyes went to the door off the kitchen. Behind it, the remnants of a life I didn't remember were preserved like a tomb. The thought of going back in there made my stomach turn.

The light in the house changed suddenly as the clouds drifted in, and outside, the wind caught the leaves of the tobacco, making a sound that reminded me of the ocean. Eamon's eyes found the window, a distracted concern surfacing in his expression.

"What were you searching for yesterday," I asked, "when you looked at my arm?"

He considered the question, taking his time with the answer. "I was checking for something."

"What?"

The muscle in his jaw clenched. "A scar. A couple of years ago, June burned herself on the stove." He glanced to the kitchen, like he was remembering it. "It left a scar on the inside of her wrist."

That was how he'd figured it out. I'd never been burned because I'd never been here. But the fact that he'd known my body that well made my pulse race. For a fleeting moment, I thought I could feel the remnants of heat there, below my palm. A faded, throbbing pain.

"Why did you come here?" His tone was flat, but there was a strained sound beneath it, like he'd been biting back the words since I'd walked through the door.

It was a question that didn't have an easy answer. I wasn't sure I even knew what it was. How *had* I ended up here, exactly? Gran's photograph? My mother's disappearance? The episodes? They'd all converged into a woven thread that had been pulling tighter and tighter until I opened that door.

"It's not that simple," I said.

"Then explain it to me, June. I'm not an idiot."

Again, I shivered at the sound of him saying my name, the way the *u* stretched deep in his faded accent. It was, impossibly, both familiar and foreign at the same time. My hands tightened into fists every time I heard it.

"I didn't mean—"

"What *did* you mean, then?"

"I was trying to find out what was happening to me. What happened to my mother." My voice rose, defensive now. "I don't know anything about you or . . ." I couldn't bring myself to say the little girl's name.

"Annie." He enunciated the word.

My mouth opened before it clenched shut again. I couldn't say it. I didn't want to. "So, she's . . . ?"

"Mine. And June's."

I could feel the dress pulling tight across my chest as my breaths deepened. "If she's mine, then why doesn't she seem to recognize me?" I asked, grasping for any thread I could.

"She'd only just turned three when you disappeared, but children aren't the fools we are. She knows you're not her mother. Not really."

I wasn't sure if he'd meant to, but that last sentence felt like a line drawn in the sand. A boundary and a warning not to cross it.

"I just don't see how any of this is possible." I said.

"It is. I've lived it."

"You don't understand, none of this makes sense. I never—"

"Your plans changed," he snapped.

I stilled. "My plans?"

"To never marry. To never have a family. To be the last Farrow."

I bristled, stung by how bitterly he'd said it. Almost mocking. And the way he'd plucked the thought from my head was unnerving, because he was right.

"Yes." He swallowed. "I *know* you."

"You don't."

He leveled his eyes on me, his expression darkening. "There's a diamond-shaped window in your bedroom—the one you grew up in. It's in the house that hasn't even been built yet," he began. "You drink too much coffee. You kept that notebook beneath your bed. In a few weeks, once the summer's come, you'll have freckles just here." He gestured to the rise of his own cheekbones, and immediately, I felt myself blush. "Your neighbor's name is Ida and your friend Mason will be looking for you, right?"

It was the mention of Mason that made my stomach drop. What else did he know about me? What else had I told him? Everything, I realized. If I'd been married to this man for four years, if I'd trusted him enough to tie my own life to his, then I'd told him all of it.

He exhaled. "Believe me, I wish it wasn't true, too."

"I just . . . I don't understand. . . ."

"Why you would come here and make a life with me? Why you would choose this?" He looked around us, to the house. "That's what you're thinking, right?"

"No. That's not what I'm saying."

He laughed, but it was a tight, coiled thing in his chest. "You're unbelievable."

"I'm only saying that if I was here and then I left, there has to be a reason."

"There's no reason good enough. Not for what we've been through." The word hardened that line. I stood on one side, he and Annie on the other. "You swore to me that you would never go back through that door."

He went quiet, and for a flicker of a moment I could see that heartbreak Esther mentioned. It was rolling off of him like heat, filling the room around us.

I'd left him and Annie. I'd broken a multitude of promises. But I had no idea how I'd gotten there or what I could say that would make any of it better.

"Why did I leave?" I asked, my voice barely rising above a whisper.

"I don't know."

Like Esther, he wasn't telling me everything. Of that, I was sure. But if I was going to understand what happened here, how I ended up in this place, I needed them to talk to me.

"You have to at least have a guess. A theory."

"You had secrets. You could have trusted me with them, but you didn't."

"I'm not her!" The words finally broke, my whole body trembling.

I was desperate for them to be true, but they weren't. I'd been here. These people knew me. *That* June, the one who'd married this man and had his child, was *me*. The space between the two was narrowing fast, like a crashing wave seconds from hitting the sand.

Eamon stared at me, his eyes widening just enough for me to see something else behind that hard, stony look. Like that fracture in me had sharpened his focus.

"You have to know something," I whispered.

His arms dropped from where they were crossed over his chest, and he closed the space between us. I'd forgotten how tall he was. How he towered over me when he looked down into my face. His eyes jumped back and forth on mine, like he was searching for something there.

"The only thing I really know about you, June—"

My fingernails bit my palms.

"Is that I never really knew you at all."

He stood there, waiting for me to speak, but no words came to my lips. Those few seconds felt like hours, the invisible rope between us cinching until I could almost feel its pull at my center. When he finally took a step back, it took every ounce of will I had not to let out the breath I was holding.

He stalked out of the house, pushing through the back door, and then he was disappearing into the field. But the breeze that poured in before the door closed was colder than it had been moments ago, carrying with it the scent of winter jasmine. It curled around me, making me shiver.

The prickle was sharp and painful on my skin, making me wince, and the familiarity of it made me go still. I unclenched my fists, trying to focus. It was happening again, my consciousness splitting in two.

I didn't move, trying to control my breathing as I leaned in to the feeling instead of instinctively pushing it away. It was like pressing into air so thick that I could taste it on my tongue—the bite of woodsmoke and the churn of river water. The little farmhouse dissolved around me, and I held out a hand, propping myself against the counter as it all came into view.

A starry sky breaks through the branches of a dark canopy of trees. I'm outside somewhere, the night beetles buzzing in the silence.

"Are you getting in?" Mason's voice rings out around me, so clear and close that I turn.

He's standing waist-deep, his pale skin stark against the black water. He's missing his shirt, his hair swept to one side. His beard is darker. Thicker. He's smiling at me.

The sound of the water grows louder, and I look down to see river water running over my bare feet. I can feel the wind on me, every inch of my skin, and I realize I'm in my underwear. My clothes are tossed to the rocks, where a small fire is burning in a makeshift ring of stones.

When I look back to Mason, he's watching me. One of his hands lifts up, out of the water, reaching in my direction.

But the moment I moved, the image was already pulling from my mind, fading fast. The sounds melted into silence, the bright sunlight of the house returning, and the image of my bare feet in the water was replaced by the view of my boots standing on Eamon's wooden floor.

I pressed a trembling hand to my chest, where my heart was beating so hard I was almost sure it would stop. I'd been standing by the Adeline River, a fire glowing on the bank and the moonlight dancing on the water. And Mason was there. It had the sharp detail and nostalgic echo of a . . . *memory.* That was the only thing I could think to call it, but I was sure that it had never, ever happened.

THIRTEEN

I was trapped in a museum of another life.

I could hear Eamon up and moving when the light broke in the sky, but I sat still on the edge of the bed, studying the frozen world around me. The bedroom took on a dreamlike quality in the early morning light, the tiny remnants that had made up my life coming into focus.

There was evidence everywhere that this place had been home to me, down to the way the clothes were folded and how things had been arranged on the dressing table. The stones and feathers and seeds that littered the windowsill. That was something I'd done even as a child, dropping little treasures into my pockets only to forget about them until later. There was a similar collection in the eave of my bedroom window at home.

I picked up one of the spotted feathers, brushing its tip against my fingers. There was no mistaking that I'd chosen this place, like Eamon said, and I'd been happy here. Somehow, I was sure of that. So, why had I left?

I'd spent hours replaying that vision of Mason in my mind. It felt embedded there. As if I'd only stumbled upon something that had been buried long ago. I could recall every single detail, but I couldn't place that night anywhere. We'd been at the river more times than I could count, but this had been different. There'd been something about the way he'd looked at me.

My feet found the floor and opened the wardrobe, letting the door swing open. This time, I let myself study its contents. My fingers skimmed along the soft cotton dresses and shirts that hung inside, a small but utilitarian array of what a woman in a 1951 farming town might need. They were colors I would have picked, I thought. Colors I *did* pick.

My hand stopped on a fold of delicate white lace tucked behind the others, and I twisted a finger into it, my throat closing. It was a wedding dress. In a series of lightning-quick flashes, I could see it. The weave of the lace draped over my arm. The brush of the hem along the floor and the milk-white color that warmed against my wavy hair. A string of bluntly spliced moments, a cracked mirror of reality, skipped through my mind. They were colors in a kaleidoscope that changed without warning to make a new picture.

I pulled my hand back, pressing my knuckles to my ribs, where my heart was pounding, and pushed the images from my thoughts before that picture could fully come alive.

I shoved the clothes to one side of the wardrobe, hiding the white lace from view, and pulled a blue dress from one of the hangers. The door of the wardrobe closed, making the whole thing rattle, and I stepped away from it, swallowing hard. I tugged the nightgown over my head and folded it neatly. The locket watch still hung around my neck, the air making gooseflesh rise on my skin despite its warmth. With any luck, that door would appear before the sun went down again, and the mark I left on this place would be almost undetectable. I'd go back to Mason. Back to the Jasper I knew.

I shrugged on the dress, buttoning it up and letting the locket fall inside. The fabric was soft and lived in, a bit loose around my frame, and I tried not to think too hard about why. Had this body changed after I had a child? Had love and marriage softened my curves in the five years I'd been here?

I turned toward the mirror, my skin crawling as I studied the image of me standing in that room. It was me, painted onto the canvas of a life I hadn't lived. The worst of it was that I looked like I belonged here, seamlessly rendered into the scene.

I smoothed my hands over the dress before running my fingers through my hair and letting it fall over one shoulder in an attempt to make my reflection more familiar. On the outside, I was like any of the women in those photographs that were stored in our basement. It was convincing, even if I didn't feel anything close to normal on the inside.

My eyes fell to the little dish on the dressing table that was made of abalone or some kind of oyster shell. In its center, the gold ring stared up at me. It was just a simple, smooth band, too small for Eamon's hands. When I blinked, I could see it on my own finger. I'd left that behind, too. It hadn't occurred to me until then how strange it was that for an entire year, he'd kept the room that way, filled with my things. *Her* things. Had he still been hoping his wife would come back?

When I finally got the nerve to open the bedroom door, the hinges creaked, filling the silence of the house. I came around the corner of the kitchen, steps halting when I saw Margaret. Not Eamon.

She stood in the middle of the sitting room, folding the afghan that had been draped over the sofa the day before. Eamon had slept there, leaving the blankets behind, but he was nowhere to be seen now.

"Morning," she chirped, a bright smile finding her lips when she saw me.

Her blond hair was curling at her temples, her cheeks pink. I couldn't get over how impossible it was to stand there in front of Gran, but a whole different version of her.

"Morning," I said. "What are you doing here?"

"Gran thought it would be good if I came over today." She draped the afghan over the back of the sofa. "Keep an eye on the three of you."

It took me a moment to understand that the Gran she knew, her grandmother, was Esther.

The curtain on the other side of the sitting room moved just slightly, and small fingers pulled the checkered fabric back enough for Annie to peek out at me. She was perched on her little bed, her shoes toppled to the wood floor.

The stockings that covered her small feet were dusted with the same dirt that stained the hem of her dress, a characteristic that made her feel more real to me. I'd only caught glimpses of her before, like a photograph taken out of focus. But now I could see her. *Really* see her.

Her lips twisted to one side of her mouth as she pulled the curtain back farther, but she only looked at me with those wide, brown eyes. They were the exact same color as Eamon's, another detail that felt like something clicking into place.

I could feel more pieces just like it lined up and waiting to fall like dominoes. I waited, half bracing myself for another speeding train of images to push back into my thoughts. But they didn't come.

"Hi," I said, the lonely word carrying with it a thousand questions.

What was an appropriate introduction between a mother and child who didn't remember each other? What did it mean that this girl had come from me and yet, I could hardly bear to look at her?

Margaret's eyes went from me to Annie, waiting.

"I'm June," I tried again.

I didn't know what else to call myself, and I figured it was the least confusing thing to say. Surely, she would have known me as Mama. Or Mommy. Thinking this gave me that falling sensation again, like I was dropping through the air.

Without a word, Annie climbed from the bed. Her eyes were fixed on me as she stepped with silent feet across the floor, toward the kitchen. Then she was out the back door.

"Does she talk?" I stared at her little bed, where a rag doll had been left behind. "I haven't heard her say a word."

Margaret smirked. "She talks plenty. But she's something of a quiet creature, like Eamon."

Eamon hadn't struck me as the quiet type in the couple of days I'd known him. Half of the time, he'd been shouting at me. But her answer to my question made me feel embarrassed.

"I don't really know anything about children," I admitted, though I wasn't sure if I was talking to Margaret or myself now.

"I know."

She gave me a sympathetic smile, like she could tell what I'd been thinking when my eyes landed on Annie. I'd spent years faced with my own death, lived and breathed grief since I was a child, but that was nothing compared to this. I didn't even have a name for the feeling inside of me.

Margaret's eyes sheepishly dropped from mine, and she went into the kitchen, taking the percolator from the stove and dumping the grounds inside.

"Where is he?" I asked.

She glanced at the window. "Working. He's out there before sunup most days."

I went to the back door, watching the wall of tobacco rustling in the wind. "Who helps Eamon with the crop? I haven't seen anyone in the fields."

"You did. You did it together." She turned on the water, pulling the block of soap closer to the sink. "He had a couple hired hands from town, but . . ." She didn't finish, her lips pressing into a line as if she'd caught herself before she said something she shouldn't.

I couldn't tell where exactly her and Esther's loyalties lay. Esther had seemed almost protective of Eamon, and she hadn't hidden the fact that she expected me to keep my distance from Margaret. We were blood, but I'd abandoned them, too, along with a husband, a child, and a farm. The list of things I'd left behind was growing.

If Eamon was running this place alone, I didn't know how that was possible. I leaned into the door with one shoulder, studying the faint yellowing tobacco leaves along the rows farthest from the house. I'd noticed them yesterday, and it wasn't good, no matter what decade of farming we were in. During an uncommonly wet season, the water would have drained down those hills, and if blight had taken hold, it could ruin the whole crop before Eamon could harvest. From the look of it, he'd barely been able to keep this place going.

Margaret turned off the water, scrubbing the pot in the sink and I took the dry rag that hung above the stove, drying the bowl she'd already finished.

"How old are you?" I asked.

"Sixteen."

Sixteen years old. I'd guessed she was about that age, but hearing her say it made her look even younger to me. She carried herself like someone who wasn't a child, but that youth in her face was unmistakable. There was a shine to her that was untouched. She had maybe ten years left with Esther before she died, according to what Gran had told me. Then she'd take over running the farm herself.

I watched her from the corner of my eye. If I was here now, did that mean that all this time, Gran remembered me? She grew up knowing Eamon and Annie, yet Gran had never said a word about them. I'd always thought there weren't things hidden between us, but that wasn't true. Gran had kept a multitude of things from me.

"You know . . ." I set the bowl on the shelf, trying to decide how to ask the question. "You know who I am, right?"

"Yeah."

"That you're my . . ."

"Grandmother?" She looked amused by the question. "Yes."

A laugh escaped me. The situation was so bizarre that I didn't know how to feel about it. What would it have been like to grow up knowing about all of this? The door. The episodes. The splitting of time. Gran had been given all that knowledge so young, but she hadn't given any of it to me.

She bit down on her bottom lip, like she was second-guessing whatever she was thinking. "It's strange. I feel like I have so much to tell you, but then I remember." She stopped herself.

I knew what she was going to say. That I didn't know her. The dimming excitement in her eyes when she'd come down the stairs yesterday had told me the same thing.

"Were we close?" I asked. "Before, I mean."

She nodded, the half smile on her face turning a little sad.

"But you don't seem angry with me, like the others." I took a chance in saying it.

Margaret's full lips pressed into a line again, exactly the way I remembered Gran doing when she was thinking hard about something. "I think you have your reasons."

Have. I twisted the rag in my hands, staring at her. I wasn't sure what I'd expected her to say, but it wasn't that. There was something strange about the words. They were so present. Like the future me she knew and loved, the one who'd lived here, wasn't really gone.

I wanted to ask her what she thought those reasons were. If she knew where I went and why. But Esther's warning came back to me. This Margaret was still just a kid.

"So, Esther really sent you to watch me?"

Margaret gave me an apologetic look.

"I get it. They don't trust me."

"They're angry because . . ." Her hands stilled on the pot. "You left Annie." She looked up at me.

"I know."

"No, I mean . . ." She took the rag from my hands, wiping the suds from her arms as she turned toward me. Her voice lowered. "The day you left, Eamon came home and Annie was alone. You'd left her here."

My fingers slipped from the edge of the counter. "That's not possible."

Margaret's mouth twisted to one side, almost exactly like Annie's had.

I could feel the tremble in my hands now, an ache traveling up my arms, to my shoulders.

"No," I tried again. "You don't understand. That's *not* possible."

"I'm only telling you because—" She hesitated. "I mean, that's why they're so angry. Why they don't trust you."

I stared at her, speechless. There was no way I'd left my own child. I knew what it was like to be abandoned by a mother. I'd never do that. Ever. So, why did it turn my stomach? Why did I have the feeling that she wasn't lying?

"Sorry." Margaret paled. "I just thought you should know."

She returned her attention to the pot, sinking her hands back into the water, and I bit the inside of my cheek. I didn't know what else to say. I certainly wasn't going to ask any questions. Not when the weight of the answers could crush me.

I pushed out the back door, following the wall of tobacco so closely that the leaves brushed my arm as I passed. When I saw Eamon through the open doors of the barn, I stopped short. He stood with Annie braced in one arm, her little legs swinging around him as he unspooled a line of wire on the ground. Even when he lowered down on one knee to cut it, she still clung to him, a small white flower twirling in her fingers.

I walked toward them slowly, arms wrapped tightly around myself. Annie's hand was hooked around Eamon's neck, her wispy blond hair falling down her back. I scrutinized every detail of those tiny hands and that round face. The way she looked cradled in Eamon's arms. Even if I didn't want to believe it, this child was mine. A part of me did know her, even if I couldn't remember her. It was the same feeling I'd had when I'd stood in front of that crumbling house two days ago.

When Eamon rose back to his feet, I took a step in the other direction, moving out of his line of sight before he could spot me. My hand found the fence posts of the small, overgrown garden tucked against the house, and I lifted the gate latch, letting myself inside. The plants had been overtaken, strangled by weeds that rose almost halfway up the fence. It had been left untended, maybe for as long as I'd been gone.

There were tomato plants, onions, squash, and herbs. In one corner, I could see the sprouts of a sweet potato vine and the leaves of a cu-

cumber plant withering on the chicken wire. It was a garden of dying things.

I sank to my knees, impulsively tearing at the mounds of clover and dandelion and nut grass. I ripped them from the earth, frantically trying to clear the overgrowth as the panic rose inside of me. My heart was still racing, my throat aching with the scream that had been trapped there since the moment I'd seen Eamon's face. It was a growing, spreading fever inside of me. A feeling that had edges sharp enough to cut me deep. This was a nightmare. All of it. And I couldn't wake up.

I wrenched another handful of weeds from the earth as I blinked back the tears in my eyes. Again, I looked to the fields in the distance, desperately searching for any sign of the red door.

It would appear, I told myself. It was only a matter of time.

And when it did, I would be ready.

FOURTEEN

By the time the sky was glowing gold over the hills, I'd cleared an entire section of the little garden. The once-buried plants were now haloed in dark, rich soil, their leaves open to the sun, and when I looked at them, I felt like I could breathe just a little deeper.

I stretched my hands open in front of me, knuckles stinging. The cuticles of my fingernails were torn and bleeding, my palms scraped and red. But that aroma—the sweetness of rich soil and the bright, sharp scent of green—was a known thing to me.

The smell of smoke had filled the air for most of the afternoon, and I scanned the sky until I spotted the drifting trail over the field. It was moving. The pillar of gray reached the edge of the plot, and Eamon appeared, pushing through the leaves on the other side of the house with a rod cast over his shoulders. A handkerchief was pulled up over his nose, a ring of sweat staining the neck and chest of his shirt.

He'd been in the fields all afternoon, coming from and going to the barn with the same rig. It was a wide wooden dowel that reached out to either side of him, and from both ends, a chain was fixed that suspended two metal containers that looked like lanterns. Smoke spilled from the holes in the metal, creating a cloud around him.

It wasn't the same smell that came from an active fire, I thought. It was more like something smoldering buried beneath a pile of ashes. He set the whole thing down and pulled the handkerchief from his face, letting it hang around his neck. When he looked up, he caught me watching him. The wind curled around his frame, his black-stained hands hanging at his sides, but he dropped his gaze as soon as it met mine.

Smoking crops was an old method, but I'd never seen it done before. It had different applications, and in my time, it was really only employed by primitive practice farmers. I'd heard of it being used to control pests, but it also helped control moisture on the plant. In this case, I guessed Eamon was using it for the latter.

Behind him, the strands of wire he'd been cutting that morning were hung in a crisscrossing pattern from the rafters like the face of a checkerboard suspended in the air. I didn't know much about tobacco crops, but I could tell by looking at the plants that they were almost ready to harvest, and my guess was that Eamon was rigging the drying lines. The barn hardly looked big enough for it.

He disappeared around the corner of the porch just as the sound of an engine came to life. A few seconds later, Esther's truck was pulling onto the road, Margaret behind the wheel. As soon as it was gone, I exhaled, looking back to the house. It loomed over me, an infinite number of forgotten moments living beneath its roof. But *forgotten* wasn't the right word, was it? How could I forget something if I hadn't lived it yet?

I closed the rickety gate to the garden, and the mare snorted when she saw me, pacing the paddock fence with her tail flicking behind her. Her head lifted, ears perking in my direction, and she stopped. She was looking me in the eye again, neck craning toward me as if she was waiting.

I moved toward her. That black eye shone in the setting sunlight, her nostrils flaring. Annie might not remember me, but this creature did.

Callie.

The word popped into my head like a bubble reaching the surface of water.

Callie. Was that the horse's name? I was suddenly sure that it was. But how did I know it?

That tingle on my skin returned, but I could already feel the memory dimming, drawing away like a pinprick of light. A sense of déjà vu. I frantically tried to keep hold of it, my eyes focusing on the glint in the mare's eye.

It came on in a rush, the barn and the paddock vanishing, replaced by the electric colors of spring.

I know where I am.

I'm standing at the back corner of the flower farm, where a small spring-fed pond is shaded by a cluster of wild dogwood trees. Before it, a chestnut mare with a mane that looks like tarnished bronze watches me.

I hold out a hand, taking a step toward her, and at first, I expect her to run. But then she's dipping her head, coming toward me, and my fingers slide up her nose.

This isn't a tear in the fabric. It's more terrifying than that. This is a hidden seam, and the longer I am still and let it unwind, the clearer it becomes.

I'm remembering.

"Callie!"

A man's voice echoes out around me before he appears in the trees ahead.

It's Eamon. A younger, narrower version of him. His white shirt is rolled up to his elbows, his hair cut shorter and his face shaven. He stops short when his eyes land on me and I go rigid, realizing that he can see me. Actually see me.

I look down to my dress. My boots. I'm really standing here.

"I see you found my horse." His accent makes the words sound like a song.

A smile lifts on one side of his face, and there is something both surprised and embarrassed about it. It makes my heart skip. I can feel myself smiling, too, a heat rushing to my cheeks.

"I think she found me," I say.

The words leave my mouth without my permission. They haven't so much as moved through my mind before they find my lips, and I suddenly know that this moment is happening without me, like skipping to a scene in a movie.

Eamon steps forward, a leather lead clutched in one hand. When I say nothing, he twists it nervously between his palms. "Sorry about this. I didn't realize the fence was down."

"That's all right." I hook my fingers into the mare's bridle, walking her toward him.

When he has hold of her, he clips the lead to the buckle beneath her jaw and then wraps it around his fist once. The veins on the back of his hand are thick beneath his skin. "Thanks."

"Her name's Callie?" I ask. Again, the words come on their own.

"Yeah. Callie."

"She's beautiful."

Something I can't decipher passes over his face and he smiles again, eyes catching the light. They are a deep, tawny brown.

When he says nothing, I nod, letting my hand glide down the horse's neck. He moves to lead her away, but stops when he crosses the fallen fence post, turning back to me. "I'll get that fixed." He gestures to it.

I don't know what to say, I just know that I'm hoping that he doesn't really go. So, when he speaks again, I instantly smile.

"I'm Eamon, by the way."

"June."

What is that flutter in my chest? That buzzing beneath my skin? I want to chase after it, to blow on its embers until it's a fire.

"June," he repeats, in that way that I know in my bones now.

He looks at me another moment before he finally turns back into the trees and disappears. I watch him go, absently twirling something between the tips of my fingers. I look down, as if just remembering it's there—a perfect bluebell.

All at once, I came back to myself. The barn, the fields, the paddock, and the horse. The memory was gone, and I could feel it drawing away from me inch by inch.

Callie pressed her nose into the flat of my palm. My skin was still warm with the afternoon sun, but I was burning now, that image of Eamon rooting itself deep within me. We'd met that day. That had been the moment when everything changed, but when I tried to push past it in my mind, in search of another memory, there was nothing.

I washed up in the water bucket out back, scrubbing as much dirt from my hands as I could manage in the near dark. I almost couldn't bring myself to open the door as I stood on the steps, fireflies dancing in the dark.

The kitchen was warm when I finally stepped inside, a humid breeze drifting in through the open windows. The whole house smelled of something herbal, and I eyed the lidded pot on the stove. Things had been tidied, the rest of the dishes from the morning washed. There were wet clothes hanging by the fire and shoes lined up by the front door. It looked as if it wasn't Margaret's first time looking after Eamon and Annie, and the thought made me cringe.

I lifted the lid of the pot and the steam curled into the air. It was some kind of stew with bits of meat, carrots, and potatoes in a broth. But it rattled closed when Eamon came from the bedroom, startling me. There was a stack of clothes folded in his arms.

He was as still as the frozen river in winter, his eyes roaming over me like he was seeing someone else. This man I'd never seen before knew me. Not just who I was, but also the intimate details of my life. He'd *been* with me. Made a child with me.

His gaze moved over my shape slowly, his face set like stone. That look in his eyes wasn't anger anymore. It was pain. Like seeing me standing there in his wife's dress, with his wife's face, was almost more than he could take.

"I'm sorry, I just thought . . ." I pressed my damp hands to the blue fabric, suddenly flustered. "I don't have any clothes or anything."

"It's fine." He cleared his throat, casting his gaze to the floor. "I've taken some of my things out of there for the time being."

I glanced to the bedroom, and that memory of him by the pond leapt back to the front of my mind. We'd shared that room. Slept in there together.

He dropped the folded clothes to the couch before he came back into the kitchen and started setting the table without a word. I followed his lead, taking a few of the glasses from the open shelf and setting them down beside the three bowls he'd put out.

His hair was wet, like he'd also washed up in the water bucket on the back steps when he came in. His shirt and trousers were filthy, and the soot from the smoke was still clinging beneath his fingernails even after he had finished drying them. I didn't look much better, but his face had a drawn look, like he'd barely slept in days. If he was smoking the fields by himself, he was probably doing it around the clock, and I'd heard him get up last night when Annie started to cry.

When the silence grew so awkward that I couldn't stand it, I desperately searched for something to say.

"Does Margaret always cook for you?"

"Sometimes" was his only answer.

Men were always left on the fringes of every story I'd heard about the Farrows. But here, even a year after I'd gone, Esther and Margaret were still treating him like family. Taking care of him, even. I didn't know how long that would go on or how long Eamon would even live in Jasper. The very house we sat in had been crumbling when I saw it. At some point, they would leave this place.

He took the heavy pot from the stove and placed it at the center of the table. As soon as his chair scraped over the floor, Annie came running. Her little smile widened when she saw me, and she climbed into the seat beside Eamon. I took the one on the other side, not wanting to get too close to her.

He stared at my hands as I unfolded my napkin, eyes inspecting the cuts on my fingers. "You didn't need to do that with the garden." He motioned for me to help myself to the stew.

I filled my bowl, feeling uneasy in the scene that was playing out. The three of us, sitting around the table, like a family. I wasn't sure how to respond to what he'd said, either. Was he saying I didn't have to, or that he preferred I didn't? Was he angry that I'd done it?

"You're smoking the fields," I said, changing the subject.

When I reached for Annie's bowl next, Eamon stopped me.

"Don't." The word was low but heavy, and his eyes didn't lift to meet mine. It was a warning. Another boundary. He'd let me stay in this house for all our sakes, and he'd let me eat at their table, but he didn't want me acting like his daughter's mother.

I sat back down as Annie's gaze drifted back and forth between me and her father.

"Here, love." Eamon spoke under his breath, reaching toward her, and she picked up her empty bowl, setting it into his open hand.

"Is it to stave off the blight?" I tried again as he served her himself.

The smallest hint of a reaction reached his face, and again, I couldn't read it. Maybe he didn't want me knowing anything about the crop, or maybe he was surprised that I'd spotted the blight.

"I saw the color change on the east side of the field. Is it spreading?"

"It's something my father used to do." Eamon answered the first question, but not the second.

"Does it work?"

"We'll see, won't we?"

The fields that were visible through the open back door looked to be at least ten or twelve acres, and that wasn't counting anything he might have planted on the other side of the hill. Sowing, tending, and maintaining that much crop for an entire season was at least a three- or four-man job. I had no idea how he was doing it alone.

"I could help you tomorrow, if . . ." I said, thinking better of finishing that sentence. If I was lucky, I wouldn't be here in the morning.

"No, thank you."

I watched him carefully. His attempt at manners might have been for Annie's sake, but he was obviously irritated. I wasn't sure why I was even offering. Maybe out of guilt.

"It's just that—" I paused. "It looks like you could use a hand."

"I've got it." The shift in his tone made it clear that he was finished discussing it.

He gave Annie a nod, as if to coax her into eating, and she picked up her spoon silently. Her legs kicked under the table, an excited gleam in her eye. It almost seemed as if she was enjoying this.

She watched me as she stirred the stew, the expression on her face making me wonder exactly what was going through her head. I had a feeling it was more than I could possibly pretend to know.

We ate in silence, and when I tried to help clean up, Eamon shrugged me off. He was stiff and uncomfortable around me. That was clear. Anytime I stepped too close to him, he moved farther away, and his eyes never met mine. Not since the day I'd shown up and he'd looked down into my face, so close I could feel the warmth of him.

Annie disappeared into her little nook off the sitting room, and I watched Eamon at the sink. Again, that feeling of familiarity found me. Like this floor under my feet was one I'd stood on countless times. It flickered back and forth like a flame, going as fast as it came.

I almost didn't ask it. "What's the horse's name?"

Eamon stopped, setting the dripping bowl in his hands into the sink before he turned to face me. "The horse?"

"The mare out in the paddock." I gestured to the window. "What's her name?"

"Callie."

A horrible, strangled feeling sank from my throat down into my chest.

"Why?" he asked.

"No reason."

His gaze turned inspecting, running over my face like he could hear every single thought sprinting through my mind. I reached behind me, hand searching for the doorknob to the bedroom.

"Good night." I closed myself inside, pressing my hot forehead to the back of the door.

My body, bones and all, felt so heavy that I thought I could fall through the floor. And I wouldn't stop there. The weight was so overwhelming that it could pull me straight into the center of the earth.

I stood there for a long time, staring into the growing darkness. That name—Callie—now felt like a rooted thing inside my head. And I could feel it growing, expanding into something else. Esther had described the madness as a fraying rope. Threads of time. But that didn't explain what had happened with the memory of Mason last night or what happened tonight at the paddock.

I could feel the memories brimming, some of them so close to the surface that if I reached out to touch them, they'd take shape. But I didn't want them to. I didn't want to *remember*, as Birdie had put it, and that's exactly what this was—remembering. A slow and steady carving, like a river eroding the earth.

I looked around, frantically searching for something, anything, that would help me understand what I'd been doing here. Why I'd left.

I took a match from the jar on the bedside table and lit the candle, my eyes adjusting to the dim glow. The room was full of shadows. Ghosts with stories I didn't yet know. But I'd had my secrets, just like everyone else did. For an entire year, I'd kept the detailed records of my episodes hidden. Years before that, I'd kept my research on Susanna from Gran.

I lowered down onto my knees, shoving both hands beneath the old mattress and working my way around to the other side. If Esther, Margaret, and Eamon didn't know why I'd left a year ago, there had to be some clue they'd missed. Some piece of evidence they'd overlooked.

I tore back the quilts, lifting the pillows to feel down the wood-paneled wall. When my fingers hit something, I froze.

Carefully, I shifted the object back and forth until it was sliding up. It was rough, like a roll of coarse fabric or a flattened spool of thick twine. When I finally had it free, I sat down on the bed, pulling it into my lap. It was a wide fold of burlap.

I lifted one corner, revealing a stack of gray paper. Newspaper. Two big, black block letters stared up at me.

MI

I pulled them free, unfolding them in my lap.

MINISTER SLAIN

It was a clipping of the same article I'd found when I was looking in the state archives online, but these were the originals, printed and distributed in 1950s Jasper.

The next one was another I recognized.

BODY FOUND IN ADELINE RIVER

Several others were with them, some of which I'd never seen, but all were pieces from local newspapers chronicling the investigation into the murder of Nathaniel Rutherford. My father.

Even thinking the word was foreign to me. I'd lived in the shadow of my mother's story, but a father was something that had never been talked about, never seemed to matter. All this time, he'd been in the past, further back than I could have imagined. And I couldn't help but think that the curse on the Farrows had touched him, too.

If he died a year ago, that meant I must have met him while I was here, and if I was remembering things from that time, I'd eventually remember him, too. So, what was this? Another collection like the one I'd had about Susanna back home? If it was, then why had I kept it hidden?

Tucked in between the newspaper clippings were more scraps of paper, and when I slid them out of the way, the light reflected off the glossy surface of a photograph.

It was the same one that Gran sent me. When I turned it over, the inscription was there.

Beneath it was a small rectangle of paper. It was a series of years written down in one long column. But this handwriting was unmistakably mine.

1912

1946

1950
1951

My eyes landed on the year 1951. That was now.

I went still when I heard a soft sound seeping beneath the bedroom door. Outside the window, the moon had risen over the crest of the mountains. I hadn't even noticed that the house had gone quiet.

At first, it sounded like wind. I slipped the papers back into the envelope and tucked it beneath the quilts before my feet found their way across the cold floor. When I opened the door of the bedroom, I realized the sound wasn't the wind. It was Annie.

A soft whimper echoed in the house, her tiny voice heavy with sleep. I peered around the corner of the kitchen, freezing when I saw a shadow moving in the dark. Eamon was sitting up on the sofa, pushing back the quilt draped over his legs and getting to his feet. The moonlight rippled over his skin as he moved through the sitting room, toward Annie's little nook. I watched as he climbed into the bed with her and she curled into him, a tiny ball beneath the blanket.

I stared at them, unable to pull my eyes from the sight. My fingers curled around the corner of the wall, that hollow ache inside of me waking. For years, I'd shielded myself with the claims that I didn't want love or a child of my own. I'd even, at times, prided myself on the independence that my fate as a Farrow ensured me. But deep beneath that pretense was a longing I'd always kept tucked away from the world.

As I stood there watching Eamon's arms fold around his daughter, I found myself in one of those vulnerable moments when the truth came for me. I'd stayed unyielding because I'd had to, but the June who'd married Eamon and had borne his child had been weak. She'd been the worst kind of selfish, and I was broken into two pieces—one that was ashamed of her and one that was envious of her.

The crying stopped, followed by a few quiet sniffs, and then the house was silent again. They lay like that until their breaths drew deep and long, and I stood watching them because I couldn't stop. His arm draped around her little frame. Her head tucked beneath his chin. They fit together like puzzle pieces, and the thought made a pain erupt inside of me that I could hardly bear.

This was the field that I had planted. With my very own hands. And then I'd left it all to rot.

FIFTEEN

I had to remember. All of it.

I woke before Eamon and Annie, when the sun was just beginning to paint a blue haze on the mountain peaks in the distance. The farm was quiet when I came down the back steps, and the faint call of birds was muted by a soft breeze that swept over the tobacco.

I'd been up half the night thinking about it. If I was somehow triggering memories of my unlived life, then it was only a matter of time before I knew exactly what happened before I left. There was no way to go back and undo it. What was done was done. But I'd had years here, filled with the things I'd never been brave enough to admit that I wanted. Now I needed to know why Gran had lied, and why I'd chosen to leave.

My boots waded through the tall, wet grass that stretched between the barn and the house as Callie watched me from the paddock. I tried to let my mind and my body follow the faint rhythm that was humming beneath my thoughts. It was at the tip of my fingers, under my tongue. A routine I was on the verge of remembering. One I'd done every morning.

I fetched the water and the eggs, testing myself with the little things I couldn't possibly know. Which trays in the chicken coop would have eggs and which were always bare. How the pump at the well needed a firm tug to the side before I pushed it down. I'd been so careful not to touch anything, afraid I would disturb the precarious balance between me and this place. But with every surface my fingertips grazed, I was filling in the edges of a picture. It wasn't just Eamon's home. It had been mine, too.

I stepped out of my boots, leaving them outside the back door as I came into the kitchen. I didn't let myself think, moving with nothing more than muscle memory. It was stilted, but it was definitely there. I placed the kettle on the burner, and my gaze was instinctively pulled like a magnet to the coffee can on top of the icebox. I knew this choreography. I'd probably done it hundreds of times.

I smiled to myself, excitement brimming in my blood. It was a drip, but it was steady.

I had to search to find the jar of shortening, but other things came more easily. When I reached into the cupboard for the sugar bowl, it was exactly where I'd expected it to be. My hand even seemed to recognize the feel of the lid and the shape of the spoon as I stirred two spoonfuls into my coffee.

As the kettle whirred on the stove, I started the biscuit dough, folding the milk into the peaks of flour with one hand while I turned the mixing bowl with the other. My blistered knuckles burned as I stirred. It was the same recipe that I'd grown up making with Gran and that she'd grown up making with Esther. I'd decided to start here, with things I knew I would have brought with me through the door the first time, and it was working. In fact, it was working better than I'd expected.

The groan of the little bed in Annie's nook made me look up from the wide-mouthed bowl. Through the doorway, I could see Eamon sitting up stiffly, as if his whole body hurt. He'd slept the rest of the night in that bed, him and Annie tangled together, and I'd had to force my eyes to stop finding them as I moved quietly through the house. They, too, felt like a fixed point. A gravity relentlessly pulling at my edges.

Eamon's gaze scanned the house, eyes blinking against sleep, and when they found me, his brow furrowed. He stood, making a half-hearted attempt to comb his hair back with his fingers, and his white T-shirt hiked up on one side to reveal his hip. I immediately dropped my eyes, heat flaring along my collarbone. Eamon was the kind of handsome that was carved from forests and rivers. He had the look of someone who'd spent his life in the sun, hands in the dirt. Every color, curve, and angle of him was shaped with it. That stomach-dropping feeling inside of me when I looked at him was a reflex, I told myself. Just a different kind of recall.

When he made it into the kitchen, he leaned into the wall with one shoulder, watching me. His jaw flexed as he swallowed, the seconds reconstructing themselves into a white-knuckled silence.

I stopped stirring. "What?"

He shook his head as if trying to break loose whatever train of thought was there. "Nothing." His voice was a deep rasp. "It's just—" He didn't finish.

I set my hands on the table, waiting and noticing that for once, he wasn't angry. He seemed almost upset, like he was swallowing down that same pain in his chest that I could feel expanding behind my ribs.

"It's just that sometimes"—he paused—"it's hard to look at you." His accent was thicker. With sleep or emotion, I couldn't tell. But it made that spreading pain find my hollow places.

I bit the inside of my cheek, unsure of what to say, but Eamon didn't give me the chance to respond. He turned back into the sitting room, taking something from the side table next to the sofa. When he came back, he held it out to me.

It was a pair of gloves. Small leather gloves.

My eyes traveled up to meet his, but they were off of me now. "Are these . . . ?"

"Yours," he answered.

I glanced down at my hands. They were torn up from working in the garden yesterday, my calluses useless without gloves. My skin was striped with cuts, my nails rimmed in red. He'd noticed.

I took the offering, pressing the soft, worn leather between my fingers. "Thank you," I said, softly.

He nodded once, filling the kitchen with that silence again before he gestured to the percolator on the stove. "May I?"

I looked at him in confusion before I realized he was asking permission to pour himself a cup of coffee. "Oh, yeah," I stammered awkwardly, tucking the gloves into the back pocket of my jeans.

He turned to the side, moving past me in the small kitchen, and when he reached over me for the cup, the space between us grew narrower. A feeling like static surfaced on my skin, an electric hum that made me draw away from him just slightly. I couldn't help it.

When he noticed, he stepped backward, putting more space between us.

I picked up the spoon, stirring, and I watched him from the corner of my eye as he took a sip of coffee. "I knew her name," I said.

His cup stopped midair, eyes locking with mine. "What?"

I let out a long breath, trying to decide how much I wanted to tell him.

"The horse. Yesterday, I remembered her name before you told me what it was."

Eamon was still rigid, his eyes fully awake now. "How?"

"It just . . . came to me."

"What else do you remember?" His voice was tight, nearly defensive, and a fragmented recognition flickered to life inside me when I heard it.

I studied the tension in his shoulders. The clench in his jaw. "Almost nothing. Just little things here and there."

"How can you remember something if it hasn't happened to you yet?"

"I don't know."

Eamon seemed anxious, but I didn't know why. It was almost as if he was afraid of me knowing something, and I couldn't help but wonder what it was. I'd been planning to ask him about the newspaper articles I'd found last night, but now I thought better of it.

"I wanted to ask you." I paused, taking a different tack. "Did I keep a journal?"

He set the coffee cup down. "No."

"Maybe a notebook of some kind?"

"Nothing like that."

I stared at the floor, thinking. That could mean that I'd stopped having episodes after I came here, or maybe I'd just stopped writing them down. That, or Eamon wasn't telling me the truth. The thought hadn't occurred to me before now. What reason would he have to lie?

"What about—"

"The answer is no," he said again.

"I'm just trying to think of anything that might help me make sense of why I left. Where I went."

"I know where you went."

I looked at him, shifting on my feet. I hadn't expected him to say that, but he looked directly at me, a confidence in his gaze that couldn't be mistaken.

My voice was a breath. "Where?"

"Back." The single word was a heavy, solid thing between us.

If that was true, there had to be a reason. I wouldn't have just left. Somehow, I knew that.

The screech of the gate out at the road drew Eamon's attention to the front window, and with his eyes off me, I finally exhaled. Margaret was here, and she and Esther seemed to be the only buffers between me and Eamon. The vulnerable, sleep-infused first moments of morning were gone, and it had taken only seconds for him to put his guard back up and shut me out. He was a field of buried land mines.

If he wasn't going to talk to me, I'd have to rely on my own memories, maybe even find a way to trigger more of them on my own. That, or find a way to get answers somewhere else. Margaret, I suspected, could help with that. Esther was prudent and careful, but there was a version of Margaret I knew better than anyone.

Three heavy knocks pounded on the door, and the shadow of a figure moved over the wall in the sitting room. Eamon and I looked to each other, the house settling uneasily around us. It wasn't Margaret, I thought. Yesterday, she hadn't knocked.

There was a new tension in the air now, and I could feel it almost right away. Eamon's hand lifted, gesturing for me to stay quiet. He was watching that shadow, gaze moving to the rifle hanging on the wall.

I pulled my flour-covered hands from the bowl, taking a step backward. "Eamon?" I whispered.

The knock sounded again, rattling the glass window on the door, and he finally moved, leaning to catch a glimpse out the kitchen window.

His hand slipped from the curtain. "Shit."

"What is it?"

"*Shit*," he said again, turning toward me.

Quietly, I moved closer to him so I could see what was out there. A police car was parked inside the gate, a drift of dust still swirling in the air from when it pulled in. I looked to Eamon. The muscles of his arms and shoulders were flexed beneath his shirt, his entire body stiff.

"Don't say a word." His voice was so low I could hardly hear it.

I searched his face, the fear in his eyes now flooding into my own veins.

He came closer, hand finding my arm and gripping me tight. It pulled me toward him until I was looking up into his face. "June, do you hear me?"

I glanced down to where his fingers touched my skin before my eyes lifted back to his. I nodded.

He let me go, and I slipped into the bedroom silently. I watched around the corner of the door as he went back into the living room, his gaze landing on that rifle again. There was a split second when I was sure he was going to reach for it.

What the hell was going on?

Again, the pound on the door echoed, and Eamon finally opened it, letting in a blinding light. My mouth went dry when the man on the other side came into view. It was a police officer. Not the man we'd seen on the riverbank. This was someone else, and as soon as my eyes focused on him, the house seemed to fill with a bitter cold. He took the hat from his head, tipping it in Eamon's direction. His blond hair was cut short and combed in a neat, waving swoop over his dark, narrowed eyes.

His chin lifted in a greeting, and the door swung wider. "Eamon."

I pressed myself into the wall, not making a sound.

"Caleb." Eamon was doing his best to look relaxed, but he wasn't succeeding. He was still wound up tight, the line of him like stone.

"Heard June finally made it home."

The man Eamon had called Caleb was peering into the house now, and I drew away from the crack in the door.

"Just got in a couple of days ago," Eamon said.

"I heard." A pause. "Thought I'd come welcome her back to Jasper myself. Have that little talk I've been waiting so long for."

"It can wait, Caleb. She just got back."

"Now, you're not the only one who's been waiting for June to come home." There was something dark beneath the smooth cadence of his voice. I could almost hear a smile in it.

"Another time." Eamon's tone didn't waver.

I couldn't tell if my breath sounded as loud in the room as it did in my ears. My head was light with it. I chanced a look through the crack again to find Eamon's hand gripped tight on the edge of the front door.

"Well, it's waited this long. I suppose another day or two couldn't hurt." Caleb's mouth pulled in a sterile smile as he set the hat back on his head, but there was a threat in his eyes. A menacing glint. "You all have a good day now."

He turned, going down the steps, and Eamon closed the door. He stood there, waiting until the sound of the car was gone. When I came around the corner of the sitting room, he ran a hand through his hair, exhaling.

In the nook, Annie was awake, sitting on the edge of her bed with her knees drawn up into her chest. She looked from me to Eamon, her small mouth crooked like she might cry. In an instant, something thorned was growing inside of me, and I could feel myself moving toward her. But Eamon was already crossing the room, scooping her up, and her arms hooked around his neck as she buried her face in his shoulder. He brushed the hair from her face, avoiding my gaze.

"What was that?" I asked, going to the front window to check the road. The police car was out of sight now.

Eamon's eyes found me over Annie's blond head. I could see him trying to decide how to answer. Or maybe deciding if he would answer at all. It was the same look he'd had a few minutes ago.

He passed me, going into the kitchen and taking an apple from the bowl on the shelf. "Why don't you go say good morning to Callie?" His deep voice softened, his mouth pressing into Annie's hair as he placed it into her hands.

Her fingers closed around it, and he set her down, her nightgown swaying around her skinny legs. Then she was pushing out the back door, letting the screen slap behind her.

He watched her go. "It's not important. He just has some questions."

"About what?"

Eamon hesitated, and my eyes narrowed on him. He was sifting information again, deciding exactly what to say.

"Not long before you left, something happened." His hands slid into his pockets. "He's interviewed everyone in town about it as part of his investigation, and now he wants to talk to you."

Slowly, the pieces strung together in my mind. "The murder," I said.

Eamon hesitated just enough for me to notice. "Yes."

"What does that have to do with me?"

"Nothing. He's the sheriff, June. It's his job. That's all."

That definitely wasn't all. Eamon didn't want me talking to him, and I suppose the fact that I didn't actually remember anything was the reason. If I was questioned about the murder, I'd have no clue what to say. But that didn't explain why those newspaper clippings and a photograph of Nathaniel Rutherford were hidden in the bedroom or why Eamon had gone white when he saw that police car outside.

This was what Esther was talking about when she said I'd come at a complicated time.

Eamon glanced out the window again, jaw ticking. Down by the barn, Annie's small frame was clinging to the fence of the paddock. The mare was sniffing her tangle of blond hair, and Annie's hand was hooked around her snout as if the horse were a puppy.

The sheriff had shaken him, that was clear. There'd been no mistaking that panic in his eyes before he opened the door. I could still feel the place on my skin where he'd touched me, the way his fingers had slid down my arm and squeezed. He'd been afraid in that moment. For me, or for him, I didn't know. But Eamon had something to hide.

SIXTEEN

I'd abandoned all hope of waking up.

I tore into the weeds, ripping them up from the soft earth one fistful at a time. The overgrown vines hid me from view as I worked, clearing another section of the garden inch by stubborn inch.

Eamon had left for Esther's as soon as Margaret arrived, and I'd caught her watching me out the window more than once. Even now, decades before I'd know her, she couldn't hide that concern on her face.

I'd known for days that this wasn't a dream, but that morning had been the first time I'd felt like what I was doing here was actually dangerous. Nathaniel Rutherford's murder happened only a couple of weeks before I left, the same day as the Midsummer Faire. I hadn't put that part of the timeline together before and judging by Eamon's reaction in the kitchen that morning, I had to question whether it was a coincidence.

What would have happened if I'd been questioned by the sheriff, unable to account for anything he knew to be true about me? Jasper was the kind of town where you couldn't hide things. It was too easy to unearth them when you knew so much about everyone. And people talked. You could always count on that.

I'd walked the edge of the field for more than an hour after Eamon left the house, scouring the horizon for any sign of the door. I counted back to the time I'd seen it in the churchyard and then tried to remember the time before that. I needed a pattern. A sequence that I could dissect in order to make some kind of prediction. But if recording my episodes had taught me anything, it was that they seemed to be completely random.

The locket watch around my neck was growing heavier by the day, a tightening noose that felt more and more like a ticking clock. Esther had been sure that the door would reappear, and Eamon was sure that the last time I'd left, I'd walked through it. That I'd gone back home, to my time, where Birdie, the house on Bishop Street, and Mason waited.

Every time I thought about Mason, my heart twisted. He'd be frantic by now, doing whatever he could to find me. If it had come out that I'd been going to see Dr. Jennings, the sheriff would likely determine that I was unwell, and that my condition was linked to my disappearance. They would draw connections between me and Susanna, maybe even before I was officially designated as a missing person. My name, description, and photo would be sent to neighboring counties, but I knew what most people would say. That what had happened to my mother had happened to me. That the madness was to blame.

I raked my hands through the soil as I kneeled in the garden. There wasn't a single cloud in the sky or even a hint of a breeze, making my hair stick to my face and neck. I didn't care, digging until the muscles in my arms were weak. I ignored the ache in my hands and the beginnings of a sunburn cresting my cheeks. The inside of my head was a maze, one I couldn't find my way out of. And the more I tried to escape, the more lost I was becoming.

My hands stilled around a newly unearthed tomato plant when I felt the soft whisper of someone's gaze on me. I looked over my shoulder to see Annie watching from the makeshift fence. Her small hands were curled around the wood planks, her brown eyes blinking at me over the top of the railing.

I pulled off my gloves, wiping my damp forehead with the sleeve of my shirt. "Hi." There was that pathetic word again.

She waited a moment before she came through the gate. Eamon had gotten her dressed in a little green jumper and white collared shirt that made her blond hair appear even paler. She didn't seem wary of me, exactly, but she was definitely curious. Her gaze roamed over the half-cleared garden before finding me.

We stared at each other, and that feeling woke in me again—like the tug of the river pulling me downstream. A tide of memories was there, dammed in my mind by something I couldn't see. It was too far out of reach.

I waited for her to come closer, but her feet didn't move. I looked around until I spotted a golden cherry tomato hiding in the leaves. I fished it out, plucking it from the vine and holding it out to her. It was warm, the ripened flesh soft between my fingers, and her eyes brightened before she finally stepped forward. Carefully, she took it from me. Then she turned the tomato around, inspecting it, before she popped it into her mouth.

A smile broke on my lips. She settled down on the ground beside me, sinking her knees into the sun-warmed soil, feet tucked beneath her bottom. The edge of her skirt touched my leg, and I felt myself lean toward her. We were only inches apart.

I sat there, studying her face, her hands, the color of her hair. Those embers of memory were glowing now, and I was terrified of the moment they would reignite, like they'd burn all of me down if they could.

She was studying me, too, and I wondered if she was comparing me to her faded recollection of the mother she knew. I wasn't sure what Eamon had told her about me or if Annie had even asked to begin with. I still hadn't heard her speak a word, but I could see that same quietness about her that Margaret had mentioned in Eamon. The two were cut from the same cloth in countenance, but in the look of her, Annie was more like me.

Her attention snagged on my throat before she reached up, almost impulsively, to draw the locket watch from the collar of my shirt. I sat very still as she took it into her hands, turning it over so that the sunlight hit its surface.

She inspected it, more focused than what I imagined was natural for a four-year-old girl. Almost as if she could sense that it wasn't just a trinket. I remembered feeling like that, too, opening and closing the locket in a compulsive rhythm as I sat on Gran's lap. She'd sing that song I loved . . . what was it? The words wouldn't quite come to me now, but the broken melody was there, like a badly tuned radio cutting in and out of the silence.

The one place I hadn't let my mind wander was to the thought that if this child was mine, that meant she was a Farrow. And if she was a Farrow, we shared a fate that ran in the blood. It flowed through her veins like it flowed through mine. One day, she would be like Susanna and the rest of us, with a mind frayed between time.

I swallowed against the thick emotion curling in my throat, the question bearing down on top of me until I could hardly draw breath. *How* could I have done it? This perfect creature would wither and fade, and it occurred to me all at once that maybe that's exactly why I had left. Maybe I was afraid to watch the consequences unfold. Maybe I'd been running from this, from her, when I went back through that door.

Annie snapped the locket closed, looking up at me, and her gaze took me in. There was a calm intensity behind her eyes, giving me the sense that she knew what I was thinking. Or, at least, that she could feel what I was feeling. I hoped that wasn't true.

"Annie." My voice was strangled as I said her name. I was suddenly overwhelmed with the need to know if she knew, *really* knew who I was. "Annie, do you—"

The sound of a truck made both of us turn our attention to the road, where Eamon was pulling in, tires cracking on gravel. The locket slipped from Annie's fingers as she sprung up, pushing back through the gate and running toward him. The hollow space she left beside me was palpable in the air.

She was in Eamon's arms seconds later, and I got to my feet, tucking the locket watch back into my shirt. It stung where it brushed my skin, as if Annie's touch had electrified it somehow.

Margaret came down the porch steps. The thought hadn't occurred to me until just then that she had most likely been waiting for Eamon to return before she left. I couldn't blame her. I wouldn't trust me with Annie, either.

She kissed Annie, exchanging a few words with Eamon, and though they didn't look in my direction, I could feel the weight of their attention. Whatever they were discussing, it had to do with me. She waved before she climbed into Esther's truck, and then she was gone.

Eamon walked toward me, his face turned toward Annie's. Her mouth moved around words I couldn't hear, and I found myself concentrating hard, trying to comb the sound of her voice from the wind. I came through the gate, pulling the gloves from my hands. The distance Eamon had put between us earlier was still there, and I thought back to that morning, when he'd watched me in the kitchen. When he'd said it was hard to look at me. There'd been an unraveling in that moment, one that had made me trust him. But the man who'd given me those gloves and the one who'd lied to me didn't fit together in a way that made sense.

He set Annie down, meeting me halfway between the house and the fence. We stood there in silence for several seconds before he finally spoke.

"Esther will be by in the morning. She'll be heading to town to drop off flowers for the Faire, and I think it would be a good idea if you go with her."

I blinked, sure I wasn't understanding him. "Into town?"

Annie crouched behind him, picking a cluster of dandelions and gathering them in a ragged bouquet.

"Caleb coming by means that people in town are doing more than talking. The longer you stay out of sight, the more they'll be curious, and we can't afford to have people paying too close attention."

I glanced at the road behind him. I'd seen more than one neighbor slow down as they drove by, sometimes the same car multiple times a day. Only minutes after Caleb's visit, Eamon had gone to see Esther, and this was what they'd decided. Without me.

"I don't think that's a good idea," I said, that choked sound resurfacing despite my best efforts.

"You can't just hide here. Caleb isn't the last person who will knock on that door. Trust me."

Trust me. Those were the same words written on the envelope that had convinced me to walk through the door in the first place. At the time I'd thought they were the words of my mother. Now, I wondered if they were mine.

I shook my head. "I can't. What if someone talks to me? What if I say something wrong?"

"You won't."

"Eamon—"

"Look, this town has been waiting for its chance to avenge Nathaniel Rutherford. You don't want to know what can happen if they think they can get it here, at my door. In a place like this, no one is going to stop them, do you understand? No one is going to come to our rescue."

I winced, bristling at the fierceness of his tone.

"First, it's a knock on the door; then, it's a fire in the barn. It doesn't stop there, June. If you're here tomorrow, you're going to town with Esther. You'll make an appearance, and we'll show them we have nothing to hide."

His voice held a finality that said he was done talking about it, and before I could argue, he started for the barn. That was what had been in his expression that morning, when he'd looked to the rifle hanging on the wall. He wasn't just afraid of the sheriff, he was afraid of what Jasper was capable of. And what he was implying was that there was more than one person in town who wanted to know what I knew about the night Nathaniel died.

As soon as he was through the door, he started on the smoking rig, lifting the lid off one of the aluminum bins and scooping what looked like wood shavings into the canisters suspended at either end of the dowel.

I didn't know if Eamon was used to giving me orders, or if he was just scared enough that he wasn't going to give me the option of refusing. I had a feeling it was the latter. He was a man on the verge of coming apart. That was obvious now. He'd already lost his wife, and at any moment, he could lose his home, his farm, his livelihood.

I looked up to the sun, now falling from the center of the sky. He was getting a late start on the fields, which meant he'd be working late into the night. Much too late if he was going to get any amount of sleep.

"Let me help you, Eamon," I called out.

He ignored me, striking a match and sinking low to light the canister at his feet.

I sighed, shoving the gloves into my back pocket. If he was stubborn enough to do the job of three men on his own every day, then I wasn't going to convince him. I don't know why I was trying to help in the first place.

I stalked toward the house, where the chimney was smoking, the curtains fluttering behind the open windows. The kitchen smelled like pot roast when I came inside, and I stopped when I saw the trimmed carrot tops on the butcher block. They were cut bluntly at the base and stuck into a jar of water.

Gran had always done that, never wanting to waste anything. She'd save the tops to sauté with greens or to chop and cook into a meatloaf. Whatever was left was tossed out for the chickens, but until then, they sat like a wild bouquet of greenery in the window above the sink.

I could see her barefoot in our kitchen, hear her humming that song. What was it called? It was on the tip of my tongue, the very edge of my thoughts. But every time I tried to bring it into focus, it only blurred, floating farther away from me.

Gooseflesh snaked up and around my entire body, like the trail of a flame. No matter how hard I tried, I couldn't recall it. Second by second, more of it vanished. The bits of melody, the words . . . it was all slowly disintegrating.

I knew it. I'd known that song my whole life, heard her sing it countless times. So, why couldn't I remember?

SEVENTEEN

Esther's old truck was waiting on the side of the road when I came outside, its wood framed bed filled to overflowing. Buckets of greenburst sunflowers and peach melba gladiolas filled every square inch of the back, their blooms heavy and drooping over the rails.

Esther's hand was resting at the top of the steering wheel when I made it to the passenger side window, her eyes appraising as I climbed inside.

"Well, you haven't killed each other," she said. "Guess that's something."

I looked to the moving pillar of smoke already drifting over the tobacco fields. I'd been asleep by the time Eamon came in last night, but the moment Annie's cries sounded in the dark, the sound of his footsteps crossed the sitting room on the other side of the wall. Each night it pulled me from sleep before the house went silent again. I didn't like knowing those rhythms.

He'd already been in the fields when I came into the kitchen that morning, which meant that he'd gotten no more than a few hours of sleep. He was working almost around the clock and for the most part, it looked like he'd managed to keep the color change at bay. But the blight was still there, waiting for its chance to take the field. It was only a matter of time before it did. Eamon just had to make it to harvest first.

Esther took her foot off the brake, guiding the truck back onto the road. "How are you holding up?"

I looked at her, unable to muster anything that resembled an answer. "Why didn't you tell me the sheriff wanted to talk to me about the minister's murder?"

She arched an eyebrow in response to my tone. "Honestly, I didn't think you'd be here long enough for it to matter. It's just some nonsense between him and Eamon."

"What kind of nonsense?"

"The kind that men always seem to find themselves in."

She said it with a weariness she hadn't had the last time I saw her. When I'd gone to the farm, she'd been controlled and direct, almost cold. Now, I could see an undercurrent of worry in her.

"This isn't a good idea." I said, my pulse quickening as we turned onto the river road.

"People are starting to wonder why you haven't shown your face. Even the hands at the farm are starting to talk. The longer you're out of sight, the more cause they have to start creating their own explanations. You'll smile at a few people, give a few waves, and then we'll be on our way."

"And if people talk to me? Ask me questions?"

"Stick to the story, and we'll be fine."

We. The subtle reminder that this bore a weight on all of them wasn't lost on me. She had herself, a family, and a farm to look after, but no one was looking after me. I'd come all this way to learn the truth about Susanna, and I'd discovered only that I was more alone than ever. But on this side of the door, June had knit herself into the fabric of a whole life only to leave it behind. I needed to know why.

Eamon seemed genuinely concerned about what the town would do if they thought we knew anything about what happened to Nathaniel. What he hadn't said was exactly what that might be.

Esther fell quiet, her carefully constructed answers lingering between us. The first time I'd seen her, I'd been overwhelmed with relief. Like she and the flower farm were a safe place that would catch me. But I was beginning to think there was more Esther *wasn't* saying than what she was. Just like Eamon.

Her silver-streaked hair lifted into the air as we picked up speed and the wind poured into the truck. I wanted to press her, to make her tell me what was really going on here, but this woman wasn't the one who'd raised me. I studied her from the corner of my gaze, looking for some reflection of the woman Gran had become, but I couldn't find it. She and Esther were different in more ways than one.

We made it around the next turn, and the view opened up to the wide vista of the Blue Ridge Mountains. Soft, dusty blue peaks rolled like waves in both directions, a thread of clouds coloring the morning sky. In a few hours, when the sun reached its zenith, that vista would turn a vibrant green, and then several shades of purple as the sunset loomed.

My hand gripped tighter on the lip of the open window as downtown Jasper appeared in the distance. The buildings that stretched ahead were like perfect copies of the ones I knew. The reflection of a reflection in a mirror.

The shop fronts looked almost the same, but some of the doors were different, the old parking meters on the street not yet installed. There were things that still had the shine of being new, like a sign over the hardware store that had apparently been an appliance repair shop. Or the chrome-framed stools that glinted behind the windows of the Jasper Diner, which was, in my time, Edison's Cafe. There was a small produce shop front in what was now . . . I couldn't remember. I could see the windows of the little building wedged between Dr. Jennings's office and the grocery in my mind, but what was it?

There was no streetlight at the crossroad that led over the river bridge, and the courthouse doors were propped open, along with the windows that faced the street. Across the intersection, a painted sign for the Midsummer Faire was strung up over an iron archway that framed the bridge. A six-pointed white tent had been erected behind it.

"This is . . ." My voice trailed off. I wasn't sure what word to use. It was strange and unsettling. The sight made my skin crawl.

"Yeah" was all Esther said, as if she actually knew what I meant.

If she was already experiencing the side effects of crossing time, then she'd walked through that door, like me and Susanna. She'd said almost nothing about it, and I had to imagine that was on purpose. My fate had been sealed when my mother brought me through that door. When had Esther opened it?

The truck came to a stop as two women crossed the street, and the man on the sidewalk beside us stopped in his tracks, eyes squinting as they focused on me. Esther pulled to the side of the road and set the parking brake, letting the engine cut off.

"Now, you just let me talk." She waited for me to give her a small nod before she got out.

I sat unmoving for several seconds before I finally followed. The truck rocked as she let the tailgate swing open, and as soon as I was standing on the sidewalk, several pairs of eyes from the courthouse to the river bridge had found me.

"Ignore them," Esther murmured, pulling the first of the full buckets toward her. She hauled it up into her arms, the stalks of flowers towering over her head.

I did the same, following her across the brick-paved street to where the large white canvas tent had been raised. This was exactly how we still did it, tenting the bridge and filling it with lights so that the Faire felt like it was suspended over the river.

Every farmer and business owner in town made a contribution, and the flowers were Esther's. I'd grown up doing the same delivery with Gran each year, and our blooms hung in garlands from the corners of the tent, adorned tables, and decorated booths from one end of the bridge to the other.

The pound of a hammer rang out, the busy street loud at our backs. Esther hoisted the bucket higher in her arms, leading us to the mouth of the bridge, where a man with a clipboard had spotted us.

"Morning!" He looked up from his pen, eyes skipping to me.

Esther gave him a nod. "Morning, Robert."

"June." A woman unpacking a crate of jam jars said my name in greeting as we passed and I smiled, keeping myself half-hidden behind the flowers.

"Beatrice Covington," Esther whispered beside me. "Her husband used to work on your farm before Eamon had to let him go."

Had to. I wanted to ask what she meant by that, but she was already motioning toward someone else.

She gave a wave to a black man crouched at the corner of the tent with a hammer in hand. He was wearing suspenders, his hat tipped back to reveal a wrinkled forehead.

When he saw me, he grinned widely, giving me a nod. "Mighty good to see you, June."

I smiled in return.

"That's Percy Lyle. He owns the pig farm down the road from you."

Lyle. That family was still living in Jasper in my time.

"Claire White," Esther said under her breath as a woman waved us toward a line of tables. "Should probably watch out for that one."

"I'm never going to remember all of this," I muttered.

"You won't have to."

Esther set the bucket of flowers down beside the stage and I did the same, keeping my hands busy with untangling the stalks. There was an assembly line started, where three women were wiring together branches of willow. They were already whispering, eyes shooting in my direction every few seconds.

"Heard you were back."

The voice at the end of the table belonged to the woman Esther had called Claire. She had a spindly branch in one hand, a small pocketknife in the other.

I gave her a placid smile. "Hi, Claire."

Esther's eyes met mine in another silent warning before she picked up her bucket, heading to the other side of the stage.

Claire snapped the branch, working it into the garland. Her thin, pale pink lips were crowned by a perfect cupid's bow. "Was startin' to think Sam was lyin' about seein' you. Thought maybe you'd come by to say hello, but it seems you've been very busy since you got home."

She didn't look up at me, as if to demonstrate that she was clearly in control of the moment. There was more to what she wasn't saying than what she was.

"You know, we've been prayin' hard for you. Thank God your mama is better." Her gaze finally flickered up.

"Thank you."

The words were flatter than I wanted them to sound, but I wasn't a stranger to this kind of arms-length inquiry. The morbid, superior curiosity of people who pretended to be good Christian folk was something still alive and well in Jasper.

"We took a few suppers over to the house; poor Eamon was practically starvin' to death." She gave a hollow laugh. "And you know the town has tried to do what they can to help out at the farm. A real shame to see it fall into such a bad state. It just breaks my heart." She frowned.

I could feel a fire burning in my chest, her words like gasoline, but I couldn't quite put my finger on why. Eamon wasn't mine. He didn't belong to me. Still, I couldn't stand that look on her face when she said his name.

"Hello, Claire." Esther was suddenly beside me again, her hand tightening on my arm before I could speak.

Claire gave her a wooden smile. "I was just tellin' June how much she was missed while she was away."

"Yes, well, that's very kind of you." Esther's tone was placating at best.

"None more than Annie, surely." Claire locked eyes with me.

Again, the words singed. Whatever the reason, I *had* left Annie, and I still couldn't even begin to wrap my head around that. The shame of it was growing heavier by the day, and Claire didn't seem the slightest bit concerned about offending me. I recognized that cool judgment in her tone. The sweetness-laced insult. I'd known a lot of women like that in my life.

"June, honey, would you mind popping into the diner and getting a pie for supper?" Esther pressed a couple of bills into my hand, and I fought to unclench my fingers.

"Sure." But I didn't move. Esther had to turn me toward the opening of the tent and give me a nudge before I started walking.

I could feel Claire's scrutinizing eyes follow me as I stepped out of the shade of the tent and into the sunny street. Once I was out of sight, that same attention found me from three women gathered on the sidewalk.

I ignored them, pinning my eyes on the diner, where the words COFFEE, SANDWICHES, and PIE were painted on the windows that overlooked the river bridge. Behind the glass, almost every table was filled.

Other than the paint color, it didn't look that different from Edison's Cafe. My reflection moved over the windows as I came up the walk, and I reflexively tucked my hair behind my ear, trying to look relaxed. Like everyone wasn't already staring at me.

The string of copper bells tied to the knob jingled as I pulled open the door, and more than one head turned in my direction. The haze from the kitchen griddle filled the air, along with the smell of thick-cut bacon. I could feel the eyes instantly. Not sympathetic glances or concerned appraisals, but a sifting kind of gaze.

I headed toward the stool-lined counter, where orders were hung like little waving flags in the window to the kitchen. For the most part, everyone returned their attention to their plates when I found a place to stand in front of the cash register. But as soon as my eyes settled on the wall beside me, I almost recoiled.

A simple wooden frame was hung above the counter, holding a portrait of Nathaniel Rutherford. He was wearing a jacket and tie, a stoic expression on his face. It looked like the kind of photograph that might have been taken for the Presbyterian Regional Assembly directory, or an official picture that would hang in the church.

In 2023 there was another photo that hung there. A different one, with a different frame. Maybe it had become some kind of tradition that Rhett Miller followed when he bought the place. I'd seen the picture at Edison's many times, but there was something that struck me differently about this one. Nathaniel's eyes bored into mine, the black pupils almost seeming to widen and stretch. I could feel myself falling into them, my stomach dropping with the sensation.

Those shoulders and even the shape of his ears made me think of that man I'd seen in the church window as I stood before Gran's grave. The same figure had been on the porch that night. There'd been a cigarette in his hand, the glow of it illuminating in the dark. Was it possible that it had been him?

"June?"

The man pouring coffee on the other side of the counter stopped before me, steaming pot in hand.

"I'm sorry." I blinked. "What?"

"I said what can I get for you?"

"Oh." I glanced again at the portrait almost involuntarily before I turned my back to it altogether. "A pie, please." I squeezed the bills in my palm.

He put down the coffeepot and went to a shelf on the wall where six pie plates were set in a row, waiting to be cut. "Cherry or blueberry?"

"Blueberry," I answered automatically, an emptiness materializing between my ribs. All I could think about was the blueberry pie on the kitchen table between me and Mason. That night felt like years ago.

I handed over the money, and the man hit the stiff keys of the register before the drawer popped open. I glanced at his name tag as he dropped the change in my hand.

"Thanks, David."

He gave me a nod, and I picked up the pie, winding back through the tables to the door. By the time I was outside, Esther had unloaded the last crate of flowers. I didn't meet anyone's gaze as I climbed into the truck, setting the pie in my lap. I could feel the sweat beading at my brow, my pulse still elevated from what Claire had said. I hadn't been the one to marry Eamon or have his child or choose to leave, but the nagging feeling of being responsible for it all was impossible to ignore.

The truck door opened, jolting me from the thought, and I gasped, the pie almost toppling from my lap.

"You alright?" Esther climbed in, fitting the keys into the ignition.

"I'm fine."

She started the truck, and I pressed my back into the seat, still keenly aware of the eyes on us. The air poured through the open window as she hit the gas, and I felt myself relax a little as the buildings disappeared in the side mirror. I was suddenly desperate to be as far away from all of it as possible. The urge to be home, at the farmhouse, was all-consuming.

Home.

I caught hold of the thought the moment it floated into my mind. I had only fragments of memories there, but somehow, it did feel like the farmhouse was a home. To a part of myself, anyway. Right now any place felt safer than this.

"You have any trouble in the diner?" Esther asked, shooting a glance in my direction.

I turned the question over in my head. There'd been no trouble, but that portrait of Nathaniel had shaken something loose in me. Instead of tugging on the feeling and bringing it into the light, I pushed it away. I wanted the memories, I wanted to know what happened, but that felt different, somehow. When I'd seen him at the church and on my porch, it had almost felt like he was watching me. Were those memories, too?

"No," I answered.

"Good." She looked relieved. "That's good."

The farther we went into the hills, the more I felt like I could breathe. The oppressive weight of Nathaniel's empty gaze and Claire's cutting words was like a tightly wound vine loosening its grip. Again, that thought of *home* resurfaced, my eyes finding a fixed spot in the distance, where I was waiting to see the turn onto Hayward Gap Road.

Beside me, Esther was quiet.

"What will you tell them when I'm gone again?" I asked.

Her eyes cut to me, revealing that it wasn't the first time she'd thought about it. In fact, she and Eamon had likely already discussed the subject.

"We'll cross that bridge when we get there."

The ominous tone in her answer made me wonder if they'd tell people I'd died. When Susanna had put me back through that door, leaving me in 1989, they'd let people believe she'd lost a daughter. They'd even erected a headstone with my name on it. Esther and Eamon could tell the town anything they wanted: that I'd run off and left my family for good, or maybe even that I'd thrown myself from the falls like one of the other lost souls of Jasper. Was that what they'd tell Annie, too, when she was old enough to ask why she didn't have a mother?

Whether the town would really believe it was another thing. Eamon's concern wasn't unfounded. The line between suspicion and fear was a thin one. Jasper was like the still, serene surface that was visible on the deepest parts of the river. It was the undertow you had to worry about.

"You said Eamon had to let his help go. Why?"

Esther looked at me. "Same reason anyone would have to. He couldn't pay them."

"What's going to happen to his farm?"

She didn't answer right away. "I can't see into the future, June. If you're asking what I *think* will happen, I suppose it's only a matter of time until he loses it. Maybe not for another couple of harvests, but I'm not sure there's a way to recover his losses."

"What happened?"

"Well, you left. Things were already tight, but the two of you were making it work, turning out enough crop to keep you afloat. We helped where we could, but there was only so much we could do since that was our busiest time at the flower farm. He lost a large portion of the harvest, couldn't keep the help on, so he planted significantly less this year to tend it himself."

I stared into the dashboard, that vision of him disappearing into the tall tobacco projected across my mind. The flash of his white T-shirt as the leaves swallowed him up, the last sight of him gone.

"I suppose if you really want to know, you can find out when you go back," she said.

I looked at her, resisting that slow churn in the pit of my stomach. She was right. How hard could it be to retrace Eamon Stone's steps and find out what became of him, where he went, when I returned to my time? But the idea of going *back* meant something different now. It wasn't just returning to the place I knew; it was also letting go of everything I'd learned since I'd been here. I didn't know how to just pick up my life again and go on like my entire world hadn't changed. I didn't know how to move on from this.

"Dammit." Esther's eyes went to the rearview mirror, her hands tightening on the steering wheel.

I turned around, peering through the dusty back window. Behind us, a police car had appeared, the single red light on its roof flashing. I exhaled unevenly before I faced forward, watching the car in the side mirror.

"*Dammit,*" she said again, reaching toward the glove compartment. It fell open, nearly hitting my knees, and she reached inside.

She moved so fast that I barely saw what she had hold of before she dropped it into the pocket of her door. It was a handgun.

My heart broke into a sprint. "What the hell are you . . . ?"

"Listen to me." She cut me off, eyes still on the mirror.

The police car was getting closer.

"June!" Esther's voice rose.

When I finally looked at her, the truck was beginning to slow.

"You were home all night," she said, one of her hands reaching out to take hold of my sleeve.

"What?"

"That night, you were home. With Eamon and Annie. Just the three of you."

I searched her face, the panic in her eyes now flooding into my own veins. "I don't know what you're talking about."

"Just say it!" Her hoarse whisper made me tremble. "Repeat what I just told you."

"I was home," I stammered, trying to remember. "All night."

She let me go, and I leaned away from her, pressing myself to the passenger door as she guided the truck over onto the shoulder.

My mouth went dry when the police car followed. We came to a stop, and Esther shifted the gear into park. There was a calm on her face now, a forced steadiness as she drew in a long breath. As soon as she had herself composed, her hand silently drifted to that pocket in the door and stayed there.

It was a few seconds before the police officer got out, and when I saw his face, my teeth clenched painfully. It was Caleb, the man who'd knocked on Eamon's door. He took measured, easy steps toward the truck, one hand at his belt, where his gun was clipped into a holster.

"Esther," I whispered.

She ignored me, leaning out the window just a little. "That you, Caleb?" Her tone had completely shifted to match her relaxed expression.

When he reached the window, he pulled the hat from his head. "Esther."

Then his dark eyes fixed squarely on me. His mouth pulled in a half smile. I mimicked it, but it felt all wrong. I could tell by his expression that it looked wrong, too.

"Good to finally see you, June."

There was a knowing undertone to the words, as if he were referring to the fact that he hadn't actually laid eyes on me when he came by the house yesterday. But he'd known I was there.

"Just got in a few days ago." Esther spoke before I had to.

"I heard. You didn't say she was headed back to Jasper." He was still watching me. "How's your mother?"

"Better." My voice was tight in my throat.

"That's good to hear," he said. "People 'round here sure will be glad to see you. Been a long time."

My eyes cut to Esther, looking for any clue as to what was about to unfold here, but she was unreadable.

"I'm sure Eamon's told you I've been looking forward to sitting down and talking. I thought now would be a good time."

I couldn't tell if my breath sounded as loud in the truck as it did in my ears. Had he followed us? Had he been watching us in town?

"Talk?" I echoed.

"You have some time to come down to the station?"

Esther laughed nervously. "Now?"

"As good a time as any." He smirked.

"Can this wait? We're just headed back to the farm."

"You're not the only one who's been waiting for June to come home, Esther." He set a heavy hand on the lip of the door, a seemingly innocent gesture, but something about it felt distinctly threatening. "We'll make it quick. I'll tell you what, I'll even have her home before supper."

Esther's gaze moved to me. She was scared, her hand still half-hidden in the pocket of the door. She was considering. Weighing her options. But if she pulled out that gun, I had no idea what would happen. Would she really shoot him? Just threaten him? What would he do when he saw it? Turn his own gun on us?

"Sure." I smiled, hands still clutched around the pie in my lap.

Esther's eyes bored into me.

Caleb's smile widened. "Great."

He waited, and when I didn't move, he gave a nod toward my door. My hand was unsteady as I reached for the handle and opened it. I left the pie on the seat, locking eyes with Esther one more time as I got out.

I came around the truck, catching another glimpse of the gun at his hip as he fell into step beside me. He opened the door to the police car, and his hand clamped down on the top of the window as he waited. My eyes fell to the badge on his chest.

MERRILL COUNTY was engraved in an arc over the word SHERIFF. Beneath it was a name.

RUTHERFORD

My pulse skipped. He was still smiling, but he had the look of someone who'd gotten what they wanted, confirming that there was something very, very wrong about what was happening here.

If his name was Rutherford, then he had to be related to Nathaniel. Too young to be a brother, too old to be a grandson. A nephew, maybe.

I pulled up my skirt, sliding onto the bench seat in the back of the car, and the door closed a little too hard behind me. Then he was rounding the car, climbing into the driver's seat. He turned the ignition, hand reaching for the switch on the two-way radio that was fixed to the dash.

Esther sat completely still in the truck in front of us, but I could feel her eyes in that rearview mirror. The car turned around, and I swallowed hard before I looked back, one hand clutching to the hot leather of the seatback as I watched her through the dusty rear window. A few seconds later, she was erased from view, disappearing behind the hill.

EIGHTEEN

The courthouse loomed over me as the door of the police car opened, and I stared up at it, a lump in my throat.

If the sheriff wanted to cause a scene, he'd been successful. Nearly everyone on the street had stopped to stare as we climbed the steps. The birds nesting in the eaves above the entrance took off, darting over the roof and out of sight as the doors opened.

"This shouldn't take long." Caleb gave me another tight smile, gesturing for me to walk ahead of him.

I tucked my hair behind my ear as I stepped inside, avoiding the gazes of the men and women who passed me. The lobby of the courthouse was more refined than the one I knew, with shining marble walls and floors. The lights were brighter in the chandeliers that hung from the ceiling, the murmur of voices making the place feel alive in a way it never had to me before.

The window to the police station was open, a brass placard engraved with the county's name. Behind the glass, Sam, the deputy who'd pulled over at the river, was seated behind a desk. He got to his feet, opening the door to let us in.

"Mrs. Stone," he said, the words echoing eerily around us.

I tensed, realizing he was speaking to me. *June Stone.*

Behind the door, warm wood paneling covered the walls of a narrow room. Papers littered a series of low desks fit with bronze lamps, and I could hear the click of a typewriter somewhere up the hall.

"They didn't believe me when I told 'em I'd seen you the other day."

The younger officer looked to Caleb with a satisfied smile. He was missing the taut, awkward energy that Caleb carried, but there was still something unspoken in the air that I wasn't following.

Caleb took off his hat, setting it on one of the desks. "Do we have a room ready, Sam?"

He nodded. "Room four is all set up."

That meant that he'd planned this. Eamon and Esther had wanted people to see me in hopes that it would keep the town from boiling over with curiosity. They hadn't thought about giving Caleb the opportunity he wanted.

I forced myself to follow the sheriff down the claustrophobic hallway. It felt like it was narrowing by the second. He turned into an open doorway, and I stopped at the threshold, scanning the small room. A wooden table and four chairs were arranged at its center, where a cardboard box sat unopened. Beside it, a large machine fit with ancient turntables was rigged with shiny black ribbon. It looked like the kind of tape you'd pull from an old cassette. An exact replica was sitting on another small table in the corner.

"June?" Caleb pulled out one of the chairs, waiting.

I stepped inside, swallowing down the sick feeling in my throat as the door closed behind me. I took a seat in the open chair and set my shaking hands into my lap. I didn't know what I was afraid of, I was just sure that I should be afraid. Of something.

My eyes lifted to the three rectangular windows set into the top of one wall. High and small enough that no one would be able to get through them, I realized.

Caleb took the seat in front of me, scooting in the chair, and Sam stayed standing, positioning himself beside the table in the corner. After a few agonizing seconds, Caleb pressed the red button on the recording device and the wheels started turning.

"Caleb Rutherford, Sheriff, interviewing June Stone on the twentieth of June 1951." He stretched out his arm, taking a quick look at his watch. "The time is 1:11 P.M. Deputy Samuel Ferguson present."

The words blurred together as I shifted in the chair. He was watching me closely, eyes skipping from my face to my shoulders before they settled at my throat. I reached up, adjusting my collar to hide the chain of the locket watch. Is that what he was looking at?

He cleared his throat. "Now, June, I know Eamon's given you some idea of what we'd like to talk about today, but I just want to assure you that all we're doing here is trying to make the pieces fit together. Can you help us do that?"

I stared at him. The tone of his voice didn't match the words coming out of his mouth.

"Of course," I answered.

"Good."

I nodded, unable to speak past the painful lump in my throat.

"Why don't you start with where you've been for the last eleven months."

I picked at my fingernail beneath the table anxiously. "In Norfolk. Taking care of my mother." The answer was rote, repeated exactly from what Eamon and Esther had told me.

"When did you first hear she was ill?"

"I'm not sure. A few days before I left?" It was a total guess, but as long as I kept to the most logical of details, I had the best chance of getting out of whatever this was. June had left suddenly, so if she was going to see her mother, it couldn't have been planned. "I got a letter." I added.

Caleb made a note on the pad in front of him. "Do you still have this letter?"

"I don't think so. I can look."

"I would appreciate that. And what exactly happened to your mother?"

"She'd had a stroke and needed me to come look after her."

"So, you've been in Norfolk since?"

I nodded.

"Answer aloud for the tape, please."

"Sorry. Yes."

"Can you provide the name of the hospital where she was treated?"

I could feel the pulse at my wrist beating harder by the second. "I . . ." I bit down on my lip. "I can't remember it right off. I can find out."

"You do that." He met my eyes long enough to let me know that he thought I was lying. This was a game. One he thought he was winning. From where I sat, it appeared that he was. "Why haven't you come home to visit in the last year?"

"I couldn't leave my mother." I was clumsily filling in the blanks now, grasping for the most reflexive answers.

"I see." He folded his hands on the table. "Well, it's been quite a long wait for us to sit down with you. You can imagine that we're relieved to finally get some of these questions answered."

I looked to Sam, who still stood by the door. He was facing the opposite wall, no reaction visible on his face.

"Why don't you take me through that night again," Caleb said, setting his pen down.

That night. The only thing he could be talking about was the night Nathaniel was murdered, but he'd said *again.* That meant he'd asked these questions before.

"June?"

"The night of the Faire?"

"Yes. The night of the Midsummer Faire."

My mind was moving so fast now that I could hardly track the thoughts. They were one huge storm in my head.

That night, you were home. With Eamon and Annie. Just the three of you.

Esther's frantic words rang in my skull.

"Where did you go after the Faire, June?" Caleb pressed.

"We were home. The three of us. All night."

Caleb's eyes narrowed again. I'd said something wrong. "You went home together?"

"Yes," I said, too loudly.

Caleb and Sam met eyes across the room, and I bit down so hard that my teeth ached. I'd messed up somewhere, but I didn't know how. I was stumbling in the dark, Esther's incomplete instructions and the few newspaper articles I'd read the only things lighting my path.

"That's not exactly what you told us last time."

I smiled, but it felt misshapen on my face. "It's not?"

"No."

Caleb gestured to Sam, who moved away from the wall, reaching for the machine on the table in the corner. He pressed the button, and the tables started turning. A scratching buzz sounded in the silence, and all the air left my lungs when I heard it.

My voice.

"... maybe about five?" A pause. "I had to be there early to help Esther."

My vision tilted just a little, the room around me tipping to one side and making me feel like I was going to fall out of the chair. There was no mistaking that it was me. *My* voice. The one trapped in my throat, ready to scream.

"What did you do at the Faire?" It was Caleb's voice now. It sounded even deeper on the tape.

"We walked around awhile, danced, listened to the band."

"I see. And did you leave together?" Caleb again.

"No."

My stomach dropped. That was what had prompted the look on Caleb's face. I'd deviated from the story.

"Percy came and found Eamon to let him know Callie had gotten out of the fence again, so he went home."

"And then?"

"Annie and I followed a little while later."

"And how did you get home?"

"We rode to the flower farm with Esther, and then we walked from there."

Sam pressed the button on the machine again and the buzz of the recording cut out, leaving us in silence.

Caleb looked at me, waiting for an explanation.

"That's right." I tried not to sound as terrified as I was. "I'd forgotten that he left early."

"You forgot," Caleb echoed.

"It was a year ago," I said. "Didn't seem like an important detail at the time."

"I'm afraid that every detail is important when you're investigating a murder." Caleb reached for the box on the table, sliding it toward him.

I held my breath as he opened it.

His hand disappeared into the box, and I heard the rustle of plastic before he lifted out what was inside. It was a bundle of something I couldn't make out.

"Mimi Granger came forward to tell us she saw you that night."

My brow furrowed. Granger. Somehow, I knew that name.

"She said she saw you running through her west pasture." He pulled a sheet of paper from inside the folder, setting it down in front of him.

"... running across the field, that baby in her arms, and I could have sworn she had blood on her dress." He read the statement aloud. "I remember, because when she got to the road, she was wearing only one shoe. One blue shoe."

The edges of my vision wavered as a rush of cold came over me. The sound of water drowned out Caleb's words, a pricking dancing on my skin. From the corner of my eye, I thought I could see that field, rolling waves of gold that stretched to the black tar road. I could hear breathing, a ragged sound coming from my own mouth.

In a panic, I pushed the memory away before it could suck my mind in, focusing my eyes on the recorder that sat on the table. Caleb's voice came back to me slowly, the vision bleeding away.

He looked up from the page. "Now, that's a pretty specific detail, but there aren't too many folks around here who would put much stock into one of Mimi Granger's stories."

I suddenly placed the name. Granger was the name on that mailbox—the one in front of the house off the river road. The day I'd come through the door, the woman on the porch had seen me. I still remembered that horrified look on her face.

There was still a glimmer in the room, my surroundings like rippling water. The scene around me was threatening to give way to the rush of the memory.

"Hell, she's drunk half the time, and that's why I didn't worry too much about it," he said.

I could hear the *but* coming, riding ahead of the words.

"But I have to do my due diligence, don't I? And just when I went to check it with you and your timeline of that night, you up and disappeared to Norfolk," he said. "Now, I'm a patient man, so I figured I'd wait until we could clear all this up. Then months went by, and you never came home. And all of a sudden, a few weeks ago—" He reached for the lump of plastic, unrolling it. "Mimi came barging in here with this."

I leaned forward as the plastic came free, revealing a blue slip-on shoe caked with dried mud. A fabric buckle was fixed to one side. He set it down in the center of the table, and it took every ounce of composure I could muster not to recoil from it. I recognized it. Somewhere in the back of my mind, I was certain it was mine.

"Apparently, it got stuck in one of the forks of the tedder when they were cutting the west field and baling hay."

If there was anything to say now, I didn't know what it was. This wasn't just fitting the pieces together. He was trying to fit the pieces around *me*.

That fear in Eamon's eyes wasn't just about his wife and the entire life she'd burned down when she left this place. It was about the minister. About the night he died.

"You told me that you didn't have a pair of blue shoes. Is that right?"

"That's right." I didn't hesitate, not wanting to risk even the slightest chance it would inflame his suspicion. All I could do was bank on whatever I'd told him last time.

He nodded. "All right. Is there any reason why Mimi would think she saw you that night? Or why she thought you were covered in blood?"

If I'd walked home from Esther's, I wouldn't cut through that field. I'd walk the path along the river.

"No. I don't know what she saw, but it wasn't me."

He folded his hands patiently. "Look, June. I'm not fool enough to believe that a little thing like you could kill a full-grown man with your bare hands. I am, however, inclined to think that a loving wife would protect her husband at any cost."

My lips parted as his meaning sunk in. It wasn't me he was after. It was Eamon.

A frantic knock sounded at the door, and Sam sprung forward, opening it. A man I couldn't see stood on the other side.

"We've got a problem out here. Eamon just showed up."

Tears instantly filled my eyes, my lungs finally expanding. I resisted the urge to stand from the chair, hands twisting into my skirt. I could hear shouting down the hall and the familiar accent-laced rasp of Eamon's voice found me.

"Speak of the devil," Caleb said, flatly.

He hit the button on the recorder, making the turntables stop. The machine fell quiet as he got to his feet. "Something tells me this isn't the last conversation we'll be having. So, I'd appreciate it if you could stay where I can find you."

"I will."

The surface of Caleb's entire countenance was simmering now, an ominous underbelly to the polite manners. "You be sure that you do."

Sam opened the door, and I bumped the table as I stood, nearly knocking the box that held the shoe to the floor. I walked out, following the hallway back to the front desk.

Eamon's voice grew louder. "You can tell me where the fuck she is."

He stood on the other side of the glass barrier that separated the office from the waiting room. He was straight-backed and stern, his jacket collar pulled up around his jaw.

"Eamon." Another officer had a hand in the air, a gesture that was meant to calm him down. But Eamon looked like he was coming out of his skin.

"Open the door, Paul." Eamon wasn't asking. "Now."

Caleb pushed past me in the hallway, with Sam on his heels.

As soon as he spotted me, Eamon exhaled, the relief visible on his face. But when his eyes focused on Caleb, his fury was back in spades. "What the hell is this?"

"I ran into June today and she graciously agreed to come in." Caleb's tone was infuriatingly even.

"Ran into her?" Eamon repeated. "You expect me to believe that?"

The officer Eamon had been shouting at slinked back, happy to be freed from Eamon's attention. I moved toward the open door, hardly able to blink back the tears.

"You should have brought her in yourself when she got back." Caleb squared his shoulders to Eamon.

Eamon took one step forward, pointing a finger at the center of Caleb's chest. "I told your father. Now I'm telling you," he growled. "Stay away from my wife."

Your father.

Eamon's arm reached out for me, and I walked toward him, swallowing down the cry in my throat when his hand firmly found my waist, pulling me to his side. I didn't look back as he guided me to the door and through the entrance of the courthouse. I couldn't even feel my feet as we went down the steps.

"You all right?"

His voice was close to my ear, but I couldn't speak. I stared at my feet until we could see the truck. A smudge of black marked the bricks behind the tires, and it was parked crooked along the curb, like he'd pulled in too fast and slammed on his brakes. Esther must have gone straight to get him.

He opened my door, and I lifted myself inside as the courthouse doors opened again. Caleb stepped out, watching as we pulled away.

"What the hell was that?" I choked out, wiping at my cheeks as the first furious tears began to fall.

Eamon lifted a hand as if to reach for me again, but he stopped himself with some effort, placing it back on the wheel. "What did he say?"

I sniffed, trying to catch my breath.

"June. What did he say?"

"He wasn't just taking statements, Eamon. He thinks *we* had something to do with Nathaniel's murder. He asked where I was that night. Where you were."

"What did you say?"

"Esther told me to tell him we were home all night."

He nodded, letting out a breath. "Good. What else?"

"How could you just lie to me?"

"I knew they wanted to talk to you, but I hoped you wouldn't be here long enough for this to catch up to us," he snapped. "Did he say anything else?"

I put my face into my hands, trying to breathe. "They found a shoe and they think it was mine? I don't know."

If he reacted, I couldn't see it. I pinched my eyes closed, trying to erase myself from the moment. There had been several minutes in that room when I thought I might not leave it.

"A woman said she saw me that night. They think I'm involved, Eamon."

But Caleb hadn't been interested only in me. I looked at Eamon from the corner of my eye. Caleb had really wanted to know about him. And if what I said was true and he'd left early that night . . .

"He wants to see the letter my mother wrote me saying that she was sick."

Eamon scoffed, shaking his head. "Of course he does."

"I have to get out of here. Tonight. I can go to Asheville or Charlotte. Wait for the door to reappear."

"No. You leave and he'll be on the phone to every police station within three states telling them to look for you." When I said nothing, he ran a hand through his hair. "He doesn't have anything real on you. If he did, you wouldn't have walked out of that station. And you might be able to run from this, but we can't. We're stuck here."

I looked at him. When he'd said *we,* he was talking about Annie.

"You leave now and you'll just convince him he's right. All of that attention will shift to me, do you understand? You might not give a shit about that, but my daughter's lost one parent already."

That's what this was to him. Not concern for himself. He was trying to contain this thing before it spilled over onto Annie.

"Things had died down before you came back. I thought it was behind us."

His voice faded out, the words almost inaudible, like he'd thought better of saying them mid-sentence. I studied him, trying to pry their meaning from the silence.

"You didn't want me to come back, did you?" I said.

His whole body tensed, and his eyes found me, disbelief paling his face. "My life ended the day you left. You'll never understand what that did to me. So don't talk about what you think I wanted or what you think you know about me."

He said it with so much hurt that it was as if the words had sucked all the air out of the truck. I suddenly couldn't breathe. It was the first time he'd let me see him, *really* see him, since I'd come here. There weren't any walls built around that truth—it was unguarded. Defenseless.

Another tear fell, trailing along my jaw as I stared at the road. "Who exactly is Caleb Rutherford?"

Eamon took a long time to answer. "He's your brother, June."

NINETEEN

M y eyes were glued to the side mirror, afraid I'd see that police car again. It wasn't until the house came into view that I loosened my grip on the door handle. Esther was standing on the porch, arms wrapped tightly around herself as if she'd been waiting.

As soon as the truck stopped, I climbed out, boots hitting the ground hard. She looked from me to Eamon, waiting for one of us to speak. But I still wasn't completely sure what had just happened. Not in the police station, and not in the truck.

Beside me, Eamon looked almost as dazed as I felt.

"Annie's inside." Esther answered Eamon's unspoken question as she came down the steps to meet us.

Behind her, the windows in the sitting room were half-opened, the curtains pulling in the breeze. I had a nagging itch to see for myself that she was in there, perched on her bed with her doll.

Eamon motioned toward the barn, where Callie was pacing again. Esther and I reluctantly followed, and we didn't stop until we were standing in a pool of sunlight between the paddock and the field. From here, we were hidden from the road.

"She knows about Caleb. And the investigation," was all Eamon said.

"All right. What happened?"

I stared at them both, so exhausted that I could hardly muster the energy to speak. I'd been forced to trust them, but it was clear now they'd been looking out only for themselves.

"You should have told me about this."

"We were trying to keep you out of it," Esther answered. "It's complicated enough as is."

"You *can't* keep me out of it. The less I know, the more dangerous it is for all of us. What would have happened if I'd said something wrong in there?"

Esther and Eamon met eyes in a silent exchange. They didn't argue with that.

"Let's start with Caleb," I said.

Esther glanced at the road around the corner of the barn, as if she, too, was afraid she'd see that car again. "He's Nathaniel and Susanna's son. He was born two years after you."

I waited.

"After she left you, she wasn't . . . well. I think she thought having another baby would help or somehow undo what she'd done. But she never got over it."

"I don't understand. You keep acting like Susanna was devastated to lose me. If that's true, then why'd she do it? Why did she leave me?"

She looked past me, to Eamon. "This is how it all started last time. This very conversation. She doesn't need to know everything."

"I need to know more than what I know right now," I snapped.

She unbuttoned the collar of her shirt, opening it to the cool breeze. I could see her mind turning with the words before she finally started speaking. "She didn't leave you, June. She didn't have a choice."

I could feel the warmth bleeding from my skin suddenly, the air around me like hard, jagged ice. Esther's eyes were on the ground between us, her silver-streaked hair unraveling from its bun.

"I told you, there was something about Nathaniel that wasn't right. His mind was twisted. From the beginning, he knew that Susanna was different somehow, that she was something unnatural. But he couldn't resist her." She paused. "He thought she was touched by demons, or some other ridiculous thing his father preached about on Sundays. I think, in a way, he both loved and hated her at the same time. He thought she had some kind of hold over him and that God was testing his faith. But he couldn't give her up, so he decided he wanted to *save* her, to fix things so that he could have her and still keep his own salvation. She was baptized in the church, and not long after, they found out she was pregnant."

Beside me, Eamon was silent. He knew what came next.

"Nathaniel came to see me. He was desperate. Scared. Terrified his father would find out." Esther paused. "He offered me two hundred dollars to poison Susanna in order to kill the child growing inside of her."

"He wanted you to *kill* her?"

"Not her," she said. "You."

My stomach turned on itself, the photograph of Nathaniel resurfacing in my mind.

"A witch to do the devil's work," she muttered. "But the only devil in this town was Nathaniel Rutherford. He figured I wouldn't want Susanna to have a baby any more than he did. So, he asked me to intervene before people could find out that the minister's son had gotten a girl pregnant. And not just any girl. A Farrow."

I stared at her, speechless.

"I didn't tell Susanna what he'd asked me to do, but I convinced her to go back to her own time because she wasn't safe with him. I could see when I said it that she knew it was true. For all of Susanna's faults, she wasn't blind. She'd already seen that darkness in him. I don't know if it was because she had you to think about or if she'd already been considering it, but she went through the door the next time it appeared."

That was when Susanna showed up in Jasper, I thought. After she'd been missing for months, she'd come home pregnant with a baby no one could explain.

"It wasn't long before she came back through that door, and I'll never understand why she did it. I think in her mind, she thought that she could fix him, the way he thought he could fix her. And that was it. She'd made her choice, and there was no going back."

"She'd crossed three times," I murmured. The first time, when she'd come here and met Nathaniel; the second, when she returned to Gran pregnant. The third crossing was her last, when she came back and had me.

Esther nodded. "There was no hiding that she was pregnant, and Nathaniel's father wasn't kind or forgiving about it. They didn't approve of her—him or the town—but they couldn't turn her away. Not when the whole of Jasper was watching. After a few sermons about the prodigal son and forgiveness, they gave in. Nathaniel married her right away, and a few weeks later, his father died of a heart attack right there in the church. Nathaniel was convinced it was God's punishment for what he'd done, falling in love with a cursed soul and giving in to temptation. He truly believed she'd brought it upon them."

"Did he know? About the door?" I asked.

"No. She had enough sense not to tell him, but like I said, he knew she was different. He could sense it, and it played right into all those Bible stories he knew. I think in his own twisted way, he loved her. But he was also terrified of her, and he was consumed with guilt over his father."

A car passed on the road, making her go quiet. When it was out of sight, she started again.

"When you were born, Nathaniel just couldn't let it go. He was so fixated on the idea that he'd brought a tainted child into the world, that you had been conceived in sin. Susanna finally seemed to accept it then. She was afraid of him. Afraid of what he might do to you. I hadn't seen her in months because he'd forbidden her to have any connection with us, saying that she was a part of *his* family now. So, when she showed up that night, I didn't know what to make of it. Nathaniel was in Charlotte for weeks, meeting with the Presbyterian Regional Assembly, and she'd waited until he would be gone." She finally looked at me. "She asked me to help her."

"How?" I whispered.

"The door would no longer open for Susanna, so she asked me to take you to the other side. We waited for the door to appear, and when Nathaniel got back from Charlotte, she told him you were dead. That you died in your sleep and we'd buried you. I wasn't sure he would believe her, but he did. At least, he wanted to, thinking God had finally acted to make things right. She was pregnant with Caleb not too long after."

I pressed a hand to my mouth, trying to understand it.

"Caleb was born, but Susanna was just getting sicker. Her mind had already begun to undo itself, and it was made worse by her grief over losing you. Another baby couldn't fix that. Caleb was just a little bigger than Annie when she died. He was there when Susanna jumped from the falls."

If what Esther said was true, then Susanna thought she was saving me. And then she killed herself because of it.

I paced to the corner of the barn and back, willing myself not to completely come apart. This was all too much. Too fast. I'd wanted answers, but not like this.

Caleb Rutherford, the vengeful son looking for justice, was also my brother. But all of this still felt like only one string in the web.

"So, Caleb knows that you're family? That his mother was a Farrow?"

"He's never acknowledged it, but he knows. He was raised by a man who hates us. That kind of thing can get into the blood, I suppose. Nathaniel kept him far away from the flower farm, but people still talked about it, telling the story about when the minister fell in love with the strange girl from Norfolk."

"What else haven't you told me?"

She pressed her fingertips to her forehead, rubbing the place between her eyebrows. "A lot. It's not just Susanna's life that you don't know about, there's the one you lived here, too. It's not something that can be covered in one conversation."

"Why don't you just skip to whatever you least want to tell me, then?"

Esther looked to Eamon again, hesitating. "When you showed up here the first time, I think Nathaniel knew who you were."

"Knew what?" I stiffened.

"That you were June. His daughter."

Eamon was staring into the fields now, silent.

"How could he possibly know that?"

Esther's eyes dropped to the birthmark on my neck, and I reached up, instinctively touching it.

"You've had that since the day you were born. But it's not just that. You look like her. You look so much like her."

That was maybe the only thing Gran ever said about my mother. Sometimes I'd catch her staring at me, that lost look in her eyes growing distant.

"I'm sure that, at first, Nathaniel tried to talk himself out of it, but eventually, he became . . . obsessed with you," Esther continued. "He convinced himself that you were sent to haunt him, that God was still punishing him for his sins. A few months after you came here, I started seeing him drive past the farm, sometimes multiple times a day. I'd see his car parked down the road and he'd just sit there, smoking his cigarette and waiting. There were a few times when you thought he was following you in town."

That's what Eamon had meant when he told Caleb that he'd told his father to stay away from me.

"And that's why Caleb thinks we might have had something to do with Nathaniel's murder?" I asked.

"Yes." Eamon finally spoke. "Nathaniel and I had words more than once about it. A couple of times, there were witnesses to those conversations, so when he turned up dead, there was more than one person in town who reported it, and Caleb started asking questions about where I was that night. He thinks you're covering for me."

"If he thinks that, why hasn't he arrested you?"

"He doesn't have any real proof, because there is none. But if enough people start taking those claims seriously, we'll have bigger problems. Nathaniel was loved by this town, and I've seen people take matters into their own hands for less."

That's what they were really worried about, I remembered. The town turning on them. Maybe that was what eventually happened to Eamon. The reason his farm sat abandoned, no trace of his name in Jasper sixty years from now. He could have been run out of town. Or worse.

"I should get back." Esther's hand found my arm, squeezing. "Margaret's probably sick with worry."

I didn't argue. In a matter of days, my entire world had come undone. I was slowly being taken apart, piece by piece. Truth by truth. The life I'd lived for thirty-four years felt far away now, and when I went back to it, I would be a different person from the one who'd left it.

Esther walked back to her truck without another word, and the headlights disappeared over the hill, taking the sound of the engine with them. Then it was only me and Eamon and the wind in the tobacco that surrounded us.

Annie was sitting at the table with a piece of chalk and some torn pieces of paper when we came inside. I went to the sink, filling a glass with water and gulping it down. Eamon sat on the sofa, kicking his boots from his feet. He was so tired that the shadows on his face changed the look of him completely.

I hadn't pried much into the relationship between us, because I was scared to. I was afraid to know what exactly I'd built here and even more afraid to remember it. I could feel this place seeping into me, and these people, too. When I went back, I needed to be able to cut myself from all of it.

I opened the door of the bedroom, but my hand caught its edge. "Eamon?"

He looked up at me, and I caught a glimpse of the Eamon who'd said his life had ended when I left.

"Thank you for coming to get me," I said.

He was still for several seconds before he nodded, and his eyes lingered on me a beat too long. I knew he'd likely come out of concern for himself as much as for me, but when I'd seen him there in the police station, I'd stopped breathing. I could viscerally remember what it had felt like to be tucked into him, his arm around me and his voice close as we went down those steps.

I closed myself in the bedroom and leaned into the door, biting down on my thumbnail as my gaze drifted to the wardrobe. Caleb wasn't just a son trying to solve his father's murder. He had a history with Eamon and me. And what he'd said about Mimi Granger had been replaying in my thoughts since I'd left the station.

The woman's wide eyes as she stumbled into the house and shut the door flashed through my mind. She'd been scared when she saw me, maybe thinking of that night she said I'd run through her field, covered in blood, with Annie in my arms.

I tried to summon the splintered memory that had tried to seize me at the police station. A field. The road. The sound of my own labored breath. But it wouldn't come.

I crossed the floor of the small room and opened the doors of the wardrobe, inspecting the clothes folded on the three small shelves and pulling them out to feel along the wood. Then I searched between and behind each of the hanging pieces. There was nothing there except for the faint smell of dried lavender and the dust that had gathered in the last year.

No blue shoe like the one Caleb had.

I sank down to the floor, feeling like this was another one of those threads, unraveling so fast that I couldn't catch hold of it.

I looked at my hands, resting on the neatly folded stack of Eamon's shirts. Without thinking, I curled my fingers around the one on top and picked it up. Before I could stop myself, I was pressing my face to it, inhaling deeply.

That smell was warmth. It pooled inside of me, filling the narrowest of spaces, and I closed my eyes. It hurt, unleashing a physical ache that reached through my entire body. It was alive, that feeling. A trapped thing trying to get out.

When my eyes opened, they focused on that swath of white lace in the back of the wardrobe.

Slowly, I set the shirt back in its place and got to my feet. I took the dress from where it hung and the length of it fell to the floor, kissing my feet. It was a simply cut garment with a fine layer of lace over the top that fluttered at the shoulders and clasped at the back of the neck.

The fabric was perfect and unstained, a creamy color that tinged gold in the dim light. Beautiful. And just looking at it made me lose my grip on that pain threatening to erupt inside of me. I couldn't contain it anymore.

I'm standing beneath a willow tree, cool grass beneath my feet. Before me, a tortoiseshell button on Eamon's shirt comes sharply into focus. I'm staring into his chest, but then my eyes find his.

I'm wearing the dress. I can see two tiny pink flower petals caught in the lace below my shoulder, and I know they've fallen from the woven crown that Margaret made for me to wear.

"For as long as we both shall live." The words drip from my mouth in a softness that echoes the sting of tears I feel behind my eyes.

Eamon's mouth lifts just the slightest bit, a tiny smile meant only for me. "For as long as we both shall live," he says.

He doesn't wait to be told that he can kiss me. He just pulls me toward him, and his hand slides around my ribs, down the center of my back, so that he can hold me against him. Once I'm fully enveloped in his arms, he moves his face close. Our noses touch before his lips part on mine, and he kisses me deeply, every single atom in my body like blinking Christmas lights.

It's not a vision. This is an embedded, sleeping beast that's been wait-

*ing to wake. My head is filling with it, forming a map of memories that
stretch and connect.*

*For the first time, I can feel a tether. It stretches tight between me and
this man.*

*Eamon's fingers slide around my neck, finding the nape of my hair. His
thumb presses to my cheek, just above the edges of the red birthmark that
stains my skin.*

And then it was gone, snuffed out from the world around me, but
I could still see it in my mind's eye. I could recall it in perfect detail.

I'd been able to smell the honeysuckle in the air and feel the give
of the earth beneath my bare feet. And it hadn't been like the jarring,
head-splitting episodes that I'd had before I came here. This was as
smooth as slipping into cool, still water.

The wind picked up outside, making the house creak around me,
and a soft cry echoed on the other side of the wall. After a few seconds of silence, it sounded again.

Annie.

It was followed by the creak of the sofa as Eamon got to his feet.
The pop of the floorboards as he crossed the sitting room. I followed
the sounds, moving along the length of the wall with my fingertips
trailing the wallpaper.

I could hear Eamon climb into bed with her the same way he had
every night since I'd been here, a predictable pattern.

I met my own eyes in the mirror, still feeling the sting on my lips
where Eamon's mouth had pressed to mine in the memory. They were
a pale silver in the lamplight, shifting with the shadows in the room.
And before I could see my mother there, looking back at me, I turned
out the light.

TWENTY

That morning was different.

Eamon and I moved like planets around each other in the kitchen, the smoke from the cast iron making the light hazy and the air rich with the smell of bacon. Annie was sitting on top of the table with a bowl of black cherries, bare feet dangling over the wood floor.

There was a sudden ease in the house, like an unclenched fist, and I wondered if it was because more of the truth had worked its way out between us. Eamon had let me see what lay behind that clenched jaw and those pensive eyes. I hadn't been able to tell if he'd meant to do it, or if it had just happened, but he hadn't hidden that pain from me when he had the chance.

My life ended when you left.

The echo of it inside of me made me shudder.

He handed me a bowl without looking in my direction, but instead of an attempt to avoid me, it appeared to be more a movement that was done by memory. It felt like a lived-in thing. Was this how we'd looked, standing side by side in the kitchen as the sun rose each morning? Was this our rhythm?

He reached over my head for two mugs, and for once, I didn't lean away from him when he got close to me. I could smell that summer scent, sun-warmed wood and grass. I found myself inhaling before he pulled away, and it lit on my tongue in a way that didn't feel new anymore.

He poured the coffee with one hand, a distracted look on his face as he pushed the bacon around in the pan with the other. Without any apparent thought, he set the spatula down and moved the sugar bowl toward him. I watched as he opened it, scooping two spoonfuls into one of the cups. The cup closest to me.

I stared at it as he turned his attention back to the sizzling pan. Two spoonfuls of sugar. That was how I'd always taken my coffee, and he knew it. But there was no evidence on his face that he was even aware of what he'd done. It had been a mindless movement, a pattern that was familiar to him, with me standing in the kitchen at his side.

My hands curled around the mug, sliding it toward me. The heat burning against my palms was also waking along the crests of my cheeks. He knew me. I was still trying to wrap my head around that.

He *knew* me.

The same questions replayed over and over in my head. Why had I left this? *How* had I left this? How could I have just walked away?

I was only just beginning to think of those choices as my own. In some ways, maybe it wasn't true, but with each passing day, I found it harder to separate myself from the June who'd lived here.

I looked across the room to the rifle that was hanging on the wall. I'd spent the night thinking about what Caleb had said and that look on Eamon's face in the police station. If he was afraid that Nathaniel would hurt me, would he have killed him? Was he even capable of that? I didn't know.

I'd thought more than once about the episode I'd had in my bathroom the morning I thought I had seen blood beneath my fingernails. I remembered that ribbon of red in the water, the smell of it in the air. I could see that flash of memory that had found me in the police station, the sound of myself gasping as I ran through the field.

And I'd felt that soul-deep love in the memory I'd experienced last night. If I knew Eamon had killed someone, would I have covered for him, like Caleb said?

Eamon pulled on his overshirt, stretching his stiff shoulder as he glanced out the window, toward the barn. He started toward the door, adjusting the collar around his chin.

I hadn't said anything, but I'd been watching the color change in the field, marking the difference by the day. From the look of the tobacco, the blight was spreading. Slowly, but it was. I wasn't sure the crop would make it. Not at this rate.

"I could help," I said, chancing a look over my coffee cup.

He stopped, holding the back door open.

"I know how to irrigate the field and trim the infected stalks without contaminating the others."

"I know you do."

I stared at him. Of course he did.

"Margaret will be here soon." He changed the subject. "The Faire's tonight, so she'll be here until the afternoon."

He looked away from me, as if that would soften the meaning of the words. Each morning, he never disappeared into the fields until Margaret had arrived. And he wouldn't stay out there if I was the only one at the house with Annie. The last time he'd done that, I'd left her.

I cleared my throat, trying to loosen the thick feeling there. "I think we should go. To the Faire, I mean."

He stared at me. "I don't think so."

"There were people on the street who saw me go into the police station yesterday. If we're the only ones in town who aren't there, which we would be, then they're going to think we have something to hide."

He didn't deny it. "What about Caleb?"

"You said yourself that if he had anything real, he would have made an arrest." I waited, and when he didn't respond, I set the mug down on the counter. "If you're telling the truth about there being nothing to find, then all we have to do is keep things from getting out of hand until the door reappears."

"What do you mean, *if* I'm telling the truth?"

I leveled my gaze at him. "We both know you're not telling me everything, Eamon. But the only choice I have right now is to trust you."

He didn't deny it. He also didn't argue with the fact that going to the Faire was our best option.

"Just . . ." His hand squeezed the doorjamb. "If you're going to work in the garden, can you leave the gate open while you're in there?"

"The gate? Why?"

He ran a hand through his hair uncomfortably. "So that I can see you from the fields."

I pressed my lips together, eyes tracing that stiffness along his shoulders as he said it. He wanted to be able to check on me, to keep me in sight.

"Just call out if you need me. I'll hear you," he said. "I'll see you tonight."

I only half admitted to myself that I hoped it was true. It had been five days since I'd come through the door, and it hadn't reappeared. Now I was almost afraid that it would. That I'd cross back without ever really knowing what happened here. I didn't know if I could live with that.

The sunlight glowed around Eamon's frame as he walked toward the barn, and Callie's ears perked up behind the fence. I watched until he was out of sight and then looked back to Annie. Her feet swung softly as she watched me with a steady, focused gaze. Was there something new in her expression, or was I imagining it?

I took a step toward her, inspecting every inch of her I could take in. I still hadn't had memories of her push through, and I suspected that might be because they were buried the deepest. Still, I was getting hungrier for them, the urge to chase them down growing by the day. There was a part of this story I'd never understand until I remembered her. There was a version of me that I'd never know.

Her toes brushed my legs, their shadows painting the floor.

"We're going to the Faire tonight," I said, my voice finding a calm that I hadn't yet been able to muster. "Won't that be fun?"

She nodded, picking up another cherry with her sticky fingers. "Will there be cake?"

I went rigid, mouth dropping open as I stared at her. She was looking right at me, eyebrows raised as she waited for her answer. But I'd never heard her voice before. She'd never spoken a single word to me.

"Will there?" she asked again, that tiny sound like a bell.

If there was anything strange about the moment to her, I couldn't tell. She said it like we were continuing a conversation that already existed.

"I—I don't know," I said through a stilted breath. "We'll have to see when we get there."

"Okay."

She twirled a stem in her fingers, the sight summoning endless memories of picking cherries over the backyard fence back home. The neighbor's cherry tree drooped past its boundary in the corner of the yard, where a small pile of bricks was stacked so that I could reach the lowest branches. I'd pick every single one I could find, and after a while, she'd finally come outside with a little ladder and let me fill a basket.

The neighbor. I could see her face, her dark hair pulled back in a clip and painted fingernails. But I couldn't dredge her name up from my mind. It was just barely out of reach.

I stared into Annie's bowl of cherries, thinking hard now. I'd known the woman almost my entire life, even before we'd moved into the house next door. I'd visited her at the courthouse many times when I was trying to find documentation on my mother. She'd baked that blueberry pie Mason and I had eaten, for god's sake.

My mind snagged, an incomplete feeling souring the memory. There was an empty place where something had once existed. Why couldn't I remember her name?

A hand went to my mouth, fingers pressed to my lips, when I

placed the sensation. It was the same one I'd had when I couldn't re-member that song Gran used to sing. Like there was a hole torn through my mind and it had simply fallen out. Only now it was dif-ferent. Before, just the words had been beyond reach, but I couldn't even think of the melody as I stood there. I couldn't even picture Gran's face when she sang it.

And there'd been something else. A shop I couldn't remember downtown, even though I'd walked Main Street every single day.

Annie jumped down, leaving the bowl of cherries behind, and I struggled to feel my feet beneath me. It was almost as if the memories were fading. Slowly disappearing behind a fog.

I went to the counter beside the back door, ripping a page from the notepad. As fast as my hand would move, I wrote it down—the entire memory of the cherry tree. Those stacked bricks, the glare of the sun, the basket on my arm, the sparrows up in the branches. I recorded every detail except the woman's name, even noting her hair color and the shape of her glasses and the ring she always wore on her right middle finger with an opal at its center. When I couldn't think of a single thing more, I set down the pen, folding the paper once, then again.

Margaret pushed through the front door, making me jolt, and I moved my hand behind my back, stuffing the paper into my pocket. I hadn't even heard the truck pull up.

She stood in the doorway, twisting the long blond braid that hung over her shoulder around her fingers.

The page in my pocket was like a live coal, but I didn't know what exactly I was hiding. I only knew that I couldn't fully tell where the alliances of this family lay. I'd gotten the impression that Margaret and June had been in league with each other in a way that Esther hadn't been. But Esther and Eamon hadn't been the only ones to keep the truth about my mother and the murder investigation from me. Margaret had, too.

"You okay?" Her wide blue eyes were glassy. She looked like she might cry.

"I'm fine." I tried to smile, but it faltered when I remembered that had been my dynamic with Gran, too. Her worried and me trying to reassure her.

Margaret fidgeted again with the end of her braid, and for a moment, it felt as if she was going to say something else. But as soon as I was sure she was about to speak, she moved past me, to the kitchen.

I watched as she started on the dishes, cutting a piece of the soap block to lather on the bristled brush. She had that look on her face now that she always did when things were moments from coming apart. Her first instinct was to control what she could, whether it was changing the oil in the farm truck or cleaning out a closet or washing the dishes in the sink. Gran hadn't just been the glue of our family. She'd been that for this one, too.

I reconsidered pressing her for whatever it was she was about to say, but I wasn't the same June she'd trusted. And if this Margaret was anything like Gran, she wouldn't be pried open.

I went into the bedroom, leaving a crack in the door as I made my way to the bed and reached behind the mattress. When I found the fold of burlap I'd left there, I pulled it free.

Quietly, I slipped the folded paper from my back pocket inside, eyes catching on the next page—the list of years I'd written down.

1912

1946

1950

1951

I'd already begun to think that they must revolve around crossings. 1912 was when Esther left me on the other side of the door. I met Eamon in 1946, and I left in 1950.

If you could cross only three times, then the older me, the one who'd lived in this time with Eamon, had used all my chances when I left. Wherever I was, I couldn't come back. So why had I written 1951 at the end of this list? I couldn't return; yet, in a way, I had, hadn't I? But as a version of myself who had passed through the door only once.

Coincidence. Luck. Happenstance. This was none of those things.

I was less convinced than ever that walking through the door that day was an accident. It also couldn't be possible that of all places and times, I'd ended up at this exact point.

Had I written the year 1951 because I'd known, somehow, that I'd be back? I'd thought that Susanna had brought me through the door, but now I wondered if the person who'd sent me here was me.

TWENTY-ONE

Warm light spilled through the open bedroom door as I fit two pearl earrings to my ears. My waving hair toppled over my shoulders, and it looked lighter against the jewel hued green of the simple dress I wore.

It was the nicest one in the wardrobe, and I found it a little unsettling how much I liked it. The fabric hugged my curves like paper wrapped around a bouquet of flowers. There was a gold brooch pinned at one side of the waist, where the fabric gathered and draped over my hip. I smoothed my hands over it, inspecting myself in the mirror. I looked like . . . myself.

Slowly, the memories were stitching together to complete the spider's web. I could remember little things without much effort now, snatching them from the atmosphere around me as I put on my shoes or uncovered another reseeded plant in the garden. They were trickling in, bits of memory filling my head like drops of water. Longer, weightier memories were harder, drawing away from me almost every time I tried to chase them. When I tried to remember the moment I left, the night of the murder, or even Annie's birth, the images disintegrated faster than they could form.

I straightened the locket watch around my neck, letting it come to rest between my breasts. On the dressing table, the light glinted on the ring in the abalone dish, and I changed my mind more than once before I picked it up. The gold was scratched and cloudy in places, as if it hadn't been taken off for some time, but I'd left it here for a reason. I knew I had.

If Caleb was trying to find a crack in my story and the rest of the town was suspicious, I couldn't afford to show up as June Farrow at the Midsummer Faire.

Tonight, I was June Stone.

I slipped the band onto the ring finger of my left hand and stared at it, a slow rush of something I couldn't name running hot under my skin. When I looked at it now, I remembered vows under the willow tree. It wasn't the replay of a story I'd heard. I'd been there, the moment fusing itself to my very core.

I drew in a steadying breath before I took the shawl from the edge of the bed and went into the kitchen. The house was empty, the front door propped open, and I could see Eamon's shape through the thin curtains that hung in the window. Annie was on the bottom step, walking its edge back and forth.

I fidgeted with the thin, gauzy fabric of the shawl in my hands before I drew up the courage to step outside, and I felt the burn in my face when Eamon looked at me.

He swallowed, eyes traveling down my body to study the shape of me. The feeling made my stomach drop.

He'd shaved, making the angle of his face sharper over the white collar of his clean shirt. His brown tweed trousers and jacket were unwrinkled; the rich brown leather of his shoes shined. Even the soot had been scrubbed from beneath his fingernails.

"Ready?" I said, voice tight.

He ran a hand anxiously beneath the line of his jaw before he pulled the keys from his pocket. "Come on, Annie," he called over his shoulder, and she let go of the porch railing, jumping down.

Her white dress was rimmed in eyelets, a pair of black Mary Janes on her feet. Two long blond braids were tied with blue bows at each shoulder—Margaret's doing, I guessed.

Eamon opened the passenger door first, and I helped Annie, hands finding her tiny waist as she struggled to lift herself into the truck. When she was settled in her seat, I followed, smoothing out the skirt of my dress over my legs. She did the same, mimicking the movement and I caught Eamon trying not to look at us, his head turning away just when I felt the weight of his gaze.

The mountains were ablaze with the oncoming sunset as we drove, a cotton candy sky speckled with pinks and violets that made everything look like it was pulled from a sleepy dream. I'd been in this very truck one year ago, headed to the Midsummer Faire. Had I known then that everything was about to change?

"Is there anything I should know about us before we do this?" I asked.

"What do you mean?"

"I mean," I tried to think of how to say it without feeling stupid. "What was it like before? What will people expect from us?"

Eamon let his hand move to the bottom of the steering wheel. He was pensive, as if images of our life were flashing through his thoughts.

"We're friendly with people in town, but not too friendly. Most don't want to be too closely associated with your family, but everyone keeps up appearances for the most part. The new minister has been coming around, trying to convince me that Annie needs to be baptized."

My head snapped in his direction. "You wouldn't do that, would you?"

Eamon seemed surprised by my reaction.

"I'm serious. You wouldn't ever get her baptized, right?" The tone of my voice was almost defensive now, bordering on angry. But I couldn't account for the anxious feeling that had gripped me when he said it. I suddenly felt like I couldn't draw a full breath.

"No, we agreed we wouldn't," he answered, leaning forward to see my face. Then his hand lifted, his knuckles pressing to my cheek like he was checking for a fever. "June, you look like you're going to be sick. What's wrong?"

"Nothing." I tried to breathe. "I'm fine."

I looked at my reflection in the side mirror, realizing that Eamon was right. The color had completely drained from my face.

"What else?" I said, dropping it. The knot in my chest was slowly unwinding.

"What else do you want to know?"

"How do we . . ." I tried to think of how to ask it. "Act?"

"Act?"

"Like, do we hold hands? Do we touch?"

Eamon was struggling now, the tension radiating from him. "Yeah."

"How?"

"What do you want me to say?" He shifted in his seat, irritated. "If you're asking if we acted like we loved each other, then yes. We did."

I fell quiet when Annie looked up between us, her brown eyes trying to read the dissonance that had settled in the truck. Eamon gave her a reassuring smile, taking her small hand in his and raising it to his mouth. He kissed it, giving her fingers a squeeze before he let her go.

It was such a natural, intuitive movement, a reflex to seeing that subtle distress on her face. And it worked. Annie let her head fall against his arm, her eyes glittering as the lights of downtown Jasper came into view.

The road was the busiest I'd seen it. Even in 2023, the Midsummer Faire was something that no one in Jasper missed. But in 1951, it wasn't just an annual event, it was the one-year anniversary of Nathaniel Rutherford's murder.

Three police cars were parked in front of the diner when we neared the white tent, and I clenched my fingers into a fist. Over Annie's head, I could feel Eamon give me an appraising look. The whole town was probably talking about seeing me in the back of Caleb Rutherford's police car, and they'd have their own theories about why. It seemed like Caleb had kept his suspicion of Eamon quiet.

The tent erected over the bridge looked like the portal to another world, a blush-hued glow spilling from beneath its roof. Strands of glowing string lights stretched across the street outside, taking on the appearance of fireflies.

As soon as Eamon turned off the engine, I could hear the music—bluegrass. It was a timeless sound I could feel at home in. For a split second, the divide between the Jasper I knew and the one I'd fallen into felt almost nonexistent.

"You sure about this?" Eamon still had his hand on the keys, ready to start the truck back up and turn around.

"No," I answered.

I got out anyway, waiting for Annie to hop out behind me before I shut the door. Eamon was at her side a moment later, and she stepped into the street, sticking close to him. His hand floated into the air between us, and I drew in a deep breath before I took it, goosebumps racing over my entire body when his fingers folded between mine.

I swallowed hard when his grip tightened, pressing the wedding ring I'd put on between our fingers. He went still, lifting our hands between us, and then he turned mine over until he saw it. The small gold band gleamed in the soft light. He stared at it, a gentle summer breeze catching the collar of his shirt.

I hoped he wasn't hurt, but he didn't betray whatever it was he was thinking. A second later, he was walking again, his hand still in mine.

The light from the tent framed the mouth of the river bridge, and we walked toward it, our three shadows moving side by side. Across the water, the white glow of the church sat nestled in the trees. It was nearly dark, but it all looked the same. The small parking lot that was half gravel and half grass. The crude fences of the churchyard, though they were narrower. They hadn't moved them to expand the cemetery yet, and I found myself searching the distant green hill for the white headstones of the Farrows.

I forced myself to smile as we ducked inside, swallowed up by the sound of voices and the quick-step melody of a song. The flowers we'd brought from the farm were woven into long garlands that were draped from each corner of the tent to the next, a cascade of golds and pinks that cast a rose-colored haze around us. Beneath them, the stage propped up a four-piece band consisting of a fiddle, mandolin, banjo, and steel guitar.

I ignored the feeling of eyes on us as Eamon pulled me through the crowd.

"Hey, June!" A woman about my age with copper-red hair squeezed my shoulder as I passed, giving me what appeared to be a genuine smile.

"Hey!" The response was automatic as I tried to place her face. Hers was one I definitely knew, painted in the background of some memory that hadn't unfurled yet.

She waved, chasing a little boy toward the stage, and then she was gone, replaced by a dozen other faces.

When we spotted Margaret on the other side of the dance floor, Eamon let me go, and I was keenly aware when the warmth of him pulled away from me. He watched me until I made it to her, Annie on my heels, and then two men were drawing him into conversation.

Margaret's bright eyes were sparkling over rouged cheeks, and her hair was pinned up, making her look several years older. The sleeves of her soft pink dress whisked at her shoulders, and a simple silver necklace with a small pendant hung around her neck.

She pulled me toward her, bouncing on her toes like she could hardly contain herself. "Was beginning to think you weren't coming."

"You look beautiful." I smiled, taking her in.

Her grin doubled in size. "Thank you."

She scooped Annie up, setting her on her hip, and Annie's hands immediately went to the sparkling pin in Margaret's hair. But Margaret's eyes were drifting across the dance floor, watching a young man with a crate of glasses in his arms.

It took me a moment to recognize him as the hired hand at the flower farm I'd seen the day I'd spent at Esther's. Margaret's gaze followed him as he passed, her cheeks flushed a deeper red.

"And who is that?" I asked, giving her a knowing look.

"Just a boy."

"Does he have a name?"

She glanced over her shoulder to Esther, as if to be sure she wasn't listening. "Malachi."

"Malachi Rhodes?" The name leapt from my mouth.

Margaret's eyes widened, brows coming together. "How do you know that?"

I swallowed. "I heard someone say his name at the farm."

I still wasn't sure about the rules of interference. I was treading lightly, trying to make the fewest ripples possible, like Esther had said, and I had thought less about it with Eamon and Annie because they didn't exist in my world. But Malachi and Gran had been close friends my entire life, so close that she'd insisted he play fiddle at her burial. I'd always wondered if there had ever been something between them. I'd even gone so far as to wonder if he may have been my mother's father and my grandfather.

Margaret's curiosity died with my less-than-interesting answer, and she swayed from side to side, rocking Annie in her arms. The music changed, and the crowd around the stage shifted shape, dispersing long enough for men with glasses of beer and women on their arms to weave along the edge of the dance floor. There were children chasing one another, and a group of a few black women in A-line dresses smoking cigarettes just outside. Beside them, a table was stacked with homemade desserts on pedestal stands.

My eyes found Eamon across the tent. He stood shoulder to shoulder with two other men, listening as one of them talked, a bottle of beer in one hand. The man's red face was turned toward the lights, but Eamon's was still draped in shadow.

"Who is that Eamon's talking to?" I said, leaning closer to Margaret.

She lifted up onto her toes to see. "Oh, that's Frank Crawley."

Crawley. It took me a moment to remember. Frank Crawley was mentioned in the newspaper articles about the murder. That's where Nathaniel had been headed the night he died.

"He lives at the end of Hayward Gap. Another tobacco farm down the road from you," Margaret said.

"The Crawley barn," I murmured.

"What?"

Annie slid down from Margaret's hip, pulling at her hand.

"That's on our road?" I asked.

"Yeah. Why?"

"No reason," I lied. "Just trying to place everyone."

I watched Eamon, studying the way he stood with his arms crossed over his chest, his reserved expression contorted by the dim light. He'd left the Faire early that night when Percy Lyle came to tell him that Callie had gotten out of the paddock. He'd gone home. If the Crawleys lived at the end of our road and Nathaniel was headed there, there was every reason to believe that he and Eamon could have crossed paths.

What had the article said? That there'd been signs of a struggle?

On the tape that Caleb played, I'd said that Eamon left to go home around 5 P.M. If I'd gone home with Esther, that meant that he hadn't come back to the Faire when he was finished dealing with Callie.

"Everything okay?" Margaret looked concerned now.

I forced another smile, catching Annie's attention before I pointed in the direction of the dessert table. "Look what I found."

Her mouth opened, eyes going wide, and I stared at her in awe.

She was so beautiful that it didn't seem like she could be real, much less have come from me, and that set off a chain reaction inside of me. She was becoming so real to me now. Too real.

"Think we should go get some of that cake?" Margaret tugged one of Annie's braids playfully.

Annie nodded, and then she was running toward the tower of desserts, Margaret trying to keep up.

The flash of a bulb made me flinch, and I blinked the bright light from my eyes, finding its source across the tent. In one corner, a man in a suit stood behind a wooden tripod set with a large boxlike camera. He leaned over it, checking the settings, before it flashed again.

The pop was followed by a brief fizzing sound, and there was something about it that pulled at the edges of a thought. I focused on that feeling, trying to tug it to the surface. It was that flash. The sound of the bulb. I squinted, trying to remember.

The music cut out, and the bodies on the dance floor stopped whirling, strings of laughter drifting through the air. When the fiddle started up again, it was slow, the notes pulling long before the mandolin joined in with a melancholy tune that made my heart ache. I could hear the river in the distance. The chirp of crickets carried on the wind coming off the mountains. They were the sounds of home, but here I was, in a sea of strangers.

I searched for Eamon again, finding him still standing in the same spot, but now another man had joined them. Eamon looked like he was only half listening, eyes scanning the room until they found me. The moment they did, my throat constricted.

He murmured something to the others, and then he was stepping through the crowd gathered between us. When he reached me, he took my hand again. This time, it was with a confidence he hadn't shown earlier. His fingers weaved with mine, and our palms touched before he set down the bottle of beer and pulled me with him.

We broke through to the other side of the dance floor, and he turned to face me. I looked around us, my breaths coming quicker as we drew attention, but this was why we were here, wasn't it? To keep up appearances?

His arm came around me, his hand finding the crook of my waist with an ease that said he knew this body, its shape and form. The mere thought of it made me tremble, but the set of Eamon's mouth looked like it physically hurt him to touch me. I wasn't all that sure I wasn't hurting, too.

He held me closely as we began to move in a kind of dance I didn't know. But somehow, my feet were following his, and slowly, the people around us seemed to forget we were there. Their conversations grew louder as the song drew on, and I couldn't stop thinking that where we stood was the center of something, a place that created the kind of gravity that made galaxies.

I stared at the way our hands fit together, wishing I could ask him to tell me more about us. To recount, from his perspective, how I'd decided to stay here. What words I'd said when I told him that I wanted to marry him. He had all of those memories, a bird's-eye view of our story from beginning to end. I wanted so desperately to know it, but we couldn't have a conversation like that in a place like this. I wasn't sure we'd ever find a way to scratch its surface.

When I looked up at Eamon, he was watching me.

"What?" I asked.

He shook his head. "Nothing."

The fiddle's notes deepened, taking on a haunting tone, and I stretched my fingers between his, squeezing his hand. "Tell me."

He considered his words for longer than I liked. I was afraid that he wouldn't answer me, but then his mouth finally opened.

"It's just that, sometimes, it feels like you're back. But then I remember you're not, and that makes me feel like"—he exhaled—"like I can't breathe."

The burn behind my eyes woke, making my throat ache.

Eamon wasn't a simple man, but he had a simple life. And I'd chosen him. Margaret said that she believed I had my reasons for what I did, but I didn't think they could ever justify what I'd put him through.

Again, the flash of the camera filled the tent, and the rising tide of a memory lapped at the edges of my mind. But this time, I didn't chase after it.

Eamon didn't take his eyes from me, holding my gaze. But he didn't speak. His arm softened around my body, and I let my fingertips slide up his back, my face so close to his shoulder that I could catch the scent of him. This was the same touch I'd felt when I woke that morning in the house on Bishop Street. I'd heard his voice. Smelled him in the sheets. I had the distant sense that maybe I did really remember him, even before, like he was engraved on some part of me I couldn't see.

I closed my eyes, letting the pictures flash in my mind. The way he'd kissed me beneath the willow tree. His hand sliding into my hair. His mouth opening on mine.

I was breathing harder now, pulling him closer to me so that the space between us disappeared. I let my head tip back, and his chin brushed the tip of my nose. I could feel his hand closing around the fabric of my skirt, a clenched fist of emerald green.

His mouth was centimeters from mine, and my entire body was waiting for it. I was burning beneath my dress, a fire engulfing me as his breath touched my skin.

The sound of the fiddle suddenly snuffed out, and the world came rushing back: a smear of glowing lights, the hum of people, and the sound of the rushing river beneath the bridge.

Eamon's grip on me tightened for just a second before he completely let me go.

"I'm sorry. I can't do this," he said, voice thick with emotion. "It's too hard."

He stepped backward, and the heat that had enveloped me bled away, leaving me cold. That muscle in his jaw was flexing again, his eyes finding everything in the room except for the one place I wanted him to look—at me.

"Eamon." I said his name, and the light in his eyes changed. He searched my face with an intensity that made my blood run faster in my veins.

But then he turned into the crowd, becoming no more than a shadow moving in the darkness on the street. I pushed into the crush of people, looking for a space I could get some air. When I finally made it through to the edge of the tent where I could feel a breeze, I found myself beside the railing of the bridge. Below, the black river was invisible.

There was a pit in my stomach, a horrible, plummeting feeling that made me close my eyes. What was I doing? Why had I touched him like that? The same questions had been in that look on his face when he pulled away from me.

"Mrs. Stone." I bristled when I heard Caleb Rutherford's voice, flat as still water, at my back.

He stood a few steps away, a glass dangling from his fingertips as he leaned into the wooden post with his shoulder. He wasn't in his uniform, and for some reason, that made him even more intimidating. A light blue shirt was tucked into his gray trousers, the gold rim of his cigarette case visible from the top of the chest pocket.

"Hello." The greeting was awkward, but I didn't know what would sound the most normal. Had I called him Caleb before? Mr. Rutherford? Sheriff Rutherford?

He took a step toward me, and I inhaled the scent of stale smoke and sweat, the hair standing up on the back of my neck. I felt incredibly small next to him, and it was clear that was exactly what he wanted.

I shot a glance in the other direction, trying to spot Esther or Margaret, but the dance floor was filled with people again, blocking my view.

Caleb's gaze didn't break from me as he moved closer, putting himself between the edge of the tent and the place where I stood. "Enjoyin' the party?"

I smiled. "I am."

There was a beat of silence where his response would have naturally gone, but he let it expand, watching me shrink away from him just slightly.

"That's good," he finally said. "I'm sure you missed this place. Your family."

I found the chain of the locket watch around my neck, fighting with it to give my hands something to do. But as soon as I realized the movement was drawing his attention to it, I instinctively turned a little away from him.

"I did," I answered.

"You know, I've been thinkin' about why you might have stayed away so long."

"I was taking care of my—"

"Your mother." He nodded. "That's right."

My palms were sweating now.

"The only thing is, I think you're lyin', June. I don't know where you've been for the last year, but I don't think you were in Norfolk. And it's only a matter of time before I can prove it."

He lifted the glass, taking his time as he drank the last of the beer.

"My only guess is that you thought if you stayed away long enough, all of this would go away. But it won't."

"Caleb." His name slipped out, but I couldn't tell if it struck him as odd. "I understand that you loved your father, and that you're trying to get justice for him. But I don't know anything about what happened to him that night."

"You don't know a damn thing about him." His tone transformed, making me unsure if I'd heard him correctly. "He was a cruel bastard and no kind of father. But you already know that, don't you?"

"What?" I said, hollowly.

I was frozen, telling myself that it wasn't possible that Caleb could know who I really was. Even if he'd entertained the idea, he could never confirm it. The moment I thought it, I second-guessed myself. I had no idea when paternity testing was invented. Was there some way he *could* know?

"See, my father wasn't right after you came to Jasper," he continued. "He was consumed with this idea that you weren't who you said you were. When Eamon started makin' complaints, sayin' he'd found him parked on the road, watchin' the house, I realized somethin' was wrong."

So, Caleb's suspicions had started *before* his father was murdered.

"He wouldn't tell me the truth. Just kept sayin' that you were sent to torment him. That the devil had cursed your family and that he had to protect us from it."

"Why didn't you say any of this when you brought me in?"

He didn't answer, but I was already putting it together.

"You don't want any of that on record, do you?" I said. "Not on the tape, and not in the statements."

Caleb appeared to be amused by the suggestion. I was right.

He moved again so quickly that I didn't see his hand coming until he'd already snatched up my arm. He squeezed it, making me gasp. But the music was filling the space around us. Laughter. A glass breaking.

"I *see* you, June Stone," he murmured, his face close to mine. "You're coverin' for Eamon, and I'll get what I need to prove it. Then you're both gonna pay for what you did."

"I don't know what you're talking about." I spoke through clenched teeth, fear coursing through me so swiftly that I could feel a scream trapped in my throat.

I could see the remnants of his father, *our* father, in that crazed look. It was the fractured man who stared back at me from that portrait in the diner. In the same breath, Caleb's face blurred, interchanging with Nathaniel's, those same black eyes boring into mine. It wasn't the first time I'd tasted this fear.

The pain in my arm grew to a sharp ache before he suddenly let me go, and the easy smile returned to his face.

"Now, you enjoy your night."

Caleb stepped past me and was swallowed up by the crowd. I glanced around me, looking for anyone who may have been watching, but there was no one. I smoothed out the rumpled shoulder of my dress before I set a hand on my stomach, holding it there as a wave of nausea rolled over me.

I could still feel that cold air that surrounded him. I could feel the throb where his fingers had clenched down on my arm. There was no mistaking that look in Caleb's eyes. He wanted to hurt me.

The pop and fizz of the camera's flash sounded again and the darkness washed out, blinding me. When my eyes focused, they settled on an old woman behind the back end of the tent. She wore a burgundy dress, her white hair pinned up on top of her head. She was watching me with ice-blue eyes, her wrinkled mouth twisting.

Mimi Granger. The woman who'd seen me running through her field that night.

The terror on her face was the same expression I'd seen that day I'd stood on the road in front of her house. She shuffled backward, a hand drifting out behind her as if she was afraid she might fall.

Her gaze didn't break from mine as she shrank back into the party, and then her dress was no more than a stroke of blood red flitting through the crowd.

TWENTY-TWO

I'm dreaming of Eamon.

In the drifts of shallow sleep, I can feel his hands dragging up my body. The weight of him between my legs. I can hear him breathing until there's the break of a moan in his throat. I can taste salt on my tongue and see bare, moonlit skin.

I'm not asleep anymore. This is the in-between place, like being stuck between two stitches in a seam.

A rush of heat pours into me, spreading like wildfire as my hands find his face. His mouth is on my throat, my shoulder, leaving a tingling trail in its wake, and all I can think is that I don't want him to stop.

He doesn't.

The heat inside of me is liquid. It's simmering now, on the edge of spilling over as I move against him. I can hear myself make a sound, and his hands tighten on me, but when I finally open my eyes, he isn't there.

The dream faded and I closed my eyes tighter, trying to hold on to it. But the more my mind woke, the further it drew away from me. My hands twisted in the sheets as it bled into a sea of black, my heavy breaths the only sound in the sunlit room around me.

I could still feel him. Taste him. The smell of his body was swirling in the air, but when I turned my face to see the other side of the bed, it was empty.

It was a dream, yes. But I'd been dreaming of a memory.

I waited for my heartbeat to find its rhythm and for the burning on my skin to cool. It was like he'd really just been there. Like we'd just . . . I pressed my hands to my face, trying to think about anything else. Anything besides the slide of his skin against mine. Slowly, the live-wire feeling began to dim, and my breaths slowed, one by one.

The memories that had found me before were one thing, but this, I didn't know if I could take this. They were coming out of nowhere now, sometimes hitting me before I even saw them coming. And at the same time, there were more things that were getting harder to recall.

I reached beneath the pillow to the edge of the mattress. I'd fallen asleep trying to redraw the image in my mind—the memory of the cherry tree. But after less than one day, I'd been unable to reconstruct it.

I unfolded the paper I'd written on, my eyes moving over the words in fits and starts. I understood them. They made sense, the scene written out like the page of a book. A girl picking cherries from a tree until the neighbor comes outside with a ladder. Only now I didn't remember any of it. It was like hearing a story told about a stranger.

I refolded the paper, pressing it to my chest as my heart sank. My theory had been right. I wasn't just gaining memories. I was losing them, too.

A plate sat on the table when I came out of the bedroom, a small knife at its side. Through the open back door, I could see the empty barn, and I bit the inside of my cheek. Eamon had left me breakfast, a thick slice of crusty bread topped with a wedge of cheese. Beside it sat a hard-boiled egg and a mug of coffee.

We'd driven back from the Faire in complete silence, and when we got home, Eamon put Annie to bed. I shut myself in the bedroom, one hand pressed to the door as I listened to his footsteps move across the house. I hadn't told him about what Caleb had said to me. I hadn't told Esther or Margaret, either. All I could think about now was how I'd felt when Eamon's mouth was just a breath from mine. How his hand had twisted in my dress.

I ate and washed my plate, going out onto the porch when I saw Annie hanging on the railing of the paddock to watch Callie. I made my way toward them, fingers skipping lightly over the knotted wood fence.

"I was wondering where you were," I said, smiling when Annie looked over her shoulder at me.

The closer I got, the more still the horse was, and when I reached for her, she touched her muzzle to my palm. Her warm breath enveloped my hand as I stroked up to the place between her eyes. She leaned into it, calming under my touch.

"Callie," I said, softly, trying it out. The name felt so known to me now.

She settled, pressing her nose to my shirt, and I leaned into her, breathing through the choked feeling in my throat. I was still stuck in the dream I'd had of Eamon, drifting between the many memories that were now filling my head. Somewhere between this world and another, I was losing myself.

My eyes drifted over the fields until the sunlight glinted off the windshield of Esther's truck coming over the hill.

I exhaled, letting my hands fall from the mare's mane.

Margaret pulled in, getting out of the truck and tossing the keys to the seat. She had that glow about her from last night, like she was still buzzing from the revelry of the Faire.

"So?" I said, making my best attempt at acting as if everything was okay. "Did you dance with him?"

She blushed, shoulders drawing up around her ears. "Twice."

I laughed, and it felt good. I missed that mischievous glint in Gran's eyes. The way she could make things sound like a secret.

Margaret climbed the steps of the porch with Annie and they went inside, leaving me alone with Callie. I could finally see Eamon out in the fields, on the north side of a hill that overlooked the house. He was hauling a load of yellowed, cut tobacco stalks up onto his shoulder. They were ones he'd been forced to cut in an attempt to prevent the blight from spreading. But it was too late. It was here. The only thing to do now was to keep as much of it healthy before harvest as possible.

Another truck drove past, and the man behind the wheel lifted a hand into the air, waving. I waved back.

It was Percy Lyle, the pig farmer who ran a farm up the road.

My hand dropped back to my side as I played the evening over again in my head. The dance with Eamon, the conversation with Caleb, the eerie sight of Mimi Granger. Margaret said that the Crawleys lived on Hayward Gap, and if Percy had come to get Eamon that night to tell him Callie had gotten out, then Eamon and Nathaniel could have crossed paths. But no one was here to see it. But there was someone who saw something that night.

That look in Mimi's eyes when she saw me at the Faire wasn't from too many glasses of ale. It had been on her face that day I came through the door, when she saw me from her porch, too.

She'd known something. She'd *seen* something.

I looked up the road, where Percy's truck vanished over the hill. Beyond it, the turn onto the river road was only a mile or so from that old farmhouse with the mailbox that read GRANGER.

In the distance, Eamon was out of sight in the fields again. I knew what he'd say if I told him what I was thinking. He and Esther both would think I was insane. But if neither of them was going to tell me what really happened that night, I had to find out for myself.

I opened the driver's-side door of Esther's truck and snatched the keys up from the seat. Before I could think better of it, I shoved them into the ignition. I was up the road before I saw anyone come out onto the porch, and I figured I had maybe ten minutes before Margaret got far enough out into the field to find Eamon and tell him what I'd done.

I turned off of Hayward Gap, eyes drifting to the rearview mirror. I was half afraid that I'd see the red flashing light of Caleb's police car there, but the road was clear.

The Granger farm was the only one in at least a three-mile stretch, the driveway one long track between two fields. At its end, the house sat behind a tall golden green sea of alfalfa. I turned onto the drive, the tires sliding in the dirt when I hit the brakes.

There was a flash of a shadow in the front window of the house when I came to a stop. I got out of the truck and climbed the steps, pounding a fist on the door. I could hear the clatter of a dish inside. Footsteps.

The wind rippled through the field, an expanse that stretched all the way to the tree line, where the river narrowed after it flowed past the flower farm. I tried to picture a woman running, a child in her arms. I tried to trace her path to the road, but there was nothing.

I knocked again. This time, harder.

"Mrs. Granger! Please, I just want to talk to you."

It was a few seconds before the door swung open, and behind it, Mimi stood with a stricken look. She changed her mind almost as soon as she saw me, and she scrambled to close the door again. I shoved my boot in front of it, keeping it open.

Her rasping breath was on the verge of a cough, her pallid skin colorless as she peered up at me. "Leave! Or I'll call the sheriff!"

"I only want to ask you a question." I put my hands up in front of me, trying to calm her. "And then I'll go. I swear."

She still looked like a wild animal with those yellowed, owlish eyes, but her thin lips pursed, like she was waiting.

I lowered my hands, glancing over my shoulder to the field on the west side of her property. "I just want you to tell me what you saw that night."

"What?" she croaked.

"The night you told Sheriff Rutherford about. When you saw me running through that field."

Her eyes narrowed. "What is this?"

"I just need to know exactly what you saw."

"I told him what you did. I told him *exactly* what you did."

"I don't remember!" The words crashed into one another, making Mimi flinch.

I knew it was the wrong thing to say, a dangerous thing to admit. She could go straight back to Caleb and tell him everything. But there was something about the way she was looking at me that made the words spill from my mouth. Like if she could somehow see how lost I was, she would help me. She would tell me the truth.

Mimi's hand fell from the doorknob as she stared up at me. She was quiet for a long moment before she came outside. The shawl around her shoulders was pulled tight now, her crooked brow relaxing.

"Please," I said again, my voice tired.

She let the screen door close, turning toward the west field. Her hand lifted, and she pointed one knobby finger at the rocking chair that sat at the corner of the porch. "I sit out here at night just after the sun goes down, when it cools off and the mosquitoes clear out. I was sittin' in that chair there when I saw you."

"What was I doing?"

She shrugged. "Runnin'." The way she said it unleashed a dread within me. This woman wasn't lying.

"Where, exactly?"

That same finger traced a path from the tree line in the distance to the fence that lined the road. "You were comin' from the river."

The river. That's where Nathaniel had been murdered, but his body was found far downstream from here, closer to the falls.

"You were wearin' a white dress and it had red splotches all over it, on your chest and legs. It was on your arms, too. In your hair."

My stomach lurched.

"You had that little girl. You were carryin' her in your arms, and when you made it to the road, you just disappeared. So, I called down to the sheriff's office and told them they needed to send someone over to check on things."

"I didn't say anything?"

She shook her head. "I called out to you, but it was like you didn't hear me. You had this look on your face . . . like . . . I don't know how to describe it. You looked like you weren't really there. Almost like you were sleepwalkin' or somethin'."

My eyes fixed on that field, trying again to imagine myself there.

"You really don't remember any of this?"

"No," I whispered. "I don't."

We stood there in a long silence as I watched the field. Only weeks ago, they'd found that shoe in the tedder—the one I'd sworn I'd never seen. Mimi had no reason to lie about what she saw that night. No reason to call the sheriff before Nathaniel's body was even found. And then there was the fact that the timing lined up. If I'd walked back from Esther's, I would have passed just beyond that tree line. If I had to, I could have cut through the field.

Mimi didn't say another word as I walked back to the truck. I pulled onto the road as she stood on the porch and watched me. She had one hand up to block the sun from her eyes, the other propped on her hip.

I believed that she saw me the night of the Midsummer Faire, but it was a memory I didn't have yet. That's what this felt like, inheriting moments until they made an entire reality. Bit by bit, I was getting pieces. If that was true, then eventually, I would feel as if I'd lived this life. I'd recapture it, in a way.

It had never been clearer to me than it was now that this wasn't just about the June who came through the door five years ago. It was about Susanna and the baby she'd asked Esther to take through that door. It was about the minister's body found in the river. I still didn't know if Eamon was actually capable of killing someone, but these were single stars in a constellation I couldn't fully see.

The brush of something across the top of my leg made me look down, and I sucked in a breath as a chill ran up my spine, settling between my shoulder blades.

The world blotted out like drops of water, a broken reflection on the surface of a puddle. Esther's truck was gone, but I was still moving. My hands were still gripped to the steering wheel, but the dash was replaced by the cracked one in the Bronco. The familiar smell of oil filled the air, and the unraveling, softened leather was smooth beneath my fingers.

> *It's happening again.*
>
> *A hand is lazily draped over my knee, hooking to the inside seam of my jeans, and I follow the arm to the passenger seat, where Mason sits beside me.*
>
> *His other arm is propped on the open window, fingers raking through his hair. The top buttons of his shirt are undone, the tan line at his wrist showing. But this touch—I look down to that hand on my leg. It's the kind of touch that never passes between us.*
>
> *"Mason," I hear myself say.*
>
> *His face finally turns to look at me, no trace of surprise there. As if I never left. As if it's the most normal thing in the world to be sitting beside me.*
>
> *"Yeah?" He answers.*
>
> *I stare at him, my lips parting to say something when the car jerks around me, tearing me from the memory.*

In an instant, the interior of Esther's truck materialized, the Bronco vanishing, and my eyes focused on the road. It was curving, and the truck was drifting off the shoulder, toward the ditch.

I cranked the steering wheel to the left, slamming on the brakes, and the truck fishtailed as it came to a stop. Smoke from the tires filled the air, and as it cleared, I could see the trees that lined the river.

I looked around me, breaths heaving. There wasn't another car in sight.

Slowly, I let my head turn back toward the passenger seat, now empty. Only seconds ago, it had felt like I could reach out and touch him. But Mason was gone.

I pushed the door open, getting out. The turnoff was overgrown, with wildflowers coming up between the cracks in the tar, and the river was just visible through the trees. It was a perfect half-moon of green water with a sandy bank.

This memory had been like the other one of Mason—when I'd been on the riverbank with a fire going and he was asking me if I was going to get in. This moment, too, had never happened. I would remember him touching me like that. But if these really were memories, *when* were they from?

I reached through the open window of Esther's truck, opening the glove box. My hand pulled back when I saw the handgun, but I reached beneath it, searching for paper and a pencil. I found an invoice from a farm supply in Asheville, and I turned it over on the hood of the truck, scribbling.

There was only one time period when those memories with Mason could have taken place. I'd gone through the door in June of 2023, my time. The future me went through in 2024. There were at least six months of life that I was missing in the span of that time. These memories with Mason were what happened to the June who didn't go through the door until months after Gran's funeral. It was a period of time I'd skipped. I'd missed it, because I'd gone through the door early.

I pushed the hair out of my face, closing my eyes and drinking in that sound of the water. When Mason and I were kids, we'd climb up onto the bridge with bottles of Coke we'd bought at the grocery and swing our feet out into the air until we were so hot, we had to jump. The river was always clear and cold, and it tasted sweet on my tongue.

I'd sink down and let the roar drown everything else out as I watched the light ripple above me in bursts that looked like stars exploding. And when my lungs couldn't stand it any longer, when it felt like there was a storm in my chest, I'd shoot up to the surface, gasping for air.

That's what this felt like.

I stared at the paper, the hood of the truck hot beneath my hands. In the distance, the dragonflies skipped across the river.

I didn't know how I felt about the idea of Mason and me. Knowing it was never possible had been a refuge. So, what had changed? I couldn't help but think that maybe that night at the house, a bottle of whiskey between us as I told him I was sick, had shifted things. If I hadn't walked through that door, was that what would have happened? Was that what was waiting when I went back? If there was a world where Mason and I were more, maybe *that's* what I'd gone back to. But then why build a life with Eamon in the first place?

We'd been so good at pretending, Mason and me. But maybe our days of pretending were over.

TWENTY-THREE

The memories were coming, whether I wanted them or not.

Eamon was waiting when I came over the hill, eyes on the road like he'd been waiting for me to appear there. As soon as he saw me, he turned on his heel, stalking up the drive and toward the house. I braced myself as I got out of the truck.

Margaret was already gone, and there was no sign of Annie. The house was empty except for Eamon's sobering presence. He stood in the sitting room when I came through the door, the lines of him rigid.

"Where were you?" he asked.

My hand tightened around the keys. I could lie to him, but I couldn't see a point to it. "I went to see Mimi Granger."

Whatever Eamon had expected me to say, it wasn't that. The stern look on his face melted away, replaced by shock. "You what?"

I lifted my chin. "I went to see her. To ask about that night."

Eamon stared at me, speechless.

"I have to know, Eamon. If you and Esther aren't going to tell me what really happened here—"

"I told you what happened."

"Not everything," I said, more quietly.

His jaw clenched. "There are things you don't need to know, June."

"But I *will* know them. I'm remembering. I'm getting more memories every single day. Eventually, I will be able to recall that night," I said, feeling my stomach clench. "And everything after."

I didn't want to say it, but the moment I was really thinking of was when I left. The moment I'd decided to walk away. It was the only memory I dreaded as much as I needed it.

Eamon ran a hand over his face, breathing through his fingers. He was coming undone in places, too. I could see it. Feel it, even.

"I'm beginning to think that maybe you don't *want* me to remember," I said, more quietly. "You don't want me to know what you're hiding."

His eyes snapped up to meet mine, defensive and cold. But he wasn't even going to try to deny it. That one look made me feel like my heart was breaking—an acute, palpable pain I'd never felt before. I'd never understood that expression because I'd never given my heart to anyone. But that's exactly what I'd done in my own future— Eamon's past. Now the man who stood before me, who'd loved me, whom I'd trusted, was torn between two versions of me.

I turned, headed for the door, and Eamon's steps followed.

"June." He said my name with a tenderness that made me bite down hard onto my lip. "June, listen."

But I was already out the door, down the steps, climbing back into the truck. I started the engine and didn't look back as I left, not even thinking for a second about where I was headed. I followed the road I'd traveled a thousand times when I felt like I had nowhere else to go.

I pulled into the flower farm a few minutes later, cranking the emergency brake with my gaze fixed on the fields before me. Dahlias and sunflowers bobbed in the wind as far as the eye could see. There were a few hats moving among them, making me think of Mason, and I was so homesick for him that I could cry.

A young Malachi Rhodes was digging a shallow trench a few feet away from the southernmost plot, an irrigation technique we still used on the farm. Esther had been ahead of her time on that practice, but now I wondered how much she'd learned from the future. Had Susanna brought with her the knowledge that Margaret had learned? Had I? Which way had the wisdom traveled?

My feet were heavy as they took me up the porch, but I stopped short when I saw a copy of the *Jasper Chronicle* on the top step.

I picked it up and unfolded it.

ONE YEAR LATER: STILL NO ANSWERS

It was one of the articles I'd found in the state archives, back when all of this began. But here it was, fresh off the press and sitting on Esther's porch—the issue that marked the one year anniversary of Nathaniel Rutherford's death.

Below the headline, Nathaniel's picture stretched across the page. He was smiling, the church at his back, the edges of his white shirt invisible against it. His fedora-style hat was just a little tilted to one side, following the slope of his mouth.

The town of Jasper remembers the life of Nathaniel Christopher Rutherford, longtime minister at First Presbyterian Church of Jasper. Today marks one year since his death on the eve of June 21, 1950, a tragic mystery that his son, Merrill County Sheriff Caleb Rutherford, has vowed to solve.

Mourners gathered at the church on Saturday evening in remembrance, for a chorus of Nathaniel's favorite hymns. The songs could be heard all the way down Main Street, only a mile and a half from where Nathaniel's body was found by Edgar Owens, who was fishing on the river the morning after his death.

Those close to Nathaniel knew that he considered himself a modern-day Job, content to suffer as God saw fit. After the sudden loss of his father when he was a young man, Nathaniel then buried his infant daughter. Only a few years later, he lost his

wife, a victim of long-term hysteria. After dedicating his remaining years to the town he loved and cherished, he died at the age
of sixty-three. He is survived by his son, Caleb Rutherford, and
the congregation that knew him to be a loyal shepherd.

The man that the town remembered was a far cry from the one
Esther, Eamon, and Caleb described. He'd been beloved as a spiritual
leader and pitied for the suffering he'd endured. Revered for his ded-
ication to the people of this town. There was no hint of the crazed,
obsessive minister whom Susanna had both loved and feared. His
didn't look like the face of a man who'd wanted to kill his own child
or who'd tried to rid his wife of demons.

"Can I help you?"

*The voice finds me, sweeping me into a memory as vivid and clear as
the world around me. The moment I hear it, I let myself sink. Faster.
Deeper.*

"Can I help you?"

*The colors bubble and bleed until I'm standing before the church, eyes
fixed on that narrow steeple from below. The wind whips my hair into
my face as I stare up at it. Heavy boots crunch on the rocks, drifting
toward me.*

"Have you come for prayer?"

*I turn around, wringing my hands when I see him. Nathaniel Ruth-
erford, the man who'd been my mother's end, stands only feet away. He's
my father, a monster that lives in the church beside the river, but I had to
see him with my own eyes. I had to look into that face and try to see what
it was that had bewitched the woman who'd left me. But I don't see anything at all. I feel only like a cavern has opened inside of me that will
never close.*

*As if he can hear my thoughts, the warm smile on his face begins to
melt, falling by the second. His brow pulls as he studies me.*

"I'm sorry, have we met?" His voice suddenly sounds strained.

I blink, wondering if he somehow knows. If there's some part of him

that can sense that I'm his daughter. The one whose body is missing from
the cemetery. Would he believe it if I told him?

"I'm visiting my aunt." My mouth moves around lifeless words. I can
hardly hear myself say them, because all I can think is that this man
wanted me to die. "Esther Farrow."

The wind pulls my hair from my shoulders, and his gaze jumps down
to my throat. He takes an involuntary step backward when his eyes focus
on my birthmark.

I reach up, pressing a hand to my skin as if it's burning, and his eyes
travel up to meet mine again. They're filled with panic now.

His face blurs, evaporating with the vision, and the church disappears
in a matter of seconds.

I was standing on Esther's porch again, disentangled from the ten-
tacles of the memory.

I let the paper close in my hands, staring at the front door of the
house. The women in this family were good at keeping secrets. Margaret, Susanna, even me. And maybe that was true for no one more
than Esther Farrow.

Gran had known Susanna's story, but she'd never shared it with
me, always steering me away from digging too deep into my mother's
disappearance. I always thought it was because it hurt too much to
revisit the loss of her own daughter, but maybe she'd known long
before Susanna was ever born what end she'd meet. In fact, she'd
grown up in the wake of it.

But Esther had seen firsthand the darkness in Nathaniel when he
asked her to take my life, and she'd been so afraid of Caleb that she'd
pulled that gun from the glove box, ready to use it. Her words were
branded in my mind.

The only devil in this town was Nathaniel Rutherford.
That kind of thing can get into the blood.

If she believed that, I couldn't know what she would have done to
protect me, Susanna, Margaret, or Annie.

I found her in the kitchen when I came inside. The sleeves of her shirt were rolled up past her elbows as she worked over the butcher block. The knife came down through the carcass of a whole, plucked chicken and onto the wood with a cracking sound.

"Margaret says there was quite a scene at the house today," she said, prying the blade to one side and breaking a bone.

I felt sick when I heard that sound.

"I hope you got it out of your system."

"I'm forgetting things," I said, my voice cutting her off.

The knife stilled, and she finally looked up at me. "What do you mean?"

"I've been remembering things from my life here since before I arrived. I didn't know they were memories at first, but they are. Now I'm forgetting things, too."

"What things?"

"Memories of my life before, in 2023 and all the years leading up to it. They're just fading, like they were never there."

There was a long moment before she set the knife down. "Why didn't you say anything?"

"Because I wasn't sure what was happening. Now I am."

Esther came around the butcher block without a word, methodically washing her hands. I could see her thinking as she scrubbed the suds up her arms.

"What does it mean?"

"I don't know. I told you, this has never happened before. We've always crossed on parallel time, but somehow, you've found a loophole. Technically, you went somewhere you don't exist, but it was a place you had once been. There isn't a rule book for that. Hell, there isn't a rule book for any of it."

We stared at each other.

"What if—" My voice turned brittle. "What if the door isn't going to reappear because I've broken it somehow?"

Her forehead wrinkled. "How?"

"I don't know. But you said that for us, time was a fraying rope, right? Multiple strands. If I'm gaining memories from one life and losing them from the other, maybe that means that time is mending for me. Maybe it means that I won't be able to cross a third time."

It was a theory, one that was based on nothing but my own fear. I was grasping at straws.

Esther wrapped her arms around me, holding me close to her. "We all have to make a choice," she said softly, "and it's different for each of us. Yours will be different from mine. From Margaret's. And Susanna's."

I let myself lean into her, closing my eyes. The problem was that I'd already made my choice when I left this place. I wasn't sure I'd get to make another.

"You don't think she killed herself, do you?" I whispered, asking the question as bluntly as I could. I wasn't going to dance around things anymore, afraid to disrupt their lives. This had been my life, too. "You think Nathaniel killed Susanna."

There was no denial in her eyes or in her silence, a slow admission settling on her face. "I told you. There was something about your mother that just wasn't . . . right. She had no center to her, no inner compass. She was one of those people who was blown by the wind, at the mercy of her feelings and her fears," she paused. "She wasn't like you, June. I loved her, but she was weak."

There was a deep echo of guilt behind the words. On some level, Esther felt responsible.

"I thought she'd done the right thing, sending you through the door, but there was no going back after that. Truly. It was more than the splitting of time and what it did to her mind. She was ruined in other places we couldn't see."

"That sounds to me like someone who might take their own life," I said.

She smiled sadly. "No. She wasn't strong enough, even for that, I'm afraid."

It was such a cruel thing to say, but the love she had for Susanna was evident in her voice. It had been since the first time I'd heard Esther talk about her that way.

"They never found her." She continued. "She wouldn't be the first to die at the falls, and it might take days or weeks, but eventually, there's a body. That part was odd, though not impossible. And when the man who saw her jump was the town minister, no one questioned it."

If she was right, then the most beloved man in Jasper, the man whose own son called him a cruel bastard, was a murderer. And the only one who seemed to know it was Esther. Probably Eamon, too. What lengths would he have gone to to be sure Annie and I were safe from a man like that?

Esther wasn't avoiding my gaze anymore, letting me see for the first time what lay within her. Esther Farrow wasn't just a farmer or a grandmother or a town outcast. This woman was a flame. *She* was dangerous, too.

The thing she and Eamon had in common was that ferocious protectiveness. If he murdered Nathaniel, maybe she'd helped. It was even possible that they'd planned it together.

"Do you think Eamon did it?" I asked, not mincing words. "Do you think that Eamon killed Nathaniel?"

She knew the answer to that question. I could see it in the wide openness of her eyes.

"I don't know what happened that night, and I've never asked. But that man would have done a lot worse for you," she said.

That wasn't a complete answer, but it confirmed what I suspected—that she believed Eamon *was* capable of killing.

I drove myself back to the house, leaving the keys to Esther's truck on the driver's seat, the way Margaret had done. Eamon was waiting at the kitchen table, but I walked straight past him, to the bedroom, unbuttoning my dress and letting it fall from my shoulders. The mountain air was cool at night, even when the days were warm. I pulled on the nightdress before I braided my hair over my shoulder and turned on the lamp.

The article I'd torn from the newspaper at Esther's was still in my pocket, and I drew it out, adding it to the others hidden behind the bed. I could hear Annie's small footsteps trailing after Eamon's in the house. There was the jostle of dishes in the kitchen. The sound of the kettle. They ate dinner, and he didn't knock on my door.

I watched their shadows move where the crack of light was shifting on the floor, until the house went dark and silent. I imagined that this was what this home had been like for the last year without me in it. A shell. A tomb.

It was like the embers of a sleeping fire somewhere inside of me, the capacity I had to hold this version of a life. I couldn't quite grasp it, but that feeling I'd had looking at Eamon as we stood in the glowing lights of the Midsummer Faire had fully manifested now. I didn't know what was me and what wasn't anymore. Was I becoming someone else, or was I just finally becoming myself? I couldn't tell.

Long after the moon rose, when I still hadn't closed my eyes, I got up and went to the mirror that hung over the dressing table. I drew in a slow breath, my hand finding the thin fabric of my nightgown, and I pressed my palm flat against my stomach. The heel of my hand followed my hip bone.

This body had carried a child. The very thought was an explosion behind my ribs. My heart felt like it was going to break through my chest every time I dared to envision it.

I could see it in my fractured mind, the image of me in that mirror, barefoot and belly swollen. I could *feel* it.

I bit down on my lip, the vision painting itself in such specifics that I began to think I'd created it from nothing. But this wasn't the blurred conjuring of imagination. This was like that moment my hand moved up the planes of Eamon's back, as if it already knew its path.

A soft cry bled through the walls of the bedroom, and I sucked in a breath, my hand curling tight from where it was pressed to my abdomen. Annie was crying that delirious, sleepy sound that surfaced every night like clockwork.

I stilled, waiting for Eamon's footsteps to follow, but they didn't come, the empty silence of the house widening. When her cries grew louder, I struck a match and lit the candle on the bedside table.

The glow of the light gathered in the eaves, floorboards popping underfoot as I came out of the bedroom. Eamon's boots were toppled beside the fireplace, and I spotted his sleeping form on the sofa. One black-stained hand was resting on his broad chest, and he hadn't even gotten undressed. He was exhausted, too far fallen into a desperate sleep to hear his own daughter's cries.

Annie's whimper drifted through the dark, and I crept toward it, my eyes adjusting to the shadows as I moved by the moonlight coming through the window. The lace curtain draped over her nook cast shapes on the wall as I set the candle down on the shelf. She was sitting up, the rag doll cradled in her arms.

She sniffed, hiccuping through another cry.

"Shhhh." I crouched beside the bed, finding her cold little hands with mine.

I half expected her to call out for Eamon, but she quieted just a little, wiping her face with the doll's skirt.

"Lie down, Annie," I whispered, trying to guide her back to the blankets, but she pulled at my fingers.

Before I even knew what I was doing, I was climbing into the bed, scooting behind her so that I could lie against the wall. She settled down, tucking herself beside me. Her feet wedged themselves beneath my legs and she went still. It was only seconds before she fell back asleep.

Her hand loosened on the doll until it rolled between us, and I lay there, watching her, like at any moment I would wake and find myself somewhere else. This felt like one of those memories—where I both belonged and didn't belong to the slice of time that was playing out.

Her face turned into the candlelight, and I breathed in her smell, like sugar and soap.

The wood floor popped again, making me still, and I searched the darkness until I saw him. Eamon was on his feet, slowly crossing the sitting room until the light painted his face. It was shadowed with sleep, his hair mussed, and the expression on his face was confused, as if he thought he was dreaming. But the waking settled over his features as he looked down at us, a deep breath escaping him.

I waited for him to tell me to go, but he didn't. He was quiet for a long while, and in that space that hung between us, I could feel the tension of countless conversations that would never be had. What did he see when he looked at me? Was it still a counterfeit version of his wife? It didn't feel like that anymore.

He sat on the edge of the bed, and I watched as he lay down on the other side of Annie. His arm came around her, resting beside mine, and he met my eyes over the tangle of her blond hair fanned out over the pillow. The air grew thick with the weight of what this was— a rendering that was too real. I fit into this space. All three of us did.

The light grew dimmer as the last of the candle melted down, and when it snuffed out, the darkness fell over us. The smell of smoke bled through the air. I couldn't see Eamon's face anymore, but I could sense him, the warmth of his body on the other side of the bed. His arm so close to mine that if I moved even an inch, I could touch him. And somehow, I knew what I'd find. I could predict the feel of his skin, the hair that thickened along his forearm and the bones that framed his arm.

His hand found mine, moving up my wrist to my elbow, and my fingers slipped beneath the sleeve of his shirt. We held on to each other, Annie sleeping between us.

It was the first time since I'd come through the door that I didn't feel like I was broken in two, and it wasn't until that moment, the red door skipping through my mind, that I realized this was the first day since I came here that I hadn't looked for it.

No, I hadn't thought of it. Not even once.

TWENTY-FOUR

The only person who knew the whole truth—all of it—was me. I just had to remember.

Annie was up first, feet shuffling from the sitting room as she rubbed her sleep-heavy eyes. I had a dress out waiting for her, and I helped her into it quietly as Eamon slept, braiding her hair down her back before I tied a little satin ribbon to its end. The strands were like silk in my fingers, that sweet smell of her filling my chest.

When she was dressed, I peeled one of the boiled eggs on the counter and cut a peach into slices, removing the skins without even thinking about it. The fact that she didn't like them was another dredged-up detail that had the feel of something I'd always known.

I riffled through the chest of Eamon's clothes until I found one of his button-up work shirts, a blue cotton with brown buttons. I pulled it on, tying up my hair with a bandana while I looked at myself in the mirror.

By the time he woke, I had breakfast ready, and Annie was on her way to Esther's. I stood in the kitchen, coffee cup in hand, and I had his waiting. Black—he drank it black, I remembered.

He stalled when he came around the corner, eyes dropping to the shirt of his I was wearing.

"We're smoking the fields today," I said, before he could get out whatever he was thinking. "All of them. We'll cut and clear as we go. Re-dig the ditches that need it."

"What are you doing? Where's Annie?"

"I had Margaret take her to Esther's. She's staying there tonight, too, in case we have to work late."

Something passed over his face that I couldn't read, and it occurred to me that maybe he didn't want to stay here alone with me. Annie's presence in the house was like a safety net between us in more ways than one.

"June—"

"Look, I know you don't want my help. But we both know you need it if you're going to keep from losing that crop." I met his eyes.

His jaw clenched, and we stood there staring each other down until his gaze fell to the coffee. He picked it up, taking a sip. That was all the answer I'd get out of him, but he wasn't arguing. That was good enough for me.

I headed for the back door with my own coffee in hand. The sweet smell of honeysuckle stirred in the air as the sun warmed the wind. The soil was turned out in the rows where Eamon had already torn up the infected tobacco, and if we were going to get every single plant treated by nightfall, we had to start working.

Callie stamped her hooves excitedly behind the fence when I made it to the barn, mane flicking as she shook her head.

"Hi, Callie." I caught her nose with my hand as I passed, stroking along her chin before I opened the door.

Eamon was behind me a moment later, hanging a bucket of oats for her on his way to the barn. He got straight to work, fetching two chains from where they were hung on the post. I took another long drink of my coffee before I set it down and rolled up my sleeves.

"Okay. Tell me what to do," I said.

For a second, I thought I saw the shadow of a grin at the corner of

Eamon's mouth, but he turned away from me, crossing the barn to the racks that were stored on the opposite wall.

"What?"

"Nothing. I've just never known you to take orders."

My lips twisted to hide my own smile. Were we joking now?

I watched closely as he assembled the rigging so that I could repeat the process if necessary. First he dumped the ash from the chambers, and then he refilled them with the contents of the metal containers I'd seen him open before.

"It's chaff," Eamon explained. "Burns for an hour, sometimes more, and that's enough to cover about half an acre if you're moving fast enough."

"How many acres are there?"

"Twelve."

I did the math in my head. That meant he was getting through about four or five acres a day. Between the two of us, we might be able to manage it all by sundown.

"How much have you lost?"

He set his hands on his hips, the number making his expression change before he said it out loud. "Almost two."

So, he'd already taken a significant hit. I wondered if Esther knew the extent of it, or if he'd kept it from her.

"And how long until harvest?"

"I think I can start in another week. Maybe two."

"All right," I said, pushing away the next thought. I didn't know if I'd still be there in a week. "Show me."

He pulled two clean bandanas from his back pocket, handing me one, and we tied them around our necks. The process was a simple one, but it was tedious and time-consuming. Eamon filled the containers with chaff and lit them, and as soon as he closed the hatch, smoke began to spill from the holes punctured in the metal.

"You walk ahead of me, tear out anything sick. The bad ones need to be pulled up completely. At the end of each row, we switch."

He said it like we'd done it before. We probably had.

We walked to the corner of the field, where the tobacco was most discolored, and I started up the row first, scanning the plants from bottom to top. It was only a few steps before I had to start cutting, gathering up the leaves in bunches before scraping them from the stalk.

Eamon followed at a slow pace, letting the smoke gather as he moved. It curled around the plants, bleeding between the rows before it drifted up into the air, hiding the blue sky. There was more sick tobacco than I expected, and I was tearing out plants more quickly than I wanted to, leaving holes in the field every ten to fifteen feet. Some of them had to come up completely, like Eamon said, and after the first several were pulled from the earth, I looked back at him, searching for any sign that he was anxious. But there was no point in dwelling on what was already done. The life of a farmer was a precarious one, every harvest season bringing with it its own challenges and losses. This one could sink him, but all he could do was get the job done. That was the only thing he had control over.

When we reached the end of the row, Eamon set the rig on my shoulders and gathered up the fallen crop, hauling it to the end so it could be burned. The weight of the dowel wasn't extraordinarily heavy, but it was uncomfortable, and the balance was difficult. It took a few minutes for me to get the trick of it, and even then, one dip to the side almost sent the canisters crashing to the ground.

"You said your father taught you how to do this?" I asked.

The question caught him off guard. "Yeah." He started down the row ahead of me and I followed, squinting through the sting of the smoke to keep him in sight. My eyes were already watering.

"Where are they? Your family?"

A pause. "This is my family."

My steps faltered, and the smoke thickened around me as the canisters swung, making it harder to see him. It wasn't cutting or meant to make me feel guilty. It was just a simple, honest answer. One that made that knife in my gut twist.

"We came from Ireland when I was a boy. Everyone went their own way, eventually."

He said it with no emotion or regret. It was so matter-of-fact that I didn't know what to make of it.

"You never understood that," he added.

He knelt, cutting at the base of one of the plants and tossing the leaves to the ground. He didn't ever talk about the "us" that existed before. In fact, he seemed to carefully avoid it.

"When I met you, you had Esther and Margaret. Mason."

His voice changed just a little when he said Mason's name.

"And here I was, alone in the world. You thought it was sad. But family, for me and my brothers, wasn't the same. I didn't really have a real family until . . ." He didn't finish.

The knife twisted deeper.

Margaret was right that Eamon was a quiet creature. He spoke only when he had something to say, and he didn't lace it in false meaning or palatable words. There was something so honest about him that it made me afraid of what else he might say now that he was talking. Like whatever judgment he might render me was bound to be true.

"And the farm?" I asked.

He smiled, but I could see only half of it with his face turned to the side. "Bought the land with money I saved working on the railroad, and the only reason I could afford it was because no one wanted it. The plot was rocky compared to the others in these mountains, but I'd grown up farming in Ireland, where the ground is more stone than earth. It took two years to get it cleared."

That young Eamon from my memory came back to me, that shy smile he'd had when he appeared at the fence.

He walked ahead, cutting as he went, and we fell into a comfortable silence, working through the morning and then the afternoon with brief spells of conversation that were easier and easier to have. He told me about the first crop he ever harvested here, about building the barn and how he'd bought Callie half-starved at an auction in Asheville. They weren't so much stories as they were excerpts from a kind of archive. One that made up his life. But when he finally quieted, taking longer to answer my questions, I found I didn't have much to say. There wasn't anything I could tell him that he didn't already know.

The smoke billowed every time we refilled the canisters, and it darkened the air between the tall plants until it looked like dusk. Before I knew it, it was. The temperature cooled and we made it to the last field, my hands black with soot the way Eamon's always were. My muscles screamed under the weight of the rigging, and when I made it to the end of the final row, Eamon was waiting for me.

I watched as he lifted the end of his shirt, wiping his face with it. Beneath was a plane of sun-gold skin that glistened over the muscles of his back. I could see the indented path I'd traced with the tips of my fingers at the Midsummer Faire.

He took the rig when I reached him, and I stretched my shoulders back, neck aching. The fireflies were awake, floating over the grass, and the house was dark, but the moon was still bright. He hoisted the rig up as I peeled off my gloves and as soon as we reached the barn, he lit the lantern that hung from one of the beams.

He took the lid from the bucket that sat on the chair in the corner, and the light rippled on the water inside. When I looked at him, he tossed me a rag, gesturing toward it. The smell of smoke still permeated the air, the same scent he carried with him into the house each night. It would probably be in my hair for days.

The chirp of the crickets outside was punctuated by Callie's impatient snorts, and I looked around us, to the empty barn. We'd been working side by side all day, but I hadn't really felt like we were alone until now.

He unhooked the chains, dumping the ash into the bin against the wall, and I hung both pairs of our gloves on the hook, side by side.

I dipped my sore hands into the water, stretching my fingers beneath the surface. "Can I ask you a question?"

For once, Eamon didn't stall. "Sure."

"How did I tell you the truth about me? About where I'd come from?"

He stood from the rigging on the ground, untying the bandana around his neck. "You just told me."

"When?"

"We were together one night, and you just said out of nowhere that you needed to tell me something. That you couldn't marry me unless I knew the truth."

Together one night. The words felt intentionally nondescript.

"I just told you and you believed me?"

He shrugged. "It was too impossible a story not to be true. And it somehow made sense to me. I'd known for some time that there was something strange about you."

"Like how Nathaniel felt about Susanna?"

"Maybe." He answered honestly.

I looked around the barn and to the moonlit fields visible through the open door. This man who'd loved me, accepted me, was hanging by a thread. So was this farm. And the weight of responsibility I carried for that was unbearable.

"I want to say—" I breathed, trying to steady my voice. "I'm sorry."

"For what?"

"For everything. For ruining your life."

His brows came together as he studied me. "You don't need to apologize."

"Someone has to." I tossed the rag to him, stepping aside so he could reach the water.

He took a step toward it, turning the cloth over in his hands before he dragged it over the back of his neck and started to wash.

"You've been waiting for me to come back, haven't you?" I said.

The line of his shoulders straightened. He ran both wet hands through his hair, raking it away from his face.

"You believed I was coming back."

"I did," he admitted.

He turned toward me, and I didn't move as he came closer. My eyes followed the curve of his throat to his shoulder, suddenly wanting so badly for him to touch me. To put his arms around me like he had at the Midsummer Faire. I wanted to feel him, like I had in that dream-steeped memory I'd woken to.

I looked up to find him watching me, his gaze fixed. Now he was recognizable in a bone-chilling way that made me hold my breath.

A bead of water dripped from his chin, and I watched his mouth, knowing exactly what it would feel like. What it would taste like. But he stopped a few inches away, waiting to see if I'd cross that space.

"You may have ruined my life, June. But first, you gave me one."

My fingers found the damp fabric of his shirt and I pulled him into me, pressing my lips to his. The fever of it spilled over inside of me, the moment as sharp and precise as the edge of a blade. His mouth opened on mine, his tongue sliding over my bottom lip, and he came low, kissing me more deeply. His fingers moved down the length of me until he had a tight hold on the waist of my jeans. Then he was walking us back, pushing me up and onto the workbench without breaking his mouth from mine. The air around us was already on fire, but now I could feel it inside of me.

He moved between my legs, scooting me close enough so that he could press himself against me, and a helpless sound broke in my chest. His hands went into my hair, unraveling it down my back. He wasn't being gentle or careful or waiting to see if I would follow him. He was a crack in a dam, a man who'd gone hungry. And I couldn't pull myself from the all-consuming feeling that existed everywhere his skin touched mine. I didn't want to.

Outside the barn, Callie grunted, and the fence creaked as if she were leaning against it. Eamon went still, breaking away from me.

His eyes were unfocused. The horse was snorting, feet stamping.

Eamon let me go, sliding from my arms. He walked to the door, listening.

"What is it?" I slid down from the bench. "Eamon?"

But he was already walking. He disappeared, and I took the lantern from the beam, following after him. He was headed toward the house, pace quickening as Callie cried out. We moved through the dark with the sounds of night all around us, and when the flash of a light flickered in the window ahead, Eamon broke into a run.

I stopped short, lantern swinging. There was someone in the house.

I ran after him, losing sight of his shadow as the back door slammed closed. I lifted the lantern, hissing when the flame-heated glass burned my arm, and when I came through the door, Eamon was pushing into the bedroom. But movement in the sitting room drew my eye, and I squinted, mouth dropping open when I saw him.

Caleb.

He stared at me from across the house, feet shuffling backward, toward the front door. When Eamon came back into the kitchen, he froze, following my gaze.

Caleb made it out onto the porch, his footsteps pounding on the steps as Eamon followed. But before he reached the door, he took the rifle from the wall.

"Eamon!"

I set the lantern on the counter, nearly toppling it over as I wove around the table, past the sofa. They were almost invisible when I made it outside, Caleb's white shirt the only movement in the dark.

"Eamon!"

The sound of the rifle cocking echoed out in the night just as Caleb reached his car, parked up the road. The sound of the shot tore through the silence, and then Eamon was cocking it again, setting the gun against his shoulder and taking aim.

The headlights of Caleb's car illuminated, the engine roaring to life just as I reached Eamon, and I took hold of his arm. But the gun fired again, making me recoil when the sound exploded.

I shoved into him, forcing the gun down, and Eamon watched, his face contorted with rage, as Caleb drove away.

"What are you doing?" I screamed.

Eamon pushed past me, back toward the house, and I caught him by the wrist. "Eamon!"

He didn't answer, tucking the gun beneath his arm and pulling free of my grasp.

"Stop!" I followed him inside, but he didn't return the rifle to the wall. Instead, he took the truck keys from the hook.

I tore them from his hand, holding them away from him. "Eamon, *stop.*"

Finally, his eyes locked with mine, and he went still long enough for me to set my hand on the center of his heaving chest. He was coming back into himself now, his breaths slowing.

When he didn't move, I reached for the gun, and he let me take it. Carefully, I hung it back on the wall, staring at the gleam of light the lantern painted on its barrel.

The trembling was starting, finding my hands first. There was no doubt in my mind, when I looked at him, what he would have done. He would have killed that man right there on the road. He was ready to do it.

I blinked, forcing myself to turn back to the house. The contents of the room were toppled, drawers opened and papers littering the ground.

"What was he looking for?"

Eamon didn't answer.

"Is there anything he could have found?" I said, warily. "Anything at all? Evidence?"

He leveled his gaze at me before he shook his head once.

My heart sank. Was this an unspoken confession?

"You're sure?" I whispered.

"Everything's gone." His deep voice made the trembling in my hands deepen.

I pinched my eyes closed, my head splitting with pain. The smell of smoke was in the air again, but this time, it was different. I could see the lick of flames. Feel the heat of them. But the fireplace was cold. It was another memory, skimming the borders of my mind. It was too far away. Too fractured.

"I talked to Caleb at the Midsummer Faire." I pressed a hand to my head. "I should have told you."

"What?"

"He threatened me."

"Threatened you how?" Eamon's voice was even, but it had taken on a new tone. One that scared me.

"He said that we're going to pay. That he's going to find proof that we're lying." I pushed through the door to the bedroom, trying to breathe as I searched the room around me.

Everything was scattered. Clothes covered the floor, the wardrobe emptied. The pages of the books that had been on the shelf were torn from their spines. The wind poured through the open window, catching their edges, and they looked like the petals of a flower torn from the stem.

I went to the bed, using both hands to shift the mattress down before I reached behind it, searching for the burlap fold I'd hidden there. The newspaper clippings. The photograph. The page with the years I'd written down. But my hand found nothing.

They were gone.

TWENTY-FIVE

I picked up the crumpled wedding dress, smoothing the white lace beneath my palm. The fabric looked like it was intact, but there was a smudge of dirt along the bodice, where it had been stepped on.

Eamon's hammer echoed through the house as he drove a nail into the doorjamb. The loose hinge of the screen had come out when Caleb and Eamon barreled outside, leaving it hanging. We'd spent the day putting things back together to mimic some semblance of normality, though the disturbing feeling that someone had been in here still lingered in the air.

I'd already collected what couldn't be saved—a broken perfume bottle, torn papers, the bedside table that had toppled over and cracked a leg. The last of the mess was the clothes that had been taken from the wardrobe and the quilts stripped from the bed.

This was what Eamon had meant about things getting out of hand. Caleb was hell-bent, so fixated on us that he'd been willing to break the law to get what he needed. He was a man on the verge of becoming unhinged, making me think that Esther had been right about him. He may have hated his father, but he still had Nathaniel's blood running through his veins.

I hung up the dress, my eyes following Annie through the bedroom window. She was walking the edge of the field, tapping the wide, flat leaves of tobacco with her hands as she made her way to the house.

Eamon came inside, and I met him in the kitchen, leaning into the wall beside the back door. We'd been like that all day, quiet and not wanting to say out loud what we were thinking. Things were catching up to us, and Eamon and I were one thing. Annie was another.

"The articles and the photograph don't prove anything other than the fact that we were interested." He said, "There have to be dozens of people in Jasper who kept those same clippings. But the years that were written down, you don't know what they mean?"

"I'm pretty sure they correspond with crossings."

He tore a sheet from the notepad on the counter and set it onto the table before he found a pencil and handed it to me. "Do you remember them?" he asked.

I nodded, taking a seat before I wrote the years out in the same order they'd been on the paper that Caleb took.

1912
1946
1950
1951

Before what happened last night, I hadn't told him about the things I'd found in the bedroom, because I wasn't sure what they meant or if I'd had a reason for hiding them from him in the first place. But we were beyond that now. Eamon and I were going to have to find a way to be honest with each other if we were going to keep things from burning down.

He came to stand beside me, close enough to conjure to life the lantern-lit moment in the barn when he'd kissed me. I hadn't been able to stop thinking about it.

He set both hands on the table, studying the numbers.

I kept writing, annotating the years.

1912—Esther brings June to 1989 (age 7 months)
1946—June (age 35) arrives
1950—June (age 39) leaves

Eamon was quiet as I tried to work it out.

I set the tip of the pencil back down on the paper, filling it in.

1951—June (age 34) returns

"This is the one that doesn't make sense. Why would I write down a year in the future?"

"Maybe you were planning to come back."

I shook my head. "1950 was my third time to cross, which means I knew I couldn't go back through the door."

"Well, in a way, you *did* come back."

That's what worried me—the five-year overlap, or *loophole,* as Esther had called it.

I closed my eyes, running over every piece of the puzzle I had. There was something about all of this that felt *planned,* like Eamon said.

"You said before that I promised you I wouldn't go back through the door? Is that because you thought I was going to?"

"I don't know what I thought."

"There had to be a reason you made me promise. What was it?"

Eamon stared at the paper on the table, arms crossed over his chest.

"It started when you found out you were pregnant," he began. "You didn't want children because you knew you would have a daughter and that she would go through what you had. So, when we got married, we agreed. But things didn't go as planned. I thought you wouldn't want to have the baby, but you did."

This changes everything.

The words floated to the surface of my thoughts. I could hear my own voice saying them.

"You changed your mind because you wanted her. And then, when she was born, you became so focused on breaking this . . ." He searched for the word. "Curse. You wouldn't accept that you couldn't fix it."

This changes everything. You know that, right?

"This is what Esther was talking about," I said, remembering. "When she said that this is how it all started last time?"

He nodded. "The more time that went by, the more obsessed you became. You were coming up with all kinds of theories on how to keep Annie from getting sick, and some of them involved trying to go back through the door. I was worried. We all were. You weren't well, and I was afraid that you were going to do something dangerous."

Maybe I had, I thought.

You weren't well.

That's what Esther had said about Susanna.

"You think that's what happened, don't you?" I guessed. "You think I tried to break the curse and failed."

"Even if you did," he paused, "that doesn't answer the question of where you went."

"No, but it answers the question of why." I looked up at him.

As soon as I thought it, the cold, biting reality sank in. There was nothing to find because this trail of breadcrumbs led nowhere. By the time I went through that door, my mind could have been gone in the way Susanna's was before she died. Maybe I'd already lost myself completely.

I stared into space, that sickening feeling in my gut making my heart kick up again. It was sinking in that somewhere in time, I was gone. *Really* gone. The thought made me feel the frost-laced breath of death on my skin.

I stood up from the table, a little too quickly, and the pencil rolled, hitting the floor. I needed to breathe. To pull air into my lungs and feel the wind on my face. I needed to get out of here.

I went through the open back door and down the steps, pushing my hands into my hair. I was too cold now, even with the humid summer heat, a chill aching deep in the center of my bones. The earth was spinning, and I could feel it, the motion of the entire planet swirling and making my head spin.

I'd been trying to understand how I could have left Annie, but I hadn't considered that *she* was the reason why. I'd broken vows for her. Ones I'd made to myself and ones I'd made to Eamon. There was nothing that could have prepared me for a love like that, to sit and watch a dying thing grow. The fate of the Farrows was Annie's fate, too. Maybe I'd risked everything to change it.

I turned in a circle, scanning the edge of the field for her, but she wasn't there.

"Annie?" I called out, lifting a hand over my eyes to block the sun. She wasn't outside the barn or at the paddock fence, either.

"Annie!" I walked toward the garden, leaning over the fence, but it was empty.

Eamon came down the back steps, watching me.

"Where is she? Did she come in the house?"

"No." His eyes were on the road now, tracing the edges of the farm.

My steps quickened as I headed for the barn, and I yanked the heavy sliding door open, ignoring Callie's insistent reach over the fence.

"Annie?" I stepped inside, looking for her. "Annie!"

The stalls and the hayloft were silent.

When I came out of the barn, Eamon was jogging toward me from the house.

"She's not in there," I panted, my voice getting frantic now.

Eamon cupped his hands around his mouth. "Annie!" His deep voice carried over the fields, farther than mine could travel. We both stood frozen, listening.

"Where is she?" I studied the road. Had I seen a car pass by? "Eamon, where is she?"

My hand gripped onto his sleeve so tightly that pain pierced through the knuckles of my fingers. I couldn't feel my heartbeat anymore.

"What about the river?" It was in the distance, beyond the tree line that sat behind the hill.

He shook his head. "She wouldn't wander that far."

The entire look of his face had transfigured, a look of pure terror consuming him. We were asking ourselves the same question. Only last night, Caleb Rutherford had broken into our home. He'd threatened me. Us.

Eamon pushed me in the other direction, hand pointing to the northeast corner of the fields. "Start on that side, I'll go this way."

I ran, legs driving me forward until I was disappearing into the farthest row of tobacco. "Annie!" My voice cracked as I flew through the fluttering leaves. "Annie!"

The panic sent my thoughts scattering in every direction, but I couldn't follow them. Eamon's voice was ringing out in the distance, growing more desperate every time he shouted her name. Each time I heard it, the chill deepened in my blood.

I didn't slow as I reached the end of the row, and then I was doubling back on the next, eyes searching the field. My throat was raw as I called for her again and again.

"Mama!" A tiny voice found me.

I stopped, catching myself on the stalks before I could stumble forward. I held my breath as I listened. Eamon was still calling out, the sound muffled by the wind. Had I imagined it?

"Mama!"

The pain of hearing that word detonated inside of me, making everything tilt and shift.

I took a step in the direction of the voice, then another.

"Mama! Look!"

I pressed myself between the plants, into the next row, then the next, looking for her. When I spotted her pink dress in the forest of green, a sob broke in my chest. She was so small beneath the height of the tobacco, standing in the center of the row. Her brown eyes were wide with excitement, her hands cupped together in front of her.

"Eamon! She's here!"

I walked straight toward her, hardly able to stay on my feet. My insides collapsed as my knees hit the dirt in front of her. I hadn't realized I was crying, hot tears dripping from my chin.

I wrapped my arms around her, pulling her into my lap. My face pressed into her hair as I wept.

"Look," she whispered, her hands opening between us to reveal a ladybug.

It crawled across her palm, the vision of it blurring through my tears.

"I see it," I rasped, wiping my cheek with the back of my hand.

Eamon burst into the row a second later, chest deflating when he saw us. His face was flushed as he sank down and pulled us both into him, and I curled into Eamon as Annie curled into me. She peered at the ladybug, oblivious to the two minutes of horror we'd just gone through.

I didn't care that this crossed the line of keeping my distance or confusing boundaries. In that moment, I needed there to be no space between the three of us. I needed to feel us together, with no beginning and no end.

I'd never felt fear like that. Not ever. And I didn't think there was any way to ever come back from that explosion of light that had birthed a universe inside of me when she said that word.

Mama.

TWENTY-SIX

She wasn't safe with me. She never had been.

I stood in the center of the sitting room in the dark, my eyes pinned to Annie's sleeping form. She was tucked into her bed, lit by the moonlight coming through the window. Her peaceful face was nuzzled into the quilt, her breaths long and deep.

"June," Eamon tried for the third time. "You can't just stand there all night."

I ignored him, refusing to blink even though my eyes ached.

I'd tried to go to bed, only to toss and turn, my feet bringing me back to this spot again and again. Every time she was out of sight, that crippling fear found me, its grip closing tight. I needed to see her with my own eyes. I needed to know that she was safe.

Those few seconds in the field had torn open an ocean of memories inside of me.

This changes everything.

I'm standing on the porch in the dark, the wind pulling my waving hair across my face. Eamon is only inches away, but he doesn't touch me.

"This changes everything. You know that, right?" I say.

It's a long moment before he nods, but it doesn't feel like an agreement. It feels like a divide between us.

I blink, and I'm in our bed, naked beside Eamon, with the quilt pushed down to keep us cool. We're in the last few moments before sleep takes hold, and my eyes are heavy. Eamon's hand slides around my waist to the crest of my swollen belly, and I feel his lips press to the back of my shoulder.

I blink, and I'm at the farmhouse. I'm screaming, but not a high-pitched cry. It's a groan from deep inside of me. Eamon's hands are bracing me, his mouth pressed to my ear, but I can't hear what he's saying.

I can feel sweat trailing down my back beneath my nightgown. I can feel pain wrapping around my body, and I push. That growl breaks in my chest again, and I can see Esther between my legs. Margaret standing in the moonlit window, waiting with a cloth draped over her hands.

And then there's another cry that doesn't come from me. I hold out my arms, reaching for her, and then she's pressed against me as I sob. A deep, broken sound I've never heard before.

Warm, is all I can think. She's so warm.

Eamon's face presses into my hair, and I can feel his body trembling. Feel his arms tighten around me.

They were only a few of the dozens of memories that had worked themselves loose in the last few hours. My head was filled with them now. Annie in my arms as a baby, nursing at my breast. Eamon pacing the house with her in the dark, early hours of the morning. They were things I couldn't unsee.

Mama.

That word contained multitudes. In an instant, it had wiped me from the face of the earth.

"June." Eamon's voice only made the ache inside of me cut deeper. That voice. I *knew* that voice. I'd known it before I ever walked through the door. "You need to get some sleep."

"You should have told me I was sick," I whispered.

"You weren't sick."

That's what Gran had always said. It's what Esther had told me, too. But being stuck between time, having a mind that was frayed, that *was* being broken. We were malfunctioning, all of us. It didn't matter if it wouldn't show up on a brain scan. There was something *wrong* with me.

"This is what happens," I said. "I've seen it. With Gran. She saw it with Susanna and Esther, too. It was happening to me, even before I got here. This is what happens to us, Eamon. This is what's going to happen to her."

This was where it was always going to lead, wasn't it? I'd known this as long as I'd known myself. So why did it hurt so much?

He looked at me with eyes that said he'd heard all of this before.

"This changes everything," I repeated, watching his face.

He was watching me, too.

"That's what I said when I told you, right? I warned you that this would change everything."

I could see that he remembered standing out on the porch when I told him I was pregnant. He remembered when I spoke those words.

"How could I have left her?" My voice cracked. "How could I have just left her here by herself all alone?"

Understanding settled in his eyes. "Esther told you?"

"Margaret."

He sighed.

"What kind of mother does that? What kind of person just leaves a three-year-old little girl by herself?"

"It's not that simple."

"It is. This sickness isn't the only thing I got from Susanna, Eamon. I was never safe with her, just like Annie isn't safe with me."

"You don't know what you're saying."

"I do." I nodded, insistent. "I never should have become a mother."

Eamon looked at me with an expression that bordered on fury.

"Look, I don't know why you did what you did, but you would have died for our daughter. If you remember, then you know that."

I wanted to hold on to the words and let them pull me from the darkness. I wanted to believe him.

"You're the same person I met that day in Esther's fields. The same one who decided to stay here and marry me. To have a child with me." Tears filled his eyes as he said it. "Even if that door appears right now and you walk through it, all of that is still true."

"Eamon."

"Listen to me." He took my face in his hands, the timbre of his voice deepening. "I wouldn't change any of it. If I could walk through a door and undo all of this, I wouldn't. Do you understand?"

I stared at him, afraid to speak.

"You and Annie are the loves of my life," he breathed. "And I wouldn't change it."

My hands tightened on his wrists. I remembered the man who was holding me. I remembered the fierceness of his love and the way he felt so unwavering and safe. For the first time, I was truly afraid of the idea of leaving. I had loved Mason for who he was, but also because he was the only one who'd ever chosen me. But this—*this* was a home I'd built with my own two hands. I'd made this. It was mine.

There was a life on the other side of the door. A history. A strange disappearance. But in this life, I had something that I'd never had before.

"I need to ask you something." Eamon's voice lowered.

"What?"

He set his forehead against mine, holding me there. "Do you remember me?" He asked the question like he was scared. Like I had an answer that could destroy him. "I don't mean do you have memories of us. I mean, do you *remember* me."

I nodded, and he exhaled, like it was the first time he'd been able to breathe since I'd left.

"I do," I whispered.

He caught my mouth with his, making the space between us come alive, and I melted into him. There was only the burn of his fingers. The heat of his breath. The feeling of his teeth grazing my lip.

I was desperate to feel it. All of it.

My hands found the collar of his shirt, frantically working at the buttons. There wasn't a storm-churned sea of thoughts in my head anymore. There was only this—the way his skin felt under my palms as I pushed the shirt over his shoulders. The searing wake his mouth left on my throat. The way it hurt just a little when he touched me.

His arm came around me, guiding me backward, toward the bedroom. As soon as the door was closed, I broke from him long enough to pull at the buckle of his belt.

His hand pressed to my back, holding me closer to him, and the other reached into the thin white fabric of my nightgown, finding my breast. I exhaled against his mouth, a small cry escaping me. Everywhere he touched me, every place he returned to, was screaming.

I pulled the nightgown over my head and dropped it to the floor. I didn't want to wait. I couldn't.

He kissed me deeper as we leaned back onto the bed, the weight of him pressing the air from my lungs. There was no fumbling. No awkward searching of hands. This wasn't the breathless thrill of discovery. It didn't have the mark of a first time.

This was a homecoming.

He pulled my leg up around him, and he groaned as we came together. My chest rose and fell beneath his, and he stilled for a moment, breaths slowing as his forehead rested against mine again. There was a tear sliding down the bridge of his nose.

"I love you," he breathed.

My hands found his hips, holding him to me. I could feel him, not just inside of me. I could feel him in places that hadn't yet taken shape—all of the images and feelings that were just out of reach.

We moved together like we'd done this hundreds of times, and we had. But we hadn't. He'd never touched *this* body. *These* lips had never kissed him like this. It wasn't gentle, and it wasn't slow; it was deep and earnest. It was full of memories, and I chased them, breath for breath, before they could flicker away.

I'd been wrong about the June who came through that door five years ago. I'd hated her for the choice she made because I thought it was cruel. I thought it careless. But this aching love that was breaking ground inside of me didn't feel selfish. It felt brave.

TWENTY-SEVEN

We were quiet a long time. Long enough for morning to fully break over the fields and fill the room with light.

Eamon lay on his back with me fit against his side, and I pressed my closed mouth to his shoulder, my hand flat on his chest so that I could feel the heartbeat beneath his bones. With every thump, it was saying that he was real. This was real. It was happening.

I didn't want to move, much less speak, afraid that I would disturb that sense of stillness that had found us. It was a fragile, precious thing. A calm that I didn't want to believe would be followed by a storm.

Whatever *this* was, it wasn't simple. I was trying to stitch together the fragments, pull them into one chronological timeline that told a story I could understand. But while the pieces were coming, they weren't coming quickly, and none of them were in order.

I'd opened the red door like every Farrow had. I didn't know that it would change my life forever. In my case, it had changed twice. Now there was one more choice to make, and the only one who could make it was me.

I could still feel the drag of Eamon's touch across my skin. The heaviness of him between my legs. I could smell him in the sheets like I did that first day I woke with the warmth of his arms around me. There had been a part of me, even then, that was waking to this, like opening my eyes after a yearslong sleep.

What was so clear to me now was that Eamon was the only person who had ever really known me. Wholly. Completely. I'd been lucky to have people who loved me. Gran. Birdie. Mason. But there were parts of myself that I'd kept hidden away from them for their sakes as much as mine. I'd found a way to give it all to Eamon.

He was the only one who knew the things I really wanted. The only person I'd never kept them from. But as I lay there, listening to the sound of his breathing, I needed to know if I was that person for him, too.

"I need to ask you something," I whispered.

His fingers sleepily wove through mine on his chest, holding my hand there. "Okay."

I studied the boundary along his collarbone where the sun had darkened his skin. Once I asked it, I wouldn't be able to put the words back into my mouth. Once I heard his answer, I wouldn't be able to unknow it.

"Did you kill Nathaniel Rutherford?"

The question was a small one for the meaning it carried. But my voice didn't waver, and I didn't hesitate. I would remember, eventually, but I needed to know now. And I needed him to be the one to tell me.

He was still for a long moment before his weight shifted in the bed, and then he sat up, making my hand slip from where it was tucked against him. He raked his hair back, his feet touching the floor, and I bit the inside of my cheek.

He was shutting me out again. I could see it in the change of his posture. The way his eyes went to the corner of the room.

I pushed myself up behind him, fitting my body to his. My arms snaked around his middle, my skin pressed to him. He was rigid, but when I set my cheek against his shoulder blade, he relaxed just a little.

"Are you asking because you're trying to decide what kind of man I am?"

"I'm asking because I want to know the truth. All of it."

Eamon set his elbows on his knees and put his face into his hands, breathing through his fingers. When he looked up again, he was half-lit by the window. Slowly, he pulled my hand so that I slid to the edge of the bed beside him. His eyes stared right into mine.

"Are you sure about that?"

I knew that I was. "You can trust me," I said, and I meant it. I didn't know if there was anything he could say that would change that. Not now.

He fell silent again, his gaze moving over the room, as if he were trying to find the words. I waited, afraid that if I said anything else, he would change his mind. When he shifted, turning to face me, his hand came to my cheek, thumb tracing the curve of my bottom lip before it followed the line of my jaw.

I wasn't sure what that look on his face was. Concern, or compassion, maybe. There was a gentleness, a caution, in his voice.

"I didn't kill him, love," he said. "You did."

And as soon as the words left his mouth, I remembered.

TWENTY-EIGHT

JUNE 21, 1950

The flash of a bulb goes off, a crackling, fizzing sound that fills my head. The wash of the bright white light fades, and the soft glow of the tent settles back over me. The tinny strum of a banjo rings out, and bodies move on the dance floor; the wind catches my dress. The photographer snaps another photograph, and the bulb sizzles again.

I'm at the Midsummer Faire.

Laughter drifts through the syrupy air, and I smile when I see Margaret's and Esther's faces push through the crowd.

Margaret is out of breath, her face flushed from dancing. "Where's Eamon?"

"At the house," I answer. "Callie's gotten out again."

She frowns, eyes dropping to my shoulder. "You want me to take her?"

I glance down, just registering the warm, heavy weight I'm carrying. A small Annie is propped on my hip, her legs dangling and her arms curled into me. She's asleep on my chest.

"That's okay," I say, thinking that I like this feeling, even though my arms are aching. I've been holding her for more than an hour.

Esther is already tying a scarf around her head. "You girls ready?"

We follow her out to the truck, the sound of the Faire bleeding away behind us, and we drive with the windows down. There's a pastel sunset just beginning to gather over the mountains, and the fireflies are blinking when we pull up to the flower farm.

By the time we're out of the truck, Annie is awake, hopping up and down the steps barefoot while we eat cake. We talk about the tobacco harvest and an overdue trip to Asheville, and then I'm scooping Annie up into my arms again. I want to make it home before dark.

"Sure you don't want me to drive you?" Esther asks from her rocking chair.

I look at Annie, who's pulling one of the ribbons from her hair. The cake is like catnip, and it will have her up late if I don't get some of her energy out.

"No, it's a good night for a walk," I say.

It's not quite twilight. The bugs in the flower fields are loud as we make our way to the back corner of the land, and Annie skips ahead of me on the overgrown path until we reach the river. There's a small footbridge that serves as a shortcut through these fields, but it's not even in sight when she stops to inspect a giant silk moth that's clung to the trunk of a nearby tree. I sink down beside her, letting my finger come beneath its furry legs, and it climbs on, wings fluttering.

I hold it between us, and Annie's honey brown eyes widen in wonder, making me smile.

It's moments like these that I'm afraid to miss. It's moments like these that make me sure about what I have to do.

The moth takes off, teetering in the air as it flies away, and Annie watches it go. The water of the river is a glowing blue now, ready to fall dark in the next hour.

"Evening, Mrs. Stone."

The southern-sweet voice is slippery in the dimming light, but I immediately recognize it. I've heard it pouring from the open doors of the church many times. I've heard it in my nightmares.

I turn to see Nathaniel Rutherford standing on the path at the top of the riverbank. His nice suit is pressed, his hat in his hands, and even from here, I can see the shine of his boots. I hadn't seen him at the Faire, but I'd felt his presence. Somehow, he always seemed to be near. Watching.

I swallow hard. This isn't the first time I've found him on Esther's farm. But that feverish gaze that hovers behind his eyes is fixed on me, and tonight, it feels a little more crazed.

Did he follow us?

There's a moment when a prick of fear climbs up my spine, and I'm suddenly reaching out to put a protective hand on Annie. We're too far from the house to be heard if I call out, I realize.

"I think it's about time we talk," he says, taking a step off the path.

"We're on our way home. Eamon's expecting us."

He smiles, as if amused, but his eyes are still flat and dead. When he takes another step, it's a little unsteady, and it occurs to me that he's been drinking.

"For we know him that hath said, 'Vengeance belongeth unto me,'" Nathaniel begins. "'I will recompense,' saith the Lord. And again, the Lord shall judge his people."

My pulse quickens when he moves again, coming slowly down the bank toward us.

"We really do need to get back. Have a good night, Mr. Rutherford." I take Annie's hand and try to step past him, but he moves faster, blocking me.

I look around us, not sure what to do. There's no easy way to get past him, especially with Annie in my arms, and though the river is crossable, it's deep. What if the current is too strong? What if she slips from my arms and I lose her under the water?

"That's what this is, isn't it?" he continues. "Vengeance?"

"I don't know what you're talking about." My voice is shaking now.

"I know who you are, June. I know my own flesh and blood when I see it."

For a moment, I'm not sure if I can read the tone in his voice. But that look on his face doesn't change. He knows. We've danced around it many times before, but he knows who I am.

"You are a seed planted by my own sin. An abomination. The both of you."

I look to the trees up the slope. We're closer to the flower farm than we are to home, and we've walked that shortcut through the fields countless times. Annie could find her way back to the house, I tell myself. She knows not to go down to the water without me. She'd stay on the path until she saw the lights of Esther's porch.

"Annie, go back to the farm," I say, trying to push her toward the trees. But she doesn't move.

"He sent Susanna to torment me," Nathaniel continues. "The devil knew that I was weak."

Again, I nudge her. "Go, baby."

But she's watching him, transfixed, a single blade of grass clutched in her little fist.

"I knew there was something evil about your mother the first time I saw her. In my pride, I thought I could overcome it."

His feet come down the bank, half sliding toward me, and before I know what he's doing, his hands are gripping my shoulders tight.

I gasp, my eyes going wide.

Fingers twist into the fabric of my white dress, and I stumble backward, trying to keep my balance. "Annie! Run!"

She finally does, her dress like a flame in the twilight. I see it disappear in the brush a second later.

"I loved her." Nathaniel is crying now, his face contorted. He shakes me, hard. "I loved her more than I loved God. And that is the worst kind of sin."

He shoves me back with so much force that I crash into the shallows behind me. Rocks scrape down my back, and the current pulls my weight, but I grasp for a hold on the bank. He's on me a second later, yanking me back up.

"There's no way to clean that stain." The words twist. "I tried. I tried to clean it."

A sharp pain lances the nape of my neck, and I realize he has my hair in his fist. "Please!" I sob. "Stop!"

Nathaniel's eyes clear for only a moment before he goes still. His grip on me is like a vise as he looks down into my face.

"I took her down to the river and I held her under the water until she stopped screaming," he whispers.

Another cry breaks inside of me. "Please."

"And then I buried her under the oak tree." He sniffs. "But God's punishment isn't over for me yet. It can't be until I put it right."

I claw at his hands, tear at his shirt.

"It's all right," he says, gently, looking into my eyes. "I baptize you, June Rutherford." He plunges me down beneath the surface and the sunset disappears, replaced by rushing water. My feet slip out from under me, and then he pulls me up again. I scream, choking.

"In the name of the Father, the Son, and the Holy—"

He shoves me back down, and I scratch at his arms, the outline of him a wavering black blot above me. I kick, but I can't get my footing. I thrash, but his grip is too tight. His weight presses down on top of me harder. He pins me there, and over the roar of the water, I think I can hear him sobbing.

I understand now what is happening. I'm going to die.

Another scream is trapped in my chest and bubbles race from my mouth as I let go of him, hands desperately searching for something, anything to grab hold of. I find it when the pain in my lungs feels like it's going to explode. The black pushes in around my vision, my legs going numb.

I wrap my fingers around the shape, and with every last bit of strength inside of me, I wrench my arm through the water, swinging it in an arc until it breaks the surface and collides with his temple.

Nathaniel's hands suddenly loosen. He stumbles back, and I feel myself floating, the current pulling me from him.

I come up with a painful gasp and I'm gagging, hunched over with the rock still clutched to my chest.

Nathaniel makes a sound, and I blink furiously, the river water blurring my vision, to see him still standing. He has one hand pressed to his bleeding head. Something escapes his lips, and then he's lunging toward me.

I watch as he stumbles, falling to his knees, and my body feels so heavy that I'm sure I'm going to faint. I'm sure that at any minute, everything will go black.

I heave, raising the rock over my head with both hands. And when I bring it down, it's with a horrifying sound that tears from my throat. I hit him again. And again. I hit him even after I realize he's not moving. It's not until the rock slips from my blood-soaked fingers that I fall to the bank.

I'm flat on my back, and when my head rolls to the side, I see him looking at me. But there's no life left in those empty eyes. I don't have to check to know that he's dead.

A snap in the trees makes me scramble back to my hands and knees, and suddenly I see that little white flame.

Annie is standing on the path, watching. She blinks once. Then again.

Only then does it come to me, what I've just done. At my feet, Nathaniel Rutherford lies motionless, the water parting around his body in the shallows. His blood is everywhere. My hands, my arms, my dress. It's spattered like paint on the rocks.

I scoot away from it, suddenly sick, and I vomit on the shore, my hair tangled and plastered to my face. I've barely finished when I get back to my feet and climb the slope. Then I'm picking Annie up, and I run.

I don't look back when we make it to the trees. I don't slow, despite the burning tremble in my legs. I cross the footbridge and lift Annie over the fence of the Grangers' west pasture, then I keep running. I don't stop until I see the smoke trailing from our chimney.

"Eamon!" I scream his name as I disappear into the tobacco. "Eamon!"

My steps finally begin to drag, a sharp pain surfacing in the center of my right foot. Somewhere, I've lost a shoe.

"Eamon!"

His name crumbles on another cry, and I break through the edge of the field, just as the back screen door flies open. It slams against the house, and I can see him. He's a black silhouette against the kitchen light.

Annie is crying now, clinging to me, but I'm sure I'm going to drop her. I sink to the ground before I do, my knees scraping in the dirt.

Eamon is coming down the steps a second later. "June?"

I can't breathe.

"June?" He pulls Annie from my arms. "What happened?"

I didn't notice until now that her white dress is dotted with the blood that covers me. He's frantically pulling it off of her.

"Where are you hurt, love?" He's panicked, searching her body for the source of the blood.

"She's okay." I feel my mouth say the words but I can't hear them. "She's okay." The words stick to my tongue, because that's all that matters. "She's okay. She's okay. She's okay."

Eamon stands. Carries her into the house. Then he's taking hold of me, getting me to my feet, but I instantly collapse against him and he catches me in his arms.

"June?" He sounds so scared. "Tell me what happened." Now his hands are all over me, lifting my hair, unbuttoning my dress.

"I killed him," I say, my mouth numb.

"What?"

We're in the house now, and I can finally see his face.

"Nathaniel Rutherford. I killed him."

He sets me down in the chair, coming down onto his knees in front of me. "Where? How?"

"He followed us. He tried to—" My whole body shakes with a silent cry. "He tried to drown me in the river."

Eamon is suddenly so still that it doesn't look like he's breathing. He's staring at the center of my chest, hands still holding on to me. When his eyes finally lift, the panic in them is gone.

"Listen to me," he says.

I double over, crying again.

"June," he says, more firmly. "Take a breath."

I swallow, trying to do as he says. I'm shaking so badly.

"Tell me exactly where he is."

I try to think. "At the bend before the footbridge. He's down by the water."

Eamon stands, going to the stove, and I hear him light it. Then he's propping open the back door and hauling in the two buckets of water from outside. I watch in a daze as he dumps them into the small tub beside Annie's nook.

The kettle is beginning to hum when he fetches Annie's stained dress from outside and pulls the remaining ribbon from her hair. He takes her stockings, her shoes. Then he does the same to me, gently helping me out of the dress until I'm sitting naked on the chair.

I can't move. I can't even ask what he's doing, but I realize once the fire is going and he throws our clothes into it. That's when I finally notice my hands. The blood caked beneath my fingernails.

I move to the sink robotically, turning on the tap and shoving my hands beneath the water. I scrub violently, watching the ribbon of red circle the drain.

The kettle squeals, and Eamon pours it into the tub before he comes back for me. I wrap my arms around his neck and he lifts me, lowering me into it. He's setting Annie into my arms next, and the water sloshes over the side as she burrows into me. She's not crying anymore. Neither am I.

"If anyone knocks on that door, you tell them I've gone to help Esther with her truck. You get her cleaned up. Put her to bed."

I think I nod.

"June? Do you understand?"

"Yes."

He brushes a hand over Annie's head and kisses me, but his lips linger on my forehead just a little longer than usual. Then he's walking across the sitting room. He's disappearing out the back door.

The only sound is the crackle of the fire as I stare into the flames, watching my dress burn.

TWENTY-NINE

The night played out in my head one frame at a time. The wood plank fence that stretched along the flower fields. The aching cold in my hands as I stood over Nathaniel's body. The fireflies blinking in the dark as I ran. The clearest part of the entire thing was the sight of those clothes burning in the fireplace. I could almost smell them, even now.

"When I got to the river, it was dark," Eamon began. "I didn't see anyone on the road, but I kept my light off anyway, just to be safe. No one saw me."

I stood before the bedroom window, watching Callie graze in the paddock.

"I found him right where you told me he'd be—at the bend before the footbridge." Eamon appeared at the corner of my vision as he leaned into the wall beside the window. "I could tell by looking at him that it would be suspicious. There were marks on his arms, his face. I think maybe from when you were . . ." He couldn't finish. "If someone found him like that, there would be questions. So, I decided to drag him downriver and send his body over the falls so that it would look like an accident. Maybe he'd had too much to drink at the Faire, or maybe he'd slipped and fell. There'd been a lot of rain that week, so the river was high. The current was strong."

So, Eamon wasn't a killer, but he wasn't innocent, either. We'd done this thing together.

"I put him into the water, and I thought I was close enough to the drop to be safe. It was so dark that it was hard to see, and I didn't realize there was a fallen tree up the bank. He got caught downstream, and at first light, he was spotted by a fisherman."

I tried not to imagine Nathaniel's pale, tangled body half-submerged in the water.

"Sam came by late that night after they'd gotten the message that Mimi Granger had left at the sheriff's office. Luckily, I was already back, and we told him we'd been home all night. "But then people came forward saying they'd seen me arguing with Nathaniel in the weeks leading up to his death. Then when it got out that Mimi Granger had seen you that night, it drew even more attention."

I closed my eyes, seeing it. Hearing it. My labored breaths as I tore through the sea of waist-high alfalfa, Annie in my arms. The pain in my foot from losing my shoe—the same shoe Mimi had found in her tedder, months later.

"No one had any reason to believe it. I don't think they were even seriously considering what Mimi said until you left. The timing was suspicious, and the investigation went on, but no one could get ahold of you. When you didn't come back, they started asking more questions."

"Why didn't we go to the police? Why didn't we just tell the truth?"

"No one in Jasper would believe what really happened. No one was going to sit on a jury and fairly consider that the minister was a bad man or that he wanted to hurt you. That's not the Nathaniel this town knew."

The only other person alive who did was Caleb. That grim flash in his eyes when he talked about his father, *our* father, was unmistakable.

"I can't believe I pulled you into this," I murmured.

"You didn't pull me into anything, June. You needed my help, and I gave it to you. You would have done the same for me."

"But Caleb knows we're lying, Eamon. He looked me in the eye and he told me he knows."

"He can't prove anything."

I wasn't convinced. He had more reason than ever to pursue us as suspects, especially after what he'd found in the house. It wasn't proof, but it only corroborated that we had more interest in Nathaniel than we pretended to.

"He was willing to break the law, break into our *home*, to look for evidence."

Eamon's expression changed. I hadn't meant to say *our*, but I had.

"What if Annie had been here?" My voice rose.

"She wasn't."

"What if he knows who I really am?"

"He *doesn't*."

I pressed my fingers to my mouth, shaking my head. "There's something else here. I just can't see it yet."

That's what I'd been thinking for days. There was still more that I'd been hiding from everyone. Why leave at such a precarious time unless I had to?

The memories weren't coming fast enough to answer all of my questions. And I didn't know how much time we had to figure it out. *1912, 1946, 1950, 1951.*

The years alternated in my mind, like flash cards.

Four years, four crossings, but my crossing in 1951 couldn't have been predicted. Not unless it was planned.

I could see the two threads of my life.

The first was up to 2024, when I'd seemingly fallen for Mason and then went through the door only to meet Eamon. I made my choice. Lived five years with him, and then I'd left.

The second thread was the one I was living now. It spanned the same life until 2023, when my path was altered. I'd gone through the door early, and I'd never let myself fall in love with Mason. But somehow, I ended up where the first thread had ended.

Esther had called it an overlap, but it was more like folding time.

My eyes widened.

Eamon was watching me carefully now. "What?"

"Folding time," I said, still trying to chase the thought down. "They're becoming one. That's why I'm losing memories. That's why, in 2022, I started having episodes the exact month and day that I left here."

"June, I'm not following."

I pulled at the thought surfacing in the back of my mind, trying to gently coax it forward. I walked to the kitchen with heavy steps, yanking the drawers open until I found what I was looking for—a spool of thick brown twine and a paring knife.

I set the knife down on the small kitchen table, and Eamon came to stand on the other side, studying me. I took the end of the twine and tugged until it was strung through the air between us. Then I pulled at its end with my fingers until the threads began unraveling.

"The curse isn't the door, Eamon. It's the splitting of time. Esther says that our minds are like a fraying rope." I let the loosening fibers work their way down the length of the twine. "For every Farrow, it's the same. Because we are one long, unraveling cord. Esther, Margaret, Susanna, me . . . we're all connected."

"All right." He nodded, catching on.

"But how do you fix a fraying rope?"

"You . . ." He paused. "You cut it."

"Exactly." I picked up the knife, slicing through the twine in one motion. It left a clean edge. "Then you tie it off or burn it, whatever. You stop the unraveling."

I twisted the cord in my fingers, still thinking. "That's what I was trying to do. Fix it before Annie ever goes through the door."

"But how?"

"I don't know." I dropped the twine, pacing now. "But it wasn't an accident that I came here. It wasn't an accident *when* I came here."

I'd been retracing my steps through the unfolding narrative of my life and the winding path that had led me here. From the beginning, I'd been following a trail.

"I didn't just see the door one day and walk through it. I'd gotten the photograph first. That's what started all of this. From there, I couldn't let it go. My mother, the baptism records, the envelope with your address . . . they were like breadcrumbs. That's what made me cross, and when I did, I created a timeline that overlapped the other one."

"You could have ended up anywhere, though, right? How did you end up here?"

I sucked in a breath, putting it together. I reached up, clasping the locket watch in my fist. The door had brought me to 1951 because that's what the locket was set to. The locket that Gran gave me.

"It was Margaret." I whispered the name. "I couldn't have done it alone. I would have needed help getting myself back here, because you can't go to a time when you already exist."

That was the thing I'd missed. The fact that the locket watch was set to 1951 wasn't an accident. It had been set that way. By Gran.

We pulled Annie from bed and got in the truck, driving the three miles to the flower farm as the sun rose over the Blue Ridge Mountains. By the time I was knocking on the beveled glass window of Esther's front door, the memory was pushing into the light of my mind. It was only fragments, but it was there.

> *I need your help.*
> *I'm speaking the words, but at first, I can't completely hear them. I look around and see that I'm standing in the shade of one of the greenhouses with Margaret. Her face is softer, younger, as she looks up at me.*
> *I'm watching over my shoulder, afraid that someone will hear us.*
> *"I need your help," I say.*

Esther's door opened, making the memory vanish, and I was back on the porch again, standing beside Eamon. The younger Margaret was gone, but the slightly older one stood before me now.

"Morning." She tucked Annie's hair behind her ear, letting the door open wider. "What are y'all doin' here so early?"

Annie ran inside, but Eamon and I didn't move.

She smiled. "June? You okay?"

"What's all this?" Esther appeared in the hallway behind her, her hair long over her shoulder. She was missing her apron, too.

"It was you," I said, gaze still pinned on Margaret. "Wasn't it?"

Margaret gave a confused laugh. "What?"

"I came to you." I pulled the memory back to the front of my mind. "I told you I needed your help."

The smile on her face faltered then.

Esther looked between us. "Help with what? What are you talking about?"

I stared at Margaret. "What did you do?"

"Margaret?" Esther prodded.

Margaret was wringing her hands now, bottom lip trembling as she shot a glance at Eamon.

I took a measured step toward her. "You knew all this time."

"I can't." Her voice scraped. "I promised I wouldn't."

"Tell me!" I took hold of her arms, squeezing.

"I promised *you*!" she cried, tearing away from me.

I let her go, and she stumbled into the porch railing, catching herself. She looked at the three of us with wide, glassy eyes.

"I'm not supposed to say anything. Not until you choose."

"I gave *you* the envelope with the bluebell, didn't I?" I said it out loud as it dawned on me. "I told you to help me come back here."

Her red face was streaked with tears now, her hair falling from its braid.

"Margaret," I said, more gently. "Tell me."

When Annie appeared in the doorway, Esther shooed her back into the house. Then she came outside and closed the door.

Margaret wiped her face. "You said you had an idea about how to—" She stopped herself.

"It's all right, honey." Esther rubbed her back, smoothing her braid. "Take your time."

"You had an idea about how to make it so Annie wouldn't ever get sick, but you couldn't tell Eamon because he wouldn't understand. You said he'd stop you from doing what you had to do. You begged me."

I could see it. I could almost hear my own voice saying the words. The memory was trickling in now. Margaret whispering. The slam of a door somewhere.

"You told me to keep the envelope safe. For a long time. I'm supposed to give it to you in 2022 so that you'll come back here."

I shook my head. "Why didn't you just tell me? Why not just explain?"

Now I was asking her to account for things she hadn't yet done. That wasn't fair. I knew it wasn't, but I also couldn't make sense of this.

"You said that you couldn't know anything until the right time. If you did, it could change things. Set things off course. I'm not supposed to tell you anything until you start to remember."

My mind raced, trying to match the timeline with the one that would play out more than seventy years from now.

"But then so much time went by that . . ." Her voice broke. "I thought maybe I'd messed it up, somehow."

"What exactly did I tell you to do, Margaret?"

"I'm supposed to give you the locket. You told me to set it to 1951, not before, so that you wouldn't risk returning to a time where you were still here."

You cannot go where you already exist.

That was one of the rules.

I'd kept the hallucinations from Gran and Birdie for nearly a year. What Margaret couldn't have known was when she would die. Mailing the photograph might have been her last-ditch effort. Her Hail Mary, hoping it would start the chain of events before it was too late.

All of this was *my* doing.

"Where did I go when I left, Margaret?"

She stared at her shoes, wiping her nose with her sleeve.

"It's done now. I'm here. There's no reason to keep it from me."

She sniffed. "I need a piece of paper."

Esther opened the door, and we followed Margaret inside. She took a piece of paper from the desk drawer in the sitting room and sat down, with us peering over her shoulder. We watched as she drew two waving, intertwined lines that looked like a rope. It was eerily similar to the one I'd imagined when I was trying to explain it to Eamon.

He glanced up at me, thinking the same thing.

"This is the Farrow line. Two woven times." Margaret's face was still swollen, but she was calm now. Focused. She put an X at the right end of the rope and wrote 1950 above it. "This is where it becomes *one* timeline."

"I don't understand."

From the X, she drew a single straight line. "When you left, you sent yourself to a place on the timeline that overlaps your life here. You thought that would make it so there was only one time."

"This is insane," Eamon muttered, his irritation not hidden.

"We made the plan, and you were going to do it the next time you saw the door. But then that night at the Midsummer Faire . . ." Her mouth twisted. "I tried to convince you to wait until things had died down, but you were worried that if Caleb found out the truth about that night, you'd be arrested. If that happened, you wouldn't be able to cross like you planned."

We were all quiet, waiting.

"The next time the door appeared, you left."

"Okay, but *where* did I go, Margaret?"

She bit her bottom lip. "To 2022."

Esther's eyes went wide.

Margaret didn't drop her gaze from mine. "You went to a place you already exist."

I shook my head. "So I'm . . . gone."

If there couldn't be two of me, then I had to be. But this, what she was saying, that meant that I'd willingly ended my own timeline. My own life.

"What do you mean, gone?" Eamon's voice was barely audible.

Beside me, Esther pressed a hand to her mouth.

"I killed myself?" I said it out loud.

"No." Margaret's eyes widened. "You found a loophole. That's all."

My eyes narrowed on her. That was the word Esther had used.

"But what if it didn't work? What if I was wrong about all of it?"

"You weren't," she said. "It's already working."

"What do you mean?"

She pointed to the straight, single line on the page before she picked up the pen. She continued the line by branching it into two that didn't intertwine.

"There's only one timeline now. This one and the one on the other side of the door. They can't exist together anymore because you ended the fray. That's why you're losing memories."

I hadn't told Margaret that.

"That's what's happening right? You're losing memories?"

Esther looked at me.

"So, what? I'm just going to lose my entire life?"

"Only if you don't go back. You're going to choose which life you want to live. If you stay here, then yes, you'll lose your memories of that life. If you choose to go back, you'll lose the ones from this one. You can't have both. Not anymore."

"Are you saying it actually worked?"

She nodded. "Yes. Once you lose all your memories of one life, your mind will exist only in one time. There's no more fraying rope."

I swallowed hard, chest burning with the breath I was holding. "So, it's just . . . over?"

"For you and Annie, yes. Annie is an extension of your timeline. You thought that if you stopped the unraveling, it would keep hers from unraveling, too. If there's no longer two timelines, the hope is that there's no door connecting them. If there's no door, Annie will never go through it."

The four of us sat there in silence, the clock on the wall ticking.

"You said it was important that you had the choice." Margaret's voice softened.

When Esther had first told me that, there *was* no choice. I was going back, no matter what. And I still could. But if I crossed again to 2023, there was no returning. That would be my third crossing, and I'd forget my life here. I'd forget Eamon and Annie. If I stayed, I'd erase from my mind the entire life I'd lived before I got here. I'd never see Mason or Birdie again.

"You knew everything," I whispered. "All this time."

I'd never doubted Gran's love for me, but it went deeper and further back than I ever could have imagined. She had known that I would be left in Jasper as a baby. She probably knew the exact night that the sheriff would knock on her door with me in his arms. She'd been the person I trusted with this. The person I knew I could count on. That had always been true.

Susanna had gone to Esther to help her save her child. I'd gone to Gran.

The plan had been a detailed one. It was thought through, but it wasn't without risk. The margin of error was enormous. The only person Margaret had trusted with the truth was Birdie. The envelope she'd delivered to me that night, couriered through time by Margaret, had that been her fail-safe? The locket, too, had been entrusted to her.

I made a promise. One I've kept for a very long time, Birdie had said.

"Who is Birdie?" I whispered.

Margaret didn't look at me. Instead, her gaze went across the sitting room, to where Annie was standing on the stool in the kitchen. She was reaching for the jelly jar on the counter.

The hardening stone in my throat plummeted into my stomach, and I stared at her, her blond hair like glowing threads of gold in the light coming through the window.

Birdie.

She'd been a fixture in my life as long as I could remember. The third member of our family. Gran's oldest friend. But she'd been more than that, hadn't she?

Annie Bird.

I could hear the name ringing in my head. I'd called her that, and looking at her now, I *could* see it. There was a sparkle in Annie's eyes that hadn't changed in seventy-two years. That golden-silver hair. The rise of her cheekbones. It was all there. In the face of my daughter.

I took a step toward her, then another, not stopping until I could touch her. She held the jelly-coated spoon in her hand, distractedly smearing it across a piece of bread as I wrapped her in my arms, a steady stream of tears falling into her hair.

I couldn't begin to wrap my head around any of this. The woman I'd raised had then raised me. Then she'd sent me back in time to herself, and to her father. Did that make this a loop? A never-ending story destined to replay over and over again? All that time, she remembered me. She was just waiting for me to remember her.

"June," Esther said, her voice frail. She was holding back the curtain of the window, watching as a cloud of dust drifted over the trees.

In the distance, another one appeared behind it. Cars on the road. And they were moving fast.

A faint twist ignited in my chest, the hair standing up on the back of my neck.

The sound of the sirens surfaced just before we saw them—police cars.

THIRTY

Annie looked up at me, the spoon still clutched in her hand. Across the room, Eamon had gone white.

The sound of the sirens grew louder as I picked Annie up, hugging her to me just long enough to kiss her face. Then I crossed the room, eyes on Margaret.

"Take her," I breathed, setting Annie into her arms. "Go to the barn."

Margaret didn't hesitate, heading straight for the back door. Annie was still watching me over her shoulder before the screen door slammed and they disappeared.

"Eamon, listen," I said.

He wasn't looking at me. His gaze traveled down the hallway, where Esther was unlocking a cabinet at the bottom of the stairs.

Through the window, I watched as the cars pulled into the drive too fast, slamming on their brakes, and then the doors were opening. I saw Caleb first. He was wearing his uniform again, his hat fixed on his head and his pistol at his hip. When the driver of the second car got out, I recognized Sam's dark mustache.

. I stood in the open doorway, my heart breaking into a sprint. He wasn't here for Eamon. Caleb's eyes were fixed on me.

The door to the cabinet opened behind me, and I froze when I saw Esther take a rifle from inside. In the next breath, she was handing it to Eamon.

"Don't!" I tried to catch hold of him as he stalked outside, but he pulled free of me, going down the steps. "Eamon, don't!"

Caleb and Sam both drew their guns the moment they saw him. Eamon had the rifle at his side, ready to raise it.

Sam's hand lifted in the air. "Eamon, let's just calm down now."

"Get the hell out of here." Eamon's eyes were on Caleb.

But that smug look on Caleb's face told me everything I needed to know. Somehow, he'd gotten what he needed, and now he'd come for me.

He pulled the handcuffs from his belt just as I heard Margaret's voice behind us. "Annie!"

I turned. Annie was running up the fence toward us, Margaret chasing after her. I caught Annie in my arms, and when Caleb took a step in our direction, Eamon lifted his gun. In an instant, Sam and Caleb raised their pistols. Both were pointed at Eamon.

I turned my body, putting myself between Annie and the aim of the guns.

"Daddy?" Annie's voice was bent. She stared at him over my shoulder.

I lifted a hand slowly, setting it on his arm. "Eamon." I kept my voice even. "Stop."

He didn't look at me, every muscle in his body coiled so tight that the gun in his hands didn't so much as shake.

My fingers curled around his wrist. "You pull that trigger, and she's alone," I whispered. "Do you understand?"

His chest rose and fell for several seconds before his grip loosened on the barrel.

"Put it down before one of them shoots you."

After another breath, he listened. The barrel lowered, the butt of the gun still pressed to his shoulder, and Sam moved closer, placing himself in front of Eamon with his aim still trained at his chest.

Caleb's eyes drifted to me. "Sam, get the kid so I can place Mrs. Stone under arrest."

Sam holstered his gun, reluctantly moving toward us. Annie's fingernails scratched around my neck as he reached to pull her from my arms. She screamed.

"June Stone, I am placing you under arrest for the murder of Nathaniel Rutherford," Caleb began.

Sam tried to take hold of Annie again, and she wrapped her legs around me, hands tangling in my hair.

When she screamed again, Eamon's fist flew through the air, catching Sam in the face with so much force that he went to his knees. He wrenched Sam up by the collar, throwing him back.

I ducked, tightening my arms around Annie, one hand holding the back of her head as she cried into me. The distinct click of metal was what made them stop swinging. From where I was crouched, I looked up over Annie's hair to see Caleb with his gun drawn. Now it was pointed at me.

Eamon still had Sam by the shirt, and I could see him thinking it—wondering if he could get to Caleb before he pulled that trigger.

Margaret's feet were moving slowly in my direction, and I peeled Annie off of me, handing her over before I stood.

"Mama!" She was looking at me now with wide, terrified eyes.

"It's okay, baby." I smiled through tears as Margaret carried her, still screaming, into the house.

"Go inside, Esther." My voice wavered.

She didn't move, looking from me to Eamon.

Eamon had his hands lifted in the air now, Sam standing between him and Caleb. There were a few seconds where I didn't know what he was going to do. Charge him? Kill him? Get the two of us in the truck and run?

A sharp, familiar tingle raced up my spine, spreading until an unmistakable feeling settled inside of me. The sensation made me still,

and a cold wind bled into the hot air, twisting around the place where
I stood.

Caleb's voice drew on, indecipherable as the world stopped turning. And it did. Time stopped, and I could feel it—that same pull of
gravity. The bloom of brightness behind my vision. That floating feeling that filled my body. Slowly, I turned my head toward the fields,
knowing exactly what I would see there.

The red door.

It stood among the dahlias, their heavy blooms rocking back and
forth. The frame of the door looked like it had just sprung from the
earth, the bronze handle glinting beneath a tangle of vines bursting
through the door's cracks.

The flash of sunlight on the cuffs in Caleb's hand made me blink
again, but I could only faintly hear him talking. It was like the sound
of running water now, and the only thing that pierced that resonance
in my head was Eamon's voice saying my name.

"June?"

I blinked, eyes heavy. He looked at me over Sam's shoulder, his
brow furrowed as he studied me.

He followed my gaze in the direction of the fields, but he couldn't
see it. None of them could. No one, except Esther.

She stared at me, one hand balled in her skirt, and once Eamon
saw her, he put it together. He glanced again to the field. It was empty
to him, but he knew.

"Is it there?" he asked, voice tight.

Caleb looked between us, suspicion gathering behind his eyes. "Is
what there?"

I nodded, throat aching. I couldn't speak.

Eamon swallowed. "Go."

I stared at him as two tears fell in tandem down my cheeks. He was
telling me to leave. To save myself. But if I did, I'd never be able to
come back.

"*Go,*" he said again.

In a fraction of a second, two paths unfolded before me. The one

I'd seen in those memories of Mason, something I'd always secretly wanted. And then there was this one, with Eamon. A simple existence in the little house on Hayward Gap Road in the time I actually belonged.

It was such an easy thing—that choice. I'd already made it.

I smiled, meeting his eyes for another second, before I turned, walking straight toward Caleb. I could hear Margaret crying inside the house.

"June." Eamon's voice rose, his breaths coming quicker now. "June, don't."

But I was already holding my hands out in front of me. I locked eyes with Eamon as Caleb fit the handcuffs around my wrists.

"I love you." My mouth moved around the words, but I couldn't hear them.

"June!"

Caleb pulled me toward the car, and I closed my eyes, trying to breathe through the cry that was climbing up my throat. He put me in the back seat as Esther stood on the steps, staring helplessly.

The door slammed closed, and then the engine was running.

I could feel Eamon being torn from me as the car pulled onto the road. He was the knotted rope that had pulled me from one time to the next.

I didn't look back out that window as we reached the hill. I didn't want to see him or the house or the farm grow small. There were none of those things where I was going.

Instead, I let my eyes fall on the field, where the flowers grew, a calm flooding through me.

The red door was gone.

THIRTY-ONE

"You lied, June. And now you're goin' to pay for it."

The tone of Caleb's voice was flat as we turned right onto the river road, away from town. When Sam's car went the opposite direction, my stomach turned.

Caleb's hands gripped the steering wheel, his frame swaying left to right as the car rocked over the uneven road. I could feel him looking at me in the rearview mirror now. Those were the same eyes that had bored into me across the table at the police station. The same ones that had followed me at the Midsummer Faire.

Caleb knew he'd won, and he wanted to watch, second by second, as I realized it.

"The truth has a way of makin' itself known, doesn't it?" he said, reaching into the glove compartment for an amber glass bottle. It looked like whiskey. "My father taught me that, and it's somethin' I've never understood about people. It doesn't matter how small the town is or how well you cover things up, there are always traces left behind. There's always someone out there who saw somethin' or knows somethin' or heard somethin'. It's only a matter of time before it washes up."

He took a long drink from the bottle before he turned the wheel, taking us onto one of the county roads that wound deep into the hills. The sweet, oaky smell of the whiskey filled the car.

"I never liked you. Mostly because I had to keep an eye on my father once you came to town. He was erratic, possessed by this idea that you weren't who you said you were. I have to say, I agree with him, June. So, imagine my surprise when I found that picture of him in your house." His hand gestured to something in the front seat.

I leaned forward just enough to see it. The stack of papers he'd taken from my bedroom were sitting on the closed folder beside him, the photograph of Nathaniel and Susanna, our parents, on top.

"I had to ask myself. Why would this woman have that photograph?"

"Susanna was family," I said.

According to what the town knew, that was true. I was a relative of the Farrows from Norfolk, Virginia, just like she'd been.

"Maybe. Or maybe there's more to it than that."

I met his eyes in the mirror.

"This picture got me thinkin'. All this mystery about that shoe and no one being in total agreement about exactly what you were wearin' that night. I hadn't thought about the photographer."

The white-hot flash of the bulb ignited in my mind again. I could smell the smoke from the spark. The photographer from the *Jasper Chronicle* had been there that night. Taking pictures for the paper.

I clenched my teeth.

Caleb reached into the folder on the seat and raised something in the air, handing it to me. I pulled it into my lap, my heart sinking. It was a blown-up black-and-white photograph of the Midsummer Faire in 1950. The image was of the dance floor, a blur of people smudged across the frame. But in the background, I was in focus. I stood beside one of the tent poles, Annie asleep in my arms. We were both wearing what looked like white dresses, and I was wearing those shoes. They were exact matches to the one Caleb had at the police station. The one I said I'd never owned or seen before.

"How're you gonna explain that to a jury, June?" Caleb laughed, taking another sip of whiskey.

He was right. He had what he needed. There was a recorded tape of me saying I'd never seen that shoe before, and a photograph to prove I was lying. Then there was Mimi's statement. The items he'd found in my house. The reports of Eamon threatening Nathaniel. It was only a matter of time before they arrested him, too.

"What'd you do with the dress? Burn it?" he asked.

Those flames were like beacons behind my eyes, their glare making me wince. I could still see Eamon's black shape as he crouched before them, feeding our clothes to the fire.

"I thought it was Eamon who killed him and you who'd helped cover it up." Caleb continued. "But now I'm thinkin' you're the one who did it. Those scratches on his arms and his neck. That's a woman's work."

Caleb's foot pressed the gas, and the car picked up speed, taking the curves faster.

My hands pulled against the cuffs, metal biting into bone. "Where are we going?" I said, the prickling fear constricting my throat.

He ignored me, dumping the rest of the whiskey into his mouth. "Part of me understood when I saw you—why he couldn't leave you alone."

I braced myself.

"It's not right." He shook his head, voice straining. "It's not right how much you look like her."

I remembered that crazed glint in Nathaniel's eyes as he pushed me down into the water. The unnerving tone of his voice. He'd known. Somehow, he'd known. The question was how much did Caleb remember about our mother? And how much truth was there in what Esther had said about what was passed down in the blood? My own veins were filled with it, too.

"Why do you look like her?" His voice changed with the question. It took on an unnatural tone that made me shiver.

His eyes were on me again, instead of watching the road. The car drifted into the gravel before he righted the steering wheel.

He was really asking, really trying to make sense of this. He'd been just a boy the day Nathaniel drowned our mother in the river, but he'd been there. He'd lived with that. The ghost of Susanna had haunted him, like it had me, and now he needed answers.

"I think you know why," I said.

He went rigid, and I was glad that I'd caught him off guard. Maybe he hadn't expected me to answer, but there was no point in hiding anymore. Something told me that Caleb knew a lot more than he wanted to admit.

He jerked the wheel, and the car slid off the road completely, into the ditch that edged one of the fields. I slammed into the door as the car slid to a stop, the keys swinging in the ignition as Caleb stared out at the road.

My heart was racing again, heat licking like flames up my arms. My throat. I couldn't tell what he was going to do. Drag me into that field and shoot me? Kill me, the way his father tried to?

Without warning, he reached for the door and got out, as if he were making a move before he could change his mind. He came around to the passenger side and pulled me out of the back seat by the sleeve of my dress, shoving me into the road. I stumbled, sliding in the gravel before I got my footing.

I looked around us, to the expanse of golden fields that stretched in every direction. An unsettled sea of wheat whispered in the wind.

"Who are you?" he shouted, but his face was different suddenly. More human. His hands fell heavily to his sides as he watched me, still scrutinizing the planes of my face. He looked so tired.

"I'm June Rutherford." My throat burned as I said the name out loud for the first time in my life. I was sure of it, because what it did to my insides was something I would have remembered.

Caleb was shaking his head, hands raking through his hair. A red flush painted his skin before he pulled the pistol from his belt. "No."

"I am," I said.

"I told him he was crazy." His words warped. "That he was imagining things."

"He wasn't."

"He said that you were a demon come to haunt him. To punish him." Caleb was breathing hard now. He paced to one side of the road and back again. "June Rutherford died as a baby. She's buried in the church cemetery," he mumbled, desperately trying to reason himself out of it.

"Then dig up the grave. There's nothing there, Caleb."

He stared at me.

"He wanted me dead. She thought he was going to kill me, so she lied. She told him I died when he was in Charlotte, and he believed her."

"Then where have you been all this time?"

"Does it matter?"

Trying to explain the door to him would only convince him that I was lying about everything else. There was no chance his mind would be able to hold it.

"When I came back, he knew. Deep down, he knew who I was, and he started following me. Waiting for me in town. When he saw me walking home that night with Annie." The vision materialized so vividly across my mind that I could hardly draw breath. "He wanted to hurt me. Make the demons go away."

There was no reaction in Caleb's expression. He was placid and cold, like none of this surprised him. And that was exactly what I wanted him to think about—the fact that he *knew* his father. I couldn't imagine what kind of horrors he'd endured growing up in that man's house.

"You knew what he was," I said. "Didn't you?"

He sucked in his bottom lip, a gesture that made him look like a little boy, and I couldn't help but feel sorry for him. But then he lifted the pistol, pointing it at me.

My hands reflexively flew up in front of my face. I was shaking all over, still searching the road for any sign of a car. But this was a remote stretch. It would be a miracle if there was anyone for miles.

"You were there," I stammered. "You were five years old, Caleb. You have to remember."

His jaw clenched.

"I think you know that she didn't jump from the falls that day. Deep down, you always knew that, right?"

A gleam shone in his eyes. "I don't know what you're talking about."

"They didn't find her body because he buried her."

His lips parted, his eyebrows coming together. "What?" If he was lying now, it was convincing.

"Nathaniel told me. Right before he tried to drown me in the river."

His chest rose on a sharp inhalation of breath. This, I could tell, was the thing he really needed to know.

"Yes," I answered. "I killed him."

The gun went off, the sound exploding in my ears, and it echoed into the hills. I waited for an eruption of pain in my chest. My stomach. But when I looked down, there was no bloom of red. He'd fired the gun, but he hadn't shot me.

Slowly, my eyes lifted. Tears glimmered in Caleb's eyes as he stared at me, and I didn't know if they were for Nathaniel or for Susanna. Only one of them deserved any kind of pity.

"He held me under the water." My voice broke. "He held me there while my daughter watched from the riverbank."

He believed me. It was etched deep in the lines of his face. The tears brimming in his eyes finally spilled over, but his face didn't change. He stood there, freed from the lie he'd been telling himself for his entire life. He'd been a child who believed the story he'd been told because he needed to survive. Now it was time to let that story go.

"You'll find our mother buried under the oak tree at the corner of the woods beside the falls. She deserves a grave, Caleb."

He moved to reach for his belt, and I flinched, drawing my cuffed hands back to my chest. But he hooked one finger into a small set of keys and tossed them to the ground, turning his back to me. I watched, completely numb, as he got into the car. Stood there frozen as it pulled onto the road.

Leaflets of paper flew out the driver's side window as he took off, fluttering in the air before they floated to the ground. I walked toward them as they scattered in the road, stopping short when I looked down at the one beside my feet.

It was the photograph. Nathaniel's sharp-edged form. That cigarette in his hand. My mother, face turned as she smiled at him. She'd had no idea what that sinister love would set into motion.

THIRTY-TWO

It comes on an ordinary day, at an ordinary hour, and the moment I feel it, my whole world stops.

That buzz in the air is one I know. I can feel it reach into the house, wrapping its tendrils around me.

The door.

Moonlight is cast across the wall of the sitting room, making everything look black-and-white. I see myself in the reflection of the kitchen window, the strap of my nightgown slipping from my shoulder. I'm standing over the stove, where the kettle is whirring, my blond hair hanging in a braid that almost reaches my waist.

Not now.

This isn't how it's supposed to go.

I meet my own eyes, letting myself paint that image in my mind. Me. In this home. A mother. A wife. I've prepared for this, but I still have to press my hand over my mouth to muffle the sound that breaks in my chest. I have to breathe through it so that I don't wake her.

Through the open door of my bedroom, Annie is asleep beneath my quilts. I can hear her breathing.

The burn in my throat is nothing to the pain behind my ribs as my feet take me across the kitchen. She is bathed in blue light, her hair like silver. She's asleep, I tell myself. Eamon will be home any minute. She won't wake. She won't even stir.

I have no choice but to hope it's true.

It's been almost eighteen months since I last saw the door, and every day that passes is a day that Caleb Rutherford could discover the truth. It's only a matter of time before it finds its way into the light. When it does, I'll have lost my chance.

I step into the room, rounding the bed. Annie's cheeks frame a perfect pink mouth, and I press my lips to her temple. I inhale her scent as deep as I possibly can.

There isn't time to second-guess it or wait for Eamon's headlights on the road. My feet take me to the dressing table, and I pull the ring from my finger. I drop it into the dish below the mirror and remember the words I wrote on that envelope—a message that will be carried through time, back to me.

Trust me.

I hope that I will.

I open the back door, not bothering to wrap a shawl around my shoulders or take the lantern with me. The tobacco fields are so thick that the wind makes the leaves look like dark water in the moonlight. That vibration on the wind is even more alive out here, and I follow it into the nearest row. The plants swallow me up, my bare feet sinking in the soft, damp soil, and I walk, hands catching the leaves as I pass.

I see it a few paces later. The chipped red paint. The shimmer that surrounds it in the air.

The door sits in the middle of the field, hidden from the rest of the world.

I am a stone sinking into a deep, dark sea. And I'm not coming back.

I reach the door with a final, silent footstep, and the wind picks up, pulling my nightgown around me. It's the same door that has appeared for the last five years, and the last time I opened it, I'd been someone else. I had no idea what waited on the other side.

The weight of the locket is suddenly heavy around my neck, and I reach inside my nightgown, pulling it free. It clicks as it opens, and I turn its face toward the moonlight. The hands are set to 2022. A place where I exist, where a thirty-three-year-old June Farrow is caring for her ailing grandmother and trying to keep the farm running. Afraid of the future. Grieved by the past. And I'm putting every bit of hope I have in her.

I lift my unsteady hand, and the moment my fingertips touch the doorknob, I don't give myself time to change my mind. I turn it. Pull it open. What lies on the other side is a blackness I have never seen. It's a darkness that eats itself. A thick wall of nothing.

I'm shaking as my foot crosses the threshold. My breath is a storm inside my head, and when I pull the door closed behind me, the crack of moonlight becomes a sliver. A knife in the dark.

It disappears with a click.

I'm

I

THIRTY-THREE

Susanna Rutherford's body was exhumed from its thirty-four-year resting place on July 3, 1951.

They found her beneath the oak tree, right where Nathaniel said she would be.

I stood on the north side of the river as the men worked, shovels in hand and white T-shirts marked with dirt as they dug. On the other side, Caleb was watching, and I could tell the exact moment they found her. A silence fell over the woods, even the birds going quiet.

She was bones and dust, had been for years, and in some way, that felt not too unlike the myth I'd always known her as. She was a prism that colored me and my world with a story. We were the limbs of a broken tree with poisoned roots.

We laid Susanna to rest three days later, and those same men who'd been at the river dug another hole in the ground. The headstone that Nathaniel had erected all those years ago still stood in the church-yard, making her the first Farrow to be buried within the fence of that cemetery. But no one ever dug up the small grave beside it for her daughter, June Rutherford.

A year later, I sat on the stool in front of the dressing table in my bedroom as Margaret wove tiny chamomile blooms through the braids in my hair. She was humming a song to herself, a glimpse of that little girl I had once known visible in the reflection as I watched her.

I could remember her now. Eleven years old. Twelve. Thirteen. Now she was seventeen, on the cusp of womanhood. She'd asked me once what it was like between us before I came here, and even though I'm not supposed to talk about the future, I told her that she was a mother to me. My dearest friend. And looking at her now, it was still true.

I still had the memory of that night on the hill with the sun going down and the fiddle playing when Birdie—Annie—reached for my hand and we said goodbye to Gran. But before I was born, she'd be the one to say goodbye to *me*. Soon, that memory would be gone, and I'd have to relive it before I could remember it again.

The curse on the Farrows had broken the natural laws of the world, and with it had come so much suffering. But in this, there'd been the most unexpected of gifts. Looking back, I understood that sadness I'd seen in Birdie's eyes when I left the house that day. It was the same reason she'd hesitated before she'd handed me that envelope.

It was a goodbye.

That moment was dimming, like the rest of them. It had been a year since I left, and the memories of *this* life were still coming, but the patches were few and far between. I had a new notebook now— one where I'd written every memory I could think of that I would miss. I recorded them in as much detail as I could recall, making a kind of archive of the life I'd lived. Cooking with Gran in the kitchen. Making garlands in the shop with Birdie. Countless summer after- noons with Mason at the river.

On the other side of the door, I will become a story, not unlike my father and my mother. Children will tell stories of seeing me in the woods. There will be rumors that I'd thrown myself from the falls, but life will go on. Three years after I cross, Birdie's full, beautiful life— her timeline—will end. And with it, so will the Farrows'. Mason will inherit the Adeline River Flower Farm, and he'll eventually fall in love with a woman who comes to work as an intern one summer.

On this side of the door, I will live a life I thought I never deserved. Not even one year after we bury Susanna, Caleb will leave Jasper. For reasons I'll never know, he will keep my secret.

It takes almost two years for the door to show up again, then five and a half. Eleven years after that, once the very last of my memories have faded, it will appear a final time.

Eamon and I will plant fields and tend them. We will raise our daughter, and even after we are too old to farm, we will spend the rest of our lives in this little yellow house on Hayward Gap Road. Annie will grow. She will age. She will never see the red door.

Margaret tidied the braid pinned across the crown of my head, and I caught her hand with mine when it landed on my shoulder.

On September 19, 1966, she will bear a child and name her Susanna. My own timeline will overlap with my mother's for just over twenty years before I die. I will watch her be born, then she will watch *me* be born, and this cycle, this revolution, will begin again.

I would spend the rest of my life walking the precarious line of what I would and would not tell Margaret and Annie. What to leave to fate and what to prepare them for. They'd done the same for me, and it hadn't been perfect, but it had been a life full of love.

It was almost overwhelmingly painful to be so happy.

"Thank you," I said, emotion thick in my throat. "For everything."

Margaret gave me her sweet smile. "You're welcome."

Annie held a crystal perfume bottle to her freckled nose, and I wrapped my arms around her tightly, burying my face in her hair.

This changes everything.

And it had.

"You ready, Annie Bird?" I said.

She slid off my lap and skipped from the room in a wordless answer.

I tucked a stray, waving strand behind my ear and rose to my feet. The white lace dress draped over my curves, its delicate hem brushing the floor. I looked at myself in the mirror before Margaret handed me a bouquet of black-eyed Susans, aster, and bee balm she'd picked with Annie.

When we came down the back steps, the tobacco fields were bursting with green. It would be a good harvest. A healthy one.

Eamon and Esther were waiting beside the patch of wildflowers that lined the fence. In the distance, the mountains were a sea of rolling blue beneath a cloudless sky.

Esther gave me a kiss, taking Margaret's hand, and beside them, Annie watched with a dandelion twirling between her palms. We stood there, four generations of Farrow women, cursed to live between worlds. But in that moment, in the valley of the Blue Ridge Mountains, we existed only in one.

When his gaze met mine, Eamon's mouth tilted in a grin that I now recognized as distinctly his. I loved it. I loved him. More than I ever thought was possible for one being to hold inside of them.

Eamon had asked me to marry him again, and I'd said yes, because even though I could remember that day as clearly as if this body had been there, I would marry him a thousand times.

When I reached him, he took my hand, holding it to his chest. I could feel his heartbeat there.

This is real, I told myself.

And then I spoke my vows into the summer wind. That I'd love him forever. That I would always, always come back. That no matter what, I would find him.

AUTHOR'S NOTE

I'm incredibly inspired by the setting of Western North Carolina. The town of Jasper, although fictional, was created as a reflection of the many rural farm towns that dot the Blue Ridge Mountains. While the area's history and culture is incredibly rich, it is also fraught with the long-lasting effects of slavery, which I thought important to note in light of the time period in which a portion of this story takes place.

More than one hundred years after the abolition of slavery, Black people still faced an overwhelming amount of discrimination in Jim Crow North Carolina. While the areas surrounding Asheville wouldn't truly begin to integrate until the 1960's, there are numerous historical examples of Black entrepreneurs, farmers, artists, business owners, and inventors that span well before this period. Many of these individuals have been erased from the region's visible and recounted history, as is the case with so many non-white figures of the past. I chose to portray the mention of or reference to Black individuals in this book to reflect these examples, but it's important to acknowledge that they do not reflect the Black experience as a whole, as is true for any fictional portrayal of any member of any group of people.

ACKNOWLEDGMENTS

When I set out to write this book, I couldn't have foreseen what was to come. The seed of the idea was planted the first time I visited Asheville, North Carolina, when I stumbled across a little door fixed to the exterior wall of a building on the street. It would take a few years for me to begin to understand what this story was really about and where it would take me as a writer.

This book is dedicated to my oldest friends, Meghan Dickerson and Kristin Watson, who have borne witness to every version of me. Thank you for being the place I return to, the lens that sees me for who I really am, and for always, always, supporting me. You are two of the greatest gifts I've ever been given.

I am incredibly grateful to my publishing team for putting on their seatbelts for this ride and taking the twists and turns with me, especially my editor, Shauna Summers; Mae Martinez; and my agent, Barbara Poelle.

A lot of inspiration for the setting of this book came from the small town of Marshall, North Carolina, and I also relied on the generous contribution of Carolina Flowers owner Emily Copus and the Register of Deeds in Asheville in my research.

There is no book of mine that takes shape without the support of my writing community—my critique partner Kristin Dwyer and my fellow authors who inspire me and encourage me without fail. Thank you also to my beta reader Natalie Faria. I am so thankful for all of you.

ABOUT THE AUTHOR

ADRIENNE YOUNG is the *New York Times* and international bestselling author of *Spells for Forgetting*, the Fable series, and the Sky and Sea duology. When she's not writing, you can find her on her yoga mat, on a walk in the woods, or planning her next travel adventure. She lives and writes in the Blue Ridge Mountains of North Carolina.

ABOUT THE TYPE

This book was set in Caslon, a typeface first designed in 1722 by William Caslon (1692–1766). Its widespread use by most English printers in the early eighteenth century soon supplanted the Dutch typefaces that had formerly prevailed. The roman is considered a "work-horse" typeface due to its pleasant, open appearance, while the italic is exceedingly decorative.